I'M A CREEP

JAIMIE ROBERTS

Editor: Kim BookJunkie

Cover Designer: Dez Purington at Pretty in Ink Creations

❀ Created with Vellum

"I would like to be the air that inhabits you for a moment only. I would like to be that unnoticed and that necessary."

— **Margaret Atwood**

CHAPTER ONE

ast

Blood on the sheets.

The tap drip, drip, drips from the family bathroom down the hall—the evidence of what he did to me washed away, the act finalized.

I am no longer pure.

Drip, drip, drip.

That's the only sound I hear as I lie motionless, my eyes fixed to the tiny portion of the blue, peeling wallpaper in the corner of my room.

Physical pain is the only thing existing in my world as I carry on staring. It's the only thing I allow myself to fully zero in on.

Drip, drip, drip.

The violent act of what happened numbs me emotionally until all I have left is this hollow space in my body. It acts like a vessel with nothing left but this constant, never-ending sound.

Drip, drip, drip.

Murmuring in the room next door pricks my ears, but again, I lie completely still—unable to make a move or sound for fear I will alert him again.

Drip, drip, drip.

The voices stop, and the front door of our house closes. I grip my eyes shut, and with them falls a tear so big that it pops right out and slowly cascades the hill of my cheek before eventually falling onto my pillow.

The deathly, hollow sound of silence fills the air as I draw up my legs and hug them tightly to my chest, cocooning myself as if doing this will protect me from the evil wickedness I have been forced to meet.

In my dimly lit bedroom where the door stands ajar, I count.

One, two, three, four, five...

I keep counting until I reach the thousands, my mind solely on those numbers.

The front door opens.

Elijah appears.

My breath catches as I wait until he takes in the scene.

"Bryce?!" he calls out, his voice quaking. "Bryce, talk to me!"

He hovers over me, his body shaking with rage, anger ... fear. All the emotions he should be feeling at the evidence in front of him.

Hastily, he leaves my room to go next door, his cries of anguish filling the house.

"Brenda, what the fuck have you done?!"

I still don't move or make a sound, my eyes fixed solely on that one corner of my room. But inside, I ache. Inside, the physical pain radiates through me, trying to force me to acknowledge what's happened. I force it down, my eyes still fixated on that corner.

Heavy breathing cascades around me, and then my body is jerked down by a hand placed next to me on the mattress.

"Bryce!" When I don't move or say a word still, he takes my head and forces me to stare into those deep, penetrating violet eyes of his. They widen at my deadened expression before rage replaces his initial concern. "I'm going to run you a bath, baby. Okay?"

He disappears, leaving only the faint musky scent of his cologne behind and the static electricity from the power he elicits.

The sound of running water twitches my ears, but the emptiness still consumes me.

Blood on the sheets.

I am no longer pure.

CHAPTER TWO

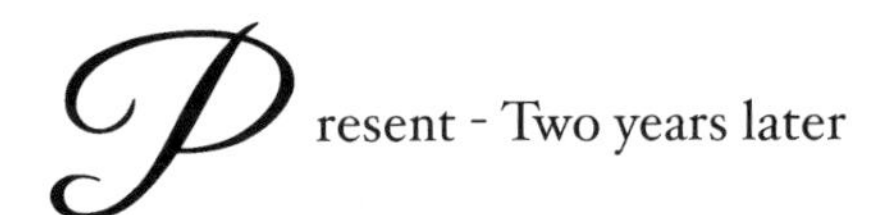

Present - Two years later

"I thought I would bring you some home cooked blueberry muffins—considering you haven't got a woman to look after you and all."

Her attempt at giggling makes the bitch sound like a crow. If I had answered the door, I would have stuffed those muffins inside those collagen duck lips of hers.

"Well, technically that's not true," Elijah responds as I wedge myself up against the kitchen door, desperate to hear what he says next. "I have Bryce here."

Damn. Fucking. Straight, he does!

Seriously, this bitch needs to back the fuck off.

Her laughter makes my ears bleed. "I know, but she's your step-daughter. Hardly a dedicated companion now, is she? She can't look after you in every ... true sense of the word."

I inhale a sharp, angry breath, the urge to pick up an ice pick and stab her in the fucking eye consumes me. I do look after him in every true sense of the word. Certainly better than Daisy fucking Duck ever could.

His laughter back at her is rich with nerves. A kind of laugh that says, "yeah, I might be laughing with you, but you're making me uncomfortable, so fuck off."

"I get by, Sharon." He pauses for a second. "Listen, I just now got home from work, and I'm beat. Would you mind... ?"

"Oh, of course not," she gasps, interrupting him from politely telling her to take a fucking hike. "I haven't even given you a chance to get out of that fine-looking uniform of yours."

I roll my eyes so fiercely that it actually hurts my eyes. No doubt Duckface got a full eye roam of his body as she said this. I don't need to see them both to know she's drooling over him.

His laughter is nervous again as he makes his excuses and shuts the door. The clomping of his boots resonates down the few steps of the hallway before he enters the kitchen, a basket of freshly made blueberry muffins in hand, smelling all nice and stuff.

Fucking bitch.

Elijah spots me straight away, standing by the door, his police uniform that Duckface so eloquently leered at hugging that tight, muscular, six-foot-four frame of his. His intensely heated violet eyes dance their way up my flimsy red dress. A dress I decided to wear absolutely no underwear underneath. I'm almost eighteen and haven't had to enhance myself like Duckface has. And I get confirmation that I don't need to when I get the exact reaction I'm looking for from Elijah.

"I see Daisy made you some muffins. Isn't that nice?"

He narrows his eyes, but a hint of a smirk he can't hide quirks up one side of his mouth. "Don't be jealous, Bryce. They're just muffins."

"Pfft," I reply, blowing a strand of my long auburn hair from my eyes. "Why would I ever be jealous of Daisy?"

"Sharon," he corrects.

"Whatever."

Elijah throws his pristine, gold-feathered insignia Kentucky police chief hat down on the kitchen island along with the stupid, amazing smelling muffins. He then ruffles what little dark strands of hair he has left on the top of his head. A sight that causes my eyes to slant with lust. Gone is the insane anger at Daisy Duckface. It's homed in on another deep emotion entirely.

"How's the new job going?" I ask, trying to be all domesticated and shit. Purely an attempt at quashing my raging hormones, but one that usually works, nonetheless.

"It's early days, but I'm enjoying more of the desk work life more than ever now considering I'm getting old."

I almost choke on my own spit. "You're almost thirty-nine. Hardly old now, are you?"

The kitchen light hits his pale violet eyes, making them sparkle like lilac diamonds. Is it any wonder the Duckfaces of this world are dying to get into Elijah's pants when he hits them with a gaze so forceful, it could zap their panties right off their bodies? Little does Duckface know ... the plans I have in store for her if she keeps up her little antics.

"For someone who's barely eighteen yet, I'm surprised to hear you say that."

My eyeroll's bigger than the London eye. Elijah has liked to bring up the fact that I'm barely eighteen for the last few months now. I think it may have something to do with our ... living arrangement.

Whatever the reason, I ignore the thousandth time he's brought it up, instead turning to stir the beef and vegetable stew I have simmering on the stove.

"Go get yourself cleaned up. Dinner will be ready in a few minutes."

He doesn't reply, but I know when he's gone as that static electricity he tends to leave lingering when he's in the room dissipates, enabling me to breathe again.

Tonight. Wait until tonight, I think to myself, grinning like a devil. For now, I play wife. For now, I cook, bake biscuits, and ask stupid fucking questions like, *"How was your day, dear?"* and, *"Go get a wash because dinner's almost ready."*

You know ... cause I'm flexible like that.

A couple of minutes of stirring the beef stew and the egg timer chimes, alerting me to the fact that the biscuits I painstakingly made are ready. Turning off the stove, I pick up the oven gloves and pull out the biscuits from the oven, the freshly baked smell pleasantly hitting my nostrils. I place them down on the counter next to the muffins, mine looking all fluffed up and perfectly bronzed.

"Try and beat that, bitch."

I have this sudden urge to take a kitchen knife and chop her perfectly formed muffins up into little tiny pieces. I'm sure I could make them look a lot less appeasing to the eye if I tried.

I sigh, forcing the thought away. As much as I want to be petty, I won't. I'm the one with the upper hand here, after all. It's just Duck-face doesn't realize that fact ... yet.

The soothing humming of his static electricity coats the air as he reenters the kitchen. With only a pair of black Adidas shorts on, his hairless chest stands proud like it's somehow meant to make an impact on the world. His jet-black hair is wet and lays haphazardly on his head like all he's done is run a towel through it. The smell of the soap he uses hits my nostrils and travels to an area I have to keep a lid on. Well, for now anyway. Pretenses and all.

"Smells amazing," Elijah sings as he takes a seat at the kitchen island, his eyes all twinkling and shit. Seriously, how can he expect me not to want to jump his bones every time he looks at me like that? I sometimes wonder whether I should tell him to dial it down a little. But then again ... where would the fun be—and also the challenge—in that?

I quirk an eyebrow at him then continue going about my business, completing my nightly dinner ritual. "I've been practicing baking these biscuits all day."

And I have been. Three separate batches and a few choice curse words later, and my biscuits are finally ready, looking and smelling like they were professionally baked. Even I'm impressed. However, the proof is always in the tasting.

"Well, I'm sure they'll taste amazing."

I place the biscuits neatly on a tray then scoop us each a bowl full of the stew before placing them down in front of us. I sit opposite him at our big island as he picks up a biscuit, ripping it in half with his capable hands. Steam rises from the cooked dough, and that freshly baked smell hits me once more.

"How was your day? Do much studying?"

My spoon hovers in midair as I clap my eyes on him. "I took a test. Scored ninety-four percent."

Even though my scores are rarely below the ninety mark, Elijah never fails to color himself impressed. His eyes light up—just like they do every time.

"That's amazing, Bryce. You should be proud of yourself. I know I am."

And again, he says the same thing every time. Of course, I soak it all up like the lap dog I am around him. Some people would be used to the praise by now, brush it off as it's the same damn thing day in and day out. Not me. Not when it comes to Elijah.

Up until a few months ago, I had been going to high school like any other kid my age. I was picked on relentlessly, so I decided to become a little ... imaginative about getting my bully's back. This resulted in a day I will never forget. The teacher's—rather than dealing with the problem themselves—instead decided that I should take my SATs earlier than everyone else. I was a star pupil and could run rings around everyone else, so why not? I didn't care for the bullying, and towards the end, I wasn't bullied anymore, but still ... I couldn't pass up an opportunity to take them early and be done with school. The reason why they stopped bullying me all of a sudden ... well, that's a whole other story entirely. One that makes me smile whenever I relive it.

Suffice it to say, I passed my SATs with one of the highest scores any pupil in the county has ever achieved, and because of it, I'm doing an accounting degree online. Totally boring, but for some reason I have a way with numbers. It all just comes so ... naturally to me. Elijah, for some reason, never wanted me to go to college. He made some excuse about me being bullied there, too, but I have a feeling he likes having me around too much. It's a pity he won't just come out and say it.

"Thanks," I reply before blowing on some stew and taking my first spoonful. The rich herbs and spices hit the back of my throat, causing my tongue to sting. Although I don't care much for spicy foods, Elijah can't get enough. Over the four years I've been living here, I've gotten used to it. I'd get used to anything for him.

"What did you do with the rest of your time?"

I notice that by the time he's asked me the question, he's already eaten one biscuit and is now picking up another. My eyes quickly flit towards the muffins. I wonder how many of those he'll be able to stomach.

"Oh, you know," I begin, being as flippant as possible. "This and that. I did some boring housework..." Spied on the neighbors. "Took a nice, long, hot bath..." Laced Mrs. Crossbrook's tea with sedatives so I could kidnap and play with her dog. "And then I read a little." I also took Elijah's electric toothbrush, got into his bed, and masturbated with it. "Boring stuff," I add with the best smile I can muster.

Conversation is light after that, and when Elijah gets up to leave so he can lock himself away in his study for the next few hours to work, I gather up our plates to wash everything and point to the muffins. "Are you not taking one of those with you?"

Elijah grimaces, his nose turning up. "Nah ... I fucking hate blueberries."

CHAPTER THREE

ast

Day one of being back at school after what happened to me three weeks ago, and already the rumor mill is rife with stories about why I've been off school. Considering my stepfather's the deputy chief at the local police station, much of what goes on behind closed doors is a well-kept secret. It still doesn't stop the tongues from wagging, though.

"I heard she takes it up the ass by her drug-dealer. I mean, it's so obvious she takes drugs. Look at the dark circles under her eyes."

I walk past the group of staring girls and clutch my folder tightly to my chest. I try not to let those words sink in, but after what I've been through, they sting more than they will ever know. Yes, I have dark circles under my eyes, but that's only because I can't sleep for fear my mum's dealer will come back for a second round with me so my mum can shoot up yet again.

"Why didn't you just do yourself a favor while you were off school and kill yourself?"

The group of girls behind me giggle as I ignore every single one of them and make my way down the school hallway. Unfortunately for me, I've been bullied for months here simply because I dress differently with my 80's rock chick style outfits and sometimes red hair to heighten my natural auburn locks. With my stunning color of hair, pouty lips, and light blue eyes, I catch the guys looking, even though they will never admit it. I can't even count the amount of times guys have laughed at the names other people call me but then act all nice and hit on me the moment school is over and no one else is looking.

Fuck them.

Fuck them all.

"Weirdo."

"Bitch."

"Freak."

"Creep."

"Slut."

"Whore."

All the same boring names I'm called day in and day out go ringing past me as I make my way down the hall to my English class. These kids ... they seriously can't think for themselves. There's Brad who is the top jock here. He's dating Chloe, the prom queen and all-round total bitch. I am no different from any of them, but because I decided to have my own style of dress, I immediately put a target on my back. Chloe won't admit it, but I believe she made me a target simply because she knew I was strong competition when I started here. I've seen the way Brad sometimes looks at me. What makes it worse is they both belong to some sexual abstinence group, so they think they're above everyone else when in fact they're just a bunch of assholes. They believe I'm not a virgin. Well, I was until three weeks ago, but even before then they were calling me a slut, so that's nothing to go by. To them I'm just a moving target. A simple outlet to enhance their own miserable lives. They may call me those names, but I know who I am. The only person I need to prove my worth to is myself. The rest of them can simply fuck off.

I take my seat, as always, in the back of the class. I've learned since coming home and having to cut gum out of my hair a few times not to sit anywhere else. One time, a bunch of kids thought it was funny to take turns, sneaking several pieces in. That resulted in me having to chop most of my long hair off. I had a pixie cut for a while after and kept it that way in fear they'd just keep doing it. In the end, I grew it back out, and I've been sitting in the back as often as I can ever since. On occasion's when I can't, I have a baseball hat I put on. Normally, you're not allowed caps in school, but the teachers never say a word to me, simply because they know how much of a rough time I have. Not that they do fuck all about it. Unfortunately, the Brads and the Chloes of this world have too much money and influence around here.

I stay seated, trying my best at acting blasé when inside my stomach ties in knots. As usual, people stare, and the dire need for the teacher to arrive takes over. As I'm praying he'll appear, a new boy walks in looking as timid as I feel. He's about my height at five-foot-six, so small for a dude. His brown waves are unruly on his head, and he wears round spectacles, which only adds to his dorkiness. He's also wearing a pair of chinos with a blue shirt underneath his brown sweater. Of course people stare when he walks in. Chesney, one of Brad's right-hand men, laughs out loud the moment he locks eyes on him.

"Look at this fucking dork."

As usual, the crowd all laughs. A part of me thinks I should be thankful that eyes are not on me anymore and are now fixated on a new target, but nothing about this situation makes me feel relieved. If anything, the fury that's constantly simmering inside me is starting to bubble.

The new boy keeps his head down as much as he can, scurrying towards the back of the class. When he's near me, I point to the desk next to me. "This one's free, if you want it."

The boy pushes his glasses up and flits his eyes to me, his face weary. When I smile reassuringly at him, his whole body seems to relax.

"Thank you."

"Oh, lookie here, everyone. Looks like weirdo has a boyfriend."

My fists clench at their mocking laughter before a flash of something wicked darts through my mind. If I knew all their secrets, I bet they'd leave me alone. No one here would be whiter than white, that's for sure. These people think they're God's gift, but I bet I could show them.

"You don't want to go near her, dorky, she's got an STD."

"Ewwwwwww," everyone says in unison as they all glance up, their eyes all fixed on us. Me and this poor unsuspecting boy are now on display for everyone to mock, ridicule, and tease.

I want to shout and scream at them, "What the fuck have I ever done wrong to you?!" but I know it would be a wasted effort. They would only make my world more miserable than it already is.

"Everyone, settle down!"

I release a breath as Mr. Brayson walks in, a copy of Shakespeare's *Romeo and Juliet* clutched under his arm. He places it down on his desk then walks to a cupboard, opens it, and proceeds to take out several copies of the same book. He hands a stack to the front row asking them to pass them to the back of the class.

"Today we are going to read Romeo and Juliet." The class groans, causing Mr. Brayson to smirk. "Now, kids, this is one of the most romantic and tragic love stories you will ever read."

"Can't we download it on our Kindles so we don't have to carry that book around with us?" One of Chloe's girls, Dina, asks.

Mr. Brayson shakes his head, tutting under his breath. "Kids these days. You know, when I was your age, we didn't have Google or smartphones or Kindles to rely on. If I needed a question answered, I would have had to take a trip to the library and sift through endless books until I found it."

"Yeah, that's because you're ancient," Chesney quips, causing everyone but me and the new boy next to me to laugh. Mr. Brayson's not ancient. He's only in his forties. Hardly ancient. Sometimes the urge to kick Chesney in the balls consumes me to a point my stomach feels like it's going to explode. The only thing that stops me is this stupid crush I've had on him since I started school. I sigh at the thought. I'm such a silly fool at times.

"Ah, I may be ancient to you, but I've lived quite the life so far. You've all still got yours ahead of you—some of whom I dread to wonder where you'll be in five years if you don't buckle down and study."

His smirk causes me to smile, too, because he's right. Some of these assholes can't distinguish between a knife and a spoon, they're so dense.

Reluctantly, the two girls in front of us hand me and the boy a copy of the book, scowling at the pair of us like we're shit on their shoes.

I take the book, completely ignoring them, then turn to the new guy. "What's your name?"

The new boy looks up, noting that the class is murmuring amongst themselves as the books are handed out. "Adam."

I hold my hand out to him. "Nice to meet you, Adam. I'm Bryce."

Wearily, he glances at my hand before looking up and finding my bright smile. Maybe something about my smile puts him at ease as he clasps his hand in mine and returns the gesture.

"How often do they talk to you like that?" he asks, his face scrunching in a grimace.

I sigh, slumping back into my chair. "Every day. But I'm used to it now."

Lies.

Adam leans over his desk towards me and whispers, "How do you get used to that?"

I don't.

"When they say it often enough it eventually starts to feel like they're saying hello to me."

"Bryce!" Mr. Brayson shouts, causing both Adam and I to jump at the same time. I fix my eyes ahead, locking them with the teacher. "Since you're so eager to use your voice this morning, why don't you read the first two chapters of the book to everyone?"

A few giggles resonate around the class, but they pipe down once Mr. Brayson stares at the girls in question. I inwardly groan but dutifully open the first few pages to start reading.

This is going to be a long fucking day.

CHAPTER FOUR

resent

After the dishes are done, I place the leftover stew in an airtight container and wrap up a couple of my biscuits before making my way out of the house to get my nightly fresh air. I skip down the three steps of our house and walk the few feet to next door, knowing that Frank will be there, smoking a joint and spying on the neighbors as usual. I round the front porch of his house, and sure enough, he's sitting in his usual rocking chair, smoking his joint under the cover of darkness.

"Hey, Frank," I greet him with a big smile. I always have the biggest smiles for Frank. For two years, I have been visiting him and having our little evening chats as we smoke pot together and bitch about the neighbors.

"Hey, rosebud," he replies. The nickname he has for me fills me with warmth. One night after about the third or fourth visit, Frank started calling me rosebud because of my pretty rosebud lips.

"I made some stew and biscuits." I hold them up in the air for him to see.

"Be a doll and put them in the kitchen for me. I'll eat it later."

I do as instructed, opening up his creaky mosquito blind before placing them on his old 70's style kitchen counter. His house is a little tired and hasn't been renovated in years, but this is how Frank likes it. As long as he's safe and happy, that's all that matters.

When I walk back out, Frank pats the rocking chair next to him for me to sit. Up until a year and a half ago, I used to have to sit on the steps in front of him, but as my nightly visits became a habit, he decided to buy me a chair so my ass wouldn't get piles—as he said. Frank is the sweetest guy I have ever known. African American, in his seventies, and living on his own in the house he once owned with his wife, who unfortunately died five years ago. Now Frank has bowel cancer, hence the self-medication with marijuana. I had tried to decline when he offered as he needed it more than me, but Frank insists. He says it's like drinking socially with friends. It'd be boring as fuck if one of them stayed sober the whole night.

I sit down in his chair and let out a long-needed sigh. The moment I'm sitting down, Frank hands me the joint.

"So what's been happening today?" I ask, inhaling my first hit, pushing my head back against the seat as I exhale. First hit is always the best.

"Nothing much," he responds. "Betty, over there," he says pointing to our neighbor right in front of us. "Had an argument with her husband about some text messages she found on his phone."

I quirk an eyebrow at Frank, handing him back his joint. "Interesting." I always thought Betty's husband John was this boring as fuck type. Go to work, come back from work, eat, go to sleep, rinse, and repeat.

"Yeeep," he drawls out before inhaling his joint. "Number twenty-five mowed the same stretch of tiny lawn for over an hour before an Amazon package was delivered to him. And I saw that Duckface came by number thirty-two."

I roll my eyes as that's us. "Yeah, tried to butter up Elijah with her sweet talk and blueberry muffins—which he hates, by the way."

Frank gives me a knowing smirk before turning back to glance out at the neighbors again. He reminds me of a king surveying his kingdom, the all-seeing, all-knowing of his little empire. I'm not sure how much he knows of my situation, but I can hazard a guess it's quite a bit. I bet he's heard and maybe even seen a thing or two from my house.

"How was your online learning today?"

"Boring," I answer, because it's the truth.

"Why do you do it then?"

"Because it's what I'm good at. Elijah always told me to do what I'm good at."

Despite his lips screwing up to one side, Frank withholds his judgement. I have a feeling he doesn't like Elijah very much, but he knows how much I love him. I guess he decides to hold his tongue for my sake. It's one of the many things I love about him.

"Every night I see you it's like you're getting older," Frank remarks, holding out his joint to me again. I take it from him and inhale before replying.

"You make me sound like a child."

His forehead crinkles, deep lines creasing his forehead. "I don't like the thought of you stuck in there all day in that big ol' house by yourself. You're only seventeen. You should be out dating guys, coming home drunk, and vomiting all over your front porch."

I rear my head back, quirking an eyebrow at him with a smile. "Sounds like hell to me. Besides, I have the life I want for now, and that's the main thing, don't you think?"

Little does Frank know, I have plenty of things to do to pass my time.

In the end he shrugs one shoulder. "I guess. It's whatever makes you happy."

I take in one last drag, handing it back to him. "Believe me when I say things are much better than what they were."

He visibly grimaces at that but says no more. Frank is aware of what happened to me two years ago, but he never brings it up. I'm grateful to him for that too. I don't want his pity. I don't want anyone's pity.

After a few more minutes of idle chitchat, I make my excuses to leave, telling Frank that I'll see him tomorrow night at the same time. I never stay for long—only for around half an hour, but it's the part of my evenings that I look forward to the most. The other being what I'm about to do next.

Licking my lips and feeling the slight buzz of the joint, I head inside, go brush my teeth to hide the smell, then pour a healthy glass of bourbon. I ruffle my hair, pout my lips, and pucker my nipples between my fingers before grabbing the drink and heading for the study.

I knock softly, but I don't allow him time to permit me entry. Elijah's head is down, a mountain of paperwork strewn across his desk as he furiously writes something down with his fountain pen. I round his desk, placing the drink down at the edge of it. "What are you doing there?" I ask, peeping over his shoulder.

Throwing the pen down, he picks up his drink, swallowing it all in one gulp, sighing deeply. "It's the yearly budget. It's making my head hurt."

Purposefully, I bend over, one hand on the back of his chair while the other leans on his desk. I'm within smelling distance and certainly within seeing distance of my top which is now open for him to gaze at my bare breasts. Sure enough, he hitches in a breath, causing a deep longing in the pit of my stomach.

"Do you want me to help?" I offer, my eyes fixed on the spreadsheet he has open on his laptop.

A relieved breath of air leaves his body. "If you could, that would be great."

Placing my legs on either side of his, I sit on his lap, bending over slightly to see the screen. His hardened cock soon greets me, causing me to wiggle my ass against his dick. His hands land on my bare legs, squeezing them ever so slightly, his desire increasing.

I try my hardest to play the part, though, my eyes still fixed on the screen. "I take it you're having trouble getting these to add up?"

"Yes," he answers, his voice wanton and desperate. Despite his resistance, he already wants me.

He always wants me.

My eyes scan down the line of figures until they land on a couple that look odd. I point to the screen. "These two are wrong, but I can fix them for you, if you want?" I rub my ass against him again, causing him to hiss with pleasure.

"Y... yes. Do it."

Standing up but still straddling him, I place my hand behind my back and pull out his awaiting cock. My heart's beating like a drum, my mind awash with nothing but the feel of having him underneath me like this. Breathless, I position the tip of his cock at my entrance and slowly slide down, the hiss of his breath again causing desire to spike in my stomach.

"Fuck!" Elijah bellows as I finally nestle him fully inside me.

Very slowly and methodically, I raise myself up, before snuggling down on his cock again, all while trying to concentrate on correcting these figures.

"This ... one," I utter, my breaths coming thick and fast as I point to the screen. "You have the two numbers mixed round. E ... easy mis ... take to ... make." I moan out as his cock meets a certain sweet spot. My head involuntarily lulls to the side, my eyes closing as my body demands that I concentrate solely on the pleasure he's giving me.

"Hurry the ... fuck up ... Bryce," he demands between pants.

I'm driving him wild, to the point of detonation. Elijah and I both don't do slow, but right now it's a necessity in order to get these figures done.

As fast as I can, I change the two numbers then glance down at the other offending number. I'm desperately trying to work it out in my head, but the longer this slow fucking continues, the harder it is for me to figure it out.

"Bryce," Elijah warns, his fingers digging into my hips. I mewl like a feral cat, but my eyes remain fixed to the screen as I type in what I think the correct number is. But it still doesn't add up. I curse under my breath, my body urging me to let go, but I also know that shit like this makes the sex we share the most climatic.

"Fuck," Elijah curses again, his breathing even more labored. The urgency in his voice forces me to focus on the task in front of me. I realize quickly that I, too, have mixed the numbers around, so I hurriedly switch them round and almost cry, "eureka" when they match up.

"Done!" I shout, my pace quickening.

"About fucking time!"

As quick as a flash, Elijah pushes me up while still inside me, bends me over his desk, and presses the side of my head against the paperwork. Once completely submissive underneath him, Elijah thrusts wildly, grunting and moaning like a fucking animal.

And I love it.

"Fucking bitch!" he roars, his feral screams causing my legs to quake.

With his other hand free, he reaches up to the top of my dress, tugging down so forcefully that it tears in his grip. My breast free, he grabs it in his palm and squeezes my nipple between his thumb and forefinger.

A deep, vibrating moan leaves my lips, causing me to close my eyes and surrender to the pleasure he's forcing from my body. The hand that's on my head fists, holding a clump of my hair as his pleasure gets the better of him. The hand on my breast squeezes my nipple again before tracing down the contour of my body and smacking my bare ass.

I jolt, the result of which has my pussy clamping down on him even harder. "Fuuuuuuccccckkkk!" Elijah screams, and it's that which has my orgasm rising and quickly spilling over in one huge crash.

"Oh, shit!" I cry, my body trembling and my moans echoing around his study.

"Fuck, shit, Bryce, you're going to make me come!"

He roars out, stilling inside me as his cum shoots against my womb. For a few seconds we stay like that, my body quivering from my orgasm, my breaths leaving me in pants.

Every time. Every time Elijah never fails to disappoint. I'm guessing it's the same for him considering he can never, ever say no to me. Despite wanting to keep away, he can't. So to compromise, I play our little charade to the outside world, just like he wants me to. It's at night when the gloves come off. Darkness falls and everything changes. In the cover of darkness, he's mine.

All mine.

"Thank you for helping me," he eventually says, pulling out of me and placing his cock back into his shorts.

Turning around, I quirk an eyebrow at him. "For the figures ... or for the—"

"The figures," he interrupts, obviously eager to get back to business.

I smirk as he sits back down in the chair, picking up a piece of paper along the way. Elijah is a funny creature. He has wants and needs like any other man and uses me as his tool to vent those desires. Anything before and after is as clinical as you can warrant. His shame at desiring his seventeen-year-old stepdaughter with a passion weighs heavily on him on a daily basis. Coupled with the fact that he's climbed the ranks so highly in his career, it would be a huge sensation if it ever got out that he came home and fucked said seventeen-year-old stepdaughter each and every night.

Sometimes even more than once.

"I'll be in my room if you need me," I murmur, moving out of his way so he can get back to his work. The only acknowledgement I get is a swift nod of his head as he focuses fully on the piece of paper he's now gripping so tightly, I'm afraid he'll rip it. Now that the deed is done, he's waiting on me to leave so he can breathe again. I'm not too stupid to realize that my presence once he's home at night makes him somewhat anxious. But the sex between us is just too sensational for him to stop. Sometimes when there's a night when I can't sleep and I'm roaming the halls, I hear him moan my name. Too tempting to pass, I often sneak into his room and make those dreams that are causing him to moan so much come true. Just the thrill of sliding under the covers without his knowledge and slowly working my way to his already erect cock tantalizes me so much that it's become a regular habit.

Up in my room, I don't bother to shut my door. I head straight for my calendar and mark off yet another day that gets me closer to my eighteenth birthday. Once I turn eighteen and all the chess pieces are where I want them, Elijah will be mine.

Permanently.

Nothing and no one will be able to stand in my way.

Not even Elijah himself.

CHAPTER FIVE

ast

"Take a look at what the cat dragged in, ladies," Chloe taunts down the hallway as I'm scurrying to get to lunch. I try to move past the giggling buffoons, but Chloe blocks my way. I glance up to her perfectly rounded face, flawless tanned skin, and the silky shine of her strawberry blonde hair that always manages to be glossier than anyone else's. She fixes me with her dull brown eyes—the only part that's dull about her—before she leisurely trails them down my overalls, sneering as she takes the journey. Once she's finished critiquing my choice of attire, she glances back up.

"Your stepdad's the deputy police chief. Can't he afford better clothes for you than ones that look like they've been bought in a thrift store?" The coterie of girls hang on her every word as she mocks and ridicules me. I'm about to ask her if she's done for the day when she suddenly gasps, holding a finger to her chin likes she's remembered something. "Or ... maybe it has something to do with the fact that your mother's a crack whore."

The girls erupt in laughter, but I don't stick around to hear anymore. This time she lets me pass because she's already dealt the blow she came to deliver. It's not well known that my mother takes drugs around these parts as Elijah keeps a tight lid on his affairs as much as he's able, but there has been the odd occasion where my mom's escaped the house and been seen passed out by the local bar or neighbor's house. Elijah has swiftly dealt with it—like he quickly deals with everything—but it still didn't stop the rumor mill from forming.

As quickly as I can, I open the door to the lunchroom, but the moment I step through, a foot is placed out in front of me. I fly forward, trying my hardest to correct myself, but it's too late. I fall flat on my face, my folder of notes along with my books flying out in front of me.

The whole room erupts in laughter, causing my cheeks to flame with complete and utter humiliation. I'm about to attempt to gather myself up and grab my things when Adam appears, bending down and picking up all my belongings from the floor. As I begin to scramble up, his hand comes out, offering me help to get up.

"Aww, would you look at that. Weirdo's new boyfriend is being a gentleman," Brad coos. I don't see Brad, but I'd know his voice anywhere.

Once I'm up and I say my thanks to Adam, I dust off my overalls and turn around. Sure enough, Brad is at the door with his minions, followed by Chloe and hers. They're all staring and smirking, no doubt enjoying the degradation they're inflicting on me. I'm assuming Chloe cornering me out there was deliberate in order to get Brad in place, ready to make his play just now.

"I wonder how much she'll love him after she knows that nerdy wets himself."

My humiliation is replaced with anger now that they're involving Adam in their petty games. I'm about to tell them all to fuck off when Brad suddenly appears with his water bottle and squeezes it in front of Adam's crotch. The water soaks in, immediately showing up, making it look like he just peed himself.

I turn to Adam who looks like he's about to cry, so I grab his hand and as fast as I can, parading him through the halls so we can go out the back entrance. The whole time, everyone's pointing and laughing, but I ignore them as best I can. I practically frog-march him to the stands by the football field, and only when we're completely away from everyone and their pathetic mocking tones, I sit him down, grabbing his hand.

"Are you okay?" I ask, knowing it's a fucking stupid question.

He dusts off his pants, even though there's no way he can get the water off. Thankfully, it's a warm day, so it'll dry quickly.

"I thought my old school was bad enough," he scoffs. He sniffles a little, trying his best to wipe away his tears so I won't see.

"Where was your old school?" I ask.

"Texas. We moved back here because my mom's from Kentucky and missed her family. She quickly found a job, and my dad his own store to run, so it was a no brainer, I guess."

Intrigued, I ask, "So you don't miss it there?"

He vehemently shakes his head. "Nope. I just wanted to get out of that school. Seems like I've jumped from the frying pan into the fire, though." He chuckles at his own joke.

"There's always going to be a school that's worse than the one before it. It's unfortunately the nature of the beast."

Adam glances behind us back at the school. "I don't want to go back in there after that. I don't think I can ever go back there again."

Deep-seated anger settles in my belly. Not because of Adam, but because those jerk-offs in there have made him feel this way. It was one thing bullying me, but it's entirely another thing now that they've involved someone else. If only I fucking knew what to do.

"We'll go back in there because we have to. If we put it off till tomorrow, the problem will still be there." I rub my knee a little as it's throbbing now. Adam notices straight away.

"What's wrong?"

"Nothing," I sigh. "Just landed a bit hard on my knee back there."

Adam's lips thin into a harsh line. "Those fuckers had no right tripping you like that. If I ever hurt a lady like that, my dad would pull me by the ear and take me to the nearest women's shelter until I could learn to show some respect again."

I giggle at that. "I bet your dad's a hit with your mom."

He smiles back, and it's then I see how cute Adam is. He's not my type, by any means, but there's definitely a hint of something blossoming there.

"He is. They've been married over twenty years and only had me. I'm their bright spark, as they call me. The only problem is my intelligence only runs so far. I seem to be great at everything, but when it comes to math, I'm a complete failure."

I crinkle my forehead at this. "What grades are we talking about?"

"C average," he grimaces.

I laugh out loud at that. "Wow, I thought you were going to tell me you get Ds or Fs. C is still passing."

"Yeah, but barely passing isn't good enough when I get As in everything else."

I quirk my brow and throw my arm around him. "Well, Adam. This is your lucky day, because I never get anything lower than an A star in math."

He rears his head back, causing a lock of his brown hair to fall in front of his eyes. "Seriously?"

I nudge at him. "Hey, don't look so shocked."

"I'm sorry. I didn't mean it like that." He looks sheepishly down at his feet.

"If your folks are okay with it, I can come over and tutor you some time." There's no way he can come to mine with my mom and the shit that happens at home.

His head snaps up. "Really? You'd do that?"

Considering Adam seems to be the only decent person in the school, it's a no-brainer. "Of course."

His face lights up with the cutest smile. He reminds me of a little puppy dog you just want to nurture and cuddle.

Remembering school, I glance down at my watch and see we only have five minutes till the next lesson. I manage to drag Adam back—albeit reluctantly, and although the rest of the day is shit and the insults still fly, they're no way as bad as they were earlier.

Once school is finished, I say goodbye to Adam and walk my way back home. Luckily where we live, I only have a fifteen-minute walk there and back, so it's a relatively painless journey. Especially since all the preppy kids have cars or have their parents drive them, meaning I thankfully get left alone. Well, I say left alone. Sometimes perverts in cars wind down their windows and shout shit at me.

"Hey, little girl, want some candy?" Or, *"Do you want a ride home from school? I'll buy you ice cream."*

Dirty fuckers.

I get home, throwing my bag down on the kitchen island before searching through the house. Elijah's at work, and my mom... Fuck knows where she is. I don't care anymore. Since what happened three weeks ago, she's been keeping a low profile. Also, Elijah has been making her do some volunteer work at a homeless shelter ever since she lost her job at an accounting firm a month or so back. I guess that's where I get my number solving from. Much to my displeasure, of course.

Seeing as I'm on my own, I retrieve all my textbooks from my bag and choose to get all my homework out the way while the house is quiet. Once done, I glance into the fridge to see if I can rustle up some dinner for everyone. Since my mom's decided to fall off the wagon, I've been the chef in the house. I learned to cook because I had to.

I'm about to take out some chicken pieces to fry them up when the sound of voices from outside prick my ears. I rush to the window to see who's outside only to find my mother with a man I don't recognize about to walk up the stairs to the front door.

Heart racing and fear like no other has me collecting all my things so it looks like I'm not here, running up the stairs like my life depends on it. I enter my new room, the one I moved into after getting raped in my old one, and promptly lock the door behind me, leaving the key inside, just in case. If I have to, I will lock myself away in the bathroom too.

As I sit on the bed, the only sound for now is my heavy breathing. I clutch my bag tightly to my body, rocking myself back and forth as I tremble with a panic so great, nausea bubbles and hits the back of my throat.

When the front door closes, I scramble as quickly and quietly as possible to my door, wedging myself up against it as much as I can. I position my ear towards the slit in the door, waiting for the sound of footsteps approaching my room.

"Elijah! Bryce!" my mom calls, causing my eyes to grip shut and my breathing to spike again. "Elijah! Bryce!" she calls again. I swallow the bile rising in my stomach and keep my ear to the little slit for any sound. "Looks like they're not here!" she chirps before giggling. Their mumbled voices rumble till they eventually fade, and then the sound of what I think is her bedroom door clicks shut.

Realizing she's not after me, I slink down the wall by the door and bring my knees up to my chest. My arms slip around them, hugging them tightly to me. As the distant murmuring of moaning punches through the walls, I cry. Hot, angry tears spill down my cheeks and don't let up. Even after whoever that man was is long gone and total silence resumes, I sob quietly into my knees.

As the day turns to dusk, I lie on my side, my knees still tucked into my chest. There I stare, my mind awash with rage. So much fucking rage that I'm sick of it. My body is urging me to scream, to cry out, "why me?!" at the world. What the fuck have I done to deserve this shit? I'm a good person. I go to class, I learn and get good grades. I'm no trouble to anyone. So why is it people seem to think they can walk all over me? Why is it that people seem to think they can punish me for something I haven't fucking done?!

So much rage, I can't think straight, so by the time Elijah is home and calling my name it doesn't register at first. Not until he's banging on my door, the urgency in his voice making me act.

Pushing myself up from the floor, I unlock the door, my eyes meeting his fiery lilac orbs of his. They're wild and unwavering as he scans my whole body for signs of possible injury.

"Are you okay? Are you safe? No one hurt you, did they?"

Questions. So many questions—each one making me angrier than the last.

"I'm fine," I reply, my teeth gritting unable to hide my fury. Elijah's eyes expand, probably shocked at my sudden outburst.

Bryce, ever the docile one. Bryce, she wouldn't hurt a fly ... bless her.

Well, no fucking more.

Without saying another word, I push past Elijah and head for the stairs. My rage is so great that scalding tears well in my eyes.

"Bryce, what's the matter?" Elijah shouts behind me, but I choose to ignore him.

By now the dusk has fully turned to dark. Normally, darkness scares me, but I inhale a sharp breath, determination setting in my rigid body.

At the bottom of the stairs, I register no sign of my mom, but I'm guessing it's because she's now shot up whatever shit that asshole gave her for a quick fuck.

Eyes on the door, I turn the handle to let myself out. But just as I'm about to walk through, Elijah grabs my arm. I stop dead but don't look around.

"Bryce, talk to me. Tell me what's happened to make you like this." He grips my arm tighter which only fuels my rage further. "Tell me what the fuck happened."

I snap my head back to him so violently that he stumbles back a bit, completely baffled by my sudden, complete change in behavior. Spotting what must be a crazed look in my eyes, he swallows hard before his mouth parts in bewilderment.

"You gave me a bath."

Those are the only words I offer him as I tear my arm away from his grip and pass through the door before slamming it behind me.

Seriously, what does he expect? He came home after I had been raped by my mom's drug dealer, and instead of taking me to the hospital and calling the police, he gave me a fucking bath. He thought he was such a fucking hero by taking care of me then sending me for a blood test to make sure I never caught anything from my rapist.

How fucking decent of him.

I hate my mom, I hate Elijah, and I hate the fucking world! All these thoughts scream in my head as I stumble down the steps before I take in a huge breath and wipe my tears away.

"I got some spinach pie I ain't gonna eat, if you want it."

The voice from the shadows next door makes me jump a little. I squint in the darkness but edge closer towards Frank. I know his name, and I know he lives on his own, but that's about as much knowledge as

I have about our neighbor. Like us, he keeps to himself the majority of the time.

I take the first step, watching Frank as he sits in his rocking chair, a joint in one hand. When he notices me staring at it, he holds it up in the air. “I got bowel cancer. This helps with the pain.”

My heart calming a little from my ordeal, I sniffle before wiping my nose with the back of my hand. “I’m sorry to hear that,” I finally say, my feet still planted on his first step.

Frank simply shrugs one shoulder. “Ah, it is what it is. I can’t grumble about what I can’t change. Besides, I have a feeling my old lady’s getting bored up there without me, so she’s helping me along the process a little.”

“So it’s terminal?” I ask, stepping up a little closer to him.

He inhales a big puff, and with a gravelly voice, he answers. “Yep. I have one, maybe two years left.”

It’s on the tip of my tongue to spout the same shit I did a moment ago. It’s everyone’s natural response, to apologize when hearing someone’s dying or dead. Instead, I clamp my mouth shut and climb up the last remaining steps to his porch, my eyes landing on the uneaten slice of spinach pie.

“I haven't got another seat, but you’re welcome to sit on my step and eat. You must be hungry.”

I’m about to ask him how he could possibly know this, but I’m guessing it’s because he lives right next door where he can see and hear just about everything that goes on in our house.

“Thank you,” I answer, grabbing the plate and shoving a huge piece of it into my mouth, the cheese and spinach flavors hitting my tongue and making me crave more.

“Hey, watch yourself there, lady. You’ll get indigestion if you keep eating like that.”

“Hungry,” is all I can answer as I’m still desperately chewing on the food.

“So I see.” He smiles at me, but the smile seems sad. I glance away because if he’s pitying me, I don’t want to see it in his eyes.

“You sit out here often?” I ask, needing something to say.

Frank stops his rocking for a moment to answer. “Every damn

night. It's amazing, the shit you see when the neighbors think no one's looking."

I swallow my last bite before placing the plate next to me and dusting the crumbs off my hands. "Really?" Suddenly this night is turning rather interesting. "Can you tell me?"

He smiles, his dark brown eyes lighting up with a mischief that causes excitement to bubble inside of me.

"Well, Sharon over there has got a huge thing for your stepfather. She's always gazing at him, every time she's out the house and when he comes home. She obviously thinks he's damn fine. I never see any men coming to her house, but I do see the local priest's wife visiting her often. She comes by for a couple of hours or less, then she leaves. I don't know what's happening. Maybe it's a cult." I snigger, causing Frank to snap his head my way. "You'll be so sorry if I'm right."

"Anything else?" I ask, my stomach fully sated and my mind finally easing.

Frank glances across at the neighboring houses before answering. "Number twenty-seven has a cat that likes to poop in the next-door neighbor's front lawn. It only ever does it at night, so in the morning when they wake and find poop on their lawn yet again, they always do that thing where they look around like the culprit has only just done it and is hiding somewhere." I giggle again, imagining that in my head. "Next week they're having cameras installed so they can find out who's doing it. That'll certainly be interesting."

It's kind of sad that Frank's all on his own, that he has to resort to spying on the neighbors to gain any excitement. But then again, the more I think about it, the more I begin to realize that Frank may or may not be lonely, but he has a wealth of information stored in his head. Another thought flicks through my mind, wondering how much he knows about my situation. I'm guessing more than enough.

And it's that final thought that has me biting my lip, considering the endless possibilities. Frank knows so much about everyone around him. Armed with enough information, he could take people down if he wanted to. What could I possibly find out if I dig around enough? What skeletons could the Brads and Chloes of this world be hiding that they're desperate not to let out?

My heart thundering at the prospect, I smile for the very first time in a long time. There's that age old saying about an eye for an eye making the whole world blind, but by fuck, wouldn't it be fun getting back at the pieces of shit who have wronged you in the world?

With renewed energy coursing through my veins, my heart flutters at the prospects ahead. No one is going to help me. That for sure has been proven lately. The only person who can help me is me.

All those fuckers better watch their backs, because like the proverbial storm, I'm coming.

And nothing and no one can stop me.

CHAPTER SIX

resent

After Elijah's long gone to bed and he believes I'm safely locked up tight in my room, I get the key I've hidden away and unlock my door, creeping out onto the landing. I have my hoodie ready to place over my head and dark Converse to quietly sneak out into the night. My phone in hand and on silent, I ever so gently shut my door behind me, lock it, then proceed to tiptoe down the stairs.

When outside, I exhale a breath and turn my head towards Frank's house. Sure enough, he's there in his usual spot, so I blow him a kiss. He waves at me, then I begin my sprint towards Duckface's house. Despite knowing her secrets for a while now, I've kept my distance from her as she's never caused me any bother.

Up until Blueberrygate, that is.

Deep in my heart, I know that Elijah would never entertain a woman like Duckface, but it doesn't stop her from constantly pursuing him, and that I definitely cannot abide by.

At the rear of her house, I enter through the unlocked back porch then very slowly creep my way into the darkness of the kitchen. As I enter the living area, faint moaning pricks my ears, alerting me to the sounds coming from upstairs. I take the steps while fiddling with my phone to hit record, making the screen go black so it doesn't alert them.

The bedroom door is ajar, so I peep through with my phone just to see if I can view what I suspect is happening.

They come into view, the priest's wife sprawled on the bed, her legs wide open as Duckface kisses her way down from her neck to her breasts where she suckles on her tiny, pink nipples. The priest's wife moans again, fisting her hand in Duckface's hair.

"That feels so good," she coos, her head back, eyes closed, no doubt enjoying the pleasure she's giving her.

Bit by bit, Duckface lowers herself down until she's in between the very married lady's legs. I can't see what Duckface is doing as the woman's leg is in the way, but I know when she starts eating her pussy when the priest's wife hisses, arching her back, and moaning out—surprisingly for a priest's wife—the word fuck.

"That feels so good. Fuck, Sharon, you're too good at eating pussy."

My eyes widen a little, and I have to cover my hand over my mouth to stop me from laughing. This shit is really too good.

Duckface stops eating her out and begins her ascent, kissing her leg up to her knee as she goes. "I'm going to rock your world, baby," she promises, turning her back to me as she straddles the priest's wife, getting into position, their pussies meeting. Duckface thrusts her hips back and forth, her ass muscles flexing as she chases her pleasure. Like a battering ram, she fucks that woman's pussy, both their moans filling the room. I'm rock still, unable to move or look away ... even If I wanted to. I lick my lips, mouth parting, and my breathing labored as I carry on staring like the perverted creep I am.

"Sharon, ahhh ... you fuck me so, so good." Her head is back, her hands fisting the sheets as Duckface does all the work.

"I'm going to make you come all over my pussy, baby. I'll make you feel so good."

I quirk an eyebrow, still recording the whole thing. Apparently, Duckface gets off on dominating her subjects. Interesting.

After a while, Duckface's movements become frantic as the priest's wife's desire-filled screams travel all around the room. I have to say, I'm impressed with Duckface's level of energy as she keeps going, her rounded ass flexing with each thrust.

The moment I note that Duckface is about to come is when she falters a little, her hand slipping off the woman's knee, but she quickly regains control thrusting like her life depends on it. A part of me thinks I should go now as I have more than enough ammo if I need it, but another sick and twisted part of me wants to witness the moment she comes. The voyeur in me is secretly excited and getting off on the display in front of me.

"Oh, fuck!" the woman cries, her head thrown back into the pillow as her body convulses with her orgasm. Soon after, Duckface follows, her gyrations slowing and their screaming moans becoming whimpers.

"You're ... the fucking best, do you know that?" the priest's wife breathlessly aims to say as she gently tucks Duckface's hair behind her ear.

"You know how much I love fucking you," she rasps back. She makes a move to climb off her, and when she does, I take that as my cue to leave, quickly scurrying down the steps and back out the door. As I approach my house, I offer a little wave to Frank then practically skip up the stairs. In no time, I'm in my room and quickly locking the door. But the moment I do, light emerges at the bottom of my door, alerting me to the fact that Elijah is awake.

Panicking, I race to pull off my shoes, throw off my hoodie and shoving down my sweatpants before climbing into bed. I consider pretending to be asleep if he enters, but my body's too pumped up to feign sleep. His footsteps sound towards my door, stopping once he reaches it. Adrenaline pumping at this point, I slide my fingers in between my folds, noting how fucking wet I am. I guess I enjoyed Duckface and priest wife's display a little too much.

I moan out, cupping my breasts, the sound of which causes Elijah to unlock my door and enter, the light shining in as he does.

"What are you doing?" he asks as I squint at the light.

"I need to come. I'm so fucking horny right now."

I throw the duvet from my body, exposing my nakedness to him. Elijah hesitates as I slide my fingers deep into my wet core, moaning as I plunge them in. I cup my breast, squeezing my nipple, and that's all the encouragement Elijah needs to slip into my room and close the door. With only the faint light from the cracks in the door illuminating the room, Elijah's figure crawls up my bed until he reaches my awaiting pussy. There he pushes my hands away, halting me from pleasuring myself. For some reason, Elijah doesn't like it when I pleasure myself. I asked him why once, but he never gave me a full answer. My own theory is Elijah is much like Duckface, he likes to dominate. Another reason why they're not compatible. Me, I'm flexible in every way, but only when it comes to the man in front of me.

Two fingers delve deep inside me, causing me to arch my back and moan out. "Fuck, Bryce. You're soaked."

I won't divulge the reason why. I'm guessing he wouldn't like it very much if he knew. "Thinking about you," I answer, breathlessly. Mostly a lie, but now that he's here it's the truth. Watching that display back at Duckface's house may have been the catalyst for this yearning to find a release, but now that he's here, my focus is solely on him.

With both fingers inside me, Elijah's tongue darts out, sliding it over my clit. My legs come together, trapping his head between them as he assaults my clit with his tongue and thrusts his fingers deep inside me. Closing my eyes, my moans are fucking loud as I allow myself this moment to only feel his pleasure. Flashbacks of what I saw assault my mind, only adding fuel to a fire that has been lit. I thrust my hips, meeting his face as his tongue flicks over and over. My body quivers and just like that, my orgasm catches me.

"Fuuuuuuuuccckkkk!" I scream, my head dizzying with my climax.

Elijah slows before kissing the side of my leg, pulling his fingers out as he goes. He raises those fingers towards his nose, inhaling my scent.

"You weren't fucking wrong about being horny. You came within a minute," he jibes, pulling himself up so he can push down his boxers.

"It's because I want you so much," I answer breathlessly as I watch his fully erect cock spring free.

Elijah hovers over me, his cock at my entrance. It slides inside without resistance, causing him to curse as he reaches the hilt.

"Why can't I ever say no to you?"

For a moment, I'm shocked at the level of vulnerability in his question. I've always known that he tries to stay away from me, but until now, he had never fully admitted his feelings out loud.

He thrusts forward again, and again curses, his body quivering with the pleasure I'm giving him.

"Why can't I stay away?"

I want to answer that he loves me, but I doubt he's ready to hear that right now. Instead, I stroke his back, encouraging him to keep going. Encouraging him to take the pleasure back that he's given me.

"I'm sick," he groans out, panting as he pushes forward, each thrust as glorious as the last. "I'm sick, but I can't fucking stay away from you."

I moan, my desire spiking at his confession until my moan is halted by his lips on mine. My body stunned, it becomes rigid at first, but within an instant of his lips on mine, I relent, pulling his head deeper into our kiss.

He's kissing me!

Fucking hell, he's kissing me!

This is something Elijah never does. The sex, always, but the kisses, never. I've desperately wanted him to and have also wanted to question why he never does, but the sex between us was always so electric that kissing became a non-essential part after a while.

But now...

Sweet, glorious, heavenly lips assault me, his tongue dancing heavily with mine as he fucks me hard. I don't know if it's the kissing or that he's just so turned on, but he comes sooner than anticipated, his body quivering with his climax.

He collapses on top of me, his breathing heavy in my ear. I close my eyes, relishing the feel of his body fully on mine, my fingers absent-mindedly stroking up and down his back. Seeing goosebumps form on his body causes me to smile. This is the most intimate moment we have ever had since the start of our insidious affair.

Closing my eyes, I relish this moment for however long it lasts, my mind counting down the days until I turn eighteen. For now, I am giving Elijah his space—honoring his need to distance himself from our situation. But once I turn eighteen, I'm setting my plan in to motion, and Elijah won't have a leg to stand on.

CHAPTER SEVEN

ast

“Have you got nothing but overalls in your wardrobe, freak?” Chloe barks the moment I approach her and her minions in the hallway on my way to class. She glances at her pack, her dull brown eyes dazzling with mischief. Sensing something’s not right, my feet hurry. “Ladies, what do you say we ... help the little, creepy weirdo to look more appeasing to the eye?”

My heart quickens, and so too does my pace, but the moment I’m about to walk past them, three of them pull out a tube of paint and squeeze the contents all over my front. I screech, causing them all to laugh at me.

“Why do you look so mad, freak? It’s a much better look with some color.”

The giggles throughout the hallway puncture my ears and sting my eyes. Wanting to get away as soon as possible, I reach the nearest room I can find which is the boy’s locker room. I know I shouldn’t be in here, but everyone’s supposed to be in class in literally two minutes, and this room won't be used until this afternoon when the asshole jocks practice football.

Once I'm in the safe confines of the room, I wedge myself up against the door and exhale a deep breath.

"Come on, everyone! Get to class!" I hear Mr. Shrouder, our vice principal shout to everyone still milling around. Their footsteps scurry, doors close, and then total silence.

Closing my eyes, I take a moment to calm myself from yet another humiliation by the Chloe harem, but when I open them back up, the blue, red, and white paint's still there in big clumps on the front of my overalls.

Heading for the sinks in the next room, I use my fingers to scoop off as much of the paint I can before eventually trying to rub off the remainder. Only through sheer determination and will do I get most of it off, but now it looks like I've been breastfeeding a baby and the milk's soaked right through.

An angered sigh leaves my lips. Patience. I have to have patience. I've been scoping out Chloe's house for the last couple of days, but so far, there's nothing salacious going on. Her minions were there last night and stayed for a couple of hours, but then they left. Boring stuff so far, but something has to give soon.

The sound of the door opening causes me to grab my stuff and go into the farthest room where the lockers are. There, I wedge myself up against one, my breathing heavy. Footsteps sound inside the room I'm in, and I close my eyes shut tight, hoping and praying whoever it is won't find me. What sounds like a gym bag slams down onto the benches, the noise alerting me to the fact whoever it is is close.

My heart still drumming, I risk a quick peek around the locker, finding Chesney on his own, rummaging through something in his bag. He's already wearing his gym clothes for football practice later, his golden waves of hair haphazardly strewn across his head. I wait with bated breath until he pulls out what it is he's after in there.

Shouldn't he be in class?

It's not long before I realize exactly why he's in here alone. He pulls out a vial of something I can't identify followed by a syringe. My breath hitches and my heart drums, thinking about the opportunity that's now presented itself. If only I could see what it is he's about to inject.

Getting out my phone, I quickly put it on silent and open up my camera. I switch to video and start recording him as he holds up the vial and pushes the needle inside. With my phone pointing towards him, I zoom in, trying to see what it is while he's holding it up in the air.

Winstrol.

Isn't that a steroid?

Deciding to hold that thought for now, I carry on filming him as he pulls his shorts down, exposing his tight ass. My eyebrow raises at the sight. Despite being a complete and utter prick, I have to admit, he does have a nice ass. Perfectly formed and muscular, no doubt aided by his exercise, and now it would seem, steroids.

I bite my lip as he injects it into his upper thigh. I fucking hate needles, so it takes everything in me not to make a whimpering sound as I watch it go in. I end the recording then quickly email the video to myself so that I definitely don't lose it.

Heart in my mouth, my head wondering if I can do this, I suck in a deep breath, waiting for him to put the needle away when I emerge from the shadows I'm in.

"So that's the reason why you're so ... fit," I say, my voice all sultry and husky. My heart is still hammering in my chest. I've never done anything like this before.

Chesney jumps at the sound of my voice, his sneer forming the moment he eyes me. "What the fuck are you doing in here?"

My body awash with nerves, I fight them back, my fists clenching, trying to hold myself together. I can do this. Don't cower. This is what he wants. I have the power now.

I know his dark secret.

"I don't think you're exactly in a position to ask me questions after what I've just seen, do you?"

One step in front of the other, I approach him, and the more I do, the more Chesney's face turns from rage to panic.

A sudden jolt of excitement crawls along my spine, making me feel tingly all over. Is this what it's like to have power? Is this what's it's like to feel empowered?

"You shouldn't be in here," he growls, trying to maintain his composure, but I still witness the fear in his eyes, the quickening of his pulse in his neck, and the way his chest heaves through the tight t-shirt he's wearing.

I ignore him, instead closing the distance between us. My eyes are zeroed in on his panic, a deep-seated longing forming in the pit of my stomach.

What is this emotion? Am I getting off on his fear?

A sudden urge to get close to him and sniff his neck takes over. Would I be able to smell his anxiety? If I darted my tongue out and licked the bulging vein in his neck, will I be able to taste his unease?

Deciding to get as close as possible, my chest meets his where I gaze longingly into those deep, chocolate brown eyes of his. I lick my lips seductively, and of course, he looks. It only adds to my sense of empowerment.

"Oh, Chesney," I begin, my voice a husky whisper. "You have been a naughty boy. What am I going to do with you?"

His pupils dilate slightly, his Adam's apple bobs as he swallows hard. I know what it is he must be thinking. This isn't like me. This isn't like me at all.

But then again, maybe this *is* me. It's just been waiting sixteen years to get out.

"What do you want?" he asks with suspicion in his tone, realizing I probably won't let what I saw go.

Too tempting to ignore, I reach up on my tiptoes and inhale the musky scent on his neck. Undertones of faint sweat fill my nostrils, his fear creeping out. I close my eyes, relishing the aroma, feeding off of it like it is sustenance.

I draw my head back, my eyes narrowing with lust. "I'm going to be honest with you. I really don't know at this point. I'm pretty sure I can think of something, though." I pull back slightly, my eyes scanning down the length of his body. Despite his anxiety, he's turned on. Something that's evident by the tent that has formed in his shorts.

"Oh, would you look at that?" I hum, my hand immediately

clamping around his cock. Chesney lets out a little whimper, his body trembling with the impact. "Can't help getting turned on by the weirdo, can we? How does it feel to be touched by the freak, huh? What would your friends say?"

His jaw tics and his eyes sharpen with anger. "You have no proof of what I've done," he sneers, causing me to tighten my hold on his cock.

The sudden jolt of his body and the trepidation in his eyes causes heat to surge throughout my whole being. I cock my head to one side and smirk. "That's where you're wrong. I recorded the whole thing on my phone." His eyes widening, he makes a grab for my bag, but I yank at his cock. "Ah, ah," I scold, pulling my other arm back so he can't grab at my bag. Luckily, my hold on his cock forces him to relent. "Do you really think I would be stupid enough not to save it somewhere safe? No matter what you do to my phone, I will always have the recording of you shooting up steroids."

Gripping his eyes shut, his breathing is labored. "It was insulin."

I laugh out loud, causing his eyes to flutter open. "I got a good shot of the vial you used so everyone will know." I practically sing the last words, I'm so high right now.

"What will it take to keep you silent?"

I inhale a long, deep breath, closing my eyes as I appreciate this moment for that little bit longer. When I open them back up and meet his dilated pupils again, I let out a noisy sigh. "I already told you ... I'm not sure just yet. I'll think of something. But I will say one thing. From this moment on, the bullying stops. No more calling me weirdo or freak or creep or whatever word of the month you fuckers probably take weeks to think up. From now on, you are courteous and kind, and when I snap my fingers your way, you will come running." I raise up on my tiptoes again just so I can get close to his lips. There, I breathe my hot breath into his mouth, his own coming in hot pants against mine. Unable to help myself, I rub his cock. The power I possess knowing I call all the shots here making me braver and hotter by the second.

"Do I make myself clear?" I whisper, my tongue darting out to lick his lips.

"Y ... y ... yes," he responds, before he lets out a croaking sound, his body jerking.

I glance down, noticing a wet patch has formed at the crotch of his shorts, so I immediately pull my hand away. "Oh, my." I giggle, realizing I just made him come.

Chesney squeezes his eyes tightly shut, his cheeks reddening by the second with embarrassment. I clear my throat, pulling my backpack up higher on my shoulder.

"I will ... leave you to clean that up."

I practically skip my way towards the doorway, but before I leave, I remember to say something else. I halt at the door. "Oh, by the way." I wait for him to turn my way, his posture completely dejected. A surge of pride courses through me that I made him that way. "From this moment on, you'll also leave Adam alone. If I get a whiff of any animosity towards him from you, I will make you pay." I then smile as brightly as a stewardess on an airplane. "You have a nice day now!"

CHAPTER EIGHT

resent

Dear Johnathan,

I just read your letter, and it made me smile. I have to admit to you that it's the highlight of my week, receiving your letters. They're the one constant I can cling on to. Just for those precious few moments, I am able to go off in to your world and escape mine. I know that sounds really selfish since you're in prison, so I apologize for that. You always told me to tell you the truth—to open my heart to you and not hold back. Well, this is me being completely honest.

I'm happy to hear that your parole hearing is coming up in just three months. You must be so excited for the possibility of being released a little earlier. I want you to promise me, though, that you won't do anything silly when you're released. I am okay. I can look after myself. You concentrate on

. . .

The front door opens, so as quickly as I can, I grab the unfinished letter and stuff it under my mattress to finish writing later.

"Bryce!" I hear Elijah call from the bottom of the stairs.

Smoothing my hair out, I perk up my breasts before appearing at the landing. "I'm here," I diligently call back. I lean my hands on the banister, my eyes taking in his perfectly formed body in that police uniform of his. Duckface was right about one thing: he certainly does look fine. Damn fine.

His bright eyes lock onto mine before they briefly trail down to my tits—just like they always do. "We've got less than two hours to get ready."

"I was just about to jump in the shower," I reply back.

Tonight I'm escorting Elijah to some police charity function where I'll have to stand and watch as all the wives and girlfriends leer at Elijah all night without being able to do a damn thing about it. The only good thing coming out of this tonight is I have a plan—a plan that will at least keep my mind occupied.

"I'm just going to do a brief workout in the basement, and then I'll hop in the shower."

I simply nod my head, smiling down at him before turning and making my way back into my room. I hesitate at the side of my bed, briefly wondering whether I should continue writing my letter, but having Elijah home makes that too risky. Deciding against it, I head for the bathroom to have that shower before getting myself dressed in one of the sexiest gowns I could find. Elijah gave me two hundred dollars to get myself something nice for tonight, and boy did I get something nice. The size four, red silk dress which hugs my body perfectly and will show off my greatest assets will certainly be a head-turner tonight. I have zero doubt about that. Even as a weirdo nerd, I am sexy. That was one thing Dick Chesney admitted to me after our locker room encounter. I smile, thinking about that day. It was the turning point to everything. Chesney being so submissive to me was what added fuel to my already lit flame. From that moment on, my confidence grew, and with that, boundaries were definitely crossed. Do I have any regrets about some of the things I've done? I should, but I don't. And I really don't care what that says about me.

I take a long, hot shower, and when I'm done, I wrap a towel around me before venturing into my bedroom. I can hear the faint noises of grunting coming from the basement below. I bite my lip, desire tiptoeing deep inside my belly.

Pulling off the towel wrapped around my hair, I let my wet auburn tendrils hang loose around me as I make my way down to the basement. There in the middle of the room is a shirtless Elijah standing on a blue mat with only his black shorts and boxing gloves on. He's already worked up a sweat, and by the way he's pounding into the punching bag right now, it's no wonder. He's fully focused on the bag in front of him as he grunts with each punch, his face full of rage and determination. He's pissed about something. I know Elijah enough by now to note these emotions whenever he decides to show them. His rage only adds to his sexiness, making me crave him even more than ever. My eyes hooded, I watch for a moment, lust pooling between my legs. It's seriously like watching porn.

"Who got you all riled up?" I start a conversation because I can't continue standing frozen in the doorway forever, lusting after him.

He doesn't even blink or look my way when I ask, he just responds, "Fucking William Schultz."

The local mayor and an occasional sore spot for Elijah. Although this is definitely the most worked up I've seen him over the man.

"What has he done this time?"

As Elijah carries on punching the bag, I walk farther in, to get closer to him. I want to smell the angry sweat that's cascading down his biceps.

"I told him we need more police," he replies, punching the bag even harder. "Says he can't afford it, it's not in the budget. The fucker can spend thousands on lavish parties with champagne, though. Unnecessary trips abroad to meet dignitaries and have lots of liquid fucking lunches at the taxpayers' expense." He punches the bag really hard two more times, grunting as he does. "But the moment crime rises a little and we need more boots on the ground, he tells me we don't have the money. Fucker!" He punches the bag three more times before he pushes it and lets his arms fall down by his sides. He's breathless, his chest rising and falling quickly with each pant. I stand in front of him, marveling at his hairless, shiny chest, waiting to be touched ... to be licked.

As if finally sensing I'm in the room with him, Elijah snaps his eyes from the bag to me. They're filled with the rage firing behind them. I lick my lips, my body humming at the sheer power he exudes from his every pore. His lips curl up into a sneer before his eyes travel the length of my body.

"Drop the fucking towel."

The growl in his voice causes the hairs to rise all over my skin. I don't have to be told twice. The moment the command leaves his lips, I undo the towel, leaving it to simply fall to the floor, my bare body completely exposed.

His sneer rising even higher, he steps forward purposefully, each stride more vigorous than the last. Once in front of me, he takes his gloves off, places a hand around my neck and forces me back towards his slightly raised weight bench. When my lower back hits the top of it, Elijah pushes me down but keeps me secured in his hands so I won't fall. His eyes foretell danger, wickedness, and terror all rolled in to one, but it doesn't scare me. Elijah would never intentionally hurt me. He's pissed and he needs an outlet. The rage that he was feeling just moments ago has been funneled in to a different, heightened emotion now that I'm here distracting him.

With my head dangling, I'm practically upside down. My ass is resting on the edge of the bench when Elijah pulls out his already erect cock. I'm a little too high for him to reach me at this point, so he has to place his foot on a pedal to lower me to the perfect height. The moment he has me where he wants me, he slips his cock inside me, his fingernails digging into my hips as he does, his eyes closing at the pleasure it no doubt gives him.

"Fuck!" Elijah bellows, his hips thrusting inside me again. "You've got the best fucking pussy, do you know that?"

I moan as he plunges into me again, his cock penetrating me to the hilt. "And you have the best cock," I answer breathlessly, my head dizzying not only from the pleasure but also from being slightly upside down.

With his hands holding my hips steady, Elijah pummels in and out of my pussy, and with each glorious thrust, his beautiful grunts echo around the basement. We're both being super loud, but neither of us cares considering this sex position fucking rocks.

"Fucking bitch!" he grinds out, his pace quickening until he roars out his release, emptying himself inside of me.

His fingernails still digging in my hips, Elijah closes his eyes for a moment as if relishing this moment. For him, he has reached his goal, but I'm still left on the precipice.

As if knowing this, Elijah opens his eyes, slides out of me, and tucks himself away. His focus solely on me, he presses the lever, and this time I'm raised even higher in the air. I start to slide back, but Elijah grabs my thighs, pulling me until I've reached the height he wants me. Without craning my neck up, I can't see what he's doing, but I don't need to see when his tongue is suddenly on my clit, dancing around it the way only he knows how. I'm completely vulnerable, totally submissive to his touch, unable to move ... even though I don't want to. With a finger inserted into my pussy, he finds my g-spot and strokes it while giving me head.

Literally thirty seconds later, I come, squirting all over his face in the process, my body jerking and convulsing from the potency of my climax.

"Fuck!" I scream, my breaths leaving my body in quick pants. Stars form behind my eyes, then I'm carefully dropped as he slides me down to a flat position. I place my shaking legs to the sides of the bench and take my time getting my breath back. Once I think I can finally see again, I open my eyes, turning my head towards Elijah who's wiping his face with a gym towel.

"Now we have less than an hour to get ready. I'm heading for the shower."

Back to being aloof, I see.

Sitting up so I'm straddling the bench, my eyes scan his perfect, over six-foot frame as he disappears through the door, his pert ass winking at me as he goes.

I sigh. I do a lot of that around Elijah.

Knowing there's not much time left to spare, I make my way up to my bedroom again, and again take another shower, needing to clean off after our little ... workout session.

Once seated at the mirror, towel wrapped around me, I get to work, making sure I pay special attention to my makeup tonight. Not too much so that I look like a slut, but certainly enough to make my smokey eyes and lips stand out. As far as I'm concerned, I want *everything* to stand out tonight.

With my natural curls, I use a spray gel to set them in place so that they don't get too wayward tonight. I place strands of my hair on top of my head then fasten them with a diamond-studded clip to keep them in place.

I take a last look in the mirror to see my reflection, and I'm impressed at what stares back at me.

Yeah, I'm the bomb.

A surge of enthusiasm escalates up my spine when I think of Elijah and what he may say when he sees me like this tonight. The excitement continues when I pull the red satin dress out of my wardrobe and run my fingers down the hem.

Wearing no underwear again, I slink my feet into the top of the dress and work the dress up to my breasts, hooking my arms inside. Again, I glance at the mirror, and what I see impresses even me. I may only be a smidge under eighteen, but tonight I look like an elegant lady in her twenties. The silk dress flows so well that it makes my body look a lot longer than it actually is.

My smile rises higher as I look even better than I'd anticipated. I had plans before Elijah's little outburst tonight, but now I know those plans are definitely going in to fruition. See, I've known for a while now that Elijah and our local mayor have been butting heads. And now it's time for me to ... settle the score.

"Are you ready?!" I hear Elijah shout before he knocks two times on my door.

I rise up from my chair at the same time he pushes my door open. Once he locks eyes on me, they widen in surprise. But then his jaw tics and his nostrils flare.

"You're not wearing that."

Inwardly, I sigh. A part of me wondered whether I would be faced with this side of him. The possessive, domineering side who wants to rule everything I do, wear, and say. I may give in to him on some things, but tonight certainly won't be one of them.

"What's the matter with what I'm wearing?"

His eyes scan the contours of my body, preparing to make his argument. "For one, it's obvious that you're not wearing any underwear—"

I cut him short. "You really think I could possibly wear underwear under this dress?" I fan my hands down the length of my body for emphasis.

"You're barely eighteen," Elijah hisses, causing my back to arch in challenge. Does he *really* want to go there? "Yet you're wearing a dress which only someone many years older than you should wear—"

"What is your problem?" I groan, wanting to get down to the real issue here.

Elijah's chest rises and falls with no doubt a deep, frustrated breath. "The problem is you're supposed to be my stepdaughter, yet you're dressed like my wife."

And there it is.

I suck in a breath of my own, my feet finding movement towards his rigid frame. He's dressed in a black, three-piece suit tonight, his white shirt as crisp as a winter's morning. He looks like James Bond, totally and completely fuckable, yet according to him, I'm the one with the clothing problem.

Once I reach within touching distance, I take my finger and lightly press it against the top of his chest before making my way down to the waist of his pants. "Just so you know, sunshine, no matter what you say, I will not be wearing anything else. You either bring me as is, or I'm going to take this dress off—if you really forbid me to wear it—and go completely naked tonight. I'm pretty sure the latter would turn more heads, so which is it going to be?"

I narrow my eyes at him to make sure he realizes I mean business. I may allow him to use me as his fuck toy whenever he damn well pleases, but I draw the line when it comes to him telling me what to wear.

His eyes narrow back as if in challenge, his breath a little ragged. I can't tell whether it's out of frustration, or if he's turned on by our little exchange. I'm betting both.

"You are to keep within eyesight of me all night. Do I make myself clear?"

I bite my lip, his words hitting me in all the wrong places considering we're about to leave shortly. His eyes dart down, then he licks his own, his tongue making my belly tie up in all sorts of heated knots.

"Crystal," I answer in a husky whisper. At some point tonight, I'm going to have to go against Elijah's wishes, but I'm sure if he realizes what it is that I'm doing, he'll forgive me.

"How are we getting there tonight?" I ask, trying to clear my mind from constantly thinking about fucking him. "Uber?"

Elijah's jaw twitches before he raises his arm to check his watch. Still unhappy with me, I see. "We have a driver coming for us in—"

As he's about to finish his sentence, the doorbell rings. "Now," Elijah continues. I smirk as he scans my dress again before meeting my eyes. "Are you ready?"

"Of course."

Elijah makes a turn before making his way down the stairs. I follow suit, my Louboutins clicking down each step as we head downstairs then outside.

Thankfully, there's a warm March breeze tonight, so I don't have to cover up. I'm not sure Elijah would be too happy to find out I'm not wearing a bra. I'm pretty sure my nipples could direct traffic in a push.

On the short journey to the fifteen-year-old modern museum holding the event tonight, Elijah's posture is rigid. With his head resting on his hand, he stares out the window, his right leg twitching. I get the sense Elijah really isn't looking forward to tonight. I'm also sensing it may have something to do with a certain mayor who is hosting tonight's event.

I inhale a breath, clutching my purse which has my phone neatly tucked inside. Elijah may not be looking forward to tonight, but I have a feeling tonight's going to be very entertaining.

CHAPTER NINE

ast

After my run in with Chesney, I feel completely and utterly invigorated. So much so that right after our encounter, I decide to wait around until Adam's physics class ends so I can haul him out of school. We both have history together next, but I'm way too pumped on adrenaline to be able to concentrate in class.

"Bryce, what the hell?" Adam snaps when I yank at his arm, pulling him down the hallway. Once we reach the end of the row of lockers, I turn to face him.

"Ditch school with me?"

Adam's nose crinkles a little, and his glasses are steamed up, no doubt from the exertion of me pulling him half a mile down the hallway.

"Why? What's going on?"

I take in a deep breath because I wasn't planning on telling him, but I think telling him will be the only reason why he'll agree to go with me.

"It's my birthday today."

His mouth parts, and a small gasp escapes. "Happy Birthday!"

He practically screams this so grabbing his arm, I yank at him. "Shh, I don't want everyone to know."

"What are you up to?"

"Nothing," I retort. "I have some money saved, and I want to buy some new outfits. It would help having a male's perspective on whether the clothes I choose are nice or not. If you don't want to come, that's fine, but I would really like you to."

Adam shifts a little before his eyes scan the hall. He bites his lip, uncertainty marring his face. I bet he hasn't missed a class in his life. Not when it comes to deliberately skipping school, that is.

"Okay," he finally relents, his mind obviously weighing it all up. I smile brightly at him then grab his hand.

"Come on then!" I shout, dragging him with me as we run towards the exit.

We walk through the doors then immediately wedge ourselves up to the side of the building when we see the principal walking across the lawn in the distance. Thankfully, he seems too focused on something to pay us any attention.

Once he's out of sight, we sprint over the lawn, and luckily, a bus heading towards town immediately appears. We hop on, showing the driver our passes before scurrying to the back of the bus, our breaths leaving us in gasps.

Adam lets out another laugh. "That was actually fun."

"It really was," I agree, realizing how much I'm missing out on life. The ever boring, suppressed Bryce has reached her end.

Within twenty minutes, we're off the bus and heading inside the mall. We enter different clothes stores where I try on anything I think will fit me. I need a new style—a new me so I can show the world I'm not the Bryce I was mere hours ago.

Eventually, we venture into a massive store filled with every conceivable style you can think of. I grab various dresses, tops, pants, skirts ... everything I can find to try on. I even use Adam to hold the huge pile I'm quickly accumulating.

"Come with me to the changing rooms?" I ask once I think I have more than enough to try. "I'll need your opinion."

I quickly dart to the changing rooms, not even waiting for his answer, where I grab a few items from his arms before I head inside. Luckily, there's barely anyone around, so we pretty much have the changing room to ourselves.

One by one, I try things on. A few outfits, some cute but mostly sexy. Some short black dresses, short checked skirts, and tight tops which show off my tits—all things I'd never even dreamed of wearing before.

"What do you think?" I ask Adam as I step out in a short, tight, lilac dress with thin spaghetti straps. The fabric clings to my body, highlighting my curves. Adam glances up from the magazine he's reading, his jaw dropping at what I'm wearing.

Yep. That's the reaction I was after.

"Bryce ... I ... you ... you really look like that underneath all your clothes?"

I bust out a giggle, unable to help reacting to his stuttering. "That's the problem, Adam. I've been hiding too long. It's time I let the real me out." I slide my hands over my curves, admiring my shape in the mirror before glancing back at him. Sure enough, he's watching my every move, his mouth still agape. "So what do you think? Keep?" I'm going to buy it no matter what he says, but it would still be nice to know he is of the same opinion.

Adam snorts. "Oh, I'd definitely keep it." I swiftly nod my head. "How can you afford to pay for all this? Did your folks give you money or something?"

"My stepdad gave me a bank card this morning and said there was some money loaded on it if I wanted to buy myself anything." I grit my teeth at the memory of this morning as I was just about to leave for school. He had come up to me, smiling like I was going to think he was the best daddy in the whole wide world. He may have given it to me today, on my birthday, but all that money he deposited in my brand-new bank account is truly hush money. Plain and simple.

The thought threatens to ruin my good mood, so I swallow the angry bile that's rising and instead, head back into the changing room to try on something new.

I've just taken the dress off and am deciding what to try on next when I notice something in the corner of my eye. I glance in the mirror to see what it is, realizing that I hadn't fully closed the curtain. Without Adam noticing me, I stare at him as he stares at the image of my body in the mirror. Although I don't find Adam attractive, the thought that he's admiring my body makes me bite my lip with fervor.

Deciding to take things even further, I unhook my bra, sliding it down my arms and dropping it to the floor. I chance a quick glance in the mirror, and sure enough, Adam is watching intently, his Adam's apple bobbing at the sight of me.

Picking up another purple dress—this one chiffon—I seductively place it over my head and let it slide down my body. The thrill of knowing he's watching me turns me on like nothing else has before. I don't know what it is about me today, but I'm quickly learning that when I experience something new, I may as well role with it.

And the feeling is exquisite.

I snap the curtain open, causing Adam to jump. "So what do you think of this one?"

Glasses slightly steamed, Adam fidgets in his spot, his magazine quickly placed on his lap. Has he seriously got a boner over me? A part of me wants to make him pull the magazine off just to curb my curiosity, but I bite my tongue.

"What is it with you and purple today?" he asks breathily.

A pair of lilac eyes assault my head, making me swarm with all kinds of fucked up emotions.

Elijah.

The one person I thought was the good guy in all this fucking shit. The one person I came to rely on, only to be the one person who viciously let me down. I used to look up to him ... loved him. Now I can't stand the sight of him.

But still, maybe my subconscious likes to play sick, twisted, little games. Why else would I be picking the same color of clothes as *his* eyes?

Not wanting to analyze this right now, I shrug my shoulders. "I guess I just like the color purple today."

I go back to the changing room where I try on a few more tops and skirts, finally deciding on around fifteen items. Once they're paid for, I drag Adam to Victoria's Secret where I purchase a few pieces of sexy lingerie, Adam's cheeks reddening by the second. By the time we've left the store he's practically hyperventilating.

I giggle, yanking at his shirt sleeve. "Want some ice cream?" Adam swallows hard before rigorously nodding his head. Smirking, I shake my head and we make our way to the Johnny Rockets, where I decide on a strawberry milkshake instead.

I take a sip of my shake and watch as Adam bites into the rocky road he ordered. "Did you talk to your folks about the math tutoring?" I ask, taking another sip.

Adam pushes up his glasses and nods his head. "Yeah, they're really happy about the prospect of you tutoring me, but I think they're even happier that I have a friend. In fact, they asked me if you were my girlfriend." His cheeks pinken at this. He glances a look at my reaction before clearing his throat. "Of course I set them straight." I nod my head, not knowing if this is the confirmation he's looking for. Adam's nice and all, but maybe a little too nice. I guess there is something naughty inside me after all.

"Want to do anything after this?" I pose the question to him, but I'm secretly beat after our shopping expedition. It's only fair I ask, though, considering I've dragged him around with me for the past three hours.

He seems disappointed. "I can't, unfortunately. I have to start work at six."

My eyes widen. "You have a job?"

He waits to finish his mouthful before responding. "My dad owns a hardware store. It closes at six, but he likes me to help him with restocking for the following morning. He pays me well for it too. During school holidays, I work there more so I can save up some cash."

"Are you saving for anything in particular?"

Playing with the ice cream with his spoon, he shakes his head. "No, not really. I just like knowing it's there just in case I ever need it."

I nod my head, and I'm about to pick up the bill when Adam snaps it away from me. "You're not paying for this. It's your birthday." I'm about to open my mouth to argue when he says, "Considering you never told me, I had no time to get you anything, so I think this is the least you can let me do."

He gives me a reproachful look that makes me smile. I let him pay since it's only a few bucks, and by the sounds of it, he can afford it.

"I have time to quickly help you back with your bags if you want?"

I glance at the time and see it's already close to six. "You'll be late. Don't worry about me, I can manage."

"I insist. I already told my dad I'll be late, and he understands. He said to wish you a happy birthday, by the way."

I smile as we head for the bus stop with what seems like a hundred shopping bags in our hands. "That's really sweet. Tell him thanks."

We get off at the stop only a five-minute walk from my house. When we reach my door, Adam puts all the bags he's carrying down on the porch. I have to inhale a deep breath because, as always, I dread going into my house. I never know from one day to the next what I may find.

"Thank you for today, Adam. I really appreciate it."

Adam's smile is wide. "No sweat. Happy birthday again. I'll see you tomorrow."

He awkwardly stands there for a moment then apparently makes the decision to leave. I watch as he walks along the street before I turn to open my door. Except, I don't have to open my door.

Elijah does it for me.

CHAPTER TEN

resent

Hundreds of bodies adorn the grand hall inside the vast art museum. All men are in black tie while all the women have long, flowing gowns of varying colors. When we walk through, Elijah is greeted by several people I don't recognize. As we pass a waiter holding out a tray of champagne, I pick one up, but the moment I do, the glass is quickly retrieved from my hand and placed back onto the tray. I narrow my eyes at Elijah.

"You know you're underage," he growls.

I desperately want to growl back that he did some pretty scandalous things to the body of someone who is supposedly too underage to drink, but I hold my tongue.

Pretenses and all.

"Elijah, how good it is to see you." A man I recognize as Ted Rosemberg, the state judge, approaches Elijah, a big smile on his ruddy face. Following close by is his wife, Sophie.

"Nice to see you too, Ted." They shake hands, then Elijah turns to me. "This is my stepdaughter, Bryce."

Ted quickly scans the length of my body before closing in and shaking my hand. "Nice to meet you, Bryce. I bet our boy here keeps you on your toes at home the same way he runs his station."

They all laugh at his joke, me pretending to join in their guffaws. "Oh, believe me, he does."

I glance a peek at Elijah, who narrows his eyes in a silent warning. Lucky for him, the judge and his wife completely miss the heated exchange between us.

"Mind if I steal Elijah away a few moments?" Ted asks me. "I just need a private word with him."

I motion with my hands for him to carry on. "Of course. Be my guest."

Ted smiles, but Elijah looks concerned as he's led away by the judge. Sophie doesn't follow them. Instead, she picks up two champagne glasses and hands one to me.

"I won't tell if you don't." She winks at me causing me to easily warm to her.

"Thank you."

"No sweat." I take a sip of my drink as I scan the crowd with her. When she spots someone, she nudges my arm. "Watch for that one over there," she points her nose at someone in the crowd. "The one with the bright green dress." Instantly my eyes land on a woman, possibly in her early forties with blonde hair and sizeable breasts. I notice when she passes some of the men, their eyes linger on her. "That's Lucy Brightmore, head prosecutor at the DAs office. She's been after Elijah for a while now. Apparently makes all kinds of excuses to go see him."

My eyes narrow to murderous slits as I gaze upon my new enemy number one. Elijah failed to tell me about this little slut. I can only hazard a guess as to why.

"A lot of people have been wondering why Elijah's been ignoring her advances so far. Lots of people think they'd make a great couple."

Murderous jealousy pools at the pit of my stomach as I gaze upon the woman in question. I watch as she laughs at something someone says, then like a missile homing in on its target, she glances in the direction Elijah is, still in deep conversation with the judge. However, my belly dances in delight when instead of looking her way, Elijah glances towards me.

I'm about to answer Sophie, to tell her that it's none of my business when she says, "But it would seem he only has eyes for one lady tonight."

I don't say anything in return because what's the point? She doesn't have hard facts about us, only speculation.

She gives me another wink, taking a sip of her drink. "Don't worry, darling. Your secret is safe with me." She then skedaddles off, waving away at some lady in the crowd she wants to talk to.

I sigh, taking another sip of my champagne, enjoying the tiny buzz it's giving me. I'm literally alone maybe five seconds when a man who looks to be in his mid-twenties approaches me, a smile dancing in his predatory, blue eyes.

"You're a new face," he starts, glancing down at my cleavage. "I'm sure I would have noticed you at one of these functions before."

I roll my eyes at his clichéd pickup line. "This is the first major function we've been invited to since my stepdad's promotion."

He turns his body so he's facing me more, his eyes still dancing around my tits. "Oh, really. And who might that..." His eyes leave my chest to look over my shoulder. "Oh, Elijah, I didn't see you there."

I turn my body around to find a rigid Elijah, rage filling his eyes as they lock onto this stranger. "Paul, I see you've met my stepdaughter, Bryce."

"Oh, you're Bryce. Nice to meet you."

Before we can even shake hands or make any further pleasantries, Elijah butts in again. "Bryce, this is Paul Brightmore. Son of the head prosecutor for the DA's office."

My eyes slightly widen at this information. This is the bitch's son. Interesting.

We nod our heads at each other, then Paul suddenly doesn't seem to know where to look. He was pretty good at knowing a moment ago.

"I'm sure my mom's going to want to speak with you at some point this evening."

Hot rage pits at Paul's words to Elijah, making me want to pluck the pretty, black painted, fake nails of hers right off her.

"There's a lot to get through this evening, so I'll see if I get the chance," Elijah responds, making me smirk at his nonchalance.

I chance another sip of my champagne, but just as I bring it to my lips, the glass is snatched from me. "Paul, will you excuse us? I need to chat with Bryce for a moment."

"Of course," Paul responds, letting us pass.

Elijah sets down my half empty glass before yanking me away from the crowd and down an empty hallway. He opens a big, wooden, mahogany door and we step inside what looks to be some sort of library. The room is dark with only the faint, fake Victorian lights flickering as if they're candles. In the middle of the room are brown leather sofas which look to be older than Elijah. Books upon books line the side walls and every crevice. This room doesn't seem like it belongs here but is beautiful, nonetheless.

Once Elijah shuts the door, cutting out any sounds from outside, he turns to me, his fists clenching. "Barely fifteen minutes here, and already you're causing trouble."

I try my hardest to hide my smirk, but it's useless. "I haven't the faintest idea what you're talking about."

Grabbing me by the neck, Elijah forces my body up against the door. "I told you not to cause trouble. The moment I turn my back, you're drinking champagne when you shouldn't, and—"

"And what?" I cut him off, my heart thundering at what he may say next.

Words he desperately wants to say. I know he does, but for some reason he's holding his tongue. His eyes gripping shut, he breathes out some much-needed air, clenching his jaw as he does.

With his hand still loosely gripping my neck, I lower my own hand to his already hardened cock. There was no guessing whether he would be hard or not. He always is around me. I'm like his own potent drug, or a thirst he desperately needs to satiate.

Fire dances in his lilac eyes as I rub his cock. "You can't say the words, can you?" I challenge. "Maybe I should remind you of the reason why you're so angry."

I unzip his trousers, pulling out his cock. Breathless, Elijah lets go of my neck, and I sink to my knees. With one hand on the door, Elijah takes his other hand and grips the back of my head. I take him in my mouth, sinking down as deep as I can go. Elijah hisses in pleasure, his body jerking at my touch.

Knowing I need to be quick, I delve up and down rigorously, sliding my tongue around his shaft as I deepen him to the back of my throat. Elijah grunts, cursing and gripping the back of my head as I mouth fuck him hard and deep.

"Fuck, Bryce!" he bellows as I continue sucking him over and over again until the inevitable explosion.

It was hard and it was quick, but by fuck has it turned me on. Taking every bit of him, I swallow his cum down the back of my throat before placing his cock back into his trousers. I rise up, hair no doubt messy, my chest rising and falling with each heavy breath. With my head pressed to the back of the door, I smirk at Elijah as he tries his hardest to catch his breath from the no doubt explosive orgasm I just gave him.

Catching my smirk, Elijah wraps his hand around my neck again, his show of dominance after I almost brought him to his knees. He presses his thumb against my lips, wiping away any remnants of what's left of my lipstick.

"These lips are mine," he grinds out, almost thumping my head back against the door.

Elijah doesn't want to admit it, but bit by bit, I'm breaking him down. Bit by bit, he's giving himself to me completely. And I will continue to until I own him the same way he owns every piece of me. He's not pissed about the champagne. That wasn't ever the reason for his dragging me away like that. He saw what he viewed as a threat, someone else daring to take what's his.

I lick my lips, putting on a show of defiance, my breaths still an effort after our encounter. Elijah may have found his release, but I'm still left hanging, my pussy throbbing as each second passes.

"Do you hear what I'm saying, Bryce?" he urges, his face inches from mine. "You fucking belong to me."

My head dizzies at his statement. A statement I've longed to hear from him. And all it took was the bitch's son to simply say a few words to me. Who knew?

"Say the fucking words, Bryce." Fervor floods his lilac eyes. A never-ending range of emotions swimming in of them. He has no clue as to why he's doing and saying the things he does, but he's doing it anyway.

"I'm yours," I finally whisper back, noticing the triumphant gleam in his eyes when I give him the words he's been looking for.

But just as our encounter gets interesting, Elijah seems to come to like he's been cast under some sort of spell. He shakes his head, his hand leaving my neck as he does.

"I need to get back before people notice I'm missing. Do you have something you can check yourself over with? A compact, perhaps? You look like..."

He's trying to find the words to say, so I help him along. "Like I've just given my stepdad the best blowjob of his life? At a police charity event, no less." I wink for extra effect, but it only seems to make Elijah's rage spring back to life.

"Bryce, this isn't fucking funny. Just answer the question."

"Yes," I snap, pointing to the floor where I dropped my purse. "I have one in there."

"Clean yourself up, then come out when you're ready."

Once he's shut the door, I get to work fixing my hair and applying a little more lipstick. When I'm done, I gaze around the books, allowing myself a few moments to slide my fingers across the old editions of Shakespeare, Dickens, and Hemingway. I inhale the pleasant odor they emit, my breathing finally calming along with my pussy. It still wants Elijah with a passion, but now that he's not here invading my every sense, I calm down.

Now ready, I exit the library and enter the vast hall where there's an auction being held, with the mayor standing on the stage. Up with him is Elijah and that fucking bitch, who's now my new enemy. They're sitting together, admiring what's going on, but also occasionally conversating. Elijah says something and she laughs, her hand sliding up his arm as she does.

I thought Duckface was a bitch, but this one takes the cake. Snapping a glass of champagne off a tray, I down the contents in one go, my anger getting the better of me.

One auction ends, then the mayor thankfully asks Elijah to stand up to conduct the next auction. He smiles, getting up and taking the microphone from the mayor to introduce himself.

"I hope everyone's having a lovely evening at this special event tonight." The crowd hums their approval before he continues. A grand painting of a meadow is brought on stage, and bidding swiftly begins. I notice the mayor stepping off the stage, so I quicken my pace towards him, deciding now is the time to make my move. He's at the bar waiting for a whiskey to be poured by the time I reach him.

"William Schultz?" I ask, standing behind him.

Upon hearing his name he turns, his eyes immediately lighting up when they clamp on mine. They search my face before glancing down to my no doubt erect nipples that are still hard from Elijah's and my little tryst only a few minutes ago.

"Oh, wow, aren't we a delight to behold." His voice is gravelly like he's trying to be sexy. I guess with his mass of silver hair and tidy beard, he does have his own uniqueness to him, but he certainly isn't sexy. "To what do I owe the pleasure, Miss...?"

"Turner," I answer, giving him the smile normally reserved only for Elijah.

His eyes dance with desire as I flutter my eyelashes at him. "What can I do for you, Miss Turner?"

"Well," I answer, placing my hand against my chest, his eyes following my every move. "I was hoping to have a very brief chat with you about something, but I don't think it should be discussed here."

My heart thunders, wondering if he'll take the bait. I slide my hand down my front, placing it on my belly. A movement William watches with interest.

"Is that so?" I nod my head. "As you can see, I'm hosting this event tonight, so I'm a little busy right now. Maybe afterwards you and I can find somewhere ... more private to discuss whatever it is you wish to."

Heart sinking, I bite my lip, but I don't dare give in. I grab his arm in my hand, squeezing it a little under my touch. I lean forward so he can get an eyeful of my braless cleavage. "Unfortunately, I can't tonight, but this will only take a couple of minutes of your time, Mayor. I swear to you. I will make sure it's worth your while."

I smile seductively at him like the promise of something risqué is afoot. He chances a quick glance at Elijah who's still fielding bids for this popular painting.

"Okay, I'm sure I can spare two minutes of my time for you, darling."

I force down the eyeroll that's desperate to form. Elijah may be old enough to be my dad, but this guy's definitely old enough to be my grandad.

"Follow me," he purrs, walking off towards the hallway Elijah and I were in. My heels are the only sound clicking against the floor as we walk farther and farther away from the grand hall. A part of me is nervous about being this far away, but I swallow it down. Whatever happens, I can't let this man see any weakness in me.

At the end of the hall we reach a room where there's a small office. He closes the door behind us then proceeds round to the desk. "So what is it you wish to discuss? Or would you prefer we were doing something where no words are spoken?"

I fake laugh at his joke before pulling out my phone from my purse. "I must admit, I haven't been very honest with you." I walk farther in, approaching the other side of the desk.

He raises a very bushy eyebrow. "Oh?" he asks, a little nervously.

"My name is Miss Turner, but my first name is Bryce. I'm Elijah's stepdaughter."

His eyes widen in surprise. "Oh, but I thought you were only seventeen?"

"Soon to be eighteen, yes."

He laughs slightly. "You look older."

Deciding to end the pleasantries, I get down to business. "I called you in here because I believe my stepfather is in dire need of new officers."

William Schultz waves his hand dismissively at me and stands up. "I am here to raise money for charity. I don't appreciate Elijah using you to hound me in this way."

He's approaching the door to leave, but I won't let him now that I have him. "Elijah has no idea I'm here. In fact, Elijah has no idea that I also know the things I do about you."

When his hand stops on the handle of the door, my smile raises in victory. Knowing he has no choice now, he turns around, fixing me with a hateful glare.

"What are you talking about?"

Taking my phone, I light it up and start playing the video of him giving a blowjob to a very young man as he's being ridden by another girl on top, their moans filling the air. I watch in delight as William Schultz takes it all in, his nervous swallow giving him away. I then stop the video and play him another of him tied up to a bed, being ridden by a girl in a school uniform.

"You certainly like them young, don't you?"

"Where the fuck did you get these?" he rages, trying to grab the phone from my hand. I quickly snap it away.

I got them from paying a mighty handsome fee to the hotel clerk who made sure Mr. Schultz was in the room I conveniently left the camera in. However, William doesn't need to know that detail.

"I'm not stupid, Mr. Schultz. You don't think I have copies?" I glance at my phone then back at him. "You don't by any chance write these prostitutes off as say ... 'meeting dignitaries' in order for the local taxpayers to fund your ... salacious affairs?"

William Schultz closes the distance between us, his face all red and flustered with rage. "What do you fucking want?"

I step back, grimacing at his bad breath. I place my phone inside my purse, deliberately wasting time before I answer. "I already told you. I want you to give Elijah what he wants."

His eyes narrow into slits. "And that's it?"

I make a sign of the cross. "Cross my heart, Mr. Schultz."

"Why?"

I sigh deeply like this whole thing is boring. It is getting kind of boring now. "Elijah has been difficult to handle lately. He's tempestuous at best, but you have made him unbearable to live with. If he's happy, I'm happy. Plus, Elijah has been my saving grace since my poor mama died. It's only fair I give him something back."

Although mostly bullshit, I am at least being honest about wanting to do this for Elijah.

"Once I do this for him, you'll destroy those videos?"

I place my hand on my chest. "I promise."

He sighs deeply, his hand swiping over his face with distress. "I don't have enough money in my budget for more police—"

"Oh, I'm sure you could tweak the budget to allow him a few more officers. Why not meet Elijah halfway? If he wants thirty, give him twenty. I'm sure you can think of something."

He grips his eyes shut. "I will need time."

"I'll give you forty-eight hours." I walk past him and place my hand on the door. "You know where to reach me if you have a problem. Have a nice evening, Mr. Schultz."

I open the door then swiftly close it behind me, letting out a huge exhale. That took more out of me than I'd expected.

With renewed vigor, I walk out to the hall again to find that bitch now on stage, taking bids, but thankfully without Elijah. As I think about this, panic surfaces, wondering if he's in the crowd, desperately searching for me but unable to find me. Just as I ponder this, my phone buzzes in my purse. I pull it out, and sure enough, Elijah's name is flashing on my phone. I answer straight away.

"Where the fuck are you?"

"I'm in the hall. Where are you?"

"I've been searching for you everywhere. Where have you been?"

I smile at a passerby then puff out some air. "I was in the ladies' room. I wasn't feeling too good, but the rest of the time I've been here."

He's silent for a moment before he answers. "Are you okay now?"

My heart lights up because despite being angry that he couldn't find me, he still cares for my wellbeing. "Yes, I'm fine now."

"Good. Meet me at the exit. We're going home."

So soon, I think. I was just starting to enjoy myself.

I end the call, making my way through the crowds. I spot Paul who salutes me as I pass by. I smile back, but my focus is now on getting outside to Elijah.

Just as he said, he's at the exit, his jacket off and slung over his arm as he waits. He spots me, his eyes narrowing in suspicion. He probably thinks my toilet excuse is bullshit, but he doesn't call me out.

"Why are we leaving so soon?" I ask as I inhale a much-needed breath of the night's air.

"I did my bit, and now I want to go home."

"Fair enough."

On the journey back, Elijah places his head back on the seat, closing his eyes. He's obviously tired, so I let him catch the few winks he can.

I take out my phone from my purse, lighting it up and going to my list of names. Lots have already been crossed off, but there are a couple that are still there. I cross off William Schultz's name, but at the bottom I add another.

Lucy Brightmore.

An evil smirk rises on my lips as I place a star next to her name.

The bitch will never see me coming.

CHAPTER ELEVEN

ast

Elijah's neck cranes, trying to locate Adam who's already quite a way down the road. When he can't find him, his angered stare glances down at my bags.

"Been shopping, I see."

I shrug at him, because a conversation with him right now is not on my list of priorities. "You told me I could spend it."

He bends down, picking up the bags and bringing them in with us. "You can spend it on whatever you want. Where do you want these? In your room?"

I nod my head, wondering why he seems so angry all of a sudden. He has no right to be angry at me.

I follow behind him as he reaches my room. "Where's Mom?" I ask, not really caring for the answer.

"She's out getting her hair done, but she'll be home in time for us to take you to dinner at eight."

I dump the bags down. "Er, no thanks. I think I'll pass."

"Who was the boy?"

His sudden question stuns me, but I answer quick enough. "He's just a friend."

His eyes narrow in on me. "A friend, or a boyfriend?"

My heart thundering at his accusing stare, I glare back at him. "It's none of your business whether he's a friend or someone I'm fucking. Is that what you want to hear, huh? That I'm fucking him?"

Elijah's jaw tics, and he inhales a sharp breath. "What's gotten in to you all of a sudden? You're not normally—"

"What? So angry? Resentful? Full of fucking rage at two people who are supposed to take care of me? I may have once been a timid, shy girl who everyone thinks they can walk all over, but not anymore." I walk to the door and hold onto the handle. "Now, if you'll excuse me, I have some clothes to try on for tonight."

Elijah stares for a moment, his eyes scanning me like he's trying to figure me out. Eventually he leaves, allowing me to close the door behind him. I plop down on my bed, a heavy sigh leaving my lips along with a couple of tears. It's funny how out of everyone I know, Elijah is the only one who can truly get to me inside. Inside my gut, heart, fucking head ... everywhere.

I lie for a moment, needing this peace to clear my head before I get to work, making myself up to look as pretty and as slutty as I possibly can for tonight. Elijah thinks I'll be getting ready for dinner, but he's sorely mistaken.

With smokey eyes, red lipstick, and a tight black dress clutching my skin, I take one look at myself, hardly recognizing the girl staring back at me.

Grabbing my purse, I open the door then hesitate on the landing to listen for any voices. I do hear faint arguing from my mother's bedroom downstairs, so I quickly and quietly head down each step, hesitating only when I hear my name.

"Is it any wonder she's so fucking angry, Brenda? What kind of mother does that to her own fucking daughter? You're nothing but a piece of shit!"

My mom yells something back at Elijah, then I hear the inevitable slap she must have given him. For a moment, I'm taken aback by Elijah sticking up for me to my mom, but I don't stick around long enough for them to leave the room and possibly see me.

Purse clutched in hand, I open the door then quietly shut it behind me, skipping down the steps as I go.

"Girl, you're dressed up like you're looking for all kinds of trouble."

I laugh at Frank, waving at him as I start my stroll down the street. "Oh, that I am, Frank. Don't you worry about that."

"Just be careful now, you hear?" he hollers back.

I turn around and blow him a kiss. "I will, Frank. Good night."

"Goodnight, rosebud."

I smile at my new nickname from Frank. He called me it a few nights ago. I asked him why, and apparently, my lips look like rosebuds. It was only when I went back home that night and looked in the mirror that I could actually see what he meant.

Walking the twenty or so minutes to the nearest bar where I know a lot of the dads from school hang out, I reach the doorway then hesitate, wondering if I can be brave enough to do this. I've never been inside a bar before let alone drank in one. I'm all alone in this, but I've come too far to back out now. Plus, I'm tired of hiding in the shadows. I'm tired of being that girl who sits silently, having had everything taken from her without so much as a please or thank you.

Hand on the door, after taking a deep inhale of air I push it open, the muffled sounds of voices now louder as bright lights force my eyes to adjust to the scene. A few tables are filled with groups of males and females mixed, but there are also some lone men at the bar, nursing beers.

My eyes scan a corner booth where a group of dads from school sit enjoying a few hours of freedom from their mundane lives.

All eyes are on me as I stand in the middle of the bar like a fish out of water. I will my legs to move, and finally, after a few seconds they do. I walk to the bar, placing my purse down before sliding onto a free stool, selecting one farthest away from everyone. The bartender immediately approaches, placing a coaster down in front of me.

"A glass of white wine, please," I request as casually as I can.

The bartender, handsome with his cropped dark hair looks to be in his mid-twenties, narrows his eyes on me. "How old are you?"

"Twenty-one," I snap back quickly.

His lips twitch a little. "Pretty convenient, huh?"

I show him the palms of my hands. "It's my age. I can't help that."

I think he's going to refuse me, so I'm totally shocked when he grabs a glass from the counter and bends down to open the fridge, grabbing a chilled bottle of wine. He places it in front of me then fills the wineglass to the top.

"That'll be six dollars."

My mouth wants to part in shock, but I will it shut. Six dollars for a glass of wine? How does anyone around here afford more than one drink?

I open my purse to retrieve a ten-dollar bill when a man approaches me. "I'll get that, David."

The bartender, who I now know as David, simply smirks, nodding his head. "Sure thing, Brian. I'll put it on your tab."

I shift in my seat, a little annoyed that he didn't even ask me if it was okay that another man pay for my drink. But when I turn to thank the stranger, I'm met with a set of brown eyes I recognize. This must be Brian Greyser. Chloe's dad.

"You're new," he says, his eyes trailing down from my face to my legs. Deliberately, I slowly place one leg over the other so that he gets a good look at what he's admiring. His eyes grow hooded before he eventually trails those same eyes up to meet mine. "The name's Brian Greyser. And you are? I think it's only fair I know your name since I bought you a drink."

Typical. I want to tell this arrogant prick that I'm perfectly capable of buying my own drink, but I force that thought down. Of all the people in the world to meet in this bar, it had to be Chloe's dad. I mean ... what are the odds?

So I smile as sweet as pie at him, holding out my hand for him to take. "I'm Bryce, and thank you for the drink."

At least in his mid-forties with black, slicked back hair and silver strands at the sides, his eyes linger on my lips for a moment. "You're very welcome, Bryce. May I ask what's brought you into this bar all on your own?"

I pick up my wine, taking a healthy sip to calm my nerves before answering him. "I was supposed to meet a friend here, but plans fell through. I figured I would have a quick drink since I was already here."

Brian pouts a little. "Aww, that's too bad. This friend of yours ... he or she?"

"She," I reply, wanting to ask him why it matters.

"I'm sorry to hear that she bailed on you, but one woman's loss can be another man's gain, huh?" He waggles his eyebrow at me as if we share a secret.

"Mr. Greyser," I begin, deliberately turning my stool to face him, so that we're intimately close. "Are you trying to seduce me?" I want to laugh at my own joke so badly, but instead, I smirk at him, causing him to laugh.

"Hmm ... nothing wrong with a bit of Mrs. Robinson in reverse. But I would only try to seduce you if you wanted me to."

I take another gulp of my wine and quirk an eyebrow at him. "That's good to know." I glance a peek over his shoulder, noticing that all of his friends are watching the scene intently, wide smirks on their faces. I point to them with my finger. "Aren't your friends missing you?"

Brian glances over his shoulder, then his friends salute him with their beers before laughing. He turns his head back to me with a knowing smile. "I doubt they will miss me too much. Besides, they know I would much prefer your company right now."

"You know nothing about me," I quip back, taking another sip. "I could be really boring for all you know."

He throws his head back, laughing before his eyes graze across my body again. "Oh, I highly doubt that."

My eyes take that moment to glance down at his wedding finger, a band securely fixed there. "Tell me, Mr. Greyser, how would your wife feel about you chatting to a young girl in a bar and buying her a drink?"

He frowns a little, like it's just dawned on him that I know he's married. My eyes flit to his hand, so he pulls it up. "Oh, this?" he fiddles with it using his thumb. "My wife and I are separated."

Bullshit.

"Then why are you still wearing your wedding band?"

He shrugs. "Habit, I guess." He then leans farther into the bar so he can get even closer to me. "You're not married, I see." He flicks his head towards my hand, not a ring in sight.

"No, it's not something I would even contemplate right now."

"So no boyfriend then? No one serious on the scene?"

I sigh as if this troubles me. "No. To be honest, men my age don't know how to look after a woman like me. I have needs that they're way too young to fulfil. Do you understand what I mean?"

Excitement swims in his eyes as he licks his lips. "Oh, I fully understand what you mean. A woman of your ..." he sweeps his eyes down my body, "caliber needs someone older to take care of her from the inside out." He puts his hand to his chin then pauses, like he's thinking about something. "Have you ever had a guy take you for a ride in a plane?" I shake my head. "I have a pilot's license and my own plane. Would you like to go with me some time?"

To a lot of women, that would be impressive, but not me. He's only using this to gain access to my panties, so armed with that knowledge, it's a turn-off. What is a turn-on, however, is knowing that Chloe's dad wants to fuck the brains out of the girl she bullies every single day of her miserable life. A flash of having her dad fuck me on his desk at home and Chloe walking in on us causes a flurry of excitement to build in my belly.

"Sounds wonderful," I reply, wondering if I could ever let it go that far with him. Could I have someone fuck me who I don't love? Could I do it simply because I want to get someone back for hurting me? Not only that, my one and only sexual experience so far was nothing but painful. Would it be just as painful again? Would it fill me with so much dread that I wouldn't be able to bring myself to go through with it?

Those questions and a million others flit through my mind, but I push them back for now.

"Are you going to introduce me to your friends while I'm here?" I ask, pointing to the booth where they're still staring at us.

Brian looks a little disappointed that I asked, but he nods his head anyway. "Sure, but I'll have to stand. There's not enough room if you sit with us."

Grabbing his arm, I pull myself up so that I can whisper in his ear. "Maybe you could let me sit on your lap?"

I watch as his mouth parts slightly, his breathing quickening which speeds up my own. I didn't know having this effect on men could fill me with such power like this. The thought turns me on like nothing else.

"It would be my pleasure." He grins salaciously at me, offering me his arm.

I get down from the stool, placing my arm through his. "Perfect gentleman," I coo.

"Only the best for the best. You're the most stunning woman I have ever come across, do you know that?"

I giggle like what he's saying is preposterous. "I bet you say that to all the girls," I joke, placing my hand on his arm as we walk to his booth.

He fixes me with a serious glare. "No, I really mean it. We don't have women like you around here, that's for sure. Tell me, Bryce. What is it you do?"

"I'm still in school," I answer honestly.

"Ah, so do you attend the local college here?"

I nod back, but nothing more is said until we reach his table. Once there, he introduces me to all five guys sitting around with their pitchers of beer, their names immediately disappearing from my mind the moment I hear them.

"Nice to meet you," I tell them as Brian sits down on the bench with my wine before tapping his knee for me.

I'm about to sit down when I notice the shit-eating grin he's showing to all his friends. I don't mind this for now since for me, this is all just a game.

I wiggle my ass onto his leg and giggle like I'm an airhead. Brian smiles up at me before sliding his hand across my belly and keeping it there.

"Comfy?" he asks.

"Very," I answer.

I take another few sips of my wine as they all fire questions, asking who I am, where I live, and what I'm studying at college. The wine is getting to my head and making me feel warm and fuzzy inside. They make some jokes that are probably not even funny, but I laugh along with them anyway.

"I'm going to look after you real good, young lady." Brian practically growls this into my ear.

I bite my lip, learning in to whisper in his ear. "A bit presumptuous of you, Mr. Greyser. How do you know it's you I want looking after me?"

He places his hand on his chest, giving me a wounded look. "Don't break my heart before I even have the chance to show you a good time."

With my arm snaked around his neck, I laugh, throwing my head back a little, but when I pull it back again, my eyes land on a pair of lilacs I know all too well.

He's scanning the crowd, but as if sensing I'm staring, he locks on to me, his eyes narrowing into slits as he takes in the scene in front of him.

Oops. Looks like I've been busted.

Striding across the room with purpose, Elijah approaches the booth, and all eyes looking up as if sensing his approach.

"Chief," one of the guys on the opposite side says, acknowledging him. "Join us guys for a beer? And girl, of course," he continues, winking at me. I smirk back, but when I spot the rage firing in Elijah's eyes, it quickly vanishes.

"Bryce," he warns, completely ignoring everyone else. "Get up. You're coming home with me."

I swiftly lift myself up from Brian's lap, because I know pretty soon Elijah's going to yank me off him anyway.

"Hey, what's going on?" Brian asks, his hands up in the air. "Who is Bryce to you?"

His lips thinning into a hard line, Elijah barks back. "She's my *barely* sixteen-year-old stepdaughter."

Brian's face drops so quickly that I almost have to cover my mouth to stop myself from laughing.

"I'm ... I'm sorry," he stutters. "I honestly didn't know, Elijah. I'm sorry. She looks a lot older, and when I asked her what she does for a living, she said she was in college." He fixes his accusing eyes on me. I could correct him that I technically didn't say that, but instead, I simply shrug my shoulders.

"Oops," is all I say back.

"You should have at least fucking realized she was too young to drink."

Brian puts his hands up in surrender. "Look, man, I'm sorry. No harm was done, so please accept my apology and be done with it."

Elijah stands rigid, his hands fisted at his sides as he glares daggers at them all—especially Brian.

"I'll leave it for now because I want to get Bryce home, but just so you know, this isn't the last you'll hear of this." He then grips my arm, yanking me away from their table.

Immediately, I'm hauled out of the bar and on to the street where Elijah's sleek, black Jaguar F Pace is waiting, looking all shiny. Once he reaches the passenger door, he turns me around, his hand still gripped tightly on my arm.

"What the fuck were you thinking, Bryce? Those men you were sitting with are even older than me. What's gotten in to you? This..." he steps back, taking in what I'm wearing. "This isn't you. Stop trying to be someone you're not."

Yanking my arm from his grip, I glare at him. "That's where you're wrong. This *is* me. And I haven't felt this free or this empowered in ages."

He crinkles his nose in anger, his head shaking. "So sitting on dirty, old men's laps in cheap bars makes you feel empowered, huh?"

Anger levels rising to new heights, I step forward, my eyes zeroing in on his. "My own fucking mother made me a whore, and you enabled her. How much *cheaper* could that possibly get?"

Anger fading in his eyes, he places his hands on my shoulders. "Listen, Bryce. I understand how difficult this must be for you. I want to be able to help if you'll just let me in. Please don't shut me out."

He wraps his arms around me in a warm embrace, and at first, I inhale that sweet, musky, cinnamon scent of his that used to drive me crazy with need. I close my eyes, relishing the feel of his body pressed against mine, but the feeling doesn't last long. Soon enough, flashbacks of the rape and subsequent bath Elijah ran for me assault my mind, causing me to violently push him away.

"Don't fucking pity me!" I snap. "I don't need your pity. I needed your protection!"

The expression on Elijah's face is like someone who's just been slapped. Well, good. He deserves to feel the guilt eating away at him. He deserves everything I unleash on him.

He remains silent as he timidly gazes into my eyes. I suppose there's nothing he can say. What's done is done, and neither of us can take it back now. No matter how much we'd both like to.

"Please, just take me home."

Elijah nods before opening the car door, waiting for me to slide in before shutting it. As he's walking around the other side, I lay my head against the headrest and close my eyes. This little hiccup may have brought me down a little, but with each kick to my gut, I'm even more determined to get back up.

CHAPTER TWELVE

resent

After Elijah and I came back from the ball, I managed to find out the new bitch's age, phone number, and address. Of course she has to live the next town over where all the rich, stuck-up tycoons reside. Elijah could afford to live there too if he really wanted, but what kept us here in the beginning was my school. It was within walking distance, which I needed since I don't have a car. Elijah wants to change that now, but I told him I would only learn to drive if he taught me.

I'm still waiting.

It's the following morning, and Elijah is getting ready for work. At eight o'clock on the dot, he's in front of me with a glass of water and my pill for the day. He's very anal about not getting his seventeen-year-old stepdaughter pregnant for some reason. He could use condoms if he really wanted to, but alas, it's me who has to bear the brunt of protecting myself from his seed.

For now, I take the pill with a smile like I do every morning, swallowing it down as he watches me. One day, I won't be so compliant.

One day, Elijah will become a daddy, and then he will have no other choice but to face us and what we are together. He'll put a fucking ring on it once he realizes he can no longer bury his head in the sand and must come to terms with the fact that he loves me as much as I love him.

"Off to work now, dear?" I ask with the best Stepford Wife smile I can muster.

"Don't." he warns, but he's unable to hide his smirk.

I cock my head to the side, pouting. "Don't what?"

He hitches his thumbs inside the waistband of his police pants, pushing them down slightly so they're resting on those oh so likable hips of his. My eyes dart to his fine form, not wanting to miss an opportunity to gawk at his proud chest, solid, powerful arms, and strong jaw that is more than capable of eating pussy.

"You don't suit this wifey shit, Bryce, so cut it out."

I raise my eyebrows at him, a quirk of a smile tugging at the sides of my mouth. "Oh, really? So you don't want your meals cooked for when you come home or your uniform washed and pressed for when you next need it? Got it."

Grabbing my chin with his hand, he tugs me closer to him so that our faces are inches apart. His lilac eyes spell danger this morning, which only heightens my desire for him. What would he have in store for me if he wasn't on his way to work, I wonder?

"You know exactly what I mean," he whispers, his warm, minty breath fanning my face. His eyes move down to my lips, and when his pupils slightly dilate, I bite my lip, my longing for him increasing with each second that passes. "You don't play wife."

My eyes narrow to slits, the yearning in them no doubt evident for him to see. "You're right," I reply, baring my teeth at him. "I play your whore instead." I dart my tongue out, licking his lips. "And you love every." Lick. "Fucking." Lick. "Minute of it."

His breathing quickens, the pulse in his neck flickering. I glance a peek down, and I'm not surprised to find his cock straining against his trousers. It makes me wonder how far I could push this.

"How bad do you want to handcuff me, bend me over, and fuck my brains out right now?"

Something swims in his eyes, his jaw ticcing as if contemplating what to do next. His desire for me is stronger than the forces at work that keep the earth spinning each day. He would hate to admit that fact, but it's true. If I were to run, he'd hunt me down ... I have no doubt about that. He's just as obsessed with me as I am of him.

"Stop this fucking shit, Bryce. I have to get to work."

When he turns to head out of my bedroom, I fall to the bed, opening my legs to him so he can see my soaked, swollen pussy. "So a quick, rough fuck is out of the question then?"

He scrubs a hand down his face, ready to admonish me when his eyes snap to my elicit display. "Fuck's sake, Bryce. Cover yourself up!"

"But I'm so horny. Look how wet my pussy is. Don't you want to slide your cock inside me? Don't you want to pound my pussy so that's it's so sore it'll remind me of who was there all day?" I sink my fingers in between my folds, excitement bubbling inside of me when his eyes pool with desire. His cock jerks inside his trousers, and then he steps forward. I smirk, a triumphant gleam forming on my face.

And then his phone rings.

"Fuck!" he curses, pulling the phone out of his pocket. "Hawthorne," he barks into the receiver.

As he's listening to whoever it is on the line, I plunge my finger into my pussy then pull them out to start circling my clit. Elijah's mouth parts, but he doesn't look away. Pushing my head back, I close my eyes, a tiny moan leaving my lips. The fact that he's watching my every move is turning me on like crazy.

"I'll be there in twenty," he snaps before ending the call. A moment later, my legs are being hauled to the end of the bed, his cock sliding in another second later. "You couldn't fucking let it go, could you?" he growls, pounding into me so hard I see stars. "You couldn't leave me to get on with work."

"I love your cock," I grunt back. "Sue me."

Elijah roars, his pounding relentless as he holds my legs up in the air. His movements are so furious and so fast that an orgasm quickly robs me, causing me to scream out his name. Within a few seconds, he follows suit, his breaths coming in quick succession.

My smile is victorious as I watch him pull up his pants and

straighten his shirt. He fixes his hair before his eyes land on me again. "Be a good girl today. Don't get in to any kind of trouble, you hear?"

I bite my lip, looking down like a timid little girl. "Yes, Daddy."

He opens his mouth like he's about to retort, but he stops himself, and instead, shakes his head. "I'll see you later."

He's walking out of my room when I shout, "Enjoy your day, dear!"

I hear him mumble, "Fucking hell," causing me to laugh as his steps lead him down the stairs and eventually out the door.

I sit up, a delighted sigh leaving my lips. There's nothing like an orgasm and a sore vagina to start your day, I must say.

Despite having already showered, I grab a quick one again to freshen up. It's going to be hot today, so once I'm dry, I slip on a strapless, short, white dress before touching up my makeup. I place my hair up in a messy bun then pull out my pair of Tiffany sunglasses from my bedside, placing them on my face. I grab my purse then head out into the warm day. As I stand on the step, my face to the sky, I inhale the new morning ahead. I turn my head to Frank's house, noting that he's not out doing his normal spying on the neighbors' routine just yet. I suppose it is kind of early.

I take the three steps down then start my stroll down the street. It's quiet as most people are already at work and getting on with their day. I take the bus, smiling the whole way, especially when men, and even some women, gawk at me. After five stops, I get out to walk the five-minute journey to a café where I order coffee. I sit at the window, a strategic point to the courthouse which will give me the view I'm after. There I sit and I stare, watching people going about their day, growing bored as every minute passes. I'm on my second cup of coffee when I spot the moment I have been waiting for.

Lucy Brightmore.

Queen bitch.

As if her bitch tendencies couldn't get any bitchier, she walks towards Elijah who appears, his focus on his watch for whatever reason. When they greet each other, she smiles up at him like he's the only man in the universe.

What the fuck is she playing at?!

They start walking together, and with each step, my anger rises. Where's he going with that bitch?

Unfortunately, I realize all too quickly that they seem to be heading my way. "Fuck," I hiss under my breath.

I grab my purse, heading for the back of the café as quickly as my legs can carry me. I spot an employee there, so I poke him with my finger, my anxiety palpable. He spins around, his face a mixture of surprise and intrigue.

"Is there an exit in the back? My ex-boyfriend who doesn't want to take no for an answer is coming into the café, and I really don't want him to see me."

His face forms a frown, concerned for my welfare. "Of course. Follow me."

As I do, I quickly glance back to find that Elijah and Bitchface are about to enter. I quicken my pace after the guy, letting out a sigh of relief when he opens the back door and ushers me through. He points to the right and says, "If you follow the path along here, it'll lead you out to an alley next to the park."

I grab his hand, surprising him a little. "Thank you. You don't know how much this means to me."

The young, preppy looking guy quirks a smile at me. "No sweat. Listen, if you ever want a coffee some time, I'm here most Sundays, but I get off at three."

I turn around momentarily to smile back at him. "Thanks. I'll remember that."

I walk away, knowing full well he'll probably be in the toilet jerking himself off at the prospect of me coming back for a coffee with him—which I won't.

I follow the path he told me to, and it does eventually lead to an alley where the dumpsters are. Although it's a bright day, the alley still freaks me out, so I quicken my pace. Eventually, the courthouse comes into view, just a few stores down from the café. My anger surfaces again when I think about them in there, cozying up together over coffee and fuck knows what else. My feet quicken, heading in the direction of the courthouse where there's a rooftop patio where I can sit. Once I reach the top and sit down, I turn in the direction of the café, and sure enough, they're already sitting at a table outside, enjoying coffees or whatever they are drinking together, deep in conversation. My breath hitches when she slides her hand over to his, patting it then leaving it there like some kind of bitch in heat. I smile when he pulls away, but it still doesn't stop the murderous thoughts flitting through my mind. I would have so much fun with that bitch before I watched her die.

"Bryce?" a male voice calls, making me jump out of my skin. "Bryce, is that you?"

I turn towards the voice, surprised to find Paul, Bitchface's son standing there, the sun a halo around his form. I squint my eyes, trying to see him. "Sorry," he says, moving out of the way and coming to sit next to me. He's in a gray business suit, white shirt, and blue tie, a briefcase in hand.

"I thought that was you." His eyes trail down my body before meeting my eyes again. "What are you doing in this neck of the woods? Been in trouble with the law?" he teases. "I happen to know a good lawyer if you need one."

I laugh falsely at his attempt at humor, wishing he would just piss off already so I can continue spying on his bitchface mother and Elijah.

"No, I'm just enjoying the sun today. I like it around here with the old buildings. It makes me feel ... calm, being around old relics."

He checks his watch a moment, biting his lower lip with uncertainty. "I've got around twenty minutes free before I have to get to court. You want to grab a coffee?"

"Where?" I ask, a little too brusquely.

He points in a different direction to where Bitchface is. "I know a good place a two-minute walk from here. Most people go to that one," he says, pointing to the café I just came from. "But too many of the old court fogeys go there, and they'll want to join in. I'd actually like to have you to myself for a few minutes."

I cock my head. "Oh, really? Why's that?"

He smiles, running a hand through his hair. "If you come and have a coffee with me, I'll tell you." He winks, nudging my arm.

I hesitate so he says, "Please. Just one quick coffee. I don't have much time left."

"Okay," I reply, getting up and walking beside him. I would

normally have said no, but a part of me is intrigued to hear what he has to say. Plus, another part of me wants to stick it to Elijah. I have a feeling if he ever caught me with another guy having coffee, the guy wouldn't live to see another day. The thought makes my sore pussy come to life again.

Once we reach the other café down the street, Paul quickly orders us both lattes before we sit by the window, admiring the view outside.

"You created quite the stir last night," he begins, blowing on his coffee.

A stab of anxiety hits my belly when I think of me blackmailing the mayor. Surely Paul doesn't know.

I swallow my nerves and ask, "How so?"

He raises an eyebrow at me. "As if you don't know?" Trepidation levels hit critical point as I shake my head with confusion. "Wow," he says on a sigh. "This just makes you even more beautiful than you already are ... if that's even possible."

I shake my head. "You've completely lost me."

He straightens his jacket, a smirk creasing his face. "There have always been these whispers about you. About the young, vivacious, sexy vixen who lives a very quiet life with the police chief. He's done a good job at keeping you hidden since you left school a while back, and last night, people found out why. You are, Miss Bryce, the most stunning woman in our county. Perhaps the whole state and country."

My cheeks heat at his compliment because hey ... who doesn't like a compliment like that? I can at least breathe a sigh of relief that what he wanted to say had nothing to do with my ... extra-curricular activities.

"And now here you are, as if you landed at my feet, ready for me to try and sweep you away from the rest of the suitors who will surely be after you. I assume many will be chivalrous and wait until you're at least eighteen. Me ... I'm an impatient bastard. If there's something I want, I go after it."

Cocky asshole.

"So being seventeen isn't putting you off?" I ask, needing to hear it.

"It's not illegal in Kentucky. A moral issue, maybe, but you're the age of consent."

I think the Pauls of this world secretly get off on the knowledge that they can fuck a seventeen-year-old girl in a state where it's legal, knowing full well there is still the moral side of it. They're all just dirty perverts at the end of the day.

"I'm not looking for a relationship," I answer, picking up my coffee to blow on it before taking a sip.

"Who said anything about a relationship?" he grins, leaning on the table so he's closer to me.

So he's just interested in sex. Good to know.

When I don't respond right away, his eyes widen as if realizing something. "You're a virgin, aren't you?"

Laughter bubbles at the pit of my stomach, but I push it down. If this idiot knew the things I have done over the past couple of years, it would not only make his head spin, he'd probably run a mile from me.

"You got me." I wring my hands, feigning innocence as I lie through my teeth.

Paul slumps back in his chair. "Wow. I would never have thought it. No wonder Elijah keeps you hidden away. He doesn't want his daughter to be tainted." He chuckles at his own joke.

He leans forward again, getting intimately close. He then pulls out a card and slides it across the table towards me. "If you ever change your mind, you know where to call me. I'd really like to get to know you, Bryce."

Yeah, get to know my virginal body, you perverted prick.

He glances at his watch and sighs. "Shit, I have to go already." He glances down at the card. "Think about it?"

I take the card, placing it inside my purse. "Sure thing, Paul." I'm unable to hide the sarcasm from my tone, but by the way he smiles back at me, he has absolutely no clue what's going on.

"Be seeing you, Bryce." He drops a twenty on the table then quickly rushes out towards the courthouse. Once he's out of sight, I throw out my coffee and head out to walk across the road. As carefully as possible, I walk past the other café, looking inside to see if Elijah and Bitchface are still there, but they've already left. A surge of jealousy hits my stomach when I wonder where the hell they could be right now.

Gritting my teeth, I glance up at the courthouse. What I see delights me. Bitchface is talking to her son, Paul. No Elijah in sight. What doesn't delight me, however, is the glow of her skin. What could they have possibly talked about to make her look so ... animated?

I bite my lip, deciding to walk home instead of catching the bus. I have a feeling I'm going to need it.

I'm about halfway home when a police siren blares several times, causing me to jump out of my skin. I stop dead, turning to the offending car when I spot two officers I don't recognize staring at me through the rolled down window. The driver, a handsome black cop with a pair of mirrored sunglasses pushes them down so he can show me his nice, light brown eyes. I chance a look at his shoulder and find he has three stripes on his shirt, telling me he's a sergeant.

"Bryce Turner?" the handsome guy asks.

Hands on hips in a defensive manner, I purse my lips. "Yeah, what of it?" I know I haven't done anything wrong, so I will stand my ground if I have to.

"Chief wants to see you."

I stay where I am, my feet cemented to the ground. "I'm not getting in the car."

Handsome guy smirks as he gets out of the car to open the door to the backseat. Once opened, he holds it there and turns to me. "This is not a request."

Always one for a challenge, I make a show of crossing my arms in front of me, a very defiant smirk raising on my lips. Handsome guy smiles back, shaking his head.

"You know," he begins, pulling at his belt. "I was kind of hoping you'd do that."

My heart rate picks up as he stalks towards me, but I don't move. Despite Elijah using his staff to summon me, this whole debacle is rather exciting.

He rounds me like a lion circling its prey before tugging my arms behind my back. When I hear the jingling of handcuffs, I say, "I'm pretty sure arresting me without any reason is illegal, officer ... ?"

"Brent," he fires back. He then leans forward, his hot breath at my ear. "Why don't you call the cops?"

I smirk at his comeback and inhale a sharp breath when he locks the cuffs around my wrists.

"All I did was walk down the street, and now you've accosted me."

"You're quite the troublemaker, aren't you, little lady?" He makes a show of tightening the handcuffs, a little too tightly, but all that does is make me moan.

"Oh, please," I whisper huskily. "Make them tighter if you want to. I love a good handcuffing."

"Jesus," he grumbles, his voice hoarse. No doubt he's going to have trouble hiding his boner once he places me in the car.

Handcuffs firmly in place, he pushes me towards the cop car. There's no one in sight down this quiet street. I have no doubt they followed me until they could find an opportunity to do their dirty work in private. They know full well this is illegal, but then the law's the law. They all think they're way above it, eventually not knowing what's right or wrong anymore.

When at the passenger door, he pushes my head down, making me bend over. He presses his hardened cock against my ass, and then I fall forward into a heap on the backseat. He bends down a moment, pulling his glasses down to wink at me before he shuts the door behind me.

Wrestling myself up, I puff out some air to try to push a strand of hair from my face. I gaze over at the other officer, a white guy with cropped blond hair and a goatee. He glances over his shoulder, smirking when he takes in my flustered state.

Handsome guy gets in the driver's side then shuts the door, starting up the car. "Watch her," he says to the blond guy. "She's a fucking alley cat."

They both laugh as he pulls away. I'm pretty sure if I told Elijah about his sergeant's roving hips on my ass, he wouldn't be laughing for a long, long time.

I don't retort. Instead, I remain quiet the short distance to station, intrigue crawling up my spine as to the reason why I'm being summoned. Elijah has never done this before, so I must admit, I'm more than a little interested to know why.

Once we've pulled into the parking lot at the station, the sergeant takes me out of the car, facing me away from him as he uncuffs me.

"Why has the fun stopped now?" I challenge, knowing full well what the answer is—not that he'll admit it.

"It wouldn't look good pushing the chief's stepdaughter down the halls of the police station in cuffs, now, would it?"

Released from the cuffs, I turn around, arching a brow at him. "No, I don't suppose it wouldn't."

He comes in closer, his eyes darting to my chest for a moment. "Are you always this recalcitrant?"

I purse my lips, hissing in a breath. "Ooo, big word for a police officer."

He pulls away, shaking his head. "No wonder the chief always looks stressed."

I smirk because I know the reason why he's stressed, but hopefully my little chat with the mayor will resolve that issue soon enough.

"Follow me," he snaps, turning to enter the station through the back entrance.

As I follow behind him, uniformed officers glance my way, their eyes scanning me from head to toe. I simply smile mischievously at each and every one of them, my belly dancing with excitement the whole way.

We reach the end of the hallway where Elijah's name is pinned in big, gold letters on a black painted door. Brent knocks two times, and when he hears the words, "Come in," being shouted from behind, he opens it up, motioning for me to go through.

I step forward, taking in Elijah's commanding presence. Barely a few hours since I've seen him, yet he's still able to raise the hair on my skin and take my breath away all at once.

Elijah stands behind his desk, his fingertips resting on the top. His fiery lilac eyes bore into mine for a second before he has no other choice but to acknowledge that Brent is still standing by the door.

"Thanks, Brent. You can go now."

"Yes, Chief," he replies before shutting the door behind him.

I'm about to ask Elijah what the problem is when he marches around his desk, approaches me, and snaps my bag from my shoulders.

I stand, mouth agape as he reaches inside, pulling out Paul's card. He gazes down, an angered sigh leaving his lips before he hands me my bag back then proceeds to rip the card up into little pieces, discarding them in the bin.

How the fuck did he know about that?

He turns around and parks his ass on the edge of his desk, his hands fisting the edges as he fixes me with a deathly glare. "You don't think I knew where you were just an hour ago? Who you were with?"

A stab of unease hits my stomach when I comprehend that he has eyes on me. Just how much does he know? Still, I round my shoulders, determination to stand my ground at the forefront of my mind now.

"It was just a coffee."

Elijah rises from his position, causing me to hitch in a breath. He stalks towards me, each step seeming more determined than the last. Once he's close, he raises his arm so that his hand rests on the door behind me, his hot breath fanning my face.

"If you weren't in my office right now, I'd have you over my knee, spanking that bare bottom of yours."

Feeling my anger rise, I bite back, "You went for a coffee too. With Bitchface, no less."

He narrows his eyes at me. "What is this, Bryce? Tit for tat? So you're spying on me now?"

"You're obviously spying on me, so what does it matter?"

His eyes scan down to my lips, spurring me to lick them in anticipation.

"The difference between you and me is that I went to have coffee for work purposes. Pray tell," he whispers, leaning even closer until our lips almost meet. "What purpose could you possibly have to go for a coffee with the DAs son?"

My eyes scanning his, I let out a breath. "He said he wanted to talk to me."

"About what?"

"Apparently, everyone who was at the ball wants to fuck me. Including Paul."

I'm thinking at this point that honesty is the best policy, but when

I spot the deathly, cold glare in Elijah's eyes, I begin to wonder if I've chosen wisely.

Without a word, Elijah turns around to pick up his car keys and hat which he places on his head. He walks towards the door. "Follow me," he demands, like I'm an employee obeying orders.

Despite that, I do follow him out the door and out to the parking lot where more officers stare at me. A few times, I notice Elijah clenching his jaw, so I'm guessing he's noticing that I'm causing quite the stir here.

Once we're at his car, he opens the door, and I sink in. He shuts it behind me, still without saying a word. He gets in, starts the car, and silently drives away from the station. It takes around five minutes to realize where we're going.

Home.

He parks in front of the garage, then we both get out, him immediately marching up the steps to the house to open the door. When we're both inside, I'm still wondering what the hell's going on.

"Upstairs. Now," he commands.

I do as he says cause he's looking pretty darn pissed by now. I reach the top of the stairs and go into my room, thinking this is where he wants me. It's only when I'm inside and turn around that I realize exactly what he's up to.

The door slams shut, and then it clicks, locking me in my room. Immediately, I run to the door and bang on it with my fists. "Elijah, what the fuck are you doing?" I bellow.

"Keeping you in there so you can stay out of trouble. That's what the fuck I'm doing."

I kick the door with my foot. "Asshole!"

"I'll be back in three hours. I'll bring takeout."

I roll my eyes. "Oh, how nice. What am I supposed to say? Thank you?"

The front door shuts, telling me he left. I sigh, but no harm, no foul. Once when Elijah was home, I sedated his drink and took the key he uses to lock me in my room. I made a copy of it with a mold kit I had bought only a few days before. With that, I was able to get myself a copy so that I can open the lock from this side.

I pull it out and open the lock, my smile wide knowing I've gotten one up on Elijah again. He so desperately wants to rule my life, to own me and possess me in every way possible, but what Elijah doesn't realize is...

It's me who owns *him*.

CHAPTER THIRTEEN

 ast

The day after my sixteenth birthday, I decide to pull out the most outrageous outfit I can find from the montage of clothing I bought, my eyes quickly scanning the items. In the end, I select a tight, pink dress where the strings at my cleavage tie up to either cover my cleavage or let them loose, revealing the swell of my puppies. The old me would have covered my breasts, but the new me says fuck that shit. I leave them loose, so that my bust sticks out half a mile. I apply some makeup then slip on some black pumps before grabbing my bag and heading downstairs. Luckily for me, my parents are already gone, so I'm able to grab some breakfast before I leave. Grabbing the bread, I take a slice out and put it in the toaster.

"What in the hell, girl!?"

My mother's shrill voice makes me jump. *I thought she was out!*

I spin around, noting the dark circles under her eyes. She's only thirty-nine, but with all the drugs she's pumped in her lately, you would think she was in her sixties. Elijah certainly seems to think the same as he hasn't slept in the same bedroom as her since my ... incident. That's apparently the preferred word for what happened to me.

"I thought you were out," I bite back.

She groans, pulling her cardigan over her skinny frame. "Bad night. Need coffee if you're making some."

Luckily for me, my toast pops out, so I grab it along with my things. "I'm off to school. You can make your own damn coffee."

I'm walking out of the kitchen when I hear her call me a bitch. I inhale a deep breath, trying to let the comment pass over me. This is the sole purpose for my change. I'm a new girl. A girl who doesn't get affected by bad words by equally bad people.

With a shake of my head, I force back the well of tears in my eyes and walk out of the door with my head held high. The day is sunny, a little on the chilly side, but I don't dare go back in the house to grab a coat. Once I'm into my walk, I'll get warm enough.

Minutes later, I'm walking along the path up to my school, the usual preppy kids hanging around outside, chatting about the latest gossip. I keep my head held high, and it's not long before I see several heads pop up to glance my way. A flurry of whispers soak my ears, making me wonder what it is they're saying about me. Why I even care, I don't know. This is supposed to be the new me. The one who doesn't give a shit.

"Hey," a voice greets me. I glance the voice's way, seeing that it's Grant, one of Brad's entourage and all-around man-slut . "You new here?" I keep on walking as he's leering at me from head to toe, his tongue darting out to lick his lips.

Does he seriously not know it's me?

He then frowns a moment, studying my face. "Do I know you? You look familiar."

The only thing I do is smirk at him. I'm pretty sure he'll figure it out if I open my mouth. I seriously want to shake my head. The boy's so dumb he doesn't even recognize the weirdo. I guess I'm like the proverbial ugly duckling who has turned in to a swan.

"New girl playing hard to get, I see." He sweeps his eyes down the length of my body again. "Are you sure I don't know you?"

It's then the urge becomes so great that I have to speak. I stop dead in my tracks, what feels like a million eyes upon me as I glare at this scumbag. "I'm not one of your fuck bunnies, if that's what you're contemplating."

I say it so loud that several 'Ooos followed by laughter resounds around the quad. Grant is taken aback by my outburst, but then he leans towards me, staring into my eyes. "Weirdo?" he asks, causing me to roll my eyes.

"Fuck off, asshole."

More mumbles and giggles sound from the crowd, and one guy even says, "She told you, Grant," followed by a load of laughter.

"Stuck up bitch," Grant bites back, but I carry on walking, a big smile on my face, head still held high.

I get to my locker and pull out my trigonometry book, ready for my first class. After I close my locker, I walk down the hall where Chloe and her little bitches are congregating as usual, looking for victims to unleash their abuse on—namely me.

Sally—one of Chloe's crew and a major airhead—gazes up when she spots me walking towards them. My heart rate picks up a little when she nudges Chloe, resulting in all of their judging eyes falling on me. Chloe rakes her eyes up and down me before she walks forward, stopping me in my tracks.

"Oh, my gaaawd," she screeches. "Is that really you, weirdo?" She takes in my outfit, smiling that triumphant smile I so want to wipe off her face. "You've turned into a slut, I see. Following in the footsteps of your mother?" The girls snigger behind her, causing my blood to boil.

I narrow my eyes at her, and for the first time ever, I see a hint of what could be fear in her eyes. "No," I reply, my eyes snaking over her fluffy pink top and short red and white checked skirt. "I thought I'd take a leaf out of your book instead." The girls behind her laugh, but Chloe has murder in her eyes. She certainly isn't used to me biting back.

Fuck, it feels good.

Using my shoulder, I push past her, causing her to stumble a little. As I continue walking, I call out behind me. "Say hi to your dad for me."

I round the corner, almost at my next class, when I spot Chesney pulling out a book from his locker. I have five more minutes till I need to get to class, so I can't help the little devil in me who urges me to approach until I'm standing next to him. He's so engrossed in what he's doing that he fails to spot me standing there for a moment. I take that time to admire his physique as he busies himself, head deep inside his locker. He certainly is in fine form with his pert ass, long, thick, muscular legs, and—judging by what I felt the other day—an adequate sized cock. I bite my lip, wondering whether I could use Chesney to further advance my sexual prowess. But then I think about all the names he's called me and all the shit he's put me through with his fucked-up friends, and I stall. He doesn't deserve my pussy. Besides, if yesterday was anything to go by, he wouldn't last a second inside me.

He shuts his locker, only then realizing someone's there.

"Fuck!" he shouts, his eyes widening when he finally spots me and takes me in. He then squints his eyes, much like stupid Grant outside, trying to figure me out. "Bryce?"

"Wow, you should be a detective."

He takes in the length of my legs, my dress, an appreciative gleam shining in his eyes, which I must admit makes my cheeks pinken a little under his intense stare.

"Wow ... I mean ... fuck, Bryce. You were always fucking sexy, but this ... I—"

I smirk which immediately shuts him up. "You're going to be my puppy dog today. Wherever I go, you go, following behind me like a good boy. Think you can do that?"

His face pulls down in an exasperated way. This is not going to bode well for his ego, following around the weirdo girl, that's for sure.

"I'm going to look like an idiot." My eyebrow hitches, daring him to defy me. He closes his eyes and breathes out in surrender. "Fine," he finally snaps, throwing a book into his locker and shutting the door with a loud bang. "We got trig together, right?"

The only answer I give him is a wink, and despite the circumstances, he can't help but smile at my charm. He can deny it all he wants, but I know he's going to secretly enjoy today.

We walk into class together, Chesney following behind me closely. Instead of sitting in the back like normal, I decide to sit in the front near Sarah and Isabel. The moment I decide to stop in front of the desk I chose, their faces scrunch up like I'm shit on their shoes. I simply smirk at them before taking my seat. When Chesney sits right next to me, whisperings and murmurings start.

"Chesney, what the fuck, dude? You fucking the weirdo now or something?"

Sarah's voice is so loud that the whole class hears and erupts in laughter. I gaze at Chesney to get his reaction, and sure enough, he's gritting his teeth. He swings his left leg around in his chair to glare at them. "Shut the fuck up, Sarah."

Her eyes widen like she can't believe he just snapped at her like that. However, she quickly composes herself and is about to retort when Mr. Trimble walks in, immediately shouting at everyone to be quiet.

"Now," he begins, holding onto some papers. "Test results." He wiggles his eyebrows, causing everyone to groan. "I'm actually very disappointed in a few of you. There's a lot of room for improvement." He begins handing them out to the students, causing a flurry of moans across the class. I sit, patiently waiting for him to bring me mine. I say patiently as I'm flicking my pen against my notebook. I ace these tests, but there's always that brief moment of doubt when I think I may have flunked this time.

Finally, my test is placed in front of me. I note his finger hovering over the A he's given me. When I glance up, Mr. Trimble has a big, proud smile on his face. "Well done, Bryce—as always." I nod my thanks to him, then he addresses the class. "A lot of you could achieve Bryce's level if you'd just put your minds to it."

"She's probably sucking his cock," Sarah whispers behind my back.

Immediately, I put my hand up. Mr. Trimble notices right away as no one ever puts their hand up in his class. "Yes, Bryce?"

"Is there any chance you can clear something up for Sarah, please, sir?"

His forehead crinkles in confusion as his eyes dart to Sarah before moving back to me. "Go on."

"Have I ever sucked your cock?"

The whole class bursts into laughter, but Mr. Trimble gasps, unable to hide how shocked he is that I said such a thing.

"Ex ... cuse me?" he eventually splutters.

I shift in my chair, trying my best to make myself look taller in my seat before I begin. "Well, it seems Sarah thinks that I perform the art of fellatio upon your person in order to achieve my exemplary grades."

The class erupts in laughter again, and I have this overwhelming desire to gaze behind me to witness Sarah's reaction, but I remain still.

Mr. Trimble's eyes dart from me to Sarah, probably not knowing what to say. I mean, what can a teacher say to something like that?

Eventually, he clears his throat, addressing the whole class. "I think to answer that question, I will pose another. Considering Bryce achieves such high grades in all her classes, would that suggest she's performing fellatio on every single teacher in school? Perhaps she's also beguiling our very own Mrs. Beckham, our seventy-year-old history teacher who's been married fifty years and is a regular Sunday church goer." The class guffaws again at Mr. Trimble's joke. He lets them all have their fun before shouting, "Okay, settle down. We have work to do." He then flits his gaze behind me, his eyes deadly serious. "Sarah, I'd like to see you after class, please."

When I hear the word bitch being whispered behind me, I can't help the smirk that curves my lips. That'll teach the skank to mess with me.

Thankfully, the rest of the class is fairly uneventful, and after the bell rings, I get up with Chesney following close behind me. I'm down the hall when I spot Adam coming out of his class, hitching up his glasses as he fumbles with the zipper of his bag.

"Adam!" I shout, quickening my pace. He gazes up, his eyes widening when he spots Chesney behind me.

"Hi," he greets, a little unsure, his face crinkling with nerves. I gaze behind me where Chesney's glancing around the hall like a hawk. Why he's so worried about his street cred, I have no idea. I mean, Adam and I aren't *that* bad.

"Don't worry about him." I wave my hand dismissively towards Chesney, causing him to grit his teeth. "He's my bodyguard. Aren't you, Chesney?" I wink back at Adam whose face is the perfect picture of bamboozled. "You can go now." I flip my hand back at Chesney to relieve him of his duties.

"Thank fuck," he curses under his breath before scurrying away.

"Bryce, what the hell is going on?"

My eyes flit around. There are too many bodies in this hallway, so I tug at his arm. "Come with me."

This is certainly a conversation I don't want to have in public. Too many prying eyes and ears about.

Knowing the boy's locker room will be free, I decide to use that again. I check the hall before quickly pulling him through, the door shutting behind us.

"What's going on?" he inquires again, a little breathless from the jog to get here.

"I have something on Chesney, so I'm using it to stop us from getting bullied."

His mouth tugs slightly to one side. "What do you have on him?"

I'm not about to tell him. I trust Adam, but this is a secret between Chesney and me, and I will keep it that way as long as Chesney tows the line.

"Never mind about that. Just trust that whatever it is will stop the bullying from at least one person. The rest I'm working on."

Adam's mouth parts, a lock of his brown waves falling on his forehead. "I don't know about this." He bites his lip.

"What do you mean?"

"I don't want you in any danger, Bryce. I know they all deserve it—"

"Deserve what?" a familiar voice questions, making us both jump.

With three others behind him, Brad strolls in, stopping when he's right in front of us, his arms crossing in front of him. Grant, the man-slut cocks an eyebrow, a slimy smirk tilting one side of his face. The other two, David and Tony, just stand there expressionless as they stare us down.

"None of your fucking business," I snap back, my heart rate picking up. They have us cornered, and judging by Brad and Grant's smug-faced expressions, they know it too.

Brad inhales a deep breath, like my comment irks him. "You're causing quite the trouble today at school, weirdo."

Despite my increasing nerves, I cock my head to one side. "If your slut of a girlfriend and her entourage left me alone, I wouldn't need to cause trouble, would I?"

Brad's laugh is forced. "Slut?" he scoffs, his eyes raking up and down my body with malevolence in his eyes. "The only slut in this school is *you*."

I let the words that would normally cut deep wash over me like a calming breeze. "I'm pretty sure your precious Chloe isn't as virginal as you think." I have no proof of this, but I'm determined to find out if my gut instinct is correct. I just need to be patient. Watch and wait until she finally slips in some way, and then I'll have my ammo. I put a finger to my mouth as I look at Brad. "I don't think her precious Brad can get it up anyway."

The guys snigger and Grant shouts, "Dude, this bitch is trolling you, man."

Brad's eyes narrow to murderous slits. Yeah, he's mad. Still, I don't dare waver from my position. "Does it make you feel good, cornering a girl in the locker room, huh? Such a fucking big man, you are," I scowl, continuing my tirade.

"Bryce, quit it," Adam whisper-hisses as he tugs my arm.

"Yeah, listen to your boyfriend, Bryce," Grant laughs back.

"You're the slut who's in the boy's locker room," Brad mocks. "We just came in here to watch the show." He folds his arms, and this time, fear creeps through me, wondering what the fuck's going on.

"What are you talking about?" I fish out my phone quickly, holding it tightly in my hand.

Grant steps forward, causing us to step back. The delight in his eyes at making us fear him has anger swarming though my belly.

"You're in the boy's locker room with another boy on your own," Grant begins, the gleam in his light blue eyes shining. "We kind of guessed you brought nerdy in here to give him a blowjob. We just wanted to watch the show, didn't we, guys?" He turns his head to get the confirmation he's after, all of them nodding their heads while verbalizing their agreement. "So don't let us keep you, slut. I bet your just dying to suck cock."

The laughter by all the boys causes anxiety to creep up my spine, but again, I hold on to my nerve. Instead of showing how I really feel, I light up my phone, pretending to be bored, but what I'm really doing is sending an SOS signal to Chesney with just the words 'locker room' in a text.

"I'm not listening to this bullshit," I roll my eyes, quickly shutting my phone before walking towards them. "Come on, Adam. Let's go to class." I walk towards the door, but David quickly blocks my path. I glance behind me to glare at Brad, heart thumping ten million miles an hour. "Tell your minion to move out of my way. I have other important things to do."

Brad simply stands there, his arms still crossed as he smiles at me. "Not until we watch the show."

Fisting my hands together, I turn to glare daggers at him. "What is this, Brad? Are you that hard up from not getting any from Chloe that you have to resort to this? Is that it? This is how you get your kicks, huh? Perverted piece of shit."

Brad nods his head to the guys, prompting Grant and David to grab Adam who they hold in a vice-like grip. My fear quickly dissipates, pure rage taking its place.

"Let him go!" I demand, pointing my finger at the assholes. I gaze at Adam who's now perspiring with fear. Seeing him like this just makes me angrier.

"We'll let him go," Grant offers, "once you've given your boyfriend head." He then turns his steely eyes to Adam. "I'm sure you don't want pretty boy's face all messed up, do you?"

A ball of nerves bundle in my stomach. These asshole's have pulled some stunts in the past, but this one takes the cake.

"What's it gonna be?" Brad asks, making my head snap to him. "Put on a show, or watch your boyfriend get beaten to shit?"

Blowing out a huff of angry air, I gaze from Brad to Adam, who's vehemently shaking his head. "Don't, Bryce. I can take it. I swear."

"Aww," Grant singsongs, his sick tone vibrating off the walls. "Isn't that sweet of him to preserve your closeted sluttiness?"

"What's going on?"

The voice has us all turning our attention to Chesney, who's just breezed in without us noticing. He takes one look at my angered stare before his eyes land on Adam, a frown forming on his handsome face.

"You're just in time for the show," Grant jeers, nodding his head to Adam. "Bryce was just contemplating whether to give her boyfriend a blowjob or watch pretty boy get beat up."

Surprise dances in Chesney's eyes for a moment. He remains silent, taking in the scene. When he finally glances my way again, I implore him with my eyes to do something. This finally seems to make him snap out of it.

"Coach is on his way," Chesney begins. "I came in here to warn you guys, just in case you were here. He told me he'd be here in three."

"Shit!" Brad barks, raking his hands through his hair. He then points to Grant and David. "Let him go."

They do as they're told, and within an instant, Adam runs towards me and we're heading for the door. Just as I open it, I hear Brad's warning behind me.

"This isn't over."

Not wanting to look back, we quickly make our way out into the hall then rush towards the exit. Adam doesn't stop running until we're at least a hundred yards from the school.

"Adam, are you okay?" I pant, trying to catch my breath. I grab his arm, holding it in my hand.

He grips his eyes shut a moment, trying to catch his breath. "I can't believe they did that."

"Nothing surprises me anymore about those guys."

Adam holds onto his belly, grimacing. "I thought Brad belonged to the Promise Group."

I laugh out loud at that. "Yeah. It's either bullshit or he's so desperate he's willing to use us to get his kicks." As I think this, a wicked thought comes into my head, and the more I think about it, the more I want to act on it. I sink my teeth into my bottom lip, wondering if I could really go ahead with the plan.

"Are you okay?" Adam asks, snapping me from my evil thoughts.

I have renewed energy now, so I'm thinking definitely yes. What

I'm having trouble with is the fact I'm a novice at all this, so I really don't know how I'm going to go through with it all.

"I'm good, Adam. Don't worry about me."

He motions towards the school where Chesney is strolling towards us. "You going back in there?"

My gaze lingers on Chesney's physique for a bit longer than necessary. "No, I have other plans. You?"

Adam nods his head, hoisting up his bag a little. "No, I can't go back in there after that. I think I'm going to head home."

"Are you going to be okay? I can come with if you need me to."

His smile is genuine. "No, but thanks. I'll be good. See you tomorrow, Bryce."

I salute him then close the distance between Chesney and me. "Are you okay?"

I'm taken aback by the genuine concern in his frown. "Yes, thanks to you."

"I wouldn't have let them do it, you know. I doubt they were really going to take it that far anyway. They were just messing with you."

I hitch one eyebrow at him. "You seriously believe that?"

"You know Brad belongs to the Promise Group, don't you? It would be fucking hypercritical of him to make other people do sexual things when he's supposed to hold out."

"I don't care," I fire back. "Even if he wasn't willing to follow it through, it still doesn't stop how disgusting he is for doing what he did."

Chesney shows me the palms of his hands. "Hey, don't get angry at me. I agree with you. That shit wasn't okay. I told him as much afterwards."

"What did he say?" I can't believe I'm even asking that. What does it really matter?

"That's when he said he was just playing with the two of you." He gazes in the direction Adam left and says, "Is he okay?"

"No, but can you blame him? He was threatened with having the shit beaten out of him if I didn't give him a blowjob."

Chesney genuinely grimaces, surprising me yet again.

"Do you have a car?" I ask, my heart rate kicking up a notch for a different reason.

He turns his head to the side, a small indentation forming between his brows. "Yeah, why?"

Grabbing his hand, I pull him towards the parking lot. "Come on."

"Where are we going?"

"You'll see."

I lead him out to the concrete lot full of cars, stepping back once I'm there so Chesney can lead us to his car. I'm figuring he has a Dodge Challenger or something just as sporty, so I'm surprised when he takes me to a brand-new, red, four-door, Ford pickup.

He notices my surprised expression as we get in. "My dad owns his own construction company, and sometimes I help out moving materials. It's just easier," he explains. I shrug my shoulders as it's really none of my business. "Where do you want to go?"

"Bell Lake."

He frowns. "Why there?"

Yanking at the seatbelt, I pull it over me. "Just shut up and drive, Chesney."

He lets out a silent laugh before shaking his head and starting the car. We're at Bell Lake around fifteen minutes later where Chesney pulls into a nice, secluded spot. Once he turns the engine off, I unbuckle my seatbelt and immediately climb in the back.

"What are you doing?" Chesney's face is the picture of bewilderment as he asks the question.

Hooking my hands underneath my dress, I pull down my lace panties. "Giving you a reward."

His eyes widen to saucers which almost makes me laugh. "What the fuck?"

I offer him my panties and smile when he takes them from me. "You're going to eat my pussy. If you're good at it, I may offer something in return." Chesney's mouth parts before swallowing hard. "Are you refusing me?"

He swallows several times in quick succession before eventually shaking his head. I watch as he climbs over, his face a picture of nerves. Surely he's done this plenty of times before?

"Have you ever eaten pussy?" I guess my intrigue got the better of me.

He scoffs, but it's unrealistic. "Of course I have."

I scoot myself down so I'm laying flat along his seats. "Let me see how well you can do it then," I challenge, hitching my skirt up, showing him my bare pussy.

Chesney gazes down, his breath hitching at the sight of me in front of him. It makes my excitement bubble, blood pumping through my veins as my expectation heightens. He licks his lips, a wave of uncertainty crossing that cute face of his, but then he takes in a deep breath and lowers himself towards my pussy. I hitch in my own breath, waiting for his tongue to hit my clit, desire and nerves crawling along my skin. Desire because it's me calling the shots, it's me wanting this. Nerves because little does Chesney know, this will be my first time too.

CHAPTER FOURTEEN

resent

Using some of the time until Elijah gets back, I continue writing my letter to Johnathan, quickly popping out to the post office to mail it. Considering Elijah believes I'm locked in my room, I figure I'm not being followed. But still, I check several times over my shoulder, just in case.

Once back at home, I twiddle my thumbs until I get a text from Elijah telling me he's on his way. I'm not the kind of person who does boredom well, so he better be ready for the pissed version of Bryce once he's back.

Going into my room, I lock the door behind me then quickly place the key back into the secret compartment under a floorboard beneath my bed. It's about five more minutes later when the sound of the door unlocking downstairs alerts me that he's back.

When he finally unlocks my door and peers in, I take great delight in how much it unnerves him that I'm in exactly the same position as he left me. I tilt my head to one side, taking in his opulent body, his arm holding what must be our takeout. I inhale sharply, the spices hitting my nostrils and making my stomach growl.

"Come on then," he simply requests, turning to walk down the stairs again.

I stay rooted to my seat, and after a few seconds, Elijah shouts for me again. When I don't instantly respond, his footsteps pick up outside, getting closer and closer. Once he's reached the top, I wait until he appears before making a show of crossing my arms in front of me and jerking up my eyebrows.

Elijah leans his arm against the doorframe, his eyes raking down my whole body. "This is how we're going to play it, huh?"

"I'm not your prisoner."

I know my arm folding is rather childish, but this is what he's reduced me to by locking me up in my own damn room.

Pushing himself up from the doorframe, he takes a step inside, his eyes never leaving mine. "You misbehaved."

"I had coffee," I refute.

"Which is not okay when it's with someone who wants to fuck you."

My lip twitches, longing coming to life. "Why's that, *Elijah*?" I make a show of enunciating every letter when I say his name.

"I think you know why," he responds, stepping even closer.

My eyes flick to the corner. "Err ... no. I'm just a silly little girl. I don't know anything."

He smirks at my attempt at acting like an airhead. "We both know that's not true."

"So are you going to tell me?" I urge, not letting him change the subject.

"No one gets to fuck you. Are you happy now?"

I purse my lips. "You fuck me."

Elijah sighs. "Don't be flippant with me."

One day I'll get him to admit it. One day. Elijah is fully aware of why I question him about it, but he still holds out from telling me the truth. I should just give in to the fact that he won't, because at the end of the day, he is mine and will always be whether he admits to the way he feels or not. I guess I just like fucking with him too much.

Once he realizes I've dropped the subject, he sighs. "Why aren't you moving your butt? Dinner's getting cold."

I purse my lips, offering a challenging smile as I cross my arms tightly around me. I'm expecting Elijah to sigh in discontent, so I'm surprised when he squints, his sexy eyes gleaming with what looks like delight.

"Is that how we're playing it, huh?"

I round my shoulders in a defiant way. "You locked me in my room."

"I always lock you in your room. To stop you from getting in to trouble."

"You frog marched me home during the day and locked me up for over three hours. Some would call that abuse."

His eyes travel down my body, almost causing me to quiver. "Yes, you look mighty abused, don't you?" When all I do is purse my lips at him, he moves forward. "Okay, if this is how it's going down."

Grabbing my arm, he hoists me up, pushing my body over his shoulder like I weigh nothing. With my ass in the air and my head hanging towards his ass, I smack him several times. "Let me down!"

I'm jolted with each step Elijah takes, completely unperturbed by my violence on his butt. However, once he reaches the bottom step, two fingers pass by my panties to enter my pussy, causing my whole body to jerk.

"Fuck!" I scream, the impact of it taking me back.

We reach the kitchen where he withdraws his fingers before setting me down, the aroma of the noodles hitting my nostrils again.

"You prick." I glare at him, but my eyes widen in hunger when he makes a show of darting his tongue out and licking the two fingers that had just been inside my pussy.

"You taste sweet," he purrs, causing my legs to tighten with need. "It's just a pity it doesn't match the rest of you."

I puff out some air. "And if I was as sweet as my cunt, you wouldn't want me in the way that you do ... and you know it."

That's another thing Elijah doesn't want to admit. He likes me bad. He loves that I'm this devious little devil who sucks his cock like it's never been sucked before. He secretly loves that I take on this persona of a sweet, young thing who stays at home and bakes cookies all day, when at night I turn in to a freak who gives him the best sex he's ever had. Why else does he come back and keep coming back for more?

Elijah pulls out his stool a bit roughly then sits down. "Sit," he orders. So I do. He then pulls out the boxes of takeout, opening one up and handing it to me. I stare down at the noodles coated in a black sauce, filled with chicken, broccoli and carrots. My stomach growls in protest, so I pick up the chopsticks which are on the table and start eating, the tang of the soy sauce hitting my mouth and livening my senses.

For a while we sit in silence eating, my stomach getting fuller and fuller with each bite until I feel like I'll explode. I watch for a moment as Elijah carries on chewing his food like he doesn't have a care in the world. Unbeknownst to him, the little devil inside me orders me to act. *He did lock you in your room for over three hours. He deserves everything he gets.*

With not much more coaxing after that, I dig my chopsticks inside the box, picking up some slimy noodles before flinging them in Elijah's direction. They land on his forehead at first then eventually slide down until they fall inside his box. Laughter bubbles inside of me until I can't keep it in any longer. Elijah stays as still as a statue, his chopsticks still in midair from when he was going to take his next bite. His eyes narrow as he watches me laugh so hard it's starting to hurt. That is until he flicks some of his food on me, landing directly on my chest, the warmth of it immediately turning cold and causing me to shiver.

"You little shit," I snarl, but all he does is smirk in response, so I decide to fling more noodles at him, this time hitting him in the chest too. His smirk fades, the jolt of what I did obviously unexpected due to him almost jumping out of his skin at the impact. I mean, what does he really expect?

As predicted, a fight ensues, both of us throwing pieces of noodles, the juices from them getting in our hair and all over our clothes. We're giggling so loud at our little food fight that we almost fail to hear the doorbell ring.

We both fall into silence, then I scoot off my stool to glance out of the window. When I spot who it is, I groan.

"Who is it?"

"Duckface."

Grabbing a towel, Elijah picks our boxes up and throws them in the trash. "Go see what she wants. I'm not here, if she asks."

As soon as Elijah disappears, my devilish smile appears. If he doesn't want to see her, that means he doesn't like her very much.

With a skip in my step, I open the door, and when Duckface's eyes land on me, her mouth parts.

"Oh, my Lord, what happened to you, child?"

I almost roll my eyes at the child comment. With my chest all wet and my nipples sticking out half a mile, I certainly do not have the body of one.

"I had a little fight with some ... noodles."

Without offering her inside, she barges her way in. "Oh, dear. Let's get you cleaned up, shall we?"

Shocked at her audacity, I simply close the door and follow after her to the kitchen. She takes one look at all the mess on the counter, shaking her head. "Oh, my. You certainly did have a fight with your dinner, didn't you?"

Sheepishly, I say back, "kinda."

She glances around the room, peeking inside the living room like she's searching for something. "No Elijah?"

"He's still at work."

She points outside. "But his car's out front."

This bitch seriously has some issues. The way she eats out pussy, you would never expect her to come after a man as hard as she does with him.

"He got a ride in with one of the officers who's going to bring him home later."

She smiles. "Ah, the perks of the new job, huh?" She again takes in my messy state, her eyes lingering around my chest area. "Let's get you cleaned up."

As she leads me to the sink, I want to ask her why she's here, but it's gotta be to see Elijah considering she asked for him. She's all dressed up today in a nice, white, figure-hugging dress, her golden locks newly curled like she's dressed to impress.

Grabbing a cloth, Duckface wets it under the tap then gets to work on my hair, wiping a bit from my face before she rinses the cloth again. She's certainly heavily into it, considering she doesn't notice that Elijah has appeared in the crack of the living room door, his eyes watching the whole spectacle. I smirk at him as Duckface fusses around me until eventually, she gets to my chest area. She washes the sauce from my exposed bare skin, my gaze watching her as her breath hitches a little. I quirk an eyebrow. Is she getting turned on?

"What happened?" she asks, swallowing hard as she hovers the cloth over my chest like she's contemplating something.

"I put the noodles in the microwave for too long, so when I opened it they exploded all over me," I lie.

Gazing at my breasts, she licks her lips. "Microwaving food isn't good for you. If you ever need to eat, come over to my place. I'll cook you something up real nice."

Little does she know, I can cook with the best of them, but I don't correct her on this. I'm just surprised she offered. Maybe if she thinks she can get me on her side then I will, in turn, get Elijah on her side too.

Yeah, like that will happen ... not even if hell froze over.

"That's nice of you to offer. Thank you."

She gazes up into my eyes, a nervous flicker in her gaze. I smile at her then point to the cloth, giving her the permission she may be seeking. Her hand trembles slightly as she grazes the cloth over the top parts of my breasts, concentrating on getting the sauce off there. Desire pools between my legs. Not because of what she's doing, but because I know that Elijah is watching everything that's happening between us. I'm not sure if he knows about Duckface's sexual preferences, but if he doesn't, he'll find out soon enough.

She's slow and methodical at first, only concentrating on the mess at the top of my dress. Her mouth is parted, her breathing labored as her erotic behavior with me is no doubt tingling all of her senses.

And then she does it. With the least bit of cloth, she sweeps over my hardened nipple, a soft but tiny moan leaving her lips. She hesitates a moment, glancing a peek up at my reaction, but I stay still, encouraging her to continue.

She doesn't disappoint. She wipes the base of the cloth round both my breasts, wetting my whole dress so that my top half is as see-through as saran wrap. Almost fully exposed, Duckface licks her duck lips, her breathing quickening with each stroke of the cloth.

I glance a peek at where Elijah was standing a moment ago, and sure enough he's there, his eyes wide with surprise, a frown forming on his face.

Interesting.

Wondering just how far I can take this, I stay rooted so that Duckface knows I'm not exactly disgusted by the idea of her feeling me up. I'm tempted. Oh, so tempted to find out just how good her duck lips could suck on my clit. Would my orgasm with her be as explosive as it is with Elijah? I doubt it, but still ... it is tempting. Plus, I'm insanely turned on by the fact that Elijah is watching us. Would he continue to watch while she licked my pussy? Would he let it get that far?

Biting my lip, an evil smirk curves my lips. He did lock me in my room, after all.

"You're ... stunning," Duckface whispers, breathlessly.

She gazes up into my eyes, my own hooded ones showing her how turned on I am from her touching me. She sucks in a breath, momentarily hesitating like she's wondering what to do next. She sweeps her eyes over my heaving breasts, hers widening with desire. She licks her lips then makes her decision.

Pulling down one half of my dress, she exposes my breast, her gasp almost a longing hiss. She bends her head forward, taking my pebbled nipple into her mouth, her tongue darting around my nipple before her duck lips suckle tenderly.

Even I can't help the small moan that escapes me. It seems Duckface got those lips for a reason, and I now know the reason why.

Meticulously, she takes her time suckling on my nipple, my breathing now quickening with hers. While Duckface's focus in on me, I glance another peek at Elijah to gauge his reaction. By the way his nostrils are flaring and how red his face is getting, I'm thinking he's madder than hell. I would have thought he would enjoy the show, but apparently, he doesn't like the thought of anyone touching me, male or female. Still, the devil in me can't help but push his buttons, so I offer him a sardonic smile, my head tilting back slightly as I enjoy the feel of her lips on my nipple. A flash of me on top of Elijah's cock, my back to him as duckface eats me out comes to mind, causing a flurry of excitement to hit me. I would never entertain the idea of the three of us together as she would want to touch Elijah, which can never happen. Still, this is my fantasy, and in my head, that's is how it's playing out.

Moaning out again, my smirk widens, challenging Elijah further. My eyes fixed on him, my pussy throbs with the need to come. In fact, I'm about to push Duckface's head down to my pussy to make that happen when Elijah's finger comes up to his neck where he sweeps it from one side to the other in a cutting motion. He's telling me to end this. Damn. Just as I was starting to have fun.

Disappointed that I don't get to find out how good Duckface really is, I step back, covering myself up. "I think you should leave." Placing my arms around myself, I try to show her my regret and embarrassment over the whole situation through my expression, even though I'm anything but.

She gasps, taking a step back, her face reddening with panic. "I'm so sorry. I don't know what came over me." She steps forward, so I step back again. "Please forget this ever happened."

She then turns and rushes for the door, apologizing with every step she takes until the door slams shut behind her.

Well, that was certainly unexpected.

"What the fuck was that?!" Elijah seethes, bursting through the door.

I turn in his direction, a bright smile on my face. "She may be after your cock, but she likes eating pussy too. Did you not know?" I turn to start cleaning up the mess, my pussy still aching for a release.

"Why did you let her do that, Bryce? Have you let her do that before? If I didn't order you to stop, how far would you have taken it?" I hum a little as I get to work on wiping up the noodles that spilled on the table. "Bryce ... fucking answer me."

I halt what I'm doing, turning to answer his twenty questions. "I let her do it because I'm still mad at you for locking me in my room. To answer your next question, no, I have never let her do that to me before since I've never been alone with her like that before. And lastly,

I would have taken it all the way. I would have come all over her face, watching you watch me the whole time, and I would have fucking loved every second of it."

Grabbing me by the neck, he forces me back until I hit the edge of the sink, his eyes dancing with a rage so potent, it scares me. But only for a fraction of a second.

"You are not to go near her again, do you hear?"

My eyes narrow in on his. "Why? Come on, tell me why it's so important, huh?" I'm goading him again, but seriously, he needs to start explaining his reasons. When he so obviously doesn't want us to be public like a normal relationship, how I am expected to stay monogamous?

"How would you fucking like it if Simon across the road came over and started going down on me while you watched, huh?" Delight swims in my eyes at the thought. When he notices my reaction, an angered breath leaves him. "Actually ... don't fucking answer that question."

Because he now knows full well what the answer would be.

"Make me come, baby," I whine, my pussy throbbing harder than ever. Duckface may have started it, but all these erotic visions swimming in my head coupled with Elijah holding me so forcefully around my neck is making my need stronger than ever.

Elijah's jaw tics in response. He leans in, his hot breath on my face. "Duckface turns you on, and now you expect me to finish it?"

I smile because even Elijah can't resist calling her Duckface now. "I'm turned on because you were watching. Not because of what she was doing. I don't find her attractive at all." And I don't. But still, her duck lips do know what they're doing. There's no denying that. I've been more intrigued by her since her little display with the priest's wife, seeing how she made her climax so hard that her whole body trembled for a while after. She's simply an itch to scratch. A mystery that needs solving. Once I've experienced it once, I won't ever go back.

"I don't care about your reasoning, Bryce. I'm not fucking you after that bitch went near you."

I pout at him which only serves to anger him more. In an instant, I'm hoisted up over his shoulder again and being marched up to my room. Once there, he swiftly closes the door, locking it behind him.

I sigh, disappointment shrouding me as my juices start to coat my legs. A part of me is tempted to grab my key, sneak out of the house, and get Duckface to finish me off. Considering I can't get Elijah to do it for me, she really is the only option.

Despite the devilish gleam in my eye at the prospect, my ass remains cemented to my bed. I may be a lot of things, but a cheater isn't one of them. It's one thing having him watch but another entirely when it involves me sneaking around behind his back. I'm mad at him for treating me like a child and locking me in my room like a prisoner whenever he damn well pleases, but I draw the line when it comes to something that may genuinely hurt him. Based on how angry he is at what he saw, I'm guessing he would genuinely be hurt.

I sigh again, resigned to the fact that I'm not going anywhere.

Tugging at my dress, I lift it up over my head and lie on the bed. I guess the only person pleasuring me tonight is myself.

CHAPTER FIFTEEN

ast

After our little make-out session in the back of Chesney's truck, he drives me home. With instructions, he eventually made me come, and I must admit, I've been on a little high ever since. In return, I gave him a hand job, but he came after just two strokes. I told him he needed to work on that, and his response floored me. He's actually a virgin. I had to laugh at that because there were rumors last year that he took Verity's virginity at school which branded her a slut and him a hero. He never once denied it, which totally makes him a douche. I told him as much, too, and he at least seemed remorseful.

Outside of my house, I grab my bag and thank Chesney as I slide out of his truck. I say slide as that's what you have to do in his truck. He offers me a wave and a big, beaming smile before he drives away. I want to hate him, I really do. In fact, I do hate some things about him —Verity being a prime example—but I still can't help the sick, little crush I have had on him since the day I met him in school.

I'm up my front steps, bag hoisted high as I'm about to let myself in when the door is opened for me, Elijah appearing, looking pissed.

"This is becoming a habit," I quip, stepping into the house.

He closes the door behind us then follows me to the living room. There's no sign of Mom. Thankfully.

"And so is you skipping school lately. They called again, wondering where you were during your last two periods. I had to invent some appointment story like last time."

I plop my bag on the floor, smiling up at him sweetly. "Thanks for that."

Elijah's eyes widen. "Where were you?"

Realizing something, I frown. "You've been home an awful lot lately. Aren't you supposed to be at work?"

Hands on his hips, he puffs out an angry breath. "I am until I get phone calls from school, wondering where you are. Every time, I have to leave work early and come back home to make sure you're okay."

I almost roll my eyes. "That's very noble of you."

His lilac eyes zero in on me. "I'm not liking your sarcasm, young lady." When I don't say anything back, he asks, "Why did you skip school? Where have you been?"

I glance down at my growing fingernails, wondering for a moment what color to polish them. "My friend and I got cornered in the boy's locker room where the jocks decided that I should give my friend head, saying they'd beat him up otherwise. The guy you no doubt saw who brought me home luckily broke it up before it went too far. I let him eat my pussy as a thank you."

I stare at my nails the whole time I say this, my proclamation met with silence. When I chance a glance at Elijah, he's red with rage.

"You better not be bullshitting me."

I cross my arms in front of my chest. "You really think I want to be bullshitting you? This is my life, Elijah. I go to school and get shit on. I come home and get shit on."

"Why didn't you fucking tell me this shit was going on at school?"

I almost stomp my foot, I'm so fucking angry. "Why?!" I shriek back. "So you can, what? Protect me?! You did that so well last time, didn't you?! Who am I supposed to trust, huh? Cause it certainly isn't my own mom or stepdad."

My breath quickening, tears start to well in my eyes. I'm especially fucking angry at him because out of everything that's happened in my lifetime, it only takes him badgering me to bring me to tears. No one else affects me this way, and I hate him for it.

"Bryce," he starts, his voice softer.

"Don't," I fire back. "Just fucking don't."

"I'll speak to the school, figure something out so you can finish your studies at home."

My eyes widen. "What, with her in the house with me? No thanks. I would rather take on the jocks at school than her."

"Jesus, Bryce—"

"What? Do you want me to lie? Because I ain't doing it." I step towards him until we're inches apart. There, I bare my teeth at him. "I want that bitch dead."

Picking my bag up, I march past him and walk up the stairs to my room where I close the door behind me. I was on a high from Chesney earlier, but Elijah ruined it.

Taking off my shoes, I plop down on my bed, curling up on my side. The door opens, and in walks Elijah, closing the door behind him. My eyes watch his every move, his statuesque physique. The way his jeans hang perfectly, kissing those exquisite hips of his, and the way his black t-shirt clings to him like a second skin. The dark clouds forming outside help to illuminate his form as his lilac eyes dance with an unreadable emotion, watching me as he prowls around my room.

Why is he here?

My breath hitches when there's a dip on my bed alerting me to the fact that he's sitting on it. I'm bounced farther as he scoots up behind me, snaking his arm around me from behind. His musky, sweet, cinnamon aroma invades my nostrils, causing me to close my eyes and breathe him in like a fine wine.

"Why are you here?"

I hate the fact that he is, but I equally hate the fact that I love that he's here too. I hate loving his warm embrace, the contours of his body, perfectly molding to mine. I hate the flurry of butterflies in my stomach when he lays his hand on my hip just so, his fingers ever so lightly tapping the fabric of my dress. I hate that I wish I was naked so that those same fingers could scorch my skin, tearing my longing from the inside out. I hate that—even after everything he's done—I still want him with a passion that burns my soul, singeing it until there's nothing left but him.

"Because you need me."

I inhale a deep, angry breath at his words. I don't need him, not now. I needed him eight weeks ago.

"I hate you."

His chest meets my back on an inhale before his warm breath peppers the back of my neck. "I know you do. But one day, you'll realize that hate isn't warranted."

Confusion shrouds me. "I don't know what the fuck that means."

His hand tugs my body closer to him, causing me to gasp. "For now, you won't. In time you will understand everything."

I stay silent, trying my hardest to control my breathing around him. Again, I close my eyes, willing my body to tamp down the desires I have that want to push the boundaries with him, wishing I could place my hand on his and guide it to where Chesney recently had his tongue.

"That guy who dropped you off," he whispers in the increasingly darkening room. "What's his name?"

I fling my eyes open, slightly turning my head. I have no clue why I do since I can't see him to gauge his reaction. "Why?"

His nose is in my hair where he inhales a moment. "No reason."

My heart does a few skips as I remain silent for a moment. That is until he tugs at my belly. "His name," he growls, the force of it vibrating through my body, almost making me shudder at the deep-seated yearning it evokes.

Oh, my.

"Chesney Felix." I curse myself at my automatic response. His command was so severe that I instantly reacted to it. "He's only sixteen," I warn him, just in case he's thinking of doing anything stupid with that information.

Why did he ask?

"And the names of the shits who cornered you?"

I suck in a breath, the force of his words settling deep in my groin. However, this time I bite my lip to refrain from giving him the information. Instead, I say, "I'm dealing with them."

"Names," he snarls, causing my heart to slam against my ribcage.

"No matter how many times you ask, I'm not telling you. I've waited way too long to get those fuckers back. It's my time, Elijah. I need you to let me settle the score."

I wait with bated breath for him to command me to tell him, so I'm surprised when he simply sighs. He then maneuvers a little bit, snuggling himself even closer into me. "Close your eyes, Bryce. Relax for a bit."

I should be annoyed at his flippancy, but I'm way too comfy to argue at this point. Letting his comfort engulf me, I do as he asks, and it's not long before I fall asleep.

I don't know how long I sleep , but when I wake it's to raised voices coming from downstairs.

Gasping, I sit up and quickly scurry to my door, opening it so I can listen to what's being said.

"I fucking hate you for what you did!" my mother screeches followed by the sound of glass crashing.

"The feeling is fucking mutual," Elijah barks back. "You're nothing but a disgusting whore, Brenda! Just look at you!"

Ouch. I know she deserves every bit of his biting words, but it still makes me cringe to hear them.

"I'm so fucking done with your shit. Tomorrow, I'm taking Bryce and we're leaving."

I gasp, my eyes widening. She can fucking try to take me away, but it ain't ever going to happen. I hate both of them, but if there is a choice, Elijah is definitely the best of the bad bunch.

"You do that," Elijah shouts, nothing but venom in his voice. "I will fucking kill you."

I have no time to process the shocking threat I just heard when footsteps sound, getting closer to my room.

"I'm going out. I'm done with your shit."

"Yeah, that's right, Brenda. Go out and get fucking high again like you always do. Why don't you do us all a favor and leave altogether?"

I edge onto the landing and peek over the banister to watch my mother yanking the front door open. "Fuck you," is all she fires back.

Elijah throws his hands in the air. "Very mature, Brenda."

She slams the door shut, then I edge even closer until I'm standing at the landing, watching Elijah as he pinches the bridge of his nose. He then sighs and turns, stopping dead in his tracks when he spots me upstairs.

With his fiery lilac eyes locked on me, something passes between us. Fuck knows what it is, but the electricity is humming, powerful and bright, illuminating my soul. For a few seconds we stay like that, completely taken in by the power he emits. I don't know what's happening, all I know is my heart is thundering in my chest, adrenaline coursing through my veins.

But then, just as quickly as he spotted me, he disappears, walking down the hallway towards the living room, the electric moment fizzling out like a wet match.

CHAPTER SIXTEEN

resent

Armed with two batches of cookies, I set them in two separate baskets then dress in a floral but sexy maxi dress before leaving the house for the bus stop. Twenty minutes later, I'm outside of the mayor's building and about to walk in. I glance up, taking in the white stone and the big bay windows, sighing my displeasure. It's been three days, and I still haven't heard anything. Considering I sent him a text last night warning him I'd be coming here and he didn't answer, I figured I should pay him a ... friendly visit.

I'm about to step in when I feel something poking into my back. I suck in a breath when a voice growls at me.

"Don't scream, and I won't hurt you. Simply turn around and get into the black sedan behind us. We need to have a little *chat*."

Heart racing, I do as he requests, turning and walking down the steps from where I came, heading towards the black sedan, waiting at the sidewalk.

The guy with a gun stuck to my back opens the door to the backseat, waiting for me to get inside. With two baskets of cookies, it's a little awkward. Once I'm in, he snatches my purse which has my wallet and phone in it.

I take in who it is that's kidnapping me, only to find I have no clue who the hell he is. The guy looks to be in his late forties, greying hair and an equally greying moustache. He's wearing black like he's in some covert operation or something. It just makes him look like a dork.

I should be scared, but I'm surprisingly calm for someone who's being taken without any clue as to why.

When he gets inside, I show my displeasure. "I just baked these cookies, and now they're getting cold because of you."

The man pivots around to look at me, his face covered in amusement. Instead of responding, his hand comes over, and he snatches one from the basket.

"Hey!" I scorn, pursing my lips. "These are for the mayor."

Ignoring me, he bites into it then hums his approval, nodding his head. "These are good. I can pass them on to the mayor with your regards after our little chat."

Stuffing the rest of the cookie into his big, fat mouth, he pulls away from the curb, driving to God knows where. At least I know that the mayor has something to do with this. I dart my eyes to the mirror, watching as this asshole hums some shitty little tune out loud that I can't make out.

"Yeah, like that isn't annoying," I grouse.

His eyes meet mine in the mirror. "You're quite the feisty little thing, aren't you?"

After a while of driving, we eventually get to Midway where there's nothing but white picket fences and horses roaming the fields. We're driving along a stretch of quiet road when the asshole throws my handbag out of the car towards a bush.

"Motherfucker!" I shout, watching as we drive past the bush. This guy doesn't want a little chitty chat. He wants me dead. Rather, it seems the mayor wants me dead and sent his minion to do it for him.

"You've got quite the tongue on you, too, haven't ya?"

I flip him the bird, causing his body to jerk in silent laughter. What he doesn't realize is, I always come with backup.

Leaning forward in my seat a bit, I take a look around us, noting we're the only car for what looks like miles. I smile sweetly and whisper. "Would you like another cookie?"

Asshole nods his head in amusement as I reach underneath the basket for the handy ice pick stored there. Without hesitation, I pull it up, jabbing it into the right side of his neck. Blood spurts over to the seat next to him as well as on the window and on me. It annoys me, considering I will have to wash this off somehow. The prick.

I don't have much time to dwell on that as the car veers one way and then the next. I try desperately to climb over the seat so I can gain control of the car, but before I can, we're off the road, heading down a ditch, my body jerking up and hitting the roof. Placing my hands on the seat in front of me, I brace for impact as the car grumbles and revs, making all kinds of noises that cannot be good.

Finally, we come to a halt at the bottom of a small ravine, my head bashing into the seat in front of me. Pain radiates across my forehead and colors dance before my eyes, blinding me for a second. Asshole's gurgling, is the only sound I hear as I glance down, taking in all the blood on my dress, causing me to grumble again.

Angry now, I stretch forward until I reach asshole who's barely alive. I place my mouth close to his ear and whisper, "Never underestimate an angelic looking seventeen-year-old girl with a basketful of cookies."

His eyes widen as he breathes his last breath, the welcoming sound of nothing but the water from the ravine permeating my ears. I reach up to the ice pick and yank it out of his neck, his head flopping down instantly after, blood dribbling out of his mouth.

"Eww, that's gross." I glance around the car, cookies strewn all over the seats and on the floor, blood coating the right side of my dress. "My, my, you really have put me in quite the pickle here, haven't you, asshole?" I groan before trying to open the left door, but it's no use. I try the other side, and thankfully, that swings open. Unfortunately, it opens a little too enthusiastically, and I fall out, landing with a thud on the earth below, the wind momentarily knocked out of me. "Motherfucker!" I curse again, my head pounding from the impact. I place my hand there, checking for blood, but thankfully there isn't any. I'm acutely aware that I'm miles away from home now, no transportation of any kind, wearing a summer dress coated in the blood of the man I just murdered.

Great. Just great.

Knowing I can't sit here grumbling all day at a dead man, I get to work at washing what I can from the handy ravine, but the blood still shows up on my dress no matter what I do. In the end, I take the dress off, using it to wipe down any of my prints that may be all over the car. Once I feel I've done enough to wipe the evidence away, I pick up my two baskets, then I take off up the hill we'd raced down.

By the time I reach the top, I'm exhausted. With no other options, I force myself to carry on, walking towards the area where the asshole threw my bag. I spot the bush, elation replacing my annoyance as I take the last few steps at a running pace. Falling to my knees, I reach the bush and eventually find my bag. I fish my phone out, calling the only person I can think of to call. I hit dial then metaphorically cross my fingers that he'll answer.

"Justin! Can you come get me?"

CHAPTER SEVENTEEN

ast

After another week of being picked on relentlessly and spying on Chloe with no results, I start to get desperate. It got to a boiling point on Friday when, at lunchtime, Chloe and her crew decided to pour a bowl of pudding all over my head, causing the whole room to erupt in laughter. As usual, there were no teachers in sight to witness it, and I had to skip school—yet again—so I could get cleaned up. I still snapped back, surprising them somewhat by my change, but it was now becoming exhausting.

Still, I do have a plan. It's just having the balls to execute it that's the problem. But I'm getting so desperate now, I'm willing to try anything.

I get to Adam's place a little earlier than we'd planned for me to help him out with math. This is the third time I've gone to his house, and by now his parents love me. Especially his dad. I see the way he glances in my direction when he thinks I'm not looking. He's looks a lot like Adam with soft, wavy brown curls and light brown eyes. He's not exactly what I'd call good looking, but he certainly isn't ugly.

When I softly knock on the door, Adam's mother answers, a bright smile on her face when she spots me. "Oh, Bryce. How lovely to see you again. Come in, come in." She ushers me through quickly then points to the stairs. "He's in his room. Feel free to go up." I glance upstairs, and I'm about to head that way when she places her hand on my arm. "Thank you for everything you're doing."

I feel my cheeks warm at her gratitude. "It's no problem at all, Mrs. Banks."

Her blues eyes twinkle behind her glasses. "Because of you, he got a B on his test today in trig."

I nod my head, impressed. I watch as she practically dances towards the kitchen, leaving me to fend for myself. I give a little laugh at her enthusiasm then make my way up the stairs. I don't bother knocking since Adam already knows I'm coming over. I'm about to say hello when my eyes land on Adam on his bed, earphones in as he watches something. His adequate sized, erect cock is out, condom on, and he's jerking off to whatever it is he's watching on the screen. He's so focused on what he's doing that he doesn't even notice I'm there at first.

Taking my time, I watch him go to town on himself, his mouth parted, an erotic expression on his face. My eyes droop at the sight as I bite my lip, and a thought suddenly pops into my head. I sink my teeth farther into my lip, wondering if I should go there. Without another thought, I shut the door behind me and take a step towards him, my decision obviously made.

Noticing movement from the corner of his eye, Adam glances up, a yelp of surprise leaving his lips as his body jerks with fright. His phone leaves his hand and lands on the bed closer to me as he attempts to cover himself up.

"Jesus, Bryce! You should have knocked!"

There's no way he would have heard me even if I had knocked. I don't say that, though. Instead, I approach the bed, glancing down at what he's watching. A fit guy with dark hair and lots of tattoos lies on his back as a younger blonde woman with huge tits rides his cock.

"Fuck, yeah, baby ... just like that!" the woman screams as she thrusts up and down on his huge cock.

I glance up at Adam, quirking an eyebrow, impressed. "Why are you wearing a condom?"

With a deep frown, he gazes up at me in surprise, his breaths coming in gasps. "What?"

I place my bag down on the floor then move towards him until I'm standing right in front of him. "Why do you wear a condom to jerk off?"

He slams his eyes shut, shaking his head, presumably at my composed attitude towards the whole thing. "It's ... it's less messy," he finally gets out. "Plus ... I guess it's practice for when ... you know."

I bite my lip again, my mind now whirring with ideas. I tug at his duvet, but he keeps a grip on it. I fix him with my eyes. "Do you trust me?"

"I don't understand," he splutters, his confused face almost making me laugh.

"Do you trust me," I question him again.

Adam glances away then breathes out some air. "Yes."

I motion towards his duvet, and he releases his grip, letting me pull it away. His cock is still hard.

"What are you doing, Bryce?"

"Shh," I get on the bed and straddle him. I have a loose dress on, which is handy, but I have to shift my panties out of the way to place him at my entrance. Once the tip is in, Adam's eyes bulge out of his head, realizing what I'm up to.

"Bryce?" he questions, but I don't allow him to say anymore. Carefully, and more importantly going at my own pace, I sink down onto his cock until he's fully inside of me. The intrusion is a little painful, but at least I have the power. I'm the one calling the shots. He's not here, so he can't hurt me anymore. For my own sake, I need to push that fucking horrific memory from my head and concentrate solely on the here and now.

Adam hisses in a breath, his eyes gripping shut at the feel of me slinking down on him. Witnessing his reaction gives me the strength to continue. I lift up, plunging back down again. Each time I do it, the pain subsides, and replacing it is a new, warm, fuzzy sensation.

I'm in control. I've got this.

"Do you want me to stop?" I ask, giving him the chance to end this if he wants.

His mouth parts, his breathing harsh and heavy. "N... no."

Keeping my eyes on Adam, seeing the control I have over him, fuels my fire. His face twists with pleasure, his body tensing with the feel of my pussy clamping down on his cock. It makes me want to go faster, makes my own body alight with a euphoria I have never felt before. Tingles suffuse my body, causing me to moan as I move up and down on his cock, maneuvering every so often to find the best position to get the most pleasure.

"Oh, shit!" Adam hisses, his hands gripping my hips. I keep my eyes on him, my own pleasure heightening from witnessing his—knowing it's me giving it to him.

"Do you like that?" I ask, needing his words.

"Y... y... yes," he finally manages, his breaths now coming in pants. I close my eyes a moment, so that the only sense I home in on is my hearing. Adam's moans surround me, causing my body to hum to life.

"Shit, Bryce. I'm going to come!"

I'm a little disappointed he's going to come so quickly, but it doesn't stop me from chasing his climax. It's what fuels me even further.

"Aaaaahhhhhhh!" Adam groans, his body jerking with his climax. I take my time coming down from his high, watching his every feature when it goes from completely satiated to completely confused. Once he catches his breath, he glances up at me. "Why did you do that?"

I shrug my shoulders, sliding off him, knowing he'll have a million more questions just like that one. I watch as he takes the condom off then scurries into the bathroom to get rid of it. Once he's back, cock tucked in his sweatpants, he fixes me with his stare, nothing but questions filling his eyes.

Guilt shrouds me, because how do I explain that I simply used him as an experiment just to see if I could do it? I have a hunch that it would crush him to hear that, so how could I possibly tell him something like that?

"Did you not like it?"

Surprise flashes through his eyes. He shakes his head slightly. "It ... it was amazing, Bryce, but what I don't understand is why."

I narrow my eyes at him, channeling my guilt into anger. Anger is a much better emotion to hold on to than guilt. "Does it really matter why? I just wanted to try it, that's all."

He sits on his bed next to me, and I feel his eyes on me, judging me ... wondering why. It makes me want to run away and hide.

"You're not a virgin."

It kind of sounds like a question, but I know it isn't one. "No," I answer, fixing my eyes on his again. "Were you?" It's something that's only just occurred to me. Adam's only sixteen and is a bit of a nerd, like me, so I'm thinking it must be a yes.

"No." He turns his head away, and then it dawns on me.

"Oh, shit. I just took your virginity, didn't I? Why didn't you say anything to me?"

I could seriously kick myself. Looking back at how I handled this, it's not like I gave the poor guy a choice.

His eyes cast towards his ceiling before he eventually looks at me. "I guess I couldn't believe my luck. An opportunity I couldn't pass up." He then frowns. "I just don't understand what this means?"

Knowing he's talking about relationships, I get off the bed. "We can't ... be together like that, Adam. I think of you as a friend—"

"A friend you just fucked."

He has me there. "Okay, I'll give you that, but just because I fucked you doesn't mean I want anything to happen between us." I shrug. "I just wanted it, that's all. Is that a bad thing?"

Adam searches my eyes before smiling. "No, it's not."

"I'm sorry. I won't do it again."

Adam's eyes slightly widen, showing a little panic setting in. "Err ... how can I say this?" He twists his body to face me more. "If you ever want to make my fantasies a reality again, I will happily oblige."

Laughter bubbles out of me, causing him to do the same. "This won't come between us, will it?" Adam vehemently shakes his head, and my shoulders sag in relief. "Good."

"Do you want to get some studying done now?" Adam asks, causing me to giggle again.

Feeling better knowing he's totally okay with what I've done, I nod my head. "Sure thing."

~

Later that night, after my little nighttime chat with Frank, I sneak away from the house and make the thirty-minute journey on foot to Chloe's house. There I stay hidden behind a bush, knowing that she and her mother will leave soon to go to their Saturday night dance class together. I check my watch, and it's edging towards eight. Either they're late, or they've decided not to go tonight. I huff out an exasperated breath, wondering if I've made this journey in vain. But then there's movement at their front door, and out pops Chloe and her mom, all dressed up in expensive spandex, their gym bags clutched to their sides.

"Come on, we're already late," Chloe's mom calls out as they run towards their Porsche Cayenne. Quickly after, they're heading down the driveway, off to their destination.

I let out a breath, my heart feeling like it's drumming a million miles an hour. I wonder for a moment if I can go through with this, but then visions of Chloe and her idiot friends calling me disgusting names and humiliating me in front of the whole school fill my head, driving me forward.

Bag over my shoulder, I take a quick look to make sure no one is around before I emerge from behind the bush and walk the short distance to her house. Once at their front door, I ring the bell and wait for it to be answered. Seconds later it opens, and standing on the other side is Brian, Chloe's dad—the man whose lap I was sitting on not that long ago. He's dressed in white slacks and a blue polo shirt, his hair gelled back and a glass of something amber in his hand. When he spots me, he frowns, but then recognition sets in.

"What the hell are you doing here?"

I step forward, my hand out in a calming manner. "Listen, I know I shouldn't be here, but I just wanted to come by and say sorry."

He gazes around his street before addressing me again. "This is totally inappropriate of you—"

"I know," I interrupt him. "Listen, do you mind if I come in for a moment? I've been walking for miles, and my feet hurt. I promise I won't stay long."

Brian sighs, indecision marring his face. He takes another peek around the neighborhood before opening up his door for me.

Adrenaline pumping, I step forward and enter the plush, grand foyer, the sweeping staircase in front of me taking up a lot of the vast space.

"You'll need to take your shoes off," he informs me, pointing to a large shoe cabinet by the door which is filled with shoes.

I slip my sandals off, welcoming the feel of the cool floorboards that greet them. "That feels good," I whisper, closing my eyes. When I open them, Brian is gulping down his drink.

"Does your dad know you're here?" He walks off, so I follow.

"I have to be honest with you and say no. I just felt I needed to apologize to you in person for not telling you who I was."

"And your age," he sneers before entering what looks to be his study. It's dark with only a small desk lamp illuminating the room. He rounds his desk and sits down, swigging the rest of his drink down before staring up at me.

"I know, and again, I'm sorry." I place my bag down on the floor before walking around to his side and holding out my hand to him. "Friends?" I ask, a lopsided grin on my face.

He takes my hand, sighing. "I guess I can forgive you."

I smile brightly at him, and for the first time since I arrived, he seems to relax. "Thank you." I stare down at his laptop, a spreadsheet opened up to what looks like a list of accounts.

"Need any help with that?" I offer as an olive branch.

He laughs out loud. "You're sixteen and still in school. This is a little above your paygrade."

I smirk at him. "Has Chloe ever mentioned me before? I'm top in every glass and a whizz with numbers. Or are you just scared that a sixteen-year-old girl may be better at this than you?"

He laughs before getting out of his seat and motioning to his laptop. "Okay, you asked for it. Have at it. I'll give you one minute before you give up."

Taking the challenge, I place my butt in the cushioned leather chair, marveling for a moment at how comfy it is. "Any chance I could get a glass of that?" I ask, pointing to his glass.

"Don't push it, young lady," he warns, shaking his head.

I shrug my shoulders. "Was worth a shot."

I then stare at the numbers on the screen. He's working on last month, which has just ended, so I begin crunching the numbers, making sure they all correlate. It's takes about twenty minutes, but I finish, crossing my arms in triumph.

Brian, who's been busy staring down at his phone looks up, noticing that I'm finished. He smirks. "That took a lot longer than I thought. Given up now?"

I shake my head. "I finished."

With a confused frown, he rounds the desk, leaning over me to look at the screen. He moves the cursor up and down the screen, double checking the numbers against the ledger, his face conveying his disbelief.

"How did you manage to finish that so fast?"

Noting how close he is, I search his face, my voice husky. "I told you. I'm a whizz."

"You certainly..." He turns his head at that point, catching my heat-filled eyes. He stares a moment, swallows, then his eyes cast down towards my breasts for a moment. "Thank you." He pulls away, but the moment was definitely there. He wants to fuck me.

Knowing I can push this now, I rise to my feet, moving until I'm right in front of him. "You're more than welcome." I make a show of dancing my eyes around his face, not hiding the deep hunger setting in them.

He swallows hard. "Why are you really here?" He's suddenly nervous ... unsure of himself. I'm surprised at how much this actually turns me on. Knowing I have the power to turn a man of his stature in to a bumbling buffoon has my heart racing and my belly flurrying with excitement.

Raising my hand up, I stroke the edge of his shirt sleeve. "You want the truth?" I glance up to meet his eyes, his lips slightly parted. He nods his head. "I can't stop thinking about what could have been that night if we hadn't been ... interrupted."

"We can't," he shakes his head, moving away from me. "I mean, you're the most beautiful girl I have ever had the pleasure of coming across, and of course, I'm flattered, but..."

I step forward until my chest meets his, gazing longingly into his eyes. "Do you not want me?"

He closes his eyes a moment, his hardness poking at my belly. "I think you already know the answer to that."

I place my finger at the top of his chest then work my way down to the waistband of his pants. "Is there somewhere I can ... freshen up a little?"

Brian pants, his face flushed with desire. "Err ... yes. Upstairs, first door on the right."

I smooth out my hair before walking around him, picking up my bag as I go. At the door, I offer him a little wave. "Make yourself comfortable. I'll be back in a bit."

I close the door behind me, taking a deep breath before running for the stairs. I bypass the bathroom door, opening all the other doors, trying to find Chloe's bedroom. The third door opens up to pink walls and a poster of Justin Bieber above the bed. I roll my eyes at how girlie it all is before I rush inside, quickly going through every drawer, every nook, and every cranny I can find, searching for anything that can give me ammunition against that bitch. I sigh, coming up empty, when something about her pillow looks a little odd, like it's suspended in the air a little. Cocking my head to the side, I step towards it, pulling it back.

Bingo!

My eyes gleam with delight as I stare down at a pink journal. A journal no doubt full of Chloe's secrets, or at the very least, her innermost desires.

Being as quick as I can, I place her diary in my bag before positioning her pillow back where it was and heading for the stairs. When I get to the bottom, I hesitate for a moment. I should leave now. I have what I came for, so why am I hovering?

I turn, glancing towards the study door, wondering if I can do it. If Chloe found out I fucked her daddy, it would break her rotten heart.

An evil smirk curves my lips as I make my final decision and walk towards the study.

I am in control.

I am the one with the power.

CHAPTER EIGHTEEN

resent

As I wait for Justin, Adam's father, to come get me, I hide in the trees, freezing my ass off with only a bra and panties on. I'm so grateful I chose to wear both today. Fuck knows what he's going to think when he turns up, finding me half naked, carrying two empty baskets. I'm going to look like a near-naked Little Red Riding Hood, especially with the backdrop I have behind me.

With the ice pick wrapped tightly in my soiled dress, feeling satisfied there's no evidence of blood anywhere on me or the baskets, I sit and I wait it out, trying to come up with a story to explain why I'm out here, why I'm half naked, and why I have a bump on my forehead that's no doubt the size of Mount Vesuvius by now. I reach up, touching my forehead, instantly wishing I hadn't.

"Fuck this shit."

Rage bubbles inside of me when I think about the mayor and how he dared to try to kill off the police chief's daughter. Because of what that fucker's done I know I have to act on this, and it's going to have to be by tonight. If he gets word that I'm still alive, he'll surely send someone else after me. I can't let that happen.

Around twenty minutes later, I hear the sound of a car approaching. I peek around the tree I'm hiding behind, and sure enough, it's Justin's car. I step forward, waving like a mad woman to get his attention. Justin comes to a halt then races out of the car, rushing to my side, his eyes wide with anxiety.

"Bryce, what the hell happened to you?"

"Did you bring me some clothes?" I ask, not wanting to explain right now.

He nods his head quickly then heads for the trunk. He opens it up, pulling out a bag full of clothes. "I didn't think you'd want any of Jenny's clothes, so I brought some of Adam's. I hope you don't mind."

I pull out a dark grey Lexington Legends hoodie along with a pair of lighter grey sweatpants, putting them on. They're a bit big, but they'll do.

"What happened?" Justin asks again as I'm tying the strings to the sweatpants around my waist. "Did someone hurt you?"

Placing my baskets in the trunk, I push the hood down then face his concerned frown. "I had an accident."

His eyes widen to saucers. "Accident?! How? When?" His eyes dart around, looking for signs of said accident but coming up empty.

Throwing my arms around him, I hug him tightly to me. "Oh, Justin, it was awful," I begin, trying to force the tears to come. I called Justin because he's the only person I can trust not to shoot his fucking mouth, and the only reason he won't do that is because he's like a puppy dog around me. I could go to his house, shoot his wife in the forehead in front of him, and he'd still bow down at my feet.

"Please don't say anything, but I stole Elijah's car just to see if I could drive it, and I accidentally ran it off the road."

He pulls me away, searching my eyes. "Jesus, Bryce. Are you okay?"

I vigorously nod my head. "A bit knocked up, but I'm fine. For now, I just want to get out of here. Is there any chance you can take me to your store to get cleaned up?"

He places his hands on my shoulder. "Of course, but why not home?"

"Elijah won't be there, and I don't want to be alone right now after..." I glance down sheepishly at my feet.

"Of course. Let's get you in the car."

As we're both getting into the car, I chance a peek down the road to see if it looks like there's been any disturbance. There're some tire marks, but other than that, everything looks normal.

"How's Adam?" I ask once he starts driving.

"He's doing good. Enjoying college life so far. He's bringing Amy back to meet us during summer break. He really wants you to meet her too."

Amy is Adam's new girlfriend of five months. They met when they both started college and immediately hit it off. We still keep in contact via text, but not as much as we used to now that this new girl's on the scene. Still, I'm happy for him.

"That will be nice."

Justin's eyes quickly flicker to me for a moment. "Are you sure you're okay?" I nod my head. "What are you going to tell Elijah?"

I scratch my head, the stress of the last two hours really starting to hit me. "I don't know yet. I'll think of something. I guess I will have to come clean about stealing his car. Unless I can tell him someone else stole it?"

I smirk in his direction, causing him to smile back, shaking his head. But then he frowns like he's just thought of something. "Hey, how come you were half naked when I picked you up?"

Searching my mind to think of something, I eventually say, "I got gas all over my dress. I didn't think it would be good to be wearing something so ... flammable."

He shudders like the thought scares him. "No, probably not." He's silent for a moment before he clears his throat. "How have you been? I haven't heard from you in a while."

I clasp my hands together on my lap, biting my lip. Truth be told, I haven't really had a use for Justin for a while—as bad as that sounds. "Sorry, I know you rely on me to do your books. I can do some when we get back to the store, if you want?"

I see the gleam in his eye at the thought, but then he tuts. "No, you were in an accident. You need your rest."

"I just need some Tylenol and somewhere quiet. I'll be fine. I'd be happy to help."

He looks relieved, and to be honest, it's the least I can do considering he just rescued me.

"You're an angel."

"I know," I tease back, causing him to smile. Despite the baggy sweatpants, his eyes veer towards my legs. He always did love my legs.

"I don't know why you don't charge me for what you do. You'd make a lot of money."

I'm tempted to tease him by asking him what he's insinuating, but instead, I answer honestly. "Some I do charge, but people like you, I don't."

After working on Brian's books for a while, word got around about my skills. I have been making good money off of some small businesses round here, but some of them I deliberately targeted in order to gain access to certain things. Justin I do for free simply for Adam. We may have fooled around a few times, but no matter what, we've always maintained our friendship. That's the one thing we promised each other we'd never allow to be broken.

"People like me?" he parrots, wanting me to elaborate.

"You're my best friend's dad. It wouldn't be right."

I witness his slight grimace at my statement.

We reach the store where he parks in the back lot. We get out, and I take the baskets inside. When inside the store, he turns to me. "I need to open up for an hour or so. Will you be okay?"

I nod my head encouragingly. "Yes, of course. Do what you need to do." He turns to walk to the front of the store, but I grab his arm. He glances his head back. "Thank you."

His face immediately softens, his fingers lightly brushing my cheek. "Anything for you, you know that."

Yes, I do, I think to myself as he heads to the front, allowing me privacy to get refreshed. Grabbing the dress from the basket, I unroll it, taking out the ice pick that I had "borrowed" from the store a few months ago. I've been carrying it around with me since, but I never thought I would actually have to use it. Immediately, I take it to the bathroom and wash all the remaining blood off, taking my time to get every little bit I can. Once finished, I look up in the mirror, noting the bruise already forming on the bump on my forehead. I grumble. How the fuck am I going to explain that to Elijah?

Head still pounding, I go to the first aid kit behind the mirror and down three Tylenol. I dry the ice pick, grab the dress and wicker baskets then take everything out back to where Justin has a burn barrel he uses to burn all his old, sensitive docs. I grab the gasoline can, throwing everything except for the ice pick into the barrel, pouring the gasoline on it all before setting it alight.

As the flames burn everything inside, I grab the little box where Justin likes to hide his stash of cigarettes and light one up. I take in a deep, much needed inhale, closing my eyes as I exhale. I sit down on Justin's sneaky cigarette seat and close my eyes a moment, hoping that the Tylenol will kick in soon. For a while, I just sit and stare at the flames, staying there until they start to dwindle and two of Justin's cigarettes have disappeared from his pack.

My head is awash with everything that's happened and the fact that William caused me to have to kill a man. I'm pissed as hell, but I keep telling myself to stay calm.

My time will come.

For now, I'll rest. For now, all I can do are the things I'm used to doing. Like bookkeeping. Some may find it laborious, but numbers actually calm me.

Leaving the burn barrel to carry on doing its thing, I go back inside, the ice pick hidden inside Adam's hoodie pocket to deal with later. In Justin's office I get to work on the books, my head calming with each minute that passes. I'm just finishing up inputting everything when Justin pops his head in.

"Everything okay?" I glance up, smiling as I nod my head. "Sorry I was a bit longer than normal. The last customer wanted quite the order."

"That's okay. I'm just finishing up now. You have a couple of receipts missing," I add, waiting for him to come around to take a look. I point to the amounts.

"I may have accidentally left them at the counter. I'll check in the morning." He places a hand on my shoulder. "I don't know what I'd do without you. Thanks ... as always."

I rise up from my seat, smiling. "It's the least I could do after you rescued me today."

"You know I'd do that, no matter what." He smiles softly, but then the air around us turns awkward. Silence tempers the room as Justin gazes into my eyes for what feels like the longest time. He then leans forward, pressing his lips to mine.

Immediately, I pull back. At one time, I would have entertained the idea, but that was before Elijah. Before I realized he was my everything.

Justin clears his throat. "I'm so sorry. I shouldn't have—"

"It's okay," I reply, interrupting him. "It's just ... things have changed. I don't think it's a good idea—"

"Of course, of course," he agrees, putting his hands up. "I just got caught in the moment, I guess. Remembering what used to be." He closes his eyes a moment. "Do you want a ride home?"

I offer him a genuine smile. "Yes, that would be nice. I just need to use the restroom first."

He nods his head, handing me the keys. "Sure. Can you lock up behind you when you're done? I'll wait for you in the car."

Even though I have my own set, I take the keys from him then watch as he leaves through the back exit to go to his car. When I'm sure he's not within eyesight of me anymore, I quickly grab a cloth, take the ice pick out of my pocket, wipe it as clean as I can of my fingerprints before placing it on the shelf with the rest of the ice picks, leaving the murder weapon for some other unsuspecting soul to purchase.

CHAPTER NINETEEN

ast

Chloe's diary contained some riveting reading material, I must say. So much in fact that I was up almost all night reading it. She's not the innocent, sweetness and light she portrays herself to be in front of the people who matter. For one, she's not a virgin. Which I'd already suspected. She lost it to some boy she met last summer, in the Hamptons where her parents probably own an enormous vacation home. Apparently, the boy swept her off her feet, and she thought he was the one until she came home and realized he had no plan to ever contact her again. She figured this out when she tried calling his phone and found out it was no longer in service. Oh, how she cried and whined in her diary for a while after that. I have to admit, although annoying to read, I read it with a smile on my face. Yeah, Karma is a bitch.

Until two months ago, she was bumping uglies with Grant, the school man-whore. I bet Brad doesn't know a thing about that. Or Hamptons Boy. He probably thinks she's still holding out for him, waiting until they get married. According to Chloe's diary, their parents have known each other all their lives, so Brad and Chloe were matched since before they were born. I thought she would mind that, but reading between the lines, she actually likes him. The biggest surprise is that he is the one who takes this Promise shit seriously. Apparently, both sets of parents did the same when they were teenagers. Although, based on the way Chloe's dad fucked me on his desk last night, I highly doubt he's only been with one woman all his life. Some men are so eager to risk throwing their entire lives away for just five minutes of a bit of pussy. Actually, I think he lasted all of two minutes before came inside the condom. Still, I recorded our little exchange just in case I ever needed it for ammunition. I must admit, I'm very tempted to send Chloe the voice recording of her dad telling me how tight my pussy is, but for now, I will refrain. It seems I have plenty of other ammunition to use.

I smile as the thought of her realizing that her diary is missing flashes through my head. Phone in hand, I text Chesney to meet me half an hour before school at Copy & Go. I'm not going to be a total bitch. I'll start small and work my way up. I just want to see the look on her bitch face when people see what a scumbag slut she really is.

A minute later, I get a message back from Chesney telling me he can't meet me. Frowning and angry, I call him. He answers two rings later.

"What the hell, Chesney?"

He exhales down the phone, sounding stressed. "I'm not allowed to see you," he whispers.

"What do you mean you're not allowed to see me?"

"Your stepdad pulled me over two days back. I thought it was a traffic violation at first, but I knew I hadn't done anything wrong. He told me that if I ever go near you again, he'll arrest me for drugs. I told him I don't take drugs, and that's when he said that he'd be *sure* to find some in my truck if they ever did a search."

Holy fucking shit. He did what?!

I've always thought Elijah to be as straight as a board. I mean, I know he covered up what happened to me, but I just put that down to his own embarrassment of having a wife with drug issues. It's not his fault she has a drug problem, and him being married to a junkie certainly wouldn't look good to his peers and the outside world.

Equally pissed and turned on by Elijah's threats, I sigh. I guess I've lost my ally now. I don't like Chesney for what he's done in the past, but he's at least been trying to make up for that. I guess a lot of the reason is because of my threats, but I do believe he's starting to like me—although I doubt he'd ever admit it.

"I don't fucking believe this." I close my eyes, pinching the bridge of my nose.

"Bryce, I want to help you, I'm serious. It's just ... I can't have my life totally ruined over something I never did."

"But you *do* take drugs," I sass back. That's the irony of this situation.

"I did, but since you caught me, I quit. I want to be judged by my physical merit alone and not because I'm using enhancements to replace my inadequacies."

I sigh, deciding for once to be nice to him. Besides, he's still cute, and I will definitely miss him being at my beck and call. "You were never inadequate, Chesney. Just insecure. You're a good football player, so you never needed them to begin with."

I can see the smile on his face in my head when he answers. "You really think so?"

"Don't get fucking mushy on me."

He laughs down the line. "Okay, I won't." He sighs again. "Listen, I really want to see you and all, but—"

"I know," I interrupt, staring at my door as though Elijah's somehow behind it. "I'll deal with Elijah myself."

"You know, he also asked me for the names of the guys who cornered you in the locker room."

Eyes widening, I ask, "What did you tell him?"

"I gave him their names, of course. Your stepdad's a scary-ass motherfucker, Bryce."

I rub the back of my neck, sighing. Fucking asshole won't ever listen to me.

"Okay, okay," I eventually reply. "I'll see you at school in an hour."

Ending the call, I grab all my shit and head for Copy & Go. I'm there for a good ten minutes, printing off two hundred copies of a snippet from her diary. That should be enough to spread around the entire school.

Smiling, I pay for my copies then head to school, my mind still flooded with thoughts of what Elijah did. It both irks and fucking tuns me on all at the same fucked-up time.

Considering I have no ride since Chesney's blown me off, I order an Uber to get me to school as quickly as possible. On the journey there, I get a surprising text from Brian telling me that there're a few small businesses in town who would be interested in my services, if I'm interested in earning some good money. He then goes on to say that we could meet in order for him to set up the introductions. I smirk, reading between the lines. No doubt the meeting would also include a quick fuck, but that's something I'm not willing to entertain again.

I am the one who calls the shots.

I am the one with the power.

I am the one in control.

And I don't need Bryan anymore. He's served his purpose.

I write a quick message back, asking for the names of the businesses he's referring to. Then with my head held high, I enjoy the remainder of the ride.

I'm at the school early as planned. I need to get these copies out as quickly as possible before all the students arrive. There are a few students milling around already, but it's relatively quiet for now. I check my watch. I only have twenty minutes to leave as many copies as I can around the halls and classrooms before first period starts.

Walking down the main hall, I turn around to see if anyone's looking, but no one's paying me any mind. With my bag unzipped, I take all the pages out and one by one start dropping them, the pages scattering all over the floor. I sneak into some empty classes and drop a few more on desks, and then last, I scatter some in the cafeteria, in the library, the bathrooms and some more in the gym where I know there will be a morning class. I finally leave the remaining copies by the main exit of the school.

At my locker, I tuck away the diary for safe keeping then get out my textbooks for the morning's classes. It's then I decide to hang out in the bathroom until the students start to arrive. I certainly don't want to be the very first person people see when they're coming down the hall full of scattered paper.

I'm in here for around five minutes, bored out of my brain, when I get a text from Brian telling me there's a boutique shop, a bookseller, and a drugstore interested in hiring me to do their bookkeeping. I have to smile as he's not telling me the names of which ones are interested. He obviously wants to keep that vital information for when we next meet. Yeah, not going to happen. I can find out who they are by myself. The money will come in handy, but the access to one particular store interests me greatly.

Murmurings sound outside, so I take that as my cue that the students have arrived and have read Chloe's innermost thoughts and secrets. An evil smile tugging my lips, I exit the stall and step into the main hall. Sure enough, groups of students are reading the little snippet of Chloe's diary while others are picking up copies that are still on the floor. Not to be left out, I bend down, retrieving a copy and read it all over again so it looks like I'm seeing it for the very first time.

I hate Sarah. Sometimes I find her staring at Brad, and it makes me pissed. She knows he's my man, but that doesn't stop her trying to steal him from me. Yesterday while at her house, I went into her bathroom and put green dye in her shampoo. She didn't turn up for school for the rest of the week. She thought it was Grant or Chesney who did it. She's that brainless that she didn't even suspect me ... not even a little. Isabel tried to help her get rid of the dye—the stupid bitch that she is. The other day, Isabel bought this white fur coat that looked hideous on her. I didn't tell her, though. I can't stand either of them. I only keep Sarah and Isabel close because they serve a purpose, but once I go to college, I will thankfully never have to see those airheads ever again.

Loud voices fill the halls, but then all goes silent when speak of the devil enters the building, head held high as Sarah, Isabel, and a couple of other cling-ons—as I call them—follow closely behind her. I watch in sweet anticipation when Chloe realizes that everyone is staring at her, the smugness that shrouded her slowly dissipating with every whispered word. I suck in a breath when Sarah glances down to pick up a stranded paper off the floor and reads it. Halfway through, her face turns red, and she nudges Isabel, getting her to read it too. Meanwhile, Chloe stands rigid, her face flaming red due to being center of attention. Aww, I thought she loved being the center of attention.

I am loving life when Sarah and Isabel start calling Chloe every conceivable name under the sun—including slut—before storming off and leaving Chloe, her face falling and looking completely lost, for the first time ever to fend for herself. Oh, my, what a joy it is to witness the queen bitch fall from such a great height.

And this, I promise, is just the beginning.

CHAPTER TWENTY

resent

Five minutes before I arrive home, Elijah starts blowing up my phone, obviously wondering where I am and why his dinner isn't on the table like it normally is. Knowing I'm a couple of minutes out, I ignore the calls and just focus on the road.

"Someone's eager to get a hold of you." Justin's eyes flicker to my phone just as it lights up again from yet another call.

"It's Elijah. He's gotta be wondering where I am."

A concerned frown covers Justin's face. "Are you sure you're going to be okay? I'm guessing Elijah won't be too happy, knowing one of his cars got trashed."

I smile softly. "I'll be fine."

Soon after, he pulls up to the curb where I have to ignore yet another call from Elijah. I lean over to kiss Justin on the cheek, thank him again, then get out of the car. I'm up the second step when Elijah opens the door, anger painting his face. Once he spots me, though, his anger turns to apprehension.

"What the hell happened to you?" I walk past him, entering the house and making my way to the kitchen to start something for dinner.

"I fell over and hit my head on the sidewalk. Nothing major." I get to the freezer, opening it up and pulling out some burgers. "Will these do for dinner?" I ask, turning around to see his perplexed expression.

"Hold up a second, Bryce. For fuck's sake. Why didn't you call me?"

Retrieving a pan, I start the process of cooking the burgers before digging through the pantry for some buns. The whole time, I can feel Elijah at my back.

"I didn't think it was necessary to call. Justin found me and took care of me. He's the one who brought me home."

Elijah's jaw tics at this information. "You should have fucking called me." He then stalks towards me, grabbing my head to inspect the bump.

"Stop fussing," I scoff. "It looks a lot worse than it is."

Completely ignoring me, Elijah grabs some peas out of the freezer along with a cloth, orders me to sit down, then places the cold cloth against my skin. "You know, peas are useless at this point," I whine, but secretly, I'm enjoying the cool sensation. It also helps that it's Elijah who's tending to me. That's something I can never really complain about. "You should have iced your forehead as soon as you hit it."

His lilac eyes scan my face before eventually looking down and noticing my clothes. "Not something you normally wear."

I'm not about to tell him they're actually Adam's clothes. That's probably not something I should share considering his ... possessive tendencies. "I picked them up at a sale. Just felt like having a dress down day, that's all."

Suddenly tapering, his eyes cast suspicion upon me. "What were you up to when you fell? Where were you?"

The sudden urge to pat him on his head and tell him not to worry his pretty little head about it is so great that my hand itches to elevate.

"I was doing some bookkeeping for Justin when I popped out for something to eat. I wasn't looking where I was going when my foot caught on the curb, and because I was carrying two coffees, I went flying onto the sidewalk and hit my head."

He takes the increasingly cold cloth off my head, inspecting the bump. "Why do you still do that shit? You should be at home working on your degree."

"Elijah," I groan. "My degree doesn't take every hour of every day, you know. College students have some down time, and lots have side jobs." Little does he know, I should have handed in a paper today. I'll do it by tonight. It'll be the first ever time I've ever turned in a paper late, but I can just say I was sick. I have been rather occupied lately.

His expression tells me something's still irking him. "We're not exactly in need of extra money."

My own suspicions grow. "Are you trying to keep me home?"

His face is impassive when he answers. "No. I just don't get why you still need to do peoples' bookkeeping."

Leaning my arm on the kitchen island, I sigh. "Why am I getting this degree then, if I can't go out and handle business accounts? What is the point of it all?"

Placing the peas down on the counter, he gets up and turns the already sizzling burgers over. "The difference is you'll be fully qualified."

I get up, closing the distance between us until I'm a finger's width away from him. His eyes scan mine as I take in a deep breath. "What happens when I get my degree and start my new job—wherever that may be? I'll have my own money. Be independent. I'll be able to finally get out of your hair so you can have this place all to yourself."

That's not going to happen in a million years because I won't let it. Still, it's nice to witness his reaction to questions like these. It proves what his mindset really is in regard to what he thinks of our relationship.

Grabbing a couple of plates, Elijah takes out the buns and opens them up for us to eat with our burgers. "If that's what you want," he replies flippantly. He's trying to play it cool, however I see the moment his jaw tics slightly and the way his nostrils flare.

"And then you can get with Duckface."

He gives me a pointed look. "Don't start on her again, Bryce. I'm still mad at you for what you did."

"Or," I begin, my eyes lighting up. "Here's an idea. I'll stay here while you get with Duckface. She can service you at night, and once you leave in the morning, she can sneak into her new stepdaughter's bedroom and give her some under cover action, if you know what I mean." I wiggle my eyebrows for extra effect.

Elijah slams the spatula down so forcefully, it almost makes me jump. "Jesus, Bryce, will you ever learn to shut the fuck up?"

I bite my lip, trying to suppress my smile. "Don't you think that would make us one big, happy fucking family? Sausage sucker at night, bearded clam diver by morning. She'd certainly be a remarkably busy mother of our household, wouldn't she?"

He stalks towards me, so I make a run for it, yelping when I realize he's on my tail. I barely reach the living room area when his arm scales around my waist, knocking the wind out of me. With only one arm, he carries me like I'm a rag doll to one of the chairs where he forces my stomach over his knees. Facedown and across him, Elijah yanks my sweatpants down before the forceful sting of his slap meets my right ass cheek. It's so hard and so unexpected that I scream out my surprise.

"If you act like a disobedient child, then I'm going to fucking treat you like one." His words are followed by another violent smack against my ass. It fucking hurts like hell, but at the same time, my pussy aches for more.

"You need to say something to me," he warns, smacking me again. This time, a slight moan leaves my lips. When I don't say a thing, he smacks me again, the sting of it vibrating through my whole body. "I can't fucking hear you, Bryce. Say the fucking words."

"Sorry, Daddy," I baby talk, knowing this will just make him madder.

The inevitable smack comes again. "You think this is one big, fucking joke, don't you?"

I want to point out that with the way his cock is currently digging into my breasts right now, he isn't exactly taking it seriously either. After another two smacks, each followed by my moans echoing around the room, Elijah stops—I assume because he finally realized I'm getting off on what he's doing. He lifts me off his legs, turning me so

I'm sitting on the chair, pulls down his sweatpants, then forces my mouth open to take in his cock.

He may think he's punishing me, but I'm loving every single fucking minute of this. The only true punishment he ever gives me is orgasm denial. Unfortunately, he already knows that's a sore spot for me, so he's used it on more than a few occasions.

Like a frenzied animal, he fucks my face as I pull him in even deeper until his cock is hitting the back of my throat.

"Fuck!" Elijah bellows, unable to hide how good I make him feel. His breathing quickens, and just as he's about to come, he pulls out, his seed immediately hitting my lips, nose, and even eyes. My tongue darts out, licking every bit he has to offer, no doubt angering him and turning him on all at the same time. Elijah hasn't come to realize this yet, but there isn't a fucking thing he can do to me that I won't love.

Once he's finished squeezing out every last drop, he places his cock back inside his pants and pulls away. "Get cleaned up. Dinner's ready."

At this rate, I'm thinking dinner has been cremated.

Elijah disappears in the direction of the kitchen, leaving me—yet again—unsatisfied. Rising up from my chair, I make my way to the bathroom to get cleaned up. I use Elijah's electric toothbrush to get me off quickly, then after I rinse that off, I put it back in its place before making my way to the kitchen, smiling.

As we eat the burnt burgers, Elijah seems pissed at my happiness. I don't know what's getting to him lately, but something's definitely bothering him. He's probably still upset about the mayor not playing ball. Fuck. I have no option but to sort that out tonight.

I wait until I know Elijah is asleep before I grab the key, sneak out of the house with my bag of tricks in tow, and jog the distance to William Schultz's house. By the time I reach his home it's after midnight, and everything is extremely quiet. I'm a little sweaty, especially from the blonde wig I'm wearing, so I take some time to cool down.

Lights are on inside, so I make my way to the door and press the doorbell. The door is answered by one of his staff, a man who appears close to dying he's so old. Poor guy looks like he needs a good vacation.

"Can I help you?"

"Stevie sent me."

Stevie is the pimp who sends the dickhead mayor all his little playthings. Playthings ... girls I recently became acquainted with. All it took was some exaggerated story-telling and lots of alcohol for their tongues to start wagging. I had to pretend I was one of them, so I learned a lot of their habits, including the fact that he's expecting a girl tonight.

The old guy frowns, making his wrinkles stand out even more. "Mr. Schultz didn't tell me he was expecting any company."

I smile sweetly. "Stevie wanted to send me as a surprise."

According to my sources this often happens, so I'm fairly confident I will be let in.

"Wait here while I speak with Mr. Schultz."

I nod my head then wait for him to go do what he has to. My heart's racing a million miles per hour because if the mayor is savvy enough, he'll call Stevie and ask him about me. I have prepared for that possibility, but I'm hoping drastic action won't be necessary tonight.

Five minutes of nervously biting my lip later, the door opens, and the old guy motions for me to come inside. I bow my head before hitching up my red dress and walking into the hallway.

"Mr. Schultz will see you upstairs, last door on the left."

I nod my head again then make my way up the staircase until I reach the landing. There, I grab my bag and put on the gold masquerade mask I bought many months ago but never had the chance to use until now. When I reach his door I knock, and he bellows for me to come in. He's laying on his bed with only a gown covering him, a highball glass in his hand. When he sees me, he sits up, drinking me in.

"Stevie's sent me someone new, I see." His eyes trail from my head to my toes. "You are quite the surprise, aren't you?"

Delving into my bag, I pull out some handcuffs. His eyes widen with delight. "I'm going to rock your world, Mr. Schultz," I tell him huskily, my voice going several pitches lower than I normally sound so I don't give myself away. "Take off your gown," I order.

Practically salivating, William does as I ask, his small penis erect already. Unfortunately for William, his downfall is he likes to be dominated. Something he'll learn is a huge mistake once I'm done with him.

"Lie on the bed," I command again, watching with glee as he climbs on, his arms out, ready for me to handcuff.

Crawling on the mattress, I slowly make my way up, his eyes taking in the garters on my legs. Deciding to offer him a little dry humping to start with, he moans as my panties slide over his pathetic cock. Wanna get the murderous little fucker in a frenzy before I reveal who I am.

"You're so fucking sexy," he rasps softly, his breathing quickening.

I smirk as I fasten one of his hands to the bedpost followed by the other. Once secured, I delve my hand inside my cleavage, his eyes watching my every move. I pull out one of Elijah's old ties and place it inside his mouth, wrapping it around his head so he can't scream. It's then that I decide to take my mask off and reveal who I am. He's a little unsure at first, his eyes squinting. It must be the wig, so I pull that off, too, revealing who I am. His eyes widen in surprise, his body jerking.

"Aww, are we scared of the dead girl? I'm guessing you haven't heard anything back from your little hitman today, have you? I'm afraid he's ... sleeping." I lean in until our faces are inches apart. "Permanently."

Fixing my wig back on and getting off the bed, I grab my bag, taking out the needle I'm after before straddling his waist again. He hasn't stopped thrashing and trying his best to scream for help. It's rather pathetic, yet it's comical to watch.

"This won't hurt, William. It's just a little prick. Much like you." I giggle at my own joke before turning around and straddling his legs again. I hold down his foot with as much strength as I can muster, practically using my body to stop him from kicking. Using my mouth, I take the cap off the needle, holding it in my teeth as I plunge the contents between his toes.

I get off, waiting for the adrenaline to do its magic. See, the problem with William is he's got severe allergies, and consequently, heart problems. Apparently, he's had a fair few heart attacks because of his lifestyle, so the amount I've given him will no doubt cause a heart attack. Something that will definitely be fun to watch.

Once I have the cap back on the needle and it's tucked under my wig, I sit on the edge of my bed and watch as he strains against the handcuffs, his face turning redder by the second.

"You shouldn't have messed with me, William. Now some other mayor will have to take your place, and I will have to start this whole process all over again. You're really creating a lot of extra work for me, you know? And just think, all I wanted to do was bring you some lovely freshly baked cookies this morning." I sigh as his body starts to jerk, and then he starts chocking. I continue to sit, bouncing my knee in impatience, waiting for this to all be over. A few more seconds go by before he stops convulsing and he gets quieter. I take a peek, and sure enough, his eyes are starting to glaze over, his face now a beetroot red.

Getting into action, I take the tie out of his mouth and undo the handcuffs, quickly stuffing them inside my bag before gearing myself up for the best, Oscar winning performance I can muster.

Taking my dress off so that I'm completely bare, I scream as loudly as I can, forcing my hands to shake as I stare at William's dying form.

The door bursts open, causing me to scream again. In walks the guy who opened the door for me followed by some other guy with a gun. With a shaking hand, I point to William. "He ... he just started ... oh, my God! What's wrong with him?!" I cry into my hands so they won't see that I don't have any tears.

The guy with the gun springs in to action, checking his pulse then pulling out a walkie talkie to tell someone to call for an ambulance.

"What happened?" he roars.

"I ... was ... on top of him, and he ... he ... he just started ... choking!"

By this time, I'm in full blown hysterics, screaming so loud that the guy with the gun tells old guy to get me the hell out of here.

The old guy grabs my dress and my bag from the floor then pulls my hysterical self out of the bedroom.

"Calm down!" he seethes, handing me my dress.

"I ... I ... what's wrong with him?" I cry, acting like a complete airhead.

"Most probably a heart attack—" I scream out, causing him to close his eyes in frustration. "Tell me exactly what happened?"

He hands me my dress, so with hands shaking, I pull it over my head before rubbing my nose with the back of my hand. "I ... I was ... I was on top of him, riding him when he just started making these choking sounds. Oh, God!" I wail again. "Stevie's going to kill me!"

An unexpected slap stings the side of my cheek, making my head pound, but it works to stop my wailing.

"Shut up, you stupid, little girl. I can't hear myself think!" He then searches my face with his eyes, a deep frown forming. "How old are you?"

It's extremely hard to hide my smirk when I answer. "Fifteen."

Eyes widening, he shoves my bag at me. "Take this and be on your way. You can't be here when the ambulance arrives." I sniffle, taking my bag from him before quickly scurrying down the stairs. I don't take a full breath until I'm at the end of the street, turning down another. On the next street, I hide behind a tree, take the stupid wig off, stuffing it and the needle in my bag. I get changed into Adam's hoodie and sweatpants then jog the rest of the way home. I'm completely exhausted, and my bed is calling my name, but at the same time, I'm high on adrenaline. I smile as I sneak back into the house and lock myself in my bedroom before sliding under the covers.

It's like I never even left the house.

CHAPTER TWENTY-ONE

ast

"Where are you going?" my mother asks, taking in my tiny, orange summer dress.

Bag over shoulder, I spin around facing her, my expression full of hate. "None of your fucking business. How's that for where I'm going? Why don't you just go back into your little hidey hole and shoot up some more? That's all you're good at."

Her mouth sneers, making her look like a spiteful, evil witch. "You little bitch!" She lunges forward to attack me when Elijah appears from the living room, pulling her back by her waist as she spits venom, her claws out, trying to get to me.

"That's it, Elijah. Rein the bitch in."

Elijah penetrates me with his glaring eyes as my mother bares her yellowing teeth at me.

"I should have had an abortion when I had the chance, you spiteful, little whore."

I raise an eyebrow at her, completely unfazed by her words. Nothing she can say or do can harm me now.

Because she's already done her worst.

"Calm the fuck down," Elijah growls, yanking at my mother to stop her attempt at wrestling free from his grip. He then leans in, gritting his teeth to whisper in her ear. "Go back to your fucking room, Brenda. And don't you dare fucking make me repeat myself again. Do you hear?"

My mouth parts at Elijah's commanding, domineering voice. His arms are still wrapped around her, holding her tightly in his grip, his jaw ticcing in anger. The scene in front of me causes red hot fire to dance inside my belly. I have this sudden and violent urge to rip my mother from Elijah and demand that he take me raw right here in the hallway.

And I won't even care if my mother sticks around to witness it.

"Okay," she agrees timidly, causing Elijah to release his hold on her. Like a frightened little mouse, she scurries back to her bedroom, not once looking my way. I'm fucking lost for words.

Breathing calming, Elijah fixes his fiery eyes on mine, sharp and in focus. I instinctively want to squeeze my legs together to try to curb this growing longing to beg him to fuck me.

"Where are you going?"

He stands tall, his chest puffed out like the beast he is.

"I'm going to help Adam's dad with his bookkeeping."

His eyes scan my attire, causing my pussy to throb. "You're not wearing a bra."

My nipples are probably sticking out like sore thumbs considering how turned on I am after that spectacle I just witnessed. I attempt to compose myself by smiling. "So you've noticed?" He sucks in a breath as I walk forward, my pace practically stalking him. When I'm close enough to touch him, I lean forward to whisper my hot breath in his ear. "I'm not wearing any panties either."

I go the extra mile by offering him a cheeky wink as I turn and walk towards the door.

"What's happened to you, Bryce?"

I hover at the door, my hand on the handle. "You, Elijah. You and my mother happened."

Opening the door, I walk through, and it's only once the door is closed behind me that I let out a breath. I fucking wish he didn't affect me the way he does. It throws me off course, leaving me a muddled mess.

I run my fingers through my hair, skipping down the steps as I wave goodbye to Frank to catch the bus to the hardware store.

"Bryce!" Adam's dad calls out when I walk in.

I smile brightly back at him. "Hi, Justin. How's it going?"

Yesterday when I came here, I only spent an hour going through his books. I couldn't stay longer because I had already worked for three hours at Carol's, the pharmacy down the road owned by Carol and her husband. I hadn't needed Brian's help in the end; I managed to find out who it was that was interested in my services by phoning a few of the local shops. Because of the hours I've already worked this week, I have already accumulated over a hundred dollars. Something I feel I will need in order to accomplish what I have planned in the future.

"Doing good today, thanks." He then points behind him. "Adam's in the back helping to store some stock if you want to go say hi."

I nod my head, making my way to the storeroom where Adam is. Dressed in jeans and a black t-shirt, I watch as Adam places a box inside a cupboard. When he turns, he spots me, a bright smile spreading over his face.

"You're a sight for sore eyes."

Surprised by his confession, I smirk. "Why, thank you."

"Seriously, Bryce. Because of you, school has been a lot easier to handle these last couple of days. I almost don't dread going in the mornings now."

I laugh out loud and place my hand on his shoulder. "Things definitely have improved, I must say."

His eyes suddenly widen. "Oh, and did you hear about Brad, Grant, David, and Tony?" Frowning, I shake my head. "I bumped into Jessica from trig, and she told me that they got beat up pretty bad over the weekend."

Heart racing, I ask, "By whom?"

His eyes are gleaming as he answers. "No idea. Apparently, they were jumped by a masked thug. Had their wallets and shit stolen."

Heart still thundering, I close my eyes. It may sound like a simple mugging, but I know otherwise. *Fucking Elijah!* I don't know whether to hug him or kick him in the dick.

Maybe both.

"Wow, that's pretty fucked up." I laugh out loud, causing Adam to join in.

"I know, right? It couldn't have happened to nicer guys, huh?"

"Definitely not."

I glance down at all the boxes. "How many more do you need to move."

He points at a small stack. "Just those two then I'm done."

Placing my bag down, I wipe my hands together. "Four hands are a lot quicker than two." I grab one of the boxes and put it inside the cupboard. Adam follows after with the others and then we're done. "See how quick that was?"

Adam's eyes scan down my dress, causing a little spark of excitement. "You look ... pretty."

My eyes move to the monitor that shows the view from the camera at the front of the store. Justin's back is to us as he deals with some customers.

"Are you up for a quick fuck?"

Adam chokes on his own spit. "Shit, Bryce. We can't."

My eyes dart to the screen again, causing Adam to do the same. "Come on," I dare him, licking my lips. "If you bend me over the desk, we can watch your dad on the screen to make sure he stays out front. It'll be exciting."

I'm thinking he's going to say no, but then I capture the animation in his eyes. Fishing out a condom from his jeans pocket, he shows it to me.

"Wow, we're extra prepared, aren't we?"

He shrugs one shoulder. "I figure after what happened last time, I should be. You know ... just in case I ever get as lucky again."

Giggling, I sprint over to Justin's desk and bend over, ready for Adam to do his thing. as Eager as a beaver, he strolls over, ripping the paper off the condom as soon as he finishes unzipping his jeans. I place the palms of my hands on the desk and glance up, watching Justin who is still dealing with customers.

"We better be quick," I tell him.

"Oh, don't worry. With you I will be."

I let out a little chuckle, but it's cut off when Adam slides inside of me, momentarily robbing me of breath. I'm still wet and horny as hell after my encounter with Elijah earlier, so Adam slides in and out, easy peasy, a moan escaping my lips.

"Shit, Bryce. You don't realize how good you feel."

Gripping my hips, he drives forward, my eyes staying on his dad the entire time.

A customer leaves and Justin moves off the screen, making Adam jerk a little. "Oh, shit," he murmurs, but he doesn't stop fucking me. "I'm almost there."

Justin appears on the screen again, causing a collective sigh of relief and allowing us both to enjoy the moment. I'm just starting to get in to it when Adam's pants become louder, his movements jerkier.

"Shit, shit, shit!" he cries, then he suddenly stills inside me. The moment he does, Justin moves out of view from the camera again.

"Fuck, Adam, quick. Your dad's coming."

He slides out of me, so I turn around, pulling my dress down. Adam's eyes go to the screen, then he bolts for the bathroom, just about to shut the door when Justin emerges, his eyes darting around, looking for Adam.

"He's in the bathroom," I tell him.

He nods his head, glancing down at his desk. "Everything okay?"

"Yep. Was just about to get started. Adam kind of ... distracted me for few minutes."

The toilet flushes and out comes Adam, his cheeks still flushed from our quickie. "I finished with the boxes," Adam tells his dad.

"Thanks, son. Do you mind heading home so Bryce has some alone time to get on with the books?"

Adam flits his eyes to mine, smiling. "Yeah, sure. I'll see you at home later, Dad." He grabs his bag, throwing it over his shoulder. "See you tomorrow, Bryce."

I give him a cheeky wink back, causing his lip to quirk up into a smirk. "Yeah, see you tomorrow."

After Adam leaves using the back door, Justin's lips part to say something, his eyes drinking me in, when the bell sounds, alerting us that a customer is out front.

"I'll be fine here if you want to go see to your customer," I suggest.

Justin nods his head then walks away, allowing me the time to get on with the bookkeeping. It's hard to focus at first because I'm still all worked up from a lack of a climax, but luckily for me, I can do this sort of thing with my eyes closed. Around an hour in, I'm finding a rhythm, and I'm almost done when Justin walks in.

"How are you getting on?"

My hand hovers over the laptop I'm working on. "I'm almost done." I look up at the security monitor and find the store in darkness. "Are you closed?"

He nods his head. "Yep. I'll leave you to finish while I make us a drink. Coffee?"

"Yes, please."

He heads into his little kitchenette to pour us coffees as I continue entering figures into the computer. He actually had a better month this month than last month.

I'm entering the last figures when he walks back in, placing a steaming cup of coffee in front of me. "Thanks," I say, picking it up. "Your profits are up by ten thousand this month."

Justin beams at the news. "I think it's because of the weather. People want to do DIY in good weather."

"I guess so."

Getting out his wallet, he walks over and sits on the edge of the desk next to me, handing me some cash. "Here, take this. It's for the work you've done last two days." When all I do is stare, he shakes the bills. "I won't take no for an answer."

Smiling, I take the two tens from his hand, my fingers hovering over his a second. His eyes raise to mine, sucking in a small breath.

"Thank you," I answer, pulling my hand away.

Justin clears his throat. "It should be me thanking you. For helping Adam with his math and being a superstar here, you're a breath of fresh air."

My cheeks warm at his compliment. "I wouldn't go that far."

"Don't be so modest, Bryce. Credit where credit's due. You have a natural talent." I only smile in return, taking a sip of my coffee. "Do you mind me asking you a question?"

"Shoot," I reply.

"You and Adam ... are you ..?"

"Friends?" I suggest in a teasing tone of voice.

"I think you know what I'm asking."

I shake my head. "No. We're just friends, nothing more."

"Adam's mom's going to be disappointed by that news. She's already talking about you as a daughter-in-law."

I laugh out loud at that. "I'm sorry to disappoint her." I smile softly, my heart skipping at what I'm about to say next. "What about you?" I bite my lip, waiting for his answer. He watches my mouth for a moment, swallowing with what seems like nerves.

"What about me?"

So he wants to play this game, I see. Placing my hand on his knee, I give him doe eyes. "Are you disappointed to hear that I'm not Adam's girlfriend?"

His eyes fall to my hand resting on his knee, but he doesn't pull away. "We're going in to dangerous territory, Bryce."

I take my hand away and lower my gaze down to my lap. "I'm sorry."

Maybe I was completely wrong about the furtive looks he sent my way every time I visited their house. The way his eyes would linger on my body a little longer than necessary. The way he'd fist his hands together whenever I passed him, deliberately brushing my breasts or ass against him, causing him to gasp. Maybe I'd just imagined it all?

A hand comes under my chin, gently tugging me to look at him. "You're one of the most beautiful young ladies I have ever come across.

I'm an old, married man with nothing to offer you. Why would you even think to make a pass at me when there're countless other, younger, unmarried guys out there who are a lot less complicated?"

I shrug one shoulder. "I guess I prefer complicated. I don't want a relationship, so someone who doesn't want to get serious is perfect for me right now."

I seriously have no clue why I'm pursuing this. I guess it has something to do with the fact that it intrigues me to find out what it's like to be fucking both father and son. I don't know what that makes me, but I'm running with it. It would crush Adam to know I'm coming on to his dad like this, but what he doesn't know won't hurt him.

I will know, though. And I can't help the rush of adrenaline coursing through me at the thought of bagging both of them. Merely two hours ago, his son was inside me. Could I possibly snag his dad too?

Justin clears his throat, getting up from the edge of his desk, indecision evident on his face. "Twenty years married, and I've never cheated on my wife before."

He takes a seat in the chair in front of his desk and sighs. I get up, walking over to where he's seated. When I'm right in front of him, he glances up, his breathing heavy. I take a step closer, and then his hand snakes up my dress, surprising me somewhat.

His warm palm caresses my leg before he reaches up and rests it on my ass cheek. "You're beautiful," he whispers. "Simply beautiful."

I sink down onto his lap, pulling the straps of my dress down, exposing my breasts to him. His breaths are heavy as he gazes down at them and licks his lips. I grab his head, pulling him towards my nipple, moaning when he takes the already hardened nub inside his mouth and suckles.

"Bryce," he rasps, cupping my other breast.

I need his cock inside me. Not because I find him attractive, it's the possession of power I know I have to make men like him break their vows of loyalty to their wives after twenty years. It's the knowledge that his son fucked me in this very same room mere hours ago.

Unzipping his pants, I pull his cock out, placing it at my entrance before sliding down until it reaches the hilt.

"Oh, fuck!" Justin jolts, his body convulsing as I take him inside me again and again. I watch his face, the way it morphs into pure and utter ecstasy—his desire becoming mine.

Fully seated in me, I bring my chest to his and breathe heavily into his ear. "Do you like that?"

"Y ... ye ... yes. Fuck, yes. You feel incredible."

"You don't want me to stop?"

Snaking his arms around me, he holds me close to him. "No."

"Your cock feels so good," I coo, licking his ear and causing him to shudder.

He actually feels similar to Adam, which is strange. Same size and everything. The thought brings a smile to my face as I continue to ride him.

I'm getting close to orgasm when he suddenly jerks, emptying his climax inside me.

"Shit, sorry," he pants with a croak in his voice, trying to catch his breath. "That crept up on me suddenly."

"It's fine."

"No it isn't. You didn't get to finish."

His thumb immediately finds my clit and begins to circle it, causing the lost climax to rear its head again. I smile, knowing that I'm finally going to be sated.

And it's all thanks to Adam's dad.

CHAPTER TWENTY-TWO

resent

"Bryce, wake up, I have to get going to work."

I'm so tired, I could sleep forever. Doesn't Elijah realize how tiring it is killing people? I mean, two in one day is exhausting.

Groaning, I twist my body around to find Elijah making funny breathing noises like he's irritated. He shoves his palm forward, holding out the usual glass of water.

"Come on, Bryce. I haven't got all day. I need to leave for work."

Closing my groggy eyes for a moment, I sit up, taking the pill from his hand and using the water to swallow it down.

"What's gotten up your ass this morning?" I grumble, rubbing my eyes.

"The mayor had a heart attack last night. Died on the way to hospital."

I sigh in relief. I mean, what had he expected? He did try to kill me first. Seems fitting, really.

"Oh, that's too bad."

Elijah lets out a quick, silent laugh. "No, it fucking isn't, but there you go. Anyway, I have to go in now, I have crisis meetings all day." He then hands me a small yet long, rectangle-shaped wrapped gift with a pretty red bow on top. "Sorry I can't stick around this morning, but I wanted to wish you a happy birthday."

I take the gift from him, smiling. "Thank you."

He hovers a moment, causing me to glance up. He has his hands on his hips, looking all expectant. "Well, go on then. Open it."

"I thought you didn't have time—"

"I can spare two more minutes."

Rubbing my eyes again, I slide my finger through the bow, pulling the wrapping off until a fancy, blue, sparkling jewelry box appears. When I open it, there's a white gold, delicate bracelet in a beautiful woven pattern with tiny sparkling diamonds. When I hold it up, they twinkle in the light.

"It's beautiful."

"Just like you," he replies, kissing me on the top of my head. I'm a little taken aback by that compliment for a moment. It almost makes my blackened heart skip a beat. "Happy birthday."

"Thank you. It really is beautiful."

I attempt to place it on my wrist, and when Elijah spots my trouble, he leans forward. "Here, let me get that."

His fingers lightly touch my skin, causing a jolt of electricity to run through my whole body. My mouth parts, a wanton breath slipping through my lips. My eyes stare up at his chiseled features, scanning his whole face like I'm cementing it to memory. He's beautiful in an almost ethereal way.

"There," he says as he clasps it, his focus now off my wrist and on me. His eyes stare at mine a beat, witnessing the moment my eyes glaze over with adoration.

Clearing his throat, he fixes his shirt button which doesn't need fixing before giving me a swift peck on the lips. "I'll try to be home as soon as I can today, okay? We'll have dinner."

When he turns and walks towards my bedroom door, I call out to him. "Are you going to take me someplace nice?"

"I'll bring home takeout," he replies before disappearing out the door. His footsteps clomp down the stairs, and soon after, the front door closes, leaving me in total silence. I sigh, laying back on my bed. I don't know why Elijah's so reluctant to be seen together in public at times. I'm eighteen now, an adult. Why can't he take me for a nice meal to a nice restaurant ... wine and dine me like a person fucking me should? At the very least on my birthday. Deep down I know it's because we can't go public. Not yet anyway. Soon, though, my patience will run thin, and Elijah will have no choice but to face up to us being a couple.

Two more months to go. Two months, then I will set my plan in motion.

Playing with my bracelet for a little while, I lie in bed, wondering if I should try to get some more sleep, but I know it'll be useless. Besides, I have a little errand to run before Elijah gets back.

Groaning, I throw the covers off me and pad towards the shower. Once I'm dressed in a little lilac number, my black pumps accentuating my toned legs, I grab my bag and head for the post office, key in hand to collect whatever mail may be there. To my delight, there's a letter, so I take it out, quickly placing it in my purse before locking the box up and taking a trip to the local café. There I buy a coffee for myself and a cinnamon roll for Frank, enjoying the heat of the sun during my walk home.

Frank is in his usual spot, rocking in his chair as he people watches the day away. "Hey, Frank," I trill, placing the cinnamon roll on the small table in front of him. "I bought you a treat."

He smiles, but he seems tired today with deep bags under his eyes. "Thanks, rosebud."

"You're welcome." I take my seat next to him, watching as he stares out in front of him. "Something troubling you, Frank?"

"Ahhh," he grumbles, fanning his hand in the air. "It's those two across the way there. What is it you call them? Duckface and...?"

"Wartface," I remind him. Betty used to have a wart on her nose a while back before she had it removed. The name still stuck, though.

"Yeah, those two. They've been over here together, trying to get me to sell my house to them again."

"Again?" I question, my eyes panning over to their house.

Frank grumbles, rocking in his chair. "They know I'm a dying man, so they're just itching to get my house so they can turn it into a replica of every other house on this street. I told them I'm not in my grave yet, and even if I was, I still wouldn't sell to them."

My back arching as if I'm about to go to war or something, I ask, "What did they say?"

"That once I die, I won't be around to stop let alone care about who buys my house, considering I have no family to leave it to."

"Fucking bitches," I curse, suddenly realizing I said it out loud. "Sorry."

Frank rumbles out some laughter. "Don't worry. It's about the same thing I thought."

"What business is it of theirs anyway? It's not like you live right next door to either of them, so they wouldn't need your house to extend or expand one of theirs."

"I believe it has something to do with Betty's daughter wanting to live here and Sharon wanting to invest."

I highly doubt Duckface wants to invest. Expanding is probably much closer to the truth since she's still clasping on to hope that one day, Elijah will become hers.

Never gonna happen.

Frank suddenly rises from his chair. "I'm going to get a little siesta. I didn't sleep very well last night."

Concerned, I get up. "Do you need anything?"

Frank smiles before picking up the cinnamon roll. "You got me this. That's more than enough. See you later, rosebud."

I watch as Frank ambles slowly into his house, the creak of the mosquito door bashing against the frame. I turn around, eyes slitting towards Duckface and Wartface's house.

As I walk home, an idea comes to mind that I immediately spring in to action on. Setting up a fake email, I upload the video of Duckface and the priest's wife. I send it to Duckface anonymously, telling her to leave Frank alone, otherwise the video will get leaked. I also demand that she rein in her chihuahua, Wartface, while she's at it.

Laptop shut down, I take out the letter I picked up today and begin to read.

. . .

Dear Bryce,

I received your letter in the mail today, and when I did , my heart skipped a few beats. It's been so long since I felt what it was like to live in the outside world, but during those brief moments when I read your letters, I'm in it. I'm there beside you as you bake cookies or take walks in the park when the suns out or simply visiting a local store.

He visited the other day, but I guess you already know that. It pisses me off so bad that I can't say anything to him, but I hold my tongue for your sake. You made me swear I would never tell, and I will keep my promise. It's just... As you know, I have too much time to think, and every time I think about what you went through, it makes me so fucking mad. Like you, I'm counting down the days. Two months, my darling. Two months, then I will get out of here, making things right. Two months and I will be there for you, baby girl. You are in my heart and my thoughts always...

I trail off, skimming the mushy bits because quite frankly, they're boring. It takes extra special effort to pull out a pen and write another letter back. I do, though. I need this guy on my side. I need him to hold on to that vengeful, fiery anger.

Two more months.

I've waited this long...

CHAPTER TWENTY-THREE

ast

The next few days at school are glorious, and it's all because of Chloe and her little clique breaking apart because of ... well ... little ol' me. It also helps that the jocks have been nursing their sore, little heads after the beatdown they got last week. I was tempted to ask Elijah about the beating, but I decided against it in the end. I know he won't admit he was behind it, so why bother?

Two days after my initial diary drop, I scatter some new copies around the school, this time about the night she lost her virginity. When the inevitable shit hit the fan, it caused the break-up of the perfect couple, Chloe and Brad.

Boo fucking hoo.

Brad hasn't been to school since, no doubt nursing his broken heart —as well as his beaten-up face.

Today is the day I decide to help make it all better for him.

Waiting for his parents to leave for work, I sneak in at the back of his house with my bag over my shoulder. The vast black and white kitchen comes into view, the place disgustingly pristine in its cleanliness. I stand still for a moment, trying to make out any sounds in the house, but so far, all is quiet. My feet slide across the shiny tiled floor towards the door. I push it open, and I'm in the plush living room. There are photos of the whole family adorning every mantlepiece and crevice they could think of, no doubt trying to show off their happiness to whoever visits.

Inhaling a breath, I head to the stairs, being extra careful with each step just in case they make a noise. At the top of the landing, I see that some doors are open, but two are closed. I get to the first closed door and slowly open it up to find Brad laying in his bed, fast asleep. I cock my head, smiling at how angelic he looks when he sleeps, knowing full well what a monster he really is underneath.

As quietly as I can, I set down my bag and pull out a bottle of chloroform that I managed to borrow from the drugstore where I'm doing the bookkeeping. I had thought I would be watched, but the owner is so eager to get her mess of her books done, that the very first day I was there, she just plopped it all in front of me and told me to get on with it. While there, I manage to find a set of keys, and lucky me! It was that set of keys that allowed me access to her locked-up treats. I took one of the bottles, pulling the one behind it up front so she won't notice, then I placed her keys back where I found them. I am doing more bookkeeping for her later today, so I can put the bottle back then. No harm, no foul. Well, in my case I plan on doing a lot of harm and a lot of foul. Carol will no doubt notice that the bottle has been opened, but of course I will play ignorant. Any of her staff could have opened it, or even the manufacturer could have sent her the bottle like that. In any case, I have a ton of excuses to give, all of which takes the heat off of me. To be honest, if she does suspect me, I really don't give a flying fuck. Without a camera in the office she will never be able to prove a thing.

Unscrewing the top off the chloroform, I grab the cloth from my bag then walk towards his bed. Once I'm near his head, I put a good amount of chloroform on the cloth then brace myself for the inevitable fight I'll have on my hands. Knowing he's more likely to wake up the longer I stand here, I place the cloth over his nose and mouth, quickly straddling him when the surprise momentarily freezes him. He bucks and he buckles, trying his hardest to get his hands up to mine to free him from the cloth. Both my hands are clasped as tightly round his mouth as I can, but his strength soon bounces me off the bed.

I land with a painful thump on the floor, and just as my ass hits the ground, I realize that I'm a dead woman. Brad isn't going to let me get away with this shit, that's for certain. I scramble to my bag, yanking out my mace, ready to spray it in his eyes. When I turn over, finger hovering over the button, I realize that Brad isn't coming after me. Breathing heavily, I look up at him, surprised to find him passed out on the bed, one leg dangling over the side.

"Shit!" I curse, my heart rate reaching new levels. I laugh out loudly at the spectacle then try to get my breathing under control. I don't know how long he's going to be out for, so I need to prepare before he starts to rouse.

Snatching my bag, I pull out a couple of pairs of handcuffs that I stole from Elijah's drawer then quickly get to work making sure Brad's arms are securely fastened to his bed. Once satisfied he won't be able to escape, I pull down his boxer shorts, cover him back up with his sheet, then sit and wait until he wakes up.

My breathing still calming, I take out my phone and start playing Candy Crush to pass the time while Brad peacefully sleeps away the chemicals currently swarming his blood.

It's about an hour later when he finally stirs, moaning out as he kicks at the sheets on his bed, almost knocking them completely from his body. When he attempts to pull his hand towards him and meets resistance, it's then he remembers. His eyes shoot open seeking the offender, widening even farther when he sees it's me who's the culprit.

"What the fuck?!" he demands, yanking at the cuffs.

"Morning, sleepyhead," I singsong. "I never thought you'd fucking wake up."

"Take these fucking handcuffs off me, Bryce!" he seethes.

I get up from the chair I had been sitting on and walk towards his bed. "So *now* I'm Bryce? I thought I was weirdo, or nerdy, or creep?"

"Okay, you've had your fun, now take these off me."

Getting onto the bed, I straddle his waist and lean forward, his eyes widening with trepidation. "Oh, but Brad. The fun hasn't even started yet."

"What the fuck does that mean?"

His breathing quickening, I lean even closer, my tongue darting out to lick his lips. "Hmm, you taste sweeter than I expected for someone who's got such a disgusting mouth." I pull away, smiling brightly at him. "Don't worry. I have no plans to hurt you, Brad. Quite the opposite, in fact."

"What does that mean?" he pants out.

I slide off his bed, my hands already at the hem of my t-shirt, ready to pull it up.

"I'll leave you alone in school, I swear. I'll get the other guys to stop bullying you too. Whatever it is you want, I'm sure we can come to an arrangement."

I turn around to face him, taking my top completely off so that my black, lacy bra is showing. "We already are coming to an arrangement, dear Brad." My eyes light up, showing him the fire, the rage, and my desire for revenge. "*My* arrangement."

Panic sears his eyes as he strains against the handcuffs. "Please don't hurt me," he whines, his voice sounding like a scared child's.

I pull down my sweatpants, a rush of excitement coursing through me. I have been dreaming of this moment for so long that I never thought it would ever get here.

"I already told you, I'm not going to hurt you, baby," I coo, desire flooding me as I touch my bare stomach. His fear is my hunger. His anxiety is my titillation. His uncertainty is my weapon.

I am the one in control.

I have the power.

His eyes dart around me, his body jerking. "What are you going to do?" His breathing is labored, beads of sweat forming at his brow.

For a few seconds I stand there, staring as he whimpers, taking in as much of this as I can. I suck in a deep breath before unhooking my bra and letting it slide down onto the floor. Brad watches my every move, his eyes widening when he takes in my breasts. I slide my panties down next until I'm completely bare in front of him. I allow him to drink me in like a fine wine, his eyes feasting on my body like a starved man. His brain may want to resist me, but in time his body won't. And that is what turns me on the most.

"Why are you naked?"

I smile at his question before pulling his covers back and exposing his nakedness. His cock is still flaccid but has every potential to get hard once I work my magic. Using my hands, I prowl like a lion, climbing on top of him until I'm straddling his waist.

"What are you doing?" He strains against the handcuffs again, his fear creeping up even higher.

I don't answer him with words. My actions will speak so much louder. Bending forward, I lay the gentlest of kisses to the side of his neck, brushing my nipples against his chest.

"S ... stop," he pants, already getting worked up.

My pussy throbs in response to his unease, desire flooding my veins. I don't think I've ever been this turned on in my life.

I take my time, kissing and licking his chest, letting out the smallest moans to fill his ears with. I rise up, capturing his eyes and witnessing the apprehension still laced in them. My hands at my breasts, I squeeze my nipples, moaning as they pebble against my fingers. Brad watches. He can't help but watch. This must be the most erotic thing he's ever witnessed.

"Do you like what you see, baby?" I taunt him, my voice hoarse.

Brad swallows hard, his mouth parting at my little show for him. With hooded eyes, I take my time kissing my way down to his growing cock. My eyes light up with fire when I realize I'm getting the reaction I was after. I thought it would take longer to work him up, but I guess I underestimated myself.

"You do like what you see." I practically sing the words with glee as his eyes widen.

"Wha ... what are you doing?" I bend down to answer his question by licking his shaft. His cock jerks at my touch, causing my insides to grip with need. "Pl ... please ... st ... stop." I massage his balls with my tongue before licking my way up to the tip of his cock. He buckles and jerks, hissing as I lay more kisses on his stomach.

All these months of denying Chloe, and here he is, completely at my mercy—ready for me to take him.

And I certainly won't disappoint.

Raising my hips up, I line his cock up with my entrance which causes Brad to really strain and flail. "No!" he shouts, gripping his eyes shut. He opens them up, pleading with me. "I'm a virgin. I'm saving myself for—"

Me.

I'm taking his virginity. Not anyone else.

I slide my wet, throbbing pussy down his shaft, moaning as he makes a whimpering sound.

"No," he cries out, his body depleting.

"What, baby? Don't you like the feel of my pussy around your cock? Don't you like the feel of it squeezing you. I know I do."

Gripping his eyes shut, he groans as I thrust my hips forward, taking him in deeper. Pulling up, I slink down on him once, twice, and then his body jerks, his mouth parting with a soft moan as he releases inside of me.

I glance down, sighing. "Damn, I was just starting to get in to that," I complain, sliding off of him. It's then I notice a single tear slipping down his face, so I bend forward and lick it with my tongue.

"Why did you do that?!" he shouts, his composure returning some. "You ... you ... you raped me."

I make a show of rolling my eyes. "Don't be so melodramatic, Brad. You hated it so much that you came inside me within two seconds. And now look, I'm still left unsatisfied. What are we going to do about that, huh?"

"Please let me go," he pleads, but when I simply stand there staring at him, his scared puppy dog act changes. "Let me go, you fucking creepy, raping bitch!"

I pout my lips at him. "Oooo, we are getting angry."

"You got what you came for, now let me go."

Simply turning on my heel, I leave his bedroom and make my way downstairs. The whole way there, I can hear Brad shouting, wondering where I'm going. I leave him to shout for a while as I make myself a peanut butter sandwich, and eventually, after a while his complaining stops. I bring the sandwich upstairs with me, taking small bites along the way. When I emerge in his bedroom again, I hold it up to him. "Want some? I got a bit hungry after our little ... tête-à-tête."

"You're a fucking psycho!"

I think about that word for a moment before answering. "I actually like that much better than weirdo or freak."

"I'm going to call the police, you psycho bitch. I'll tell them *everything* you did."

I chew on the sandwich before placing it down on his nightstand. "And tell them what exactly? That you came inside a girl? And what if I tell them you raped me? I have evidence we had sex." He groans, bashing the back of his head against his pillow. "And what are your friends going to think if you report me? They'll laugh their asses off at you."

Resignation resides all over his face as he grips his eyes tightly together. "Fuck this shit."

"Quite," I respond, actually agreeing with him. I know what I did was wrong, but after all the years of abuse I've suffered because of this fucker, I can't even dredge up the will to care about anything related to him. He abused me, and now I've abused him back.

Retribution complete.

"Do you want to fuck again?" I offer, walking towards his bed and glancing down at his flaccid cock.

His eyes widen in shock. "Are you fucking kidding me right now?"

"I'm pretty sure we could go again. At least the second time you should last longer. Maybe I can actually get myself to come this time. I'm still horny, you know."

He shakes his head as I climb on his lap, straddling him.

"Get off me!" he roars, but I don't listen to him. Instead, I take my time working him up again. This time I have to suck him off a little while before his cock starts to harden.

"Bitch!" he screams as I take him inside me again. I begin riding him, and this time I stroke my clit, the desire which waned earlier coming back in full force. Brad lies there completely helpless, completely at my mercy. As I ride him, he lets out small moans, unable to hide how good this feels. It's watching his face twist from rage to hunger that fuels my climax and has me screaming out his name as I come all over his cock. It's not long after that Brad comes, too, his body relaxing as I allow myself to come down from my high.

"See, that was better, wasn't it?" I murmur, sliding from his cock then immediately grabbing my clothes to get dressed. I grab my phone and rewind to the moment Brad comes, showing him just how pleasurable it looked for him. "Your face there, Brad. You fucking loved every minute of it." Disgusted, he twists his face around so he can't look at me anymore. I smile, leaning forward. "Don't you ever fucking utter a bad word my or Adam's way again. All of you and your crew will be nothing but nice and courteous from now on. Got it? If not, I will show this little video to your precious parents. The same precious parents who think you're saving yourself for marriage. I can make you pay in worse ways than you could ever imagine, Brad. You've already seen just how capable I am."

I fix him with a hardened stare before grabbing the bottle of chloroform and walking back to him.

"Don't ... don't!" he shouts as I near him with the cloth.

"Don't worry, Brad. By the time you wake up, you will be free of the handcuffs, and I will be long gone. I promise."

I take the cloth, hovering at his mouth, and just before I lay it down, I say, "Oh, and just one more thing." I whisper the next fabricated words in his ear. "I'm not on the pill."

His eyes widen to saucers, but I don't let him get a chance to speak. I place the cloth over his nose and mouth, watching as he bucks a little before eventually calming. Satisfied that he's out, I grab my things then unhook him from his handcuffs. I stand at his bed a few seconds and watch as he sleeps.

"Yes ... just like an angel."

CHAPTER TWENTY-FOUR

resent

My birthday went well last week. The meal was nice, the sex after even better. It would have been nice to go out, but after the marathon we had in bed, I didn't care.

The only thing people have been talking about all week is the mayor's death. The amount of people with their fake tears and equally fake condolences makes me want to vomit. Yesterday it was announced who the new mayor is going to be, so Elijah's happy. Apparently, he's a lot easier to 'mold', as Elijah put it. They also found the dead guy in the car yesterday. I bet he stank to fucking hell. He couldn't have been the best of sights either, that's for certain. Still, I have no concerns about anything leading back to me. I had no connection with the man up until he was ordered to murder me. No doubt they'll eventually find out who he was and that he was involved in shady shit, assuming a hit was most probably ordered on him.

Today, Elijah is off, but he's getting ready—just like he always does around this time every two weeks.

"Where ya heading?" I ask as he's yanking at his shirt sleeve.

"Running some errands, as usual."

I smirk at his lie, but I don't call him out. I never call him out. "Want me to come?"

I see him flinch slightly, but he holds his nerve. "No, it's boring stuff. You won't be interested. I tell you what, though. How about tomorrow we order in, and then we can watch something on Netflix, if you want?"

How perfectly normal.

"Why not tonight?"

He hesitates a moment before responding. "I have plans tonight."

I frown at that. "What plans?" He never told me about any plans.

"It's a ... work thing. I'll tell you about it when I get home."

I'm not liking his cagey attitude. Something's up, and it pisses me off. Whatever it is that I'm not aware of, I don't like it. Normally I know everything when it comes to Elijah, so these *plans* he's referring to throw me off kilter.

I drop it—for now—but I'm not happy with this situation. Not one bit.

He grabs his car keys after letting me know he'll be back in a few hours. I had plans to pamper myself today, maybe go to the hairdresser or get my nails done. After Elijah's half-assed admission, I'm not feeling it anymore.

The bath is what calls me in the end. After the way my body has been tensing for the last few minutes, I'm thinking it's a necessity.

For the next two hours, I bathe. After, I make a nice breakfast then decide to bake some cupcakes to calm my nerves. I'm actually feeling much better by the time the egg-timer rings, and I pull out the cakes, smelling their sweet aroma.

As I'm admiring the little bronzed sponges, the doorbell rings, causing me to frown. I'm certainly not expecting any guests.

I gaze out of the window to see who it is, huffing out an angry breath when I see it's Bitchface. "What the fuck does she want?" I grouse under my breath.

Intrigued as to why she's here, I walk to the door and answer, her white blouse slightly open for me to see her bulging puppies. She smiles in a way that looks fake, her head trying to peek over my shoulder to see inside. "Bryce, is it?"

"Yes," I respond, wiping the flour from my hands onto my dress.

"Is Elijah in? I tried calling, but he's not answering his phone. I just wanted to confirm that we're still on for tonight."

My eyes narrowing, I ask, "Tonight?"

She laughs a little, like a silly schoolgirl. "Our date. Did he not tell you?"

A flash of me taking one of our kitchen knives and stabbing this bitch multiples times in those perfect breasts of hers springs to mind. I'd probably fuck her pretty rosy-cheeked face while doing it.

"Elijah would forget his head if it isn't screwed on," she continues, laughing again. But I'm not seeing any bit of this funny. She's speaking about him like they're already intimate.

A date.

With Bitchface.

Tonight.

Did Elijah really think I would let that happen?

Of course not. That's why he didn't tell me earlier.

"No, Elijah has not said a word about you." I'm unable to hide my sneer as I answer her. "Who are you anyway?"

Bitchface's expression turns from friendly to irritated in a nanosecond. "I'm not sure I'm liking the tone of your voice, young lady."

"You're the one who came to my house uninvited," I snap back.

She smiles, but it's not a nice smile. "You're just the unwanted stepdaughter. This isn't your house, sweetheart. Just be glad Elijah's put you up for so long."

I want to ask her why, if I'm so unwanted, does he fuck me every night. The words are on the tip of my tongue, but I hold them in. Instead, I smile falsely back at her. "I'll tell Elijah you came by." Immediately, I slam the door in her face. I peek through the window, watching until she eventually walks away, calling me a bitch.

My palm itches, the need to bash that skull of hers until her brain splatters all over the floor becoming stronger by the second. I'm so immersed in imagining it all that I fail to recall until much later the reason she was here in the first place.

A date.

A date with Elijah.

I'm so angry with him that I whip my phone out, ready to send him a scathing message. My fingers hover over the keyboard, hesitating. If I tell him now, then he'll know I know. If I wait until he gets home, I can ambush him.

So for the next few hours, I pace up and down the house, my anger levels growing to new heights. Bitchface must have it wrong. He wouldn't dare go on date with someone when he knows he's mine. This and more are wrestling my thoughts right up until the moment I hear the sound of the door opening, alerting me that Elijah's home. I frog-march it to the door, his smile only ramping up my anger.

"Hey, babes."

He's just about to say something else when I pull my hand back and lunge forward, my fist meeting his cheek.

"Motherfucker!" I scream, both at him and the fact that my hand now fucking hurts like a bitch.

"What the fuck was that for?!" Elijah booms, holding his cheek. Adrenaline numbing my hand somewhat, I lunge for him again, but this time he's prepared for my onslaught.

Grabbing me by the shoulders, he hoists me towards the wall until my back meets it with a thump. "Calm. The. Fuck. Down!"

I grit my teeth at him, the urge to growl like a bear consuming me. The only small speck of happiness that courses through me is from the delight I feel seeing that the side of his cheek is already swelling slightly.

"What the fuck did you do that for?"

"If you'd care to check your fucking phone, you'd know." Logic would have it that Bitchface has left messages for him—especially after our little ... encounter.

"I had my phone switched off." Yes, like he always does when he disappears for hours every couple of weeks. "What happened?"

Narrowing my eyes to slits, I grit my teeth. "Your *date* happened." His eyes widen when he realizes I know. "Yeah, that. Care to fucking explain?"

Elijah shakes his head in frustration, but he releases his hold of my shoulders. I'm not sure how much of a good idea that is considering I'm still feeling homicidal.

"This is your way of dealing with the situation, huh?" he accuses, tutting under his breath. "Throw fists and ask questions later."

"Well, considering you're sneaking around behind my back and going on dates with bitches, then yes, I think I have the right to, don't you?"

He walks into the kitchen, so I stalk after him. I watch as he gets the peas out, wraps it in a cloth, then places it on his cheek, wincing. "Fucking hell, Bryce. For such a small girl, you can really sucker-punch a guy." His eyes travel to my raging expression and he sighs. "Listen, I'm not interested in Lucy. It's just that it's been almost two years since your mother's passing, and people are talking, wondering why I'm not at least trying the dating game yet. I figured I'd go on one or two, but I would ultimately say I'm not interested in her."

Biting my lip till I draw blood, I scowl at him. "One or two dates? One or two dates!?" I shriek, the last sentence louder than the first. I step forward, causing Elijah to step back. He glances down, no doubt noticing the blood on my lips but also noting that I don't give a fucking shit.

"It means nothing."

"Oh, how fucking cliché," I bellow, stepping forward again. "In the same way as Duckface sucking on my nipples was nothing?"

Anger swarming in his eyes now, he sneers at me. "You know full well there's a fucking big difference between me pretending to be on a date and you having your tits sucked by our fucking neighbor!"

I have an inkling that that was part of his rationale for going on a date with Bitchface. It's to get me back for what I let Duckface do to me.

Tit for date.

"What is it with you and having to keep up these fucking pretenses, Elijah? What does it matter if you haven't dated anyone in two years? It's none of anyone's fucking business!"

Flinging the peas down on the counter, he inhales a breath. "I'm the chief of police in this town. Everyone knows me, knows the power

I possess through my job. I'm a pillar of the community, and I need to keep it that way in order to keep you and I in the lifestyle we've become accustomed to."

Crossing my arms, I ask, "So what happens after the one or two dates? Please tell me because I'm just *itching* to know!"

"I'll tell her it's not working out, and that I don't feel that way about her."

"And then what?" I press. "You go on another date with someone else and then another and then another? How many dates are you going to go on while I sit at home, waiting for you to come back and fuck me?"

He closes his eyes, stress clearly showing on his face. "Stop being ridiculous."

I laugh out loud. "Oh, *I'm* being ridiculous? Are you even listening to yourself?!"

Elijah pinches the bridge of his nose a moment before his lilac eyes land on mine. "I know things are difficult right now, but it won't always be this way."

"Ha!" I puff out. "If you could, you'd get married, have kids, and keep me in the basement as your secret fuck pet to use whenever you need one."

"Stop this, Bryce. You know that isn't true."

"Oh, really?" I scoff, walking out of the kitchen and into the living room, Elijah following after me. "I'm always going to be your dirty, little secret, Elijah. I don't know why you can't just fucking admit that." He's about to protest when I add, "It doesn't matter anyway. You're not going on that date."

Elijah throws his hands up in the air. "It's just a date. Not even a date. A fake date. And yes, I *am* going on it. There's nothing you can do to stop me."

I raise my hand, pointing my finger ready at him. "If you go on this date, I will kill the bitch. And you know full well I'm capable of it."

"You're so melodramatic." He rolls his eyes, apparently not letting it sink in that I'm serious. "I haven't got time for this shit. I need to get ready for dinner."

"It's not happening!" I scream after him, ready to stand in his way. Instead, he grabs me, throwing me over his shoulder, my arms and legs kicking and fisting his back as he drags me upstairs.

Once he's in my room, he sets me down by my bed. "If you're going to behave like a bratty child, then I'm going to treat you like one."

I jump off the bed then stalk forward, ready to pounce. "If you dare lock—"

Too late. By the time I reach the door, it's shut behind him, then he swiftly locks it.

"Asshole!"

How the fuck does he manage to shut me in and lock it so fast? He must be carrying the key around with him at all times. I don't know who's more twisted in this relationship: him or I.

Sitting at the edge of my bed, I bite my lip, tempted to retrieve the key and let myself out. But if I do that, Elijah will know I have a spare.

"Shit!"

I want to stop this motherfucker from leaving, but I can't give myself away either. I sit, tapping my leg against my bed for a few minutes, wondering what the fuck I should do. In the end, the only logical thing I can do is let him go on this fucking date, following the little shit once he leaves.

For over an hour I sit on my bed, biting my nails as I listen to Elijah getting ready. As he's running the shower, I quickly sneak out of my room and search through his phone for text messages to Bitchface. Sure enough, I find the message I'm after which divulges the name of the restaurant they're going to. Luckily for Elijah his messages to her are rather short and formal.

Shower off, I quickly darken his phone before running back to my room to lock myself in. Absolutely ridiculous, but that's Elijah all over. As if I'd do anything remotely like this to him.

When I hear the jangling of keys downstairs, I jump up, retrieving my key on my bed and unlock the door. I run down the staircase and glance out of the window to see him backing out of the driveway.

I curse under my breath that I don't know how to drive yet. How the fuck am I going to follow him? Sighing, I light my phone up and hire an Uber.

The entire time I wait for it to get here, I'm on edge, biting my nails and thinking of all the wonderful ways I can kill Bitchface. The devil in me takes great pleasure when I imagine sneaking into the restaurant they're going to and slipping some arsenic in her food.

When it finally pulls up, I rush outside. In the corner of my eye, I spot Frank on his porch. I wave goodbye to him as I dash for the car, not waiting to hear if he replies.

The journey is only fifteen minutes, and by the time I get there, sure enough, Elijah and Bitchface are already sitting at a table, their glasses of wine poured.

Opposite the restaurant is a bar, so I head in there, taking a seat by the window. I order a Coke then watch them as I slowly sip on my drink. Bitchface has gone all out tonight, I see. Her blonde hair is a mass of wavy curls, her makeup light, and her tits so high up, they're almost hitting her chin. She's wearing a red dress with thin straps, and a diamond necklace hangs around her neck.

I scowl as she throws her head back, laughing at something Elijah says, her body language screaming that she wants him to fuck her. She's leaning forward, obviously into Elijah, so I'm glad to find that his posture is the complete opposite. Wearing navy slacks and a pale blue shirt with a couple of buttons undone at the top, he's leaning back in his seat, his arms resting on the arms of the chair. He looks every bit the sex God that he is, appearing to be carefree and relaxed, but his chair is pushed back a bit from the table which makes me a little happier about the situation. Bitchface is leaning so far over the table, it's squashing her tits. Her hand rests in the middle by a romantically lit candle. I bet in the hopes he will reach over and place his on top of hers, lightly dancing his fingers over her knuckles like he sometimes does to mine.

"Hey, beautiful," some random guy greets as he takes the seat next to me.

Without even looking his way, I say, "Fuck off."

"Stuck up bitch," he responds, shoving the chair in and walking away. At least he had the curtsey to do as he was told.

I roll my eyes. I can't even sit with a drink and stalk my man without some asshole chancing his luck. This happens another two times while I'm watching Elijah and Bitchface eat their meals. I'm starting to think maybe the first guy made some sort of bet with his friends to see if any of them will be able to sit with me. If that's the case, each one will lose. I'm in the middle of telling the third guy to go take a hike when I spot Elijah and Bitchface leaving the restaurant.

Getting to my feet, I leave a ten-dollar bill on the table, grab my things, and race outside of the bar. Across the street, they look like they're taking a stroll together. They are having a conversation but they don't seem intimate right now. I follow as they keep walking another five minutes until they reach what I assume is Bitchface's house. I smile, remembering exactly where it is for future reference.

I quickly order an Uber because I need to be home before Elijah is. I have no clue where he's parked his car, so I can't be too reckless.

Seeing that the Uber is two minutes away, I glance back up, my stomach dropping when they face each other. I'm about to witness the inevitable, awkward goodbye moment after a first date. She motions with her head towards her house, no doubt inviting him in. If he dares to go inside, I'm going to gouge his eyes out and cut his dick off.

Thankfully, he points behind him then steps back, a look of disappointment shining on Bitchface's pretty, little face. Somehow this doesn't deter her as she raises up on the balls of her feet, trying to kiss him on the lips. My jaw grinds at her audacity, and then I have a flash of an image of what her precious blonde hair would look like covered in her own blood. I bet she'd look rather beautiful, actually. In a sense, I don't blame Elijah for dating her. Even I would be tempted to go inside and have her show me how nice her tits look without that tight dress covering them. I'd even have fun playing with them too. A perverted thought suddenly comes to my mind. I wonder if her nipple would be big enough to stick in my vagina. The fantasy of it makes me laugh out loud, but I don't have time to dwell on how that would work when Bitchface makes the first move to kiss him.

A relieved breath has my whole body relax when Elijah's head turns, only letting her kiss his cheek. However, my breath catches when he turns his face her way, smiling down towards her lips before backing away. Her eyes are fixated on him. Hell, it almost looks as though she's fucking head over heels for him. She has that glazed gleam in her eyes like he's her whole world or something.

Thankfully, he then turns to walk in the opposite direction, allowing me to breathe again. My Uber arrives, so I quickly get inside, my mind whirring with what I just saw. As we're driving away, I watch the sadness cover her face at him leaving, the inevitable loss of not getting fucked by him tonight sinking in that pretty head of hers. I almost feel sorry for her.

Who am I kidding?

Once home, I quickly rush out of the car and dash for my house, noticing Frank is still outside. "Hey, Frank," I call out again, but he doesn't respond. I'm about to turn around and walk over to see if he's okay when I spot headlights coming down the street.

"Shit!" I curse, knowing it may be Elijah. I dash inside and run for the stairs, taking two steps at a time before I lock myself in my room, put the key under my bed, and quickly undress before sliding into my bed.

Around ten minutes later, my door unlocks and light shines into my room, silhouetting his commanding frame.

"Bryce?" he asks in barely a whisper. I don't respond. I'm not going to. I hate the bastard. "I brought you some food."

"Fuck off," I reply, pulling the covers over me more.

Elijah steps inside my bedroom, a small bag of what smells like fries filling the room with its aroma. He places it down next to me then sits on my bed, taking his shoes, shirt, and slacks off before climbing in my bed and spooning me from behind.

Sweet clementine fills my nostrils, making them flare with anger. "You smell like Bitchface."

His nose nuzzles the back of my head as he inhales, making my body thrum with hunger. Even angry at him, I still manage to get turned on.

"It was just a meal, I swear. I never touched her, nor did I want to."

Luckily for him, I already know this, but it still makes me angry that he locked me in my room just so he could take a woman out for a meal. Something he's never done with me.

As he snakes his hand down towards my pussy and I slightly part my legs for him to start rubbing my clit, I begin to fantasize about what I'm going to do to Bitchface. I know exactly how this should be handled. I mean, I did tell Elijah what I was going to do.

I did warn him.

CHAPTER TWENTY-FIVE

ast

On Monday I walk into school with a renewed sense of vigor. For the first time in a long time, I don't have a row of dumbasses waiting, ready to call me the new mean word of the week.

Over the weekend, I used up all my available free time to do as much bookkeeping as I could, just so that I was away from home as much as I could be. I even offered to help out Justin again, much to his eagerness. I let him fuck me over his desk before I said goodbye and went over to Adam's where I fucked him too. The whole day turned me on so much that I actually came on Adam's dick for the first time. The delight in his eyes that it happened... his whole face was animated for the rest of the day. I know it's wrong on every level that I'm having sex with both of them. It's just ... I can't fucking help myself.

Sunday, I did the books at the drugstore again, and in between sorting out Carol's records, I sneaked through her array of drugs. It made me smile inside, realizing how much power I possess simply by holding her most private business dealings in the palms of my delicate, little hands. Because she trusts me with her books, I assume she feels I can be trusted with everything. Silly fool that she is. There's certainly been no mention of the opened bottle of chloroform so far. Maybe it's not even been noticed yet.

I really don't give a shit.

During break, everyone is whispering about how one of the students apparently caught Miss Pashmore kissing another woman over the weekend, much to the disappointment of some males here that have huge crushes on her. Even I've admired her at times in class, with her long, slender frame, perky rounded tits, and her long, flowing, blonde hair. Only in her late twenties, she's the youngest teacher in the school, and she's also actually good at her job. In fact, she is who I have next—not that much work will get done in her class now with this news running rife.

With ten minutes before the next lesson, I quickly pop into the restroom. While I'm in there, I hear quiet sobs coming from one of the stalls farther down. I sit on the toilet and wait, wondering if I should say something, but I decide to hold my tongue. About a minute or so later, I peep through the crack in the door to see Sarah emerging from the stall. She has something in her hand, but I can't make out what it is. She throws the object in the trash before washing her hands and wiping the tears from her eyes. She touches up the rest of her makeup, takes a look at herself, and then walks out.

The moment she's gone, I flush the toilet then race out of my stall, delving my hand in the trash can to search for whatever it is, rummaging through all the damp, wet tissues that are in there. I screw up my face but keep on searching because whatever it is may have been the cause of her upset.

I'm about to curse out in frustration when my hand hits a long, hard object. I grip it, pulling it out to find it's a positive pregnancy test. My smile grows wide when I get an idea that's simply too irresistible to ignore. It will make me late for class, but it'll be totally worth it.

Wrapping the pregnancy test in a paper towel, I wash my hands then make my way outside to a classroom I know will be empty. There, I grab some tape then race to Sarah's locker. With everyone in their classes now, I quickly stick the test on her locker and smile triumphantly.

I'm making my way to Miss Pashmore's class when I spot Brad and Grant at the end of the hall. As if knowing I'm coming, Brad glances up and stiffens, his eyes like a frightened child. Pride courses through me that I did this to him.

He deserved every minute of it.

Both of them remain silent as I approach, Grant smirking while Brad remains stoic next to him.

"Hey, Brad," I coo, offering him a mischievous wink. Grant opens his mouth to say something to me, but Brad's hand grips his arm, halting him. The words, "Good boy," are titillating my tongue, I'm itching to say it, but I keep the words in.

"What the fuck, man?" Grant mutters as he shakes Brad off of him.

With no time to stall, I stroll into class, everyone's head popping up at my sudden entrance. Miss Pashmore's head darts to me, an unamused expression on her face.

"Well, hello, Bryce. Nice of you to join us. May I ask why you were over ten minutes late?"

I place my best winning smile on then reply, "I'm sorry, Miss Pashmore. I didn't feel too well and had to spend some time in the ladies' room to calm down a bit."

A flash of concern creases her forehead. "Are you okay to sit through the rest of the class?"

I nod my head, so she motions for me to take a seat. My head still feels dizzy from the encounter outside. I hadn't realized till lately just how sexual I really am. It's like that first encounter with Adam created the beast I've become.

Only when I'm in control.

Only when I have the power.

Miss Pashmore writes *The plague of 1346* on the chalkboard, and as she does, my eyes land on her rounded ass which is being tightly hugged by the red and white checked pants she's wearing. She turns around to address the class, her white shirt unbuttoned enough to show a tiny bit of cleavage. Not too much that it makes her slutty, but enough of a tease so that my eyes scan as far down as they can in an attempt at taking in as much of her as possible.

After a minute or so of staring, I realize that I'm actually leering at my female teacher. A strange sensation ripples through me, an odd sense of wonderment at the surprise that my sexuality doesn't start and end with men. I had always thought Miss Pashmore was attractive —much like every male, or even female, at this school—but I had never sat here admiring her form and wondering what her nipples would feel like inside my mouth and on my tongue. Would her pussy be shaved? Would her lips be big and fat, allowing me to explore more of her?

The whole class, I simply stare like the creep everyone calls me, my curiosity growing by the second. Evidently, the more sexual explorations I try, the more I want to.

When the bell rings ending the class, everyone makes their way to lunch. Whisperings and murmurings surround the hall, and for a brief moment I wonder why. I had completely forgotten about Sarah and her little bundle of news.

"Bryce!" Adam screeches, running up to me like an excitable child. "Did you hear the news?"

I smirk, deciding to humor him. "No, I only just now got out of class."

As he pushes his glasses up, I glance at his NY hoodie, noting for the first time that he's decided to change his wardrobe too. He doesn't look nerdy anymore, that's for certain. In fact, he looks kinda buff.

"Have you been working out?" I ask, cutting him off from what he was about to say next.

His smile is proud as his concentration slips a moment. "Yeah, I have, actually. Glad you noticed." He then shakes his head. "Anyway, I was about to tell you... Guess what was stuck on Sarah's locker?"

I want to laugh, but instead I shrug my shoulders. "Go on, tell me."

"A positive pregnancy test."

"Seriously?" I gawk at him, playing along. He nods his head. "Oh wow, I wonder if it's really hers."

He leans in closer, so I mimic his movements, knowing he's going to whisper something secret. "I heard Isabel tell Samantha that when

Grant saw the test, he immediately grabbed Sarah and pulled her out of school. Apparently, he looked seriously pissed."

Interesting.

"Well, that's not really surprising if it's Grant who knocked her up. He's slept with practically every girl in school." As well as many outside of school. And one in particular is of great interest.

"Everyone, except you." Adam surprisingly smiles at that.

I grin back. "Yeah, only special people get to sleep with me."

Adam's cheeks flush, and then he bites his lip. "Erm ... I wan ... want to ask you something."

"Okay."

"I thought this Saturday after you finish work, I could pick you up and take you for something to eat. Maybe even a movie after."

My gut twists a little. "This sounds like a date to me."

Adam grimaces at my tone. "Would it be so bad if it was? I mean, we are ... you know."

I laugh when he mimics sex as he fists the air. "What's *that* supposed to mean?" I ask, copying what he just did.

He lets out a small laugh, his cheeks still flaming red. "Don't make me say it."

"What? That we've been fucking? Sex isn't a shameful subject, you know." As I finish my sentence, my eyes cross over to Miss Pashmore as she sways her hips, walking down the hall. I definitely have plans for her later.

"I know, it's just," Adam begins, bringing me back to our conversation. "It's been what, like two, three months now? I just thought it would be nice to do something other than you come over my house and we..."

"Fuck, Adam. That's always what I said it was. We're friends first, and I don't want to lose that."

I inwardly groan. I should have known he would get serious about us at some point. I've always had plans to end things with Adam after a while, but at the moment, I'm still having fun sneaking around with both him and his dad.

My stomach twists when his mouth turns down in disappointment, his shoulders drooping.

"Do you think we should stop?" I ask, causing his head to immediately snap up to look at me. "It's probably for the best, don't you think? Having sex is obviously complicating things between us."

He grips his eyes shut like the thought pains him. "No, I don't want to stop. I just thought ... shit, forget I said anything." His eyes scan down the hall, people still gossiping about the latest drama. "It's a nice day out today. Do you want to go eat lunch on the grass?"

Biting my lip, I stare at Adam, wondering if I really am a shitty friend. Screwing his dad is a pretty shitty thing to do, and something Adam definitely doesn't deserve. Neither his dad or I can afford for Adam to find out about us because what we're doing to him and his mom is despicable.

I just can't stop, though.

I inwardly sigh, knowing the fun I was having with Adam and his dad will have to end soon, before any of it gets out of hand—or worse, they find out about the other.

Looping my arm through his, I tug at him. "Sure thing. I'd like that."

After we finish our sandwiches, I tilt my face up to the sun and close my eyes, enjoying the warmth it provides. A few seconds later, Adam tugs on my arm.

"Bryce," he says, his voice shaking a little. "We have company."

My eyes snap open to see who the threat is, finding Brad standing close by us, looking all sheepish yet somehow angry at the same time.

"Can we talk?" Brad asks, his eyes motioning to his left.

I'm about to move when Adam grabs my arm. "You don't have to go with him. You know what he's capable of."

And now Brad knows what I'm capable of, I think gleefully.

Gently, I take Adam's hand off my arm. "I'll be fine," I reassure him. "Honestly."

He still looks unsure. "I'll be watching him."

I smile at Adam's protectiveness. If only he knew what I did to the little shit. I'm not sure he'd want to be as protective then.

I rise from my position, leaving my things safely with Adam while I follow Brad out of Adam's earshot.

"What do you want?" I ask, not in the friendliest way. "I thought I made my feelings clear last week."

Brad slams his eyes shut, the memory of it apparently still in his mind. "I just want to talk to you for a minute. I'll be quick." Waiting, I cock my head to one side. Brad glances over my shoulder, looking at Adam before his eyes land back on me. "I assume you heard about Sarah."

"Yes, because I was the one who stuck the test on her locker."

His eyes widen, and then he scowls at me. "You know, you really are a major bitch."

I smile. "Thank you."

"Is everything a joke to you? I mean, fucking up everyone's lives is so fucking funny."

Rage bubbles in my stomach and forces its way up my throat. Stepping closer, I narrow my eyes at him, causing his to widen in what resembles fear.

"Fucking up my life for the past few years has been one huge, massive fucking joke to you, *Brad*!" I practically spit this, my teeth gritting under my towering rage. "You thought it was a huge joke to try to force me to go down on Adam in front of you sick, perverted, little twerps."

"I would never have let it get that far," he shakes his head. "You on the other hand—"

He's about to say something, but I cut him off by stepping so close to him that I'm virtually in his face. "Tell me something. If you had a pet lion stuck in a cage and every day you went to that lion, laughing and poking at him with a stick when it was powerless to do anything about it, what do you think would happen to the person poking it every day when someone happened to release that lion from his cage?" I point a finger to my chest. "I'm that fucking released lion. Yet you want to sob and get angry about the shit that's happening to you and your so-called shitty fucking excuse for friends. Take a moment to realize that this is all your fault after the years of shit you put me through. All. Your. Fucking. Fault." Fisting my hands by my sides, I try and compose myself before I clock him. "Now, have you finished saying what you had to say, because I'm fucking done with you?"

He closes his eyes, taking in a deep breath, his hands out showing me his palms. "Look, I didn't come here to fight with you. I came here because..." He fidgets, wringing his hands together before raking one of those hands through his hair.

"Spit it out, Brad."

He exhales, making his nostrils flare a little as he fixes his eyes on me. "Seeing Sarah's pregnancy test made me remember something you said." I want to smirk so badly, but I manage to hold it down. "When you..." He's getting so flustered about saying the words that sweat is now forming at his brow. I remain silent, though, allowing him to eventually get it out. "I came inside you," he whisper yells, leaning forward. "Twice."

Now I decide to smile. "So you did. You naughty little virgin, you."

Brad wrings his hands. "This isn't funny, Bryce. You took the one thing away from me I promised to never give up until I was married."

I glance down at my nails, showing him how unfazed I am by this. Yes, I really am a bitch. "It's a pity your precious Chloe didn't promise the same, though, huh? When are you going to forgive her for her misgivings? I'm supposing soon, considering your parents will be planning your wedding in a year or so."

His jaw flexes like the thought angers him. "I'm not here to talk about Chloe. I'm here to talk about us."

I step back. "Us? Nuh-uh, Brad. When it comes to you and me, there is no *us*."

He lowers his eyes to my belly, pointing at it. "You said you were unprotected."

I shrug my shoulders. "Yeah, what of it?"

His eyes widen like he's surprised I'm that stupid. "If you're late, I'll get you a pregnancy test, and if it's positive, then I will have to tell my parents that I'm getting married to you instead."

I laugh out loud, cracking up at the absurdity of his words. Is he even listening to himself?

"Why after what I did to you would you want to do that?"

His eyes glimmer a little as he searches mine. "Because I was raised right. If you're pregnant with my baby, then I need to take responsibility."

"I could always get an abortion."

His eyes widen in shock. "You'd want to kill our baby?"

I sigh out loud. "Oh, for fuck's sake, Brad, there is no baby in this scenario *to* kill. Stop getting ahead of yourself."

I know I need to put him out of his misery soon, especially after confessing that he'll want to marry me if I'm pregnant. It's just ... this is way too much fun.

"Abortion is immoral. It's a sin." I roll my eyes at him. "If you don't want the baby, I'll raise him or her myself."

"Oh, but it's totally fine to make me be a vessel for nine months?" He's about to say something when I cut him off. "I'm on the pill, Brad. Stop fussing." His forehead crinkles with confusion. "Do you really think I would have sex with you without protecting myself? You really are a moron."

His expression becomes indignant. "I have more money than you. I just figured you'd try to trap me."

Placing my hand on his shoulder, I laugh. "Oh, Brad. If I ever wanted to trap someone for money, you'd be the last person on earth I would think of."

He steps back from my touch which makes me smirk. "Just because you're on the pill, that doesn't mean you're one hundred percent protected. In a few weeks, I'll come see you one more time just to confirm you're not pregnant, and then I'll have full pleasure in never having to talk to you again."

He's about to move away when I speak to his back. "Do you think about what happened between us often? Does your dick get hard when you do?" He stiffens, his hands fisting at his sides. "Do you pleasure yourself when you think about my hot, wet, tight pussy clamping down on your dick? Does it make you come hard when you do?"

His shoulders rise then fall before he walks back towards the school building. A big smile on my face, I turn around and head back to where Adam's sitting, leaning curiously forward.

"What did he want?" Adam asks, his eyes still brimming with concern.

Picking up my drink, I take a sip before I reply. "Nothing major.

Just that breaking up with Chloe has made him realize what a jerk he is, and that he wants to take me out."

Adam laughs out loud like he doesn't believe me. "Seriously?"

"Yeah, I think he wants to ride the Bryce train."

An angry crease forms between his brow as his eyes home in on the school. "That guy's a fucking dick."

It's my turn to laugh out loud. "Adam," I reply, tapping his knee with my hand. "I couldn't agree with you more."

CHAPTER TWENTY-SIX

resent

Elijah slept with me all night. Which I assume he only did because of the guilt he felt for going on a date with Bitchface. The next morning starts like any other morning with Elijah handing me a pill and glass of water. And just like every morning, I take the pill and swallow it like the good, little girl I am. Elijah leaves, just like he does every morning, but when the front door opens ten minutes later, I rush to the door to find Elijah on the phone to someone.

"Send an ambulance as soon as you can."

Heart thumping, I wait as Elijah ends his call, his eyes not meeting mine for a moment. "Elijah, what's happening? Is someone hurt?" When he doesn't say anything, my frustration levels spike. "Elijah, what the fuck? Talk to me."

Grabbing my arms, he looks deep into my eyes. "Whatever happens, don't go outside."

I turn my head to gaze out onto the front lawn, everything appearing normal. "What's that supposed to mean?" Of course curiosity gets the better of me, and my feet move forward to try to find out what's going on. But Elijah holds me firmly. "What the hell?" I ask again, glaring at him.

Elijah's head dips down, a long sigh leaving his lips. When he glances back up, he says, "He was a very sick man. It was obviously his time."

Eyes widening at the realization of what he's just said, my feet scramble to move again "Frank?" I scream, not wanting to believe it at first. I race to the door, but a set of arms wrap around me, trapping me. "Leave me alone!" I scream. "Frank!"

My arms reach out, trying to get to the door, but Elijah's holding onto me too tightly. "I'm not letting you go out there, baby. Remember him how he used to be. Not how he looks right now."

Relenting into his arms, tears start to brim in my eyes. "Frank," I say again, but this time it's a mere whimper.

"I'm sorry, baby. But it was just his time to go."

Elijah sits with me in the hallway, the whole time my body wracking with tears as he strokes my hair. I knew he was getting sicker, but because of how self-absorbed I've been lately, I didn't acknowledge that fact. Guilt floods my body at the thought that he must have been dead yesterday, and that's why he never answered me. It's just... I never took the fucking time to make sure he was okay.

I hardly ever cry, but I am now. I'm crying because out of everyone who has ever entered my life, Frank is one who deserves my tears.

Elijah continues to hold me until the paramedics get here, and once he releases me to go outside to talk to them, I take his advice and stay inside, making myself a cup of tea as I stare off into space. As I sip my tea, observing the commotion happening outside, I get angry at Duckface and Wartface, wondering if they're outside, rubbing their hands together in excitement that he's finally dead. It's all I can think about as Frank's body, now zipped up in a black bag, is wheeled to an ambulance. After they drive away and the chaos has calmed, Elijah heads back inside the house, his eyes searching mine.

"How are you feeling?"

In one sense, I hate seeing his concern, but in another, I love it. At least this means he cares. It's just ... Elijah and I don't do mushy shit like this.

"I'm fine. It was a shock, but I came to terms with the fact that he was going to die a long time ago. I just wasn't expecting it when it actually happened."

He places his hand on my shoulder. "I know he really liked you. He never liked me very much, but he definitely liked you."

I laugh at his sentiment. "Yeah, but the only reason why he hated you was because he knew you were fucking your stepdaughter and locking her in her own room each night."

His eyes widen with what looks like panic. "You fucking told him that?"

I shake my head, tutting. "I never told him shit, Elijah. He sat outside on his front porch for hours every day and night. You don't think he saw and heard things when he was out there? Hell, he was the one who gave me the idea about spying on all those fuckers in my school." I think back to the day it all exploded in school and sigh. Some teachers were a bitter disappointment after.

Elijah's lips thin into a firm line. "All that time, I thought Frank was good for you, yet it turns out he was an extremely bad influence."

I huff out a laugh at his hypocrisy. "Coming from the man who takes a woman out on a date just so he can hide the fact that he's fucking his stepdaughter every time he comes home."

Elijah sucks in a breath, his lilac eyes brewing with violence. "I don't want to argue with you about this. You're obviously grieving and want to take it out on someone. Because of that, I'll ignore your snide comments."

"Oh, gee. Thanks," I sass back.

"Do you want me to make you breakfast?"

He's obviously choosing to ignore my childish antics, so I decide to shut up. "No, thank you. What I want is to be left alone."

"I don't think that's a good idea. You've just been handed some awful news—"

"Elijah, just go to work. I have shit to do."

He eyes me suspiciously. "Like what?"

Like visiting Duckface so I can vent my anger on her instead.

"I have some assignments that I need to get done, plus some washing to do."

"I think you can forgo the assignments just for today, Bryce."

My head snaps up to meet his eyes. "I think doing my assignments is just the thing I need. It certainly beats sitting around the house all day doing nothing but feeling sorry for myself."

Elijah leans his hand on the counter next to me, his expression uncertain. "Are you sure you'll be okay?"

"Yes, darling," I reply, all sweetness and light.

Elijah shakes his head, an amused grin on his face. "Okay, but if you need me—"

"I know where to find you," I cut him off.

I drink the rest of my tea as Elijah gathers his things to leave. Before he does, he gives me a tender kiss on the lips which has them tingling for a while after.

Getting up from my seat, I stalk to the window and stare across at Duckface's house, noting that her Wrangler is parked out front. It's probably not a good idea to go over there right now considering how angry I am. Still, there is no logic in most of the things I do, so why should this be any different?

I look over to Wartface's house, seeing that both her and her husband's cars are gone.

Interesting.

My eyes lighting up with an idea, I grab some latex gloves from under the sink then stuff them in the pocket of my jeans. I grab a hoodie, throw that on, then stuff a black trash bag in the hoodie pocket. I walk to the nearest park which is about five minutes away. While there, I grab what I need, taking my time so I don't get caught before walking back home.

With my black trash bag now full, I glance around my street, making sure no one is watching before I walk to Wartface's house. I walk around the side until I'm in her backyard. There, I put on my gloves then pick the lock—something I've perfected over the course of my criminal career, before making my way inside her clean, white kitchen. When I enter the living room, my eyes light up at the sight of her expensive looking, plush, beige carpet, a carpet feet would no doubt get lost in.

"Perfect," I murmur to myself as I grab the black bag and get to work. The whole process makes me cringe, and the fucking shit stinks, but it's all worth it when I step back and take in all the old and fresh dog poop seeping into Wartface's precious carpet.

"That'll teach you, you crusty-faced bitch."

The scent becoming too much, I hold my nose and quickly rush outside, disposing of the trash bag and gloves in another neighbor's trash. I then walk home, but I pause when I come close to Frank's front porch, saddened by the empty chairs that now look completely out of place without him there. I close my eyes, sadness washing over me and momentarily replacing my anger. It'd already been alleviated after my retribution on Wartface, but Duckface is still on my mind as I'm washing my hands in the sink a few minutes later. My eyes are on Duckface's house when it hits me that she hasn't been around for a while.

Leaving the house again, I venture over to hers and knock on the door. It takes a while for her to answer, but she does, a white robe covering her body, her eyes all puffy like she's been crying. My anger at her is replaced by curiosity at what could be upsetting her so much.

"I really don't need this right now," she snarls, wiping her nose on a tissue. She turns, leaving the door open as she walks back inside the house. I frown at her odd behavior. Is she expecting me to leave or follow her into the house? Deciding on the latter, I pad inside, shutting the door behind me. By the time I reach the living room she's sitting on the couch, sniffling.

"Are you sick?"

She huffs out a laugh. "I wish I was sick."

It's strange. I came over here to get angry at her, but seeing how pathetic she looks has me stalling for a moment. Still, I say, "I suppose you're happy about Frank now."

Her head snaps to mine, confusion written all over his face. "I don't understand what you mean."

"I mean about him dying."

Her eyes widen so much, I instantly realize she had no clue. "Frank's dead?"

My frown takes hold as I sit next to her on the couch. "He died. Elijah found him this morning."

She closes her eyes. "I'm sorry to hear that." She then returns her gaze to me. "You must be so distraught. I know you two were really good friends."

I want to tell her yes and that's the reason why she's being blackmailed. Instead, I surprise her by smiling. "Yes, we were."

She blinks a couple of times before saying, "Listen, I want to properly apologize for my behavior a couple of weeks back. It was completely inappropriate of me. I haven't stopped thinking about my actions since."

I point to her attire. "Is that why you're stuck at home, crying?"

She closes her eyes like something pains her. "It's part of the reason, but not the main one. There's ... other stuff happening. Other things that have made me realize I'm not as good of a person as I'd thought." She swallows thickly, licking her enlarged lips. "I have to confess something to you. I wanted Frank's house. Well, both Betty and I both do. We've been talking for years about how old his house looks compared to everyone else's, and that one of us should buy it when he dies so that we can make it look like the rest of neighborhood. It was a shallow and callous thing to consider, and I especially felt bad when we kept asking him if he would sell to us once he dies."

I'm wondering if her regret is genuine or if it's because she's being blackmailed that she's finally seeing the light. It may be a bit of both.

Knowing she seems to be suffering in her own way, my anger continues to diminish. I believe I've done enough to make my point, so there's no need to dredge up the same shit. I still smile inside when I think of how Wartface will react when she gets home and realizes there's dog shit everywhere.

"Do you forgive me?"

Her question takes me back a little. And I think I speak for Frank as well when I answer, "Of course." She breathes a sigh of relief and when she does, her gown opens slightly, revealing a breast. It's big, bronzed, and pert, but her nipple is a bit smaller than I remembered from her camera fun. Still, they're nice to look at, at least.

Duckface catches my ogling, her mouth slightly parting in surprise. She doesn't cover up, though, which has me wondering for a second why. Could I push her to go there with me again if I really wanted to? For a long time, I've been curious about what it would be like to be with a woman in that way, but what held me back and will continue to is Elijah. Not that he's exactly the glowing example of loyalty after the stunt he pulled last night.

Sighing my disappointment at another lost opportunity, I rise from my seat. "I'd better get going."

Duckface nods somewhat sadly before I make my way to the door. I'm tempted to tell her that I would have let her go down on me that day, but what would be the point? She would only wonder why, which would result me admitting it's because of Elijah.

I say goodbye, feeling oddly strange by my sudden switch in emotion. An emotion I have no time to think about when I get home to find a delivery driver bringing a huge bunch of flowers to my house.

Frowning, I run the short distance, catching up to him before he knocks. "Hey, can I help you?" I get up the steps as the guy spins around.

"Are you Bryce Turner?" I nod my head. "Delivery for you." He hands me the gorgeous bouquet before walking back to his truck.

"Thank you," I call out, still frowning as I wonder who would send me flowers. I've never been sent flowers before.

Inside the house, I place the array of flowers down then reach in to grab the card. When I read who it's from, the anger which had faded earlier reaches fever pitch.

Bryce,

Thinking of you.

Elijah x

. . .

I grit my teeth. This is the sort of shit men do when they're feeling guilty about something. The thought unnerves me so much that I start baking a big batch of chocolate chip cookies. As they're cooling, I decide to have a shower to wash off any flour that's gotten on me before dressing in my usual attire of a short, sexy dresses that leave little to the imagination.

My hair up in a messy bun, I place all the cookies in a basket before taking the bus to the police station. At the front door, I bump into the one and only Sergeant Brent.

His smile is wide as his eyes peruse me from my legs to my breasts. "Well, lookie who we have here. It's the alley cat." He whistles for full affect, causing an unwanted smile to grace my lips. "What you got there?"

I pull the basket tighter to me like he's going to snap it away from my grip. "I made a big batch for everyone at the station. I thought you boys would like a bit of a ... treat."

My voice is a little teasing at the end there, and of course, Brent latches on to that. "That you are, baby girl. That you are."

I nod to the entrance. "Are you going to let me in?"

He folds his arms in front of him. "Depends."

I almost roll my eyes. "On what?"

I think he's going to say something really suggestive, so I'm surprised when he answers, "On whether I get first dibs on how many cookies I can nab before any of those other fuckers get in there."

An unexpected laugh leaves my lips. "Okay then. If you kindly let me in, you get first dibs."

His hand reaches in, grabbing five of them at once. Gasping, I smack his hand. "Hey, I didn't think you meant *that* many."

He raises an eyebrow at me. "You do realize you've just assaulted an officer of the law?"

"Yeah, after he stole the cookies from my basket," I snap back.

Brent bites his lip suggestively. "How is it you made that sound a lot more sexual than it was?"

I purse my lips at him. "You do realize that my stepfather is your boss. What do you think he'll do to you if he finds out you've been flirting with me?"

He leans forward and whispers, "Isn't that what makes this more ... exciting?" I make a show of rolling my eyes, and then he says, "Come on in. I'm sure the guys are going to love a visit from *you*."

The suggestion that it may not just be my cookies is definitely insinuated, but I don't reply as I follow him inside while he munches away on the cookies.

"Hmm ... these are good."

"You sound surprised," I reply, following him into the main office.

His gaze trails up and down my body again. "It seems your talents are endless."

"Wow, you really don't know when to stop, do you?"

He leans forward to whisper, "I believe it was you who started things when you refused to get into my patrol car."

I'm about to retort when an older looking officer approaches us. "What's this?" He points to my basket.

"I made a huge batch this morning, so thought I'd come down and share them with y'all." I offer him the basket. "Want one?"

He smiles, taking one out then biting into it. "Hmm, these are so good." He then turns to everyone in the office. "Free cookies if anyone wants one."

One by one, they all come up, taking the cookies. Eventually, I decide to leave them on a desk and place my ass in the seat next to it.

"These are really yummy," one young, blond officer says, taking a couple of bites. My eyes wander over to a couple of female officers who don't get up. In fact, they don't look like they're happy I'm here. I smirk, realizing it's probably because I'm getting all the attention.

"So tell me what it's like living with the boss?" One of them asks as they all walk over, piling around me.

I giggle for full affect as I swing my bare legs back and forth under the desk. "It's like living with the chief of police," I tell them, their laughter now filing the room.

They ask a couple more questions, hanging on my every answer. "You bake cookies like these, you can come visit us anytime," a cop with reddish hair and a moustache says. Everyone mumbles their agreement.

"You know," Brent starts, chewing on the last cookie he took.

"There's a singles' police dance coming up in two weeks. You should go."

I'm about to remind him that I'm not a police officer officer when Elijah appears in the room, his heated, lilac eyes taking in the scene in front of him.

"What is this?" he bellows, his murderous glare hitting everyone in the room—including me.

I smile sweetly at him. "I brought them all cookies. I thought it would be a nice gesture, considering they're all helping to keep our neighborhood safe." I glance inside the basket, noticing that all the cookies are gone. "I would have offered you one, but it seems the little piggies ate them all." I laugh at my own innuendo as a few laugh along with me.

His eyes stare me down a moment before they swing around the room. "Get back to work." I roll my eyes as they all scurry back to their desks. "You," Elijah points to me. "Come with me."

I want to ask what I've done wrong, but I decided to leave that until we're in his office and behind the closed door.

"What's wrong?"

"What's wrong," he echoes, pointing an angry finger my way. "Is that you've come to the station wearing a dress that leaves very little to the imagination, taking all of my officers' attention off their work and focusing it completely on you."

I shrug one shoulder. "I baked them cookies. I can't help it if they all want to fuck me because of that."

Elijah inhales an angry breath. "It's not the fucking cookies that make them want to have sex with you, Bryce." He stares at me a moment, eventually shaking his head, his eyes softening somewhat. "Listen, I understand that you've had a bad morning, but I can't let that excuse your coming here and disrupting my officers."

I step forward, placing my empty basket down on his desk before approaching him, my finger stroking down his chest. "You're not angry because I disrupted them. You're angry at *how* I did it. It's a pity you won't admit it."

"Bryce," he warns, his tone harsh. "Not here. Not now."

Picking up my little basket, I hook my arm inside. "Thank you for the guilt flowers, by the way."

He frowns. "Guilt flowers?"

"Yeah, flowers that men send after they've been with a floozy. Much like what you did last night."

His nostrils flare. "I bought them for you because of the news about Frank. I thought it was a nice gesture."

I'm momentarily stunned, realizing that I was too pent up on jealous rage to even think about that as an option. He spots the moment sadness coats my eyes, so he steps forward, cupping my chin between his fingers.

"Do you want me to come home with you? Just say the word, and we'll leave together. It's not right that you're on your own today."

I swallow the small sob that wants to escape my lips. "I'll be fine."

"You don't have to constantly put on this persona of a cold-hearted bitch, Bryce. Especially in front of me. You and I have been through too much shit together to hide what we feel."

The words are on the tip of tongue to tell him that he hides his feelings for me every day, but I'm tired of constantly fighting this man when I know damn well it won't get me anywhere. I've known all along that I would end up having to force us in the end rather than letting him choose.

Leaning his head forward, Elijah captures my lips with his, a tender kiss leaving me breathless and wanting more.

"I'm fine," I eventually proclaim, cutting off the moment between us.

Elijah smiles, stepping back. "Of course you are."

"I'll see you at home," I say, opening the door and stepping out of his office. I don't know why, but my nerves are rattling me somewhat. Apart from my momentary euphoria at defacing Wartface's house, today's been a real shitty day. There are only two emotions I allow myself to feel on a daily basis: anger and lust. Anything else just puts me off balance.

Deciding I need to walk home, I clutch onto my basket and make my way outside. However, when I get there, Bitchface is walking up the steps. She stops mid step and smirks my way like she has the superior high ground.

"Oh, if it isn't Little Red Riding Hood," she coos, deciding not to hide the bitch that she truly is.

I huff in a breath, happiness now spreading through my veins that the anger's back. I should actually thank her for that.

"Just bringing cookies for all the boys," I reply, my smile wide as I get within arms-reach of her. My eyes scan down to her bulging cleavage, not caring that she spots me.

"Wondering if you'll ever be able to have breasts as nice as mine?" she taunts, making my eyes snap up to her smug face. I want to laugh. She thinks I'm looking because I'm jealous of her.

Stepping closer to her, I lick my lips. "No, I'm wondering what your nipples would taste like if I suckled on them."

Delight swims in my veins at her completely shocked expression. Yeah, she certainly wasn't expecting that.

Puckering my lips, I blow her a kiss before walking around her to move down the steps. "Let me know if you ever want to make that happen," I call out as I begin my journey down, the whole time knowing she must be confused as fuck by me.

"Even if I was in to women," she begins to my back, "you'd be the last one I would *ever* let touch me."

I bite my lip, sniggering to myself.

Challenge accepted, Bitchface.

CHAPTER TWENTY-SEVEN

ast

Mark Twain famously wrote, "The two most important days in your life are the day you were born and the day you find out why."

Today was the day I found out why.

That's it. I've done everything I can, planned it all to the letter, and now all I can do is watch and wait with apprehension to see if all of my hard work pays off.

It's a testing day at school which means there are no classes. It's the perfect time for me to set up all my traps. I have been working through the early hours of the morning arranging it all, and now I'm ready.

Let the games begin.

Disappointment shrouds me some when I realize Chloe won't be there to enjoy the fun. She, unfortunately, took a sabbatical after her leaked diary entries and the subsequent war that ensued after. Daddy to the rescue, no doubt. He had no alternative but to leave me alone after I decided to block him after a few text messages chasing me for another "meeting".

"Today's going to suck even with no classes," Adam complains as we walk to the gym to watch a basketball match that's about to start.

"Wait, are you telling me you're not looking forward to watching Chloe's bitches when they do their dance performance later? I'm pretty sure they're wearing cheerleader outfits." I waggle my eyebrows for full affect.

Adam smirks as we take our seats together on the stands. "I would normally dig that, but knowing how bitchy they really are makes them look just as ugly on the outside."

I smile in agreement just as the principal speaks through the microphone at everyone. "Thank you to all who turned up for our annual games and activities day," he begins.

"He says it like we have a choice in the matter," Adam whispers. "I seriously feel like I'm ten right now."

I giggle in response as the principal continues. "Another year is almost over. For some it's been tough, having to work extra hard to attain your grades. For other's who treat school as a playground..." he hesitates a moment, smiling. "Not so much." A round of laughter echoes around the gymnasium. "Now, to kickstart this fantastical day, we're going to start with a basketball game played by our male juniors. Let's hear a cheer for the team!"

Claps resound as I lean over to talk to Adam. "I can't believe the principal said the word fantastical."

Adam sniggers. "Yeah, I know, right?"

The boys enter the court, some already scratching their chests. I bite my lip, trying to suppress my laughter, but it's bubbling up so much that Adam notices.

"What's so funny?"

I cover my mouth as I laugh out loud. "You'll see."

My eyes search out for Grant since he's the one I wanted to target the most—other than Brad, of course. I snigger when he starts scratching around the inside of his leg at the same time as he's scratching his stomach. He stops, but then his forehead turns down in an annoyed frown when he begins to scratch the same areas again. My eyes pan to each player to find they're all scratching in one form or another. The game begins, but the scratching continues until it starts to become apparent that all of them have a problem. The coach calls for a timeout then runs onto the floor, leaning into a huddle with them, to no doubt ask what the problem is. As the itching and scratching gets worse, giggling increases around the gym.

"Shit, Bryce," Adam whispers, a huge grin on his face. "Did you do this?" I nod my head. "Oh my God, I think I love you even more—if that's possible."

The scratching forgotten, my head snaps to Adam, but he's too busy watching what's going on to notice my shock. Did he mean to say that as a flippant, passing remark, or does he actually mean what he says, and it just slipped out?

Feeling a little nervous, my initial joy at the start of what I know is going to be a fun day is tampered down by his ... what? Confession?

Maybe I'm reading into this too much.

Deciding to ignore the remark for now, I reply. "You should see what I have planned for later."

While carnage ensues and the gym fills with the deafening laughter and voices of the students, the teachers begin scrambling around like a bunch of headless chickens, trying to calm the boys who are getting increasingly stressed by their itching.

As the boys are quickly ushered away to the locker room, my smile grows even wider. I assume they'll be rushing to the showers to wash off all that itching powder they have inside their clothing.

"Everyone, quiet down, please!" the principal, Mr. Shrouder shouts. It takes a little while for the excitable chatter to calm. "Someone in this school obviously thought it would be funny to ruin the start of our activities before they've even begun. Let it be known now that we do not tolerate such behavior in this school. I expect the person responsible to see me in my office by the end of today. If not, there will be consequences."

I roll my eyes at his stern voice which vows to make the person pay.

For so many years, I have been picked on, bullied, and abused, yet every single teacher here decided to turn a blind eye.

Fuck him. Fuck all of them!

We're told to wait in the gym until they can figure something out, then the murmuring continues.

"Are you nervous?" Adam asks me, a concerned look in his eyes.

"About what?" I pivot towards him, awaiting his answer.

"Getting caught. What if they find out it's you?"

I shrug my shoulders. "They won't, Adam. But even if they did, at this point, I don't give a fuck."

"You only have a few more months of school, then you'll never have to worry about these people again."

My lips twist up in a smirk. "Yes, but I will have so many fond memories of this day to take with me." Let alone the others I've had up to this point.

"I'm just worried about you."

Adam seriously has no clue. "Don't be. I can totally take care of myself. I'm not the timid girl I used to be."

Adam's forehead bunches up as he scrutinizes me. "No, you're certainly not."

We wait about another five minutes before being ushered out into the school hallway and outside where we can watch the girls volleyball match. Most of the girls on this team are okay, so I decided not to prank all of them for the sake of a few bad eggs.

And then the fun really starts. All the boys emerge from the locker room. All the jocks who have ever picked on me, called me names, or tripped me up in the hallways appear, each with different colors on their face and in their hair. Brad is a bright green, Grant, a blushing pink, David, a lovely orange, and Tony, a bright yellow.

The whole school erupts in laughter as they walk one by one, their expressions dark and embarrassed. Mr. Shrouder is walking behind all the boys, his head shaking with frustration. Again, we're all addressed, and again Mr. Shrouder rambles the same bullshit that whoever's responsible will feel the full brunt of the school, yadda, yadda, yadda.

The day eventually quiets, and so do I as I can't do too much too soon. However, when it's time for the bake sale where loads of people have baked cookies and cupcakes and things like that—including the batch of cupcakes I enjoyed making yesterday. Some are good, but some others have a special ingredient in them that are only reserved for the VIPs of the school.

The logistics are a little tricky, but knowing how idiotic the jocks of this school are, they won't even notice. I stand by Becca, a student a year below me and an alright kind of girl. A bit of an airhead, but otherwise harmless. As she's busy flirting with a guy in my year, I pull out of the yummy looking vanilla cupcakes I made with so much love in them and place them on the table.

"Oh, those look yummy." One of the freshman girls points at my special cakes. "Can I buy one of those?"

I shake my head. "Oh, these aren't for sale," I explain. "They were accidentally put on display. Sorry. You're more than welcome to choose another item, though."

The freshman glances around the others, her face a mixture of disappointment and irritation. "Err, no, thanks."

As she walks by, I stick my tongue out at her, going cross-eyed. A little juvenile, I know, but this is what the whole day is about for me today. I'm allowed the occasional indulgence of delinquency every now and then.

"What's that you got there, freak?" Grant chortles, as he glances down at my cleavage before looking back to my cupcakes.

I snatch them away. "Oh, these aren't for you, pinky," I smirk at his pink hair and face. "These are reserved for special people."

He actually looks indignant. "But I'm special."

"What's going on?" Tony asks, appearing at Grant's side, his bright yellow self almost blinding my eyes.

"Slutty freak here won't give us one of her cupcakes."

Tony's lips turn down in an angry frown. "Why the fuck not?"

Holding them to my side, I snipe back, "Because you don't deserve my cupcakes, that's why."

Completely whiney but also completely deliberate. What is it they say? Reverse psychology always normally works.

My body relaxes slightly, a purposeful move. It's one that allows Grant to snatch the plate from me before stuffing one into his mouth.

"Hey, you fucker! Give them back!"

Tony snaps one of the cupcakes up, stuffing it in his mouth too. "These are actually pretty good for a whore." He chews it down before nudging Grant. "I wonder if her blowjobs are as good as her baking."

Grant smirks, leering at my mouth. "With lips like that, I bet she could suck a lollipop right off its stick."

"Fuck you!" I growl, causing them to, "Ooooo," back at me.

"Does your stepdad kiss that mouth of yours?" Grant asks, his sneer menacing.

I thought Brad had reined these fuckers in. I'm guessing that because he's not around now, the last few weeks of not being able to taunt and tease me is coming out of them by the bucket load.

"I think he kisses something else of hers," Tony jokes, causing them to high-five each other as they laugh.

"Is that true, whore?" Grant continues. "Does your stepdad kiss that pink, little pussy of yours?"

Eyes narrowing, I lean over the table so he can get a good view of my cleavage. Like the perverts that they both are, they lean in too. "Every fucking night. It's so good that my orgasms make me pass out. I bet you can't make a girl pass out with an orgasm, can you, dickhead? I bet you can't make a girl orgasm at all." He's about to retort when I say, "How's Sarah doing these days? Is she glowing yet with the spawn of Satan growing inside of her?" His face falls, causing me to chuckle. "Not so cocky now, are you, *Grant*?"

He sneers, leaning forward. "Why don't you just run away and die, bitch."

Placing my hand over my mouth, I fake yawn. "How original of you. Can you seriously not think of anything better?"

He's about to open his mouth when Mrs. Harris, one of the English teacher's, approaches the table, immediately noticing Grant with the plate of cupcakes in his hand.

"Is there a problem here?"

I smile towards both Grant and Tony. "No, they were just leaving. Weren't you, boys?"

One side of Grant's lips curl up. "Yes, we were."

They turn to move, but Mrs. Harris halts them. "Err, did you pay for those cupcakes?" She points at the five still sitting on the plate.

Grant looks at me, challenging me to say something, but I just smile, crossing my arms in front of me.

Delving into his pocket, he pulls out a ten dollar bill and throws it on the table. "Always willing to give to charity," he mocks, walking away. I watch as he joins David, taking great joy in watching him eating one too.

"Are you okay, dear?" Mrs. Harris asks, an uneasy crinkle between her brows.

I smile like I always do when a teacher asks me the same damn questions every time one of these assholes get a chance to bully me.

"I'm fine, Mrs. Harris. I'm always fine."

My smile doesn't meet my eyes when I look at her. She swallows, all nervous, then scurries away with her tail between her legs.

"Fucking assholes," I mutter under my breath. No backbone. Not a single teacher here. It's shameful.

Deciding not to get angry, I turn my attention to the assholes and squeal inside when more of the jocks take a cupcake, all while they're holding them up, teasing me like it's all a big joke.

Well, pretty soon the jokes going to be on them.

When the bake sale ends, we're marched into the theatre to watch the slut squadron perform a dance routine they've supposedly been rehearsing for months. Again, I meet up with Adam, and again, we sit down to endure the show.

"I don't think I can walk," Adam complains, patting his belly.

I smile, peering over my shoulder as the jocks take their seats. Already, they're looking a bit pale. Smiling so much my cheeks are starting to hurt, I turn my attention back to Adam. "Well, you did eat one of pretty much everything being sold, didn't you?"

He grumbles. "But they were so yummy."

Lights flicker, so all the voices quiet. Mr. Shrouder comes on stage again to introduce the girls who will be doing the performance. One by one, the bitches all come out. Sarah, Isabel, Michelle, Tracy and the others, each as just as bad as the slut next to her. They're all dressed in their cheerleader uniforms, a portion of their bellies showing and their hair up in high ponytails. The guys in the crowd whistle, causing the twats on stage to giggle. I can't help but roll my eyes. They think they're so worshipped by this school, it's sickening.

It lasts only around five minutes, but right at the end when they do their final flips, before the jazz hands appear, it happens. The chord is pulled so glitter can rain down on their heads like the shining stars that they are. But instead of glitter, it's red paint. The girls' inevitable screams reverberate around the theatre hall just as the boys behind us scramble out of their seats, gripping onto their stomachs as they race for the exit.

Laughter and voices erupt around me, everyone wondering what's happening and who could be behind all of this.

"Bryce."

My head snaps to Adam, a questioning look on his face. I simply tip one shoulder up. "I may have had a little something to do with this," I reply all innocently.

He's about to respond, but the girls on stage start to scream, some even crying as they're quickly ushered off the stage. I just laugh. I can't help myself. Lots of others are laughing, too, so why not?

Nothing happens for a good few minutes, and then Mr. Shrouder appears on stage, microphone in hand, his head down in disappointment. The crowd naturally quietens without being asked, all of them eager to hear what he has to say.

Slowly, he brings the microphone to his mouth. "In all of my thirty-two years teaching, I have never come across such acts of unruly, vile, disobedient behavior. Whoever is behind this should hang their heads in shame for spoiling what should have been a memorable day." I snicker at his use of words. It will definitely be memorable for me. "A group of boys are currently sick in the bathroom while the lovely girls who worked so hard to put on a brilliant dance performance not only have red paint all over them, they will have no choice but to go home and miss the rest of the day, all because some reckless person has stolen all of their clothes."

Yeah, and put them in the trash where they belong.

He clears his throat as he surveys the crowd, his face stern. "The culprits will be found and will be brought to justice. There's no question about that. If this group of people come forward to see me by the end of the day, I *may* decide to not involve the police. You have been warned." He then scans the whole room again. "Now, considering the stage is ruined for the remainder of the acts, I will have no alternative but to dismiss you early. However, I will remain on campus until four today. I'll expect some visitors before then." His eyes pan around the room again. "You may go."

Everyone rises from their seats, voices escalating with each second that passes. I watch the animation of their faces, the gossip that they'll no doubt bring home with them to tell their families. They're all reveling in it. They all fucking love it.

"Did you seriously do all this today?" I bite my lip, nodding my head. Adam shakes his in return, laughter escaping him. "I don't know whether you're awesome or crazy."

"Maybe a bit of both." I wink at him, causing him to giggle again.

"As long as you're careful."

I place my hand on his shoulder as we enter the hallway. "Don't you worry. I'm always careful."

"I gotta go grab my bag from my locker. Meet me out front in a bit? I can walk you home."

I nod my head then take my time, strolling to my locker. Lots have already left by now, but there are still some people milling around as they grab their stuff.

I get to the end of the hall to my locker and take my bag out. I lock up, and as I'm walking back towards the exit, Grant, David, and Brad step out of the bathroom, groaning as they clutch their stomachs. Grant glances up, his eyes landing on mine. The urge to wink at him is so great that I do it without conscious thought.

Realization dawns on him, and then he rushes forward. "You fucking bitch! You did this to us, didn't you?"

Luckily, Brad and David pull him back before he does any damage. I step forward, my body language calm and collected.

I cluck my tongue at him. "Only what you fuckers deserved."

"You did this?" Brad asks, his mouth an O, his face full of disappointment. It only serves to make me angrier.

"Yeah, so fucking what? It was a long time coming."

"You fucking bitch!" Grant seethes as he bares his teeth at me. "I'm going to make you pay for this. What you did is assault."

I smirk, stepping forward to whisper something in his ear. "Do that and I will tell your precious daddy that you've been dicking his new wife for the last four months." His eyes widen in disbelief that I know. "Oh, yeah. I know it all. And I have proof." I step back, talking louder this time. "I have shit on all of y'all. Do you seriously want to test me on it?" Grant's shoulders drop, and David darts his eyes to Tony before landing back on me. I give him a mischievous wink. "I know about that too." David's eyes widen to saucers so I lean forward to whisper to him too. "Quite the fucking hot show, too, I must admit. I had to go back home and fiddle with my magic bean afterwards."

No one knows, but David and Tony have been sucking each other off for months. They still date girls, which is fucking ridiculous considering they seem to be really in to each other. Why they're hiding it is anyone's guess.

"Stay the fuck away from us," Brad demands, causing me to glare daggers at him.

"Gladly," I snap back. "Now, if you don't mind, I have more important places to be."

The boys had all switched on their hateful glares again, but they don't last long. Before I can walk away, they're turning and rushing back into the boys' room. I watch until the door closes behind them, releasing a huge belly laugh. However, when I turn, my smile instantly drops. Standing ten feet away with an intense frown on his face is Mr. Shrouder.

"I think you need to come with me, young lady."

CHAPTER TWENTY-EIGHT

resent

Two days go by, and not only am I bored stiff, I'm also frustrated at the amount of time it's taking to hash out my plan. Elijah worked late the last two nights, so I've been unable to follow through with my scheme.

I thought today was going to be like any other day until I get a phone call from a lawyer named Andrew Chester asking me to come see him. Apparently, it's got something to do with Frank. Elijah was there when he called, and he insisted on coming with me—the controlling asshole that he is.

"I don't see why you needed to come to this."

We're sitting in the reception area, waiting to see this lawyer called, his busy secretary making appointments and answering calls for him at her desk nearby.

"He's a lawyer. I just want to make sure that whatever he's bringing you in for is legit."

I roll my eyes at him. "That's seriously the lamest excuse I have ever heard."

Elijah leans forward, his eyes hooded, his irises blazing. "Tell me why you think I'm here then."

My mouth parts, the electricity between us humming. Even when I'm frustrated with him, I'm still unable to hide my wanton longing for his touch.

"Because if Frank decided to put me in charge of anything relating to his property and belongings, you want to make sure it's you who's actually in charge."

He pffts at me, shuffling his feet on the ground. He knows I'm right. "That's fucking ridiculous."

"Is it?" I challenge, hitching my eyebrow. For the past two years, Elijah has been controlling me in every sense of the word. I'm sure this is no different to any other circumstance. What he doesn't realize is that I've always let him control me. But only because I want to let him ... for now.

"Miss Turner," a male voice calls, making our heads snap his way.

Standing in the doorway, Andrew Chester greets us, his eyes a dazzling blue, his hair light blond. He reminds me a little of Chesney, making me wonder if they're related.

Both Elijah and I stand, then I close the distance, shaking Mr. Chester's hand. "Nice to meet you," I greet him.

He shakes Elijah's hand, then once greetings are over, he motions for us to go into his office and sit down. We do so, waiting for him to do the same.

"As you know, Frank Horton died a few days ago." He offers a sympathetic smile before continuing. "Around two months ago, Frank came to see me to update his will. He knew time was running out, and although he'd written an initial will many years ago, he decided to change some things." I nod, urging him to continue as Elijah remains silent, listening to the lawyer's every word.

"Now, as you're probably already aware, Frank lived a very modest life, so he was able to save a little, bit by bit. He wants to be buried next to his wife, his funeral was already arranged and paid for weeks ago. Here are the details if you want to attend." Pressing his finger on a piece of paper, he slides it forward until it's in front of me. The funeral is tomorrow, at a local church nearby.

"Mr. Horton," Andrew continues, "requested that all of his belongings go to you to do with as you wish." Gasping, I place my hand on my chest. Andrew notices and smiles. "I gather you weren't expecting that."

I snap my head from side to side. "Never in a million years. I just thought he would have given you instructions for me to carry out ... or something. Certainly not this."

He glances down at a piece of expensive, thick, slightly yellowing paper. "He also wants you to have the almost fifty thousand dollars in his bank account."

"What?!" I shout, almost choking on my own spit.

"He left you a letter, requesting that you read it once you get home."

He's speaking, but the words aren't making much sense.

Frank, what did you do? I don't deserve any of this.

Sadness shrouds me, my thoughts everywhere. I even forget that Elijah is with me until he places his hand over mine, offering me some comfort.

"I realize that this is a lot to take in," Andrew acknowledges, placing a handwritten envelope in front of me. "Go home, take your time, then call me whenever you're ready to give me instructions on where to send the money." He places another envelope in front of me along with a set of keys. "This is the deed and keys to the property, the deed's already in your name. I believe Mr. Horton has written down everything else you'll need to know."

Elijah takes the deed, keys, and the letter from the table, rising from his seat. "Thank you, Mr. Chester."

I get up, too, shaking his hand, exchanging the same pleasantries again before we leave. I still can't process everything that just happened. It's only when we're in Elijah's car that his voice snaps me out of it.

"Well, that was totally unexpected."

I turn my head to him, gauging his reaction. He seems a little ... on edge. Grabbing the documents that Elijah picked up for himself then placed in front of him on the dash, I set them on my lap, fixing him with a glare.

"I believe these belong to me." My saccharine smile greets him as he starts the car.

"What are you going to do with all this?" he asks, his eyes flickering between me and the road. "Owning a home is a lot of responsibility for someone as young as you."

"I think I can handle it."

A muscle jumps in his cheek at my indifference. If Elijah had his way, I'd sign everything over to him, that way, he remains the one with all the power. I would always be reliant upon him. In some ways, I love that he's secretly so possessive of me, but in another, I'm thrilled by this news—even if it has been born out of something so tragic.

Back at the house, I annoy him further when I decide to take Frank's letter out back to the garden to read. It's a lovely day, so why not? Sitting on a chair on our lanai, I sip on some iced tea then open the letter.

Rosebud,

If you're reading this, then I must be dead. Although we both knew it was going to happen, I'd at least wanted to see you leave home and make something of yourself first. You remind me of a trapped bird who's wings have been clipped, and that's why I decided to make the decisions I did. You must have a lot of questions, so I will answer them for you.

I don't expect you to live in my house. In fact, I would prefer that you left this town and start a new life someplace better, a place that deserves you. Someplace you can thrive and grow in to the beautiful woman I know you can be. All I ask is that you use some of the money I'm giving you to touch up the house a little before you sell. My request is that it goes to a loving family. One that will grow in that house for many years like I did. Tell Duckface and Wartface they can go fuck themselves. The house is not a cash cow they can use to make them a quick buck. My wife and I spent many happy years in that house. Now it's time someone else starts their memories here too.

You're intelligent and beautiful, Rosebud—one in a million. I don't know if my money will bring you happiness, but it's certainly a start.

. . .

Go get your wings.

All my love,

Frank

P.S. I'll tell Grace you said hi.

I laugh at the last line referring to his wife as I wipe a lone tear that falls. "Frank," I whisper, shaking my head. He always thought I was getting abused in this house. At the start, I did, but any abuse going forward was wanted. Something I came to crave.

Guilt prickles my skin when I think about the fact that he's offering me all his wealth under false pretenses. I don't deserve any of this, and yet, he must have seen something in me. Maybe he saw something I'm not fully aware of. I'm a murderer, rapist, evil schemer, and a proud slut. Where Frank's gone, they won't accept the likes of me in their entourage, and I've come to peace with that over time. The deeper I dove in to the rabbit hole, the deeper I wanted to go. All the wealth in the world won't change that or anything about me. I'm still going to get what I want. I'm still going to dive even deeper.

"Did it say what he wanted you to do with the house?" Elijah sits in the chair next to me, an expectant glint in his eyes.

I draw in a deep breath. "He wants me to fix it up then sell it to a loving family."

"So he doesn't expect you to live in it?"

I shake my head. "Quite the opposite. He wants me to find my wings and get out of this town."

Elijah purses his lips at this. "That's something we need to discuss ... for future reference."

I smirk, knowing exactly what he means by that. I've always believed that Elijah wouldn't want to let me go as much as I don't want to be let go of. Sometimes men like Elijah need a little ... push in the right direction. I'm sure we'll get there soon. Very soon, in fact. Hopefully, all my patience and biding my time will pay off shortly. I just need to hang in there a little bit longer.

"Do you want me to order in a pizza or something?"

This is Elijah's way of saying that the discussion is over. I shake my head. "How about I cook your favorite?" His favorite being juicy ribs with barbecue sauce which he always has an orgasm over.

"Some corn on the cob too?" he asks, his eyes lighting up.

"Yep, corn too."

I head into the kitchen to get to work on feeding us. For what I have planned later, I will certainly need my strength.

Dinner eaten, dishes cleaned, and my pussy thoroughly pounded, I pour Elijah a drink. My head is buzzing, my adrenaline spiking as I wait—rather impatiently—for Elijah to drop off to sleep. I fidget, wringing my hands together as we sit in front of the TV watching a predator pick off victims one by one in a forest. A lot like something I'd do but with more ... finesse.

When his eyes start to droop, my heart picks up. He's desperately trying to keep his eyes open, but the inevitable eventually happens. Once they have fully shut, I sit there waiting an extra minute or so until I'm one hundred percent sure he's asleep.

"Elijah?" I call, poking a finger into his arm. He doesn't even flinch.

Biting my tongue with renewed energy, I jump from the couch, grabbing my bag of tricks before I head out on foot in black sweatpants and hoodie. I jog, making what's usually a thirty-minute walk in twenty before creeping around to the back of Bitchface's house. At her back door, I glance around to make sure there are no cameras before I bend down to pick her lock. All the lights are off, and considering it's after midnight during the week, I'm guessing everyone is in bed.

Lock picked, I hesitantly walk through, waiting a moment just in case I hear an alarm. Luckily, there's nothing. Since most major crimes happen in the poorest areas of the city, I'm guessing everyone around here feels safe, assuming that creeps like me won't go breaking into their homes.

Fucking idiots.

With the door gently closed behind me, I take off my shoes then very slowly move up the stairs seeking out Bitchface's bedroom. After trying one room, I push the second door open to find her laying completely naked on her bed, her sheets cast aside next to her. The room illuminated just enough for me to see, which is exactly how I want it.

I step in then prowl around the bed, my eyes trailing from the blonde hair splayed against her pillow to her extra-large breasts which are sticking up to the ceiling but also drooping slightly to the sides. Her big nipples, which are not even erect yet, are a dark pink, small brown areolae cocooning those perfect little pebbles of hers. She moans softly, her breathing shallow as she sleeps. She licks her lips, her legs parting to show me her bare pussy. I inspect the area, seeing that she's had a bikini wax recently. There's not a hair to be seen.

Her pussy glistens slightly with her moisture, and her clit is hidden away ... for now.

I have always admired the female form, but I've never seen one up close like this in the flesh, completely bare and completely submissive to me.

Standing at the head of the bed, my hand darts out, caressing her left breast and marveling as her nipple becomes erect against my touch. Between my finger and thumb, I pinch it slightly, her soft moan coated with need. As I continue caressing her breast, her leg darts up then falls to the side so she's open farther as if in invitation, her back arching like she's seeking more.

"Elijah," she moans out, obviously dreaming about him. The dumb bitch is desperate for a man I won't let her have. Ever. He's mine.

All mine.

And this is the night when she will learn this.

My other hand on the voice recorder, I press PLAY, allowing Elijah's soft voice to fill the air. "Do you like that?"

Her eyes fling open, and she takes in my darkened form, my head completely covered by the hoodie. "Elijah?" she gasps, her eyes wild with fear and trepidation.

"Yes," plays the sound of his voice, having anticipated that she would ask this.

"What are you doing here?" she asks groggily.

Again, as predicted, I hit play so she can hear him tell her he wants her.

Unbeknownst to Elijah, I have been making recordings of our times together and have meticulously pieced together things he said for me to use tonight.

A smile reshapes her lips as her hand darts out to touch me. I step back, playing the next part. "Lie down, hands above your head, and close your eyes. I have a surprise for you."

Her mouth parts, no doubt unable to fathom that he's here, so I play the next part.

"You're my fantasy. This is my fantasy. Hands above your head. Eyes closed."

It took a while to piece together those parts, but it works. She lies down, her smile wide. "Wow, Elijah. You don't know how long I've dreamed of this moment."

"I want to touch your body. It's fucking perfect."

Bitchface moans before diligently placing her hands above her head, her eyes closing. As quickly as I can, I delve my hand into my bag and pull out some rope and an old tie that Elijah never wears. I secure the tie over her eyes, and she licks her lips in sweet anticipation as I tie her wrists to the bed.

"Perfect," Elijah's voice says, the wanton tone unmistakable.

"I'm going to make you come so hard, baby," his voice whispers, causing her to wriggle with need. I graze a hand over her nipple again, another soft moan leaving her lips.

With the two sets of rope, I play with her nipples a little, brushing them over and over her stiff nubs.

"Fuck, Elijah, that feels so good. I want your cock inside me. Fuck me hard like you know I want it."

Eyebrow raised at her words, I stop teasing her with the rope, using it to securely tie each hand to her bed. I straddle her waist, her hips darting up to meet me. Such an eager little beaver she is.

Taking my time, I caress her breasts more, the need to dart my tongue out and lick them all too consuming.

"You're driving me crazy," she groans, a shameless growl leaving her lips.

I suppose I did tell her I wanted to taste her nipples, so why not? She's certainly not going to tell anyone.

Bending down, I flick my tongue over her nipple, flattening it with my tongue then watching as it hardens before suckling on the solid nub again. She moans and again lifts her hips, seeking out her release. She fucking loves what I'm doing to her, and I love it too. What makes this even more entertaining is that she has no clue that it's me driving her crazy.

"Please," she begs as I continue taking my time with her breasts. They really are quite phenomenal. I'll give her that. "I need to come so badly, baby."

Watching her squirming like this because of me is making me want to come, too, so I guess we both have a problem.

Bitchface lifts her hips again, seeking me out. I'm tempted to give her what she wants, but even I know that's going a step too far. Elijah would kill me if he knew I was suckling on the DAs nipples like they're my favorite brand of lollipop.

Still with her nipple in my mouth, I move my hand up, unhooking the tie that's around her eyes. Because of the hoodie over my head, I can't see her, but she can't see me either.

"Oh, fuck, that feels good. Please, Elijah. I need to come so badly."

Intrigued to find out how wet she really is, I slide my hand down between her legs, coating my fingers with her wetness.

She's fucking soaked.

"Holy fuck!" she screams as my finger surrounds her erect clit. "I'm going to come!"

Seriously?

I want to laugh so hard, but I don't even have time to think about that as her body stiffens and quakes, goosebumps riddling her whole body as she screams her release.

It's at that moment, I glance up, her eyes meeting mine as I shove the hoodie off. I smile brightly at her shocked expression. Although her wide eyes tell me she's completely astonished, she's still riding out her orgasm.

"How do you like that, Bitchface?" I sneer before grabbing the pillow next to her and placing it over her head. "Those voices you heard of Elijah," I tell her as she desperately thrashes beneath me. "That was of him speaking to *me* like that. And do you want to know why?" She's still twisting and jerking for her life, but I keep a firm hold on her. "Because he loves fucking me and only me. He would never dare touch a bitch like you."

Becoming a little breathless from holding her down, I stop talking so I can concentrate on the task at hand. After a few more seconds of her body jerking, she stops altogether, her body relaxing, her life gone.

Taking a much-needed, deep breath, I remove the pillow from her head, her dead eyes meeting mine.

"Well, that was certainly unexpected," I say to her lifeless body. "But I guess you deserved one last orgasm before you died, so I'll give you that." I throw my leg over and slide off the bed. "Elijah would be so angry with me, though." I pause a moment. "Do you think it's cheating if I make someone come as opposed to someone making me come?" I glance to her face as if she'll answer me, giggling when I realize I'm actually talking to myself. I'm still pondering this as I untie her wrists from the bed and wipe her down with disinfectant wipes.

I take my time cleaning as much as I can, wiping away any evidence that I was here before creeping downstairs and out through the back door.

I slowly jog to Justin's hardware store, using my set of keys to let myself in. I remove everything I used tonight along with what I'm wearing then place it all in the burn barrel. I sit in my new sweatpants and hoodie, smoking one of Justin's cigarettes as I watch everything burn, eventually turning to cinders. I then leave, jogging all the way home where I quietly let myself back in the house, just in case Elijah's awake. With the amount of sedatives in his system, he should be out for at least another three or four hours.

Dropping my bag in my usual spot, I tiptoe into the living room, finally releasing my breath when I See Elijah exactly where I left him in front of the TV, out for the count The movie *Inside Man* flashes on screen, so I pick the remote up, switching it off.

My eyes flick back to Elijah, his head to the side as he peacefully sleeps. I'm still buzzing with adrenaline after my encounter, so I'm desperate for some form of release.

Damn, I never realized killing people could make me so ... well, horny.

Licking my lips, I pull down my pants then straddle his bare leg, positioning my clit against his warm skin. Once situated, I ride his leg hard until I come apart, collapsing on top of him.

He doesn't even stir.

Pulling my sweatpants up, I cuddle up next to Elijah, resting my head in the crook of his neck where I, too, fall into a lovely, restful sleep.

CHAPTER TWENTY-NINE

ast

I've been sitting outside for the last ten minutes as my teachers and Elijah talk about my "behavior" in school today. Of course it was Elijah who came—it's never my own mother. I don't think the school even knows I have one.

Realizing that Adam's probably still waiting for me, I quickly text him that something's come up and to go home without me.

The door sliding open next to where I'm sitting causes my head to snap in that direction. Mrs. Harris places one step forward, just enough to greet me. She offers a small smile before speaking.

"Bryce, would you like to come in now, please?"

I know it's not a question, so I get up, accepting whatever fate they want to hand out, expecting it to be at least a suspension.

Taking up every chair except one, are six teachers and Elijah, all silently watching me as I take the only available seat next to Elijah. His stare burns me, his irises blazing like the hottest purple flames. I hold his stare until I take my seat, which is when Mr. Shrouder speaks.

"Bryce," he starts, sighing like he's already ready for bed. "Your behavior today was not only totally out of character, but also completely unacceptable. Do you have anything to say in regard to what you did today?"

I purse my lips before I reply. "I think you all already know the reasoning behind what I did."

"Bryce," Elijah warns, obviously unimpressed by my sarcastic tone.

I give him the evil eye before returning my gaze back to my principal. He hesitates a moment before he continues speaking. "Your stepfather came to us a few weeks back, saying it would be a good idea for you to continue your studies at home." I snap my head to Elijah. He did what? "We all spoke about it, but we thought you had been coping well these past few weeks. You seemed happier than you had been in ages, so we felt, although you're more than capable of completing your studies at home, that it would be better for you socially to remain at school. However," he continues, his eyes moving towards Elijah. "Today, I believe your stepfather was correct. You've already got a college ready credit, so it's completely doable."

I've already told Elijah that I don't want to be at home any more than necessary. I certainly don't want to be there with my mother around.

"I would much prefer to continue here at school."

Mr. Shrouder glances towards the other teachers before he speaks. "It's not an option, Bryce. After your behavior today, you're lucky I'm not expelling you. You're also lucky that I spoke briefly to the boys you targeted, and they're not pressing charges."

"And you all feel this way?" I ask, my eyes scanning each teacher before they land on Miss Pashmore. I zero in on her, and she looks down at her hands.

Yeah, she knows. I haven't forgotten our little encounter after school, and neither will she.

"Yes, we all think this will be for the better. I appreciate that you haven't had the best of times at this school, it's a topic Elijah and I have had many conversations about—"

I puff out a burst of laughter, causing him to abruptly shut his mouth. "You all watched as I was picked on, tripped, called every name under the sun, and you all did fucking nothing!"

"Bryce!" Elijah scolds, causing me to snap my head his way.

How dare he condemn me and not them? How fucking dare he!?

"Well, seriously, what do you expect?" I ask, flinging my hands in the air. "They," I point my finger towards the teachers, "didn't do a thing to help me all these years, so I decided the only person who could was me. Those assholes deserved every fucking thing they got, and they all know it."

My eyes assess all the teachers, and sure enough, they all have the same guilty expression.

"Go and wait outside," Elijah commands.

"Are you just going to let them—"

"Go. And. Wait. Outside."

The warning in his tone and eyes holds me captive for a moment. I don't think I've ever seen him so angry.

Well, fuck him.

Snatching my bag from the floor, I stomp to the door. "Okay, so you want me gone. I can't say that I'll miss any of you. I hope you have a nice life, assholes."

The words, "and fuck you," are on the tip of my tongue, but I hold them in. I've already acted childish enough for one day.

I fling my body onto the seat, my bag thumping with it. "Fuck this shit," I say out loud to no one. Leaning my head back against the wall, I close my eyes and try to contain my breathing. I went in to this day knowing I could get caught and knowing that the consequences would be my expulsion, but I didn't care. If they had tried to expel me, I would have threatened to go to the press to tell them all about the teacher's lack of care for students. Sitting out here now after that, it's still tempting, but I just want to be done with this place. My one and only annoyance is that I'll be stuck at home. I guess the library plus my little bookkeeping jobs will be seeing a lot of me from now on. I certainly won't miss school. I'll miss seeing Adam every day, though.

I sigh, thinking more about that. Maybe it's for the best I don't see Adam every day. He's starting to get a little too close anyway. Maybe the separation will do us both some good.

A raised voice startles me, so I sit up, trying to figure out who is saying what, but these doors are way too good at muffling sound. The door handle turns, causing me to jolt back, and then out steps Elijah, his forceful gaze landing on me.

"We're going home," he simply states, shutting the door behind him.

He marches off, so I follow quickly behind him to the parking lot, my bag clutched to my chest. When we get in the car, nothing is said. It's only when we're on the road and the silence kills me that I decide to say something first.

"I'm not going to say I'm sorry."

Elijah's jaw tics, and without any warning, he swerves the car so violently that the tires screech in complaint. Car horns blare behind us, but Elijah ignores them, focused on slipping the car off the road onto an old, abandoned, dusty parking lot. Once he brakes, he puts the car in park and gets out. I'm so stunned by what the fuck's going on that all I can do is wait and watch to see what his plans are.

My door is opened with a violent pull, and then he's unclipping my seatbelt. He grabs my arm, hoisting me up and making me squeal.

Fucking hell, he's going to kill me!

That's the only thought I have in my mind as he grabs my arms and thumps my body against the passenger door, his eyes as blazing hot as I've ever seen them.

His hands latch onto my face and before I can even register what's happening, he brings my lips to his in such a hard, possessive kiss that my teeth bite into his lip, drawing blood. It's the most domineering, erotic thing I've ever experienced.

But just as quickly as it started, he ends it, my shock surely evident on my face. "You're scarily fucking brilliant, do you know that?"

Gasping out loud because I certainly wasn't expecting that, I stutter. "Wh ... what?"

"What you did today ... the way you planned it all out on your own. You're fucking brilliant."

I laugh out loud. "What ... you're not mad at me?"

He frowns. "Fuck no! I'm mad at that fucking school for not doing their duty."

I suck in a breath, unable to fully breathe because out of everything I could have expected, this certainly isn't it.

And he kissed me! Fuck, he kissed me! I know it wasn't a proper kiss with tongues or anything like that, but he still landed his lips to mine. Shit, I don't think I'll be able to think about anything else for weeks now—despite the fact that I still hate him.

"I thought you'd be mad at me."

Elijah smiles, but it's not a throwaway smile. It's a melt your heart and panties type of smile. "You think so badly of me, Bryce, and it's so unwarranted."

"You keep saying that," I protest.

"You'll find out soon enough."

I roll my eyes. "You keep saying that too."

"It's true." His eyes motion towards his car. "Get in. I need to figure out some sort of punishment for you once we get home."

Indignant, I cross my arms. "Hey, you just said how brilliant I was for thinking up and executing my revenge on those shits at school. How can you possibly punish me now?"

He smirks, shrugging a shoulder as he opens the driver's door. "I wouldn't be doing my duty as a parent if I didn't punish you is some way." Then he does something that completely explodes my heart. He winks at me. "Get in the car, Bryce."

Unable to form words, I do as he orders, completely robbed of speech as well as breath. I feel like I'm glued to my seat like it's a part of me as we continue our journey home.

"Was that all of it?" he suddenly asks out of nowhere.

Baffled, I respond. "What do you mean?"

"Your revenge, Bryce. I need to know if you have anything else planned." His jaw is rigid, awaiting my response.

"Why? Are you worried you're on my shit list?"

"So there is a list?"

"Maybe," I respond, playing the game. He flits his eyes to me for a fraction of a second, catching my smirk.

"I'm serious, Bryce. Tell me."

"Why, so you can prepare yourself for the storm?"

"I just don't want you doing something I know you'll regret later."

I scrutinize him for a moment, unable to figure out what his angle is. He's hiding something. That much is certain.

"You're not next, if that's what you're worried about. My mother is certainly higher on my list than you. And I want the fucker who stole my innocence."

He doesn't say anything for a moment, just stares out the windshield. I catch the tiny hint of a smile, but he quickly hides it. "I thought as much," he finally responds. "Robert Jamison."

Not having a clue who that is, I respond, "Who the hell is that?"

"When we get home, look him up."

Intrigued, I want to ask him more, but I know he's not going to offer anything further. "So you're not planning on punishing me by taking my internet privileges, at least."

His mouth twists up. "I think I'll allow it on this one occasion."

I shake my head on a smile, and when he catches it, his face lights up too.

At home, Elijah sends me to my room, his feet padding behind me as I ascend. Once I reach my room, I sit on my bed with Elijah standing in the doorway.

"You're grounded, young lady."

Like a petulant child, I cross my arms in front of me. "For how long?"

He hesitates a moment. "Until you learn the error of your ways."

"Which will never happen," I scoff.

"Well, then. I guess you're going to be stuck at home for a very long time."

He's about to shut my door when I say, "If you keep me inside this house, I will kill her." And I'm deadly serious which I think he can tell by my determined expression.

"I'll take my chances," he answers, shutting the door behind me. When the lock clicks, I snap my head to the door, rushing to it

"Motherfucker!" I shout.

He's fucking locked me in my own room!

I'm stewing over the fact that he locked me in and that I no longer have the key for this side for what feels like ages, just standing here, staring at the door like it will somehow magically unlock itself. Dropping my bag to the floor, I slump onto my bed and sigh. What the fuck am I supposed to do with myself now? I'm still pumped from today with no outlet. It's going to drive me fucking crazy.

When my eyes land on my laptop on my desk, I remember the name Elijah gave me in the car. Wanting to know what that's all about, I sit down at my desk and open my laptop. I wait for it to load, then I pull up Google, typing in the name Robert Jamison. A local newspaper article pops up from several months ago.

Man found dead in what police are saying is a gangland slaying.

Heart thumping, I click on the link and begin reading.

A man we now know is Robert Jamison was found dead on Sunday after his parole officer, Dale Wishmore, made several attempts to contact him. When Mr. Jamison failed to turn up for his appointment, Mr. Wishmore immediately phoned the police. When they arrived at Jamison's home, what they were greeted with was like something out of a horror movie.

Mr. Jamison was found on his bed, his throat cut, with his penis sewn to his head. Authorities immediately questioned surrounding neighbors, but so far, there are no suspects. Police say that Mr. Jamison was a known criminal who dealt in drugs and prostitution as well as an array of other crimes. "The investigation is ongoing," Elijah Hawthorne, Deputy Chief of Kentucky Police said in an interview with JBC News. "We have no suspects yet, but we will be looking in to the possibility that this was a revenge killing by another gang member. If anyone has any information, they should contact the Kentucky State Police Department at 502-782-1800."

Heart now well and truly in my mouth, I scroll down to find a photograph of this Robert Jamison. When my eyes meet the man who violently took my virginity all those months ago, nausea rises and burns my throat. Unable to stand to look at him anymore, I close the website page and shut the lid of my laptop with a thump.

What does this mean?

My head scrambles to come up with a reasonable explanation, but there's really only one logical possibility. His dick was cut off which suggests this was more than just a gang killing.

This was *revenge*.

At this point, everything comes crashing down on me all at once. Elijah hadn't covered it all up because he was embarrassed by how he would look if it got out. He covered it up because deep down, he'd planned... He knew he was going to kill him.

That's what he's been trying to insinuate all this time. He isn't the bad guy in this. My hate towards him isn't warranted. Because he cared enough to kill for me.

It's right then, in this moment, that I realize the reason why I was born ... why I was put on this earth over sixteen years ago.

For Elijah.

It's always been Elijah.

CHAPTER THIRTY

resent

Several weeks pass by and the shit has really hit the fan.

Bitchface's body was found the evening after she failed to turn up for work or answer any of her calls. Elijah has vowed that justice will be served, yada, yada, fucking yada.

He told me they suspect it was a disgruntled criminal she'd sent away. Considering there're so many, I am sure it will take them a lot of time to narrow them all down. Apparently, she was hated in the criminal world.

However, Elijah has been watching me. He doesn't realize I've noticed, but I definitely do. I can practically see the cogs rotating around in his head, wondering if it was really me. He certainly knows I'm capable. He hasn't said anything, and unless he brings it up, I will keep being the pretty little thing who makes him dinner and bakes scrumptious treats for him to eat. I even brought a few more batches of cookies to the station after her death, telling them all how sorry I was to hear the news. Inside, I was laughing. Inside I was joyous. She is one less bitch to worry about. One less obstacle in my way of having Elijah all to myself.

I attended Frank's funeral to say my last goodbye. Besides the priest saying a prayer as he laid Frank's body by his wife's grave, I was the only one in attendance. Elijah was planning on going, but an unexpected call from work telling him that Bitchface wasn't answering her phone had him sprinting out the door. His actions made me even happier that I done her in. She certainly doesn't deserve all this fuss, that's for sure.

While Elijah was at work today, I checked the mailbox where I received another vomit-inducing love letter from Johnathan. I responded with equal amounts of vomit-inducing gushing in return. After mailing it, I came home, crossing off yet another day on my calendar. Once done, I sit back, looking at the date that I deliberately haven't marked and smile.

Not long to go now.

Not long till *everything* changes.

CHAPTER THIRTY-ONE

ast

After feeding me this morning, Elijah locked me in my room then went to work. I knew my mother was in the house because I could hear her fumbling about, no doubt trying to find any money or jewelry she can pawn off to feed her ever-growing addiction.

Yesterday, I figured out a way to escape my room. Acting like the typical teenager that I am, I sneak out of my window, easily stepping out onto the awning over our back patio. From here, all I have to do is hang down then drop onto the patio table. Piece of cake. The tricky part will be pulling myself up later to get back in, though, so I tied a sheet to one of the slats. Hopefully it'll help me climb back up later.

I carefully drop down onto my belly then hang my legs over the edge before dropping down onto the table. Moving too quickly, my stomach scratches against the wooden awning on the way down.

"Fuck!" I hiss, clutching onto my stomach after I land with a little thud, almost twisting my ankle. Grimacing, I clamber down from the table then pull my hoodie up, inspecting my stomach. There're around six scratches and a little blood, but thankfully it's not too bad. I'm sure they'll hurt like a bitch later, though.

I climb the steps up to the back door then peep through the window to see if I can find my mother. She's not there.

I quickly let myself in then tiptoe towards the hallway. On my way, I hear the front door click shut, so I run to the window to check out front, and sure enough, she's walking down the street.

As fast as I can, I check the drawer where I hid some money and as expected, it's gone. Confirmed, I rush to the front door, close it behind me, then race after her to follow her.

Wearing a blue coat with a hood, her head hangs down, hands in her pockets as she scurries down the street like she's on some sort of mission. I deliberately keep a safe distance so she won't catch me. I highly doubt she'd look behind her even if I was close; she has money in her pocket to burn, and I bet it's scolding her hand more and more with each step she takes towards her destination.

After almost thirty minutes, we enter the poorer area of town, the kind of place you know to never visit alone at night. The kind of place decent folks would never even dare enter no matter what time of day it is.

She crosses one street, entering another. I slow down when I spot three men sitting on the front steps outside a dirty looking house. My mother approaches them, her steps quickening as she does. She says something to them then takes something out of her pocket to show them. One of the guys—an overweight, white guy with a bald head and tattoos all over his face—nods his head, taking the money from her. He waves her up, and she practically skips up the steps of the nasty looking house.

She disappears inside, so I turn around to walk home. As soon as I turn, I bash into a young girl, about my age with pixie-styled blonde hair and light blue eyes. She's chewing gum behind her ruby red lips, a small scar right beside her left eye.

"I'm sorry," I quickly apologize, going around her and heading off.

"You don't belong here," she snarls, causing me to stop dead in my tracks. I'm thinking she's being an asshole, so I'm about to call her one when she says, "This part of town isn't safe, sweetheart. You're lucky you bumped into me and not someone else."

Realizing she's not a douche, I point to the men that my mom just spoke to. "Do you know who those guys are?"

Her eyes move to the men sitting on the steps, her jaw ticcing with anger. "Unfortunately, yeah. The big guy, he recently took over for his brother after he got murdered a few months back. The other two sell drugs to the kids in the park. They're fucking scumbags. I wouldn't have anything to do with them if I were you. There're much better assholes to buy your drugs from." Her eyes trail from my head to my toes. "You don't look like you do the hard stuff."

I wonder for a moment how to answer, but then I realize this is the opportunity I need to get the ball rolling. "I don't, but my mother does. She's sick at home and in a lot of pain. She tried to get through the withdrawal, but she literally begged me to go buy some stuff for her."

Pixie girl offers me a sympathetic smile. "I'm sorry you have a shitty mom."

Tell me about it.

"It is what it is. I'm just hanging in there and waiting until I'm eighteen. Social services has been threatening to take me and my younger brother away, so we've been trying to get her cleaned up. It's been hard, though."

She closes the distance between us, placing an arm over my shoulder. "I may be able to help you out."

I frown. "How?"

"I'm a bit of a pothead. I won't do anything stronger than that, but I regularly smoke weed. I can contact my dealer and see if he can help you out. I don't think he sells anything stronger, but I'm sure he'll have a contact who does. All I know is ... it won't be those guys," she shakes her head, pointing towards the men on the steps. "They're fucking dangerous, chica. Don't go near them."

My eyes return to the supposedly dangerous men before I glance back, nodding my head. "If you could do that, I would really appreciate it."

~

Three hours later, I'm standing on the patio table, holding my bedsheet, ready to climb back up. I'm also armed with the shit I need for later. I had been weary of pixie girl, who I quickly found out is named Trix, but she was as genuine as they come. She was right in that her dealer couldn't help out, but he did know someone who could. He put her in touch with the person, and within an hour, I had the stash I needed. I had thanked her, offering her money for her help. She refused, but she gave me her number just in case I wanted to hook up with her one day. Maybe in another life I would.

With the stuff safely tucked into my bra, I climb the sheets which takes a while considering I have zero upper body strength.

Man, I need to exercise more.

Hoisting myself up as much as I am able, I press my feet on the awning post to try to help pull my heavy body along with my arms. It's awkward and takes a while, but I manage to get on top of the awning, collapsing in a heap and panting once I'm there.

"Fuck," I mutter, pushing my hands against the awning, my jelly arms barely able to take my weight. I untie the sheet, pulling it up, then wrapping it under my arm before yanking up my window. Carefully, I place one foot inside and then the other, slipping in until my ass hits the floor.

"Shit." I'm going to have all sorts of scrapes and bruises later.

"Did you have fun?"

Heart in my mouth, my head snaps to Elijah who's sitting on my bed, his eyes blazing purple fire.

He takes in my crumpled state and sighs. "Where have you been?" He concentrates on picking bits of fluff off his pants, awaiting my answer.

Deciding to counterattack instead of thinking an excuse, I ask, "Why do you keep me prisoner in my own damn room?" I wait until he glances back up at me, and when he does, I fold my arms in front of me.

"I told you I was going to look out for you, and this is my way of doing it. You're a danger to yourself—and to others, apparently."

Wondering if he's referring to the threat I made on my mother's life, I reply, "My mom isn't in the house, so that's bullshit."

Elijah simply rises off my bed, closing the distance between us. He towers over me by at least seven inches, his arms bulging as he flexes each bicep. His eyes narrow, his penetrating stare making heat surge through me. It makes me wonder if he could eventually make me come if he stared at me long enough.

"Your mom was in the house before I left. Besides," he continues, his eyes trailing down to my chest before meeting my eyes again. "You've been out, so how do you know she isn't here?"

My mind scrambles for an excuse, but I manage one quick enough. "I heard her leave. She was very loud about it too."

Elijah studies me a moment, no doubt trying to figure out if I'm lying or not. "Do you know where she is?"

I huff. "Isn't she where she'd normally be? Out getting fucked up."

"There's no money in the house."

I throw my hands in the air. "Maybe she managed to find someone who will give some shit for a bit of pussy. I don't fucking know."

He scrutinizes me again, making me nervous. "You're hiding something."

"Ha!" I let out. "Says the guy who hid the fact that he murdered my rapist from me for weeks."

A small quirk of a smile emerges, but it's gone as quickly as it appears. "Those are some serious allegations, Bryce. Got any evidence to prove that theory?"

I step forward, my confidence growing a little now. I droop my eyes, staring at his full lips before I trail them back up. "I don't," I whisper back huskily. "But you and I both know the truth, and that's all I need. I don't need your words, Elijah. Your actions speak volumes."

Elijah's mouth parts slightly, his warm breath fanning my face. "Does this mean I'm off your shit list?"

I smile, because fuck, I can't help myself. "I guess so," I shrug. "But keep me locked up in my room like I'm fucking Rapunzel, and you may just end up back on there."

His eyes light up with his smile, making my panties soak with need. The moment I'm done with my mother, Elijah will be mine.

"I know you're up to something, young lady." His voice is so low and gravelly, it causes my pussy to throb.

Placing my finger against his pale blue shirt, I tease back, "That's for me to know and for you to find out."

Elijah laughs, shaking his head. "You've changed so much, Bryce. It's like you're a different girl."

I think this is actually the real me, I've simply been hiding her all this time. Still, I don't correct him. "Ah, you love it. Go on, admit that you do."

He twists his mouth, trying his hardest not to smile again. "Fuck if I should be encouraging this."

He's encouraging this because secretly he fucking loves it. "Too late. You already let that little secret out once you told me how brilliant I was the other day."

"Don't get smug. It doesn't suit you."

I bite my lip, and my belly flutters when his eyes land on my mouth. "I think you love it when I go all smug." I've entered the territory of flirting, but Elijah seems to be coaxing it out of me somehow.

His sunken, smokey eyes turn from hot to suspicious in a fraction of a second. "You've successfully managed to distract me, and considering I'm an officer of the law, I should be fucking ashamed of myself."

I fake tut. "So you should be. But then so should I, considering I wasn't one hundred percent successful in er ... distracting you."

He sucks in a breath. "Don't, Bryce," he warns.

I frown back. "Don't, what?"

He steps forward, so I step back. He continues stepping forward until eventually, my back hits my bedroom wall. He searches my eyes, the heat of them burning a hole in my panties. "You know exactly what you're doing. This is very dangerous, unprecedented territory you're entering. Cut it out now before you lose any last remaining sweetness you have left."

I pop my mouth open. There's no way I'm heeding his warning. "Oh, I'm sweet as fucking American pie, Elijah. All tasty and succulent, leaving you aching for more. So. Much. More." My voice is husky and dripping with need, leaving no doubt on the table that I want him.

Unfortunately for me, he doesn't play along.

"You still haven't told me where you were."

Disappointed by his change in tactic, I glance away from him before I answer. "I just felt like taking a nice walk to the park, that's all."

He starts shaking his head before I even finish speaking. "I checked the park, and you weren't there. Try again, and this time, sound a little more ... convincing."

I take in a breath before I answer. "I wanted to study a little, so I headed to the library."

He shakes his head again, sighing. "Tried there, too, and nobody had seen you. Try again."

I throw my hands in the air. "What do you want from me?!"

Placing his hand on the wall right next to my head, he leans in until our lips are inches apart. I suck in a breath as wetness literally pools between my legs. This man could start a fire with his own damn eyes, they're so potent.

"I want you to tell me the truth."

Joining him in this staring match, I respond. "Why should I tell you anything? You're already locking me in my room. I don't want to find out what else you could possibly do to me."

Without warning, I'm spun around to face the wall, my hands forced to press against the cold, hard surface. With his body pressed against mine and his arms now following a trail as he searches me, I close my eyes. My breathing becomes shallow, because by fuck, this is the most erotic thing I have ever encountered.

"Where are they, sweetheart?" he growls in my ear as his hands splay under my armpits and trail around the sides of my breasts.

I can't help it. Despite worrying he's going to find what I stuffed beside my left nipple, I let out a soft moan.

"Where's what?" I somehow manage to reply.

His hand caresses my back before wandering around to my belly. My breath rushes from me, my heart thundering in my ears.

"The drugs you bought. Where are they?"

How the fuck does he know?

His hands land on my hips, and when both of them roam to my lower belly, mere inches away from my pussy, I moan out loud.

"I don't know ... what you're ... talking about," I pant.

Those same hands glide down each one of my legs, slowly and meticulously. "Take off your shoes."

His voice is so commanding that I do as he says, my hands still splayed against the wall. I need it just to support me I'm so turned on.

Shoes off, I turn my head and watch as he inspects them, obviously finding nothing. "Where is it?" he demands again, the side of his face brushing mine.

"How could you possibly know I bought drugs?"

His laughter rumbles in my ear causing my body to hum. "You don't think I have eyes on you?"

Fuck.

He's ruffled me, so I'm not going to bullshit anymore. However, I am going to play with him a little. "Inside my pussy." I smirk just as his head pops up to witness it.

"You really think I won't go in there?"

Fuck! Yes, please! God, yes!!

"You really think I'll stop you?"

"Bryce," he warns again.

"Elijah," I taunt back.

He's silent for a moment, only our heavy, hot breaths filling the room. He's not pressing his front to my back anymore, which makes me wonder why. Is he as turned on as I am right now?

He looks hesitant to say something else, so I decide to push him a little further. "Go on, I dare you. Search inside me, and feel how fucking wet I am."

His fingernails grip the sides of my hips, causing me to yelp in surprise. I stay still, my hands remaining fixed to the wall, waiting in anticipation for what he'll do next. When he digs his fingers into my hips, I groan again.

"Fuck!" I shout, my voice quivering with a violent passion. At this point, I'm not past begging.

Elijah answers by growling in my ear, his hardened cock pressing against my ass. I moan again. Shit, I need his cock so fucking badly.

"Don't push me, Bryce. I'm asking you nicely."

He's not, but hey ... tomayto tomahto.

"And I'm telling you where the drugs are. It's up to you to figure out whether you want to see for yourself." Closing my eyes, I deliberately rub my ass against his hardened cock, almost coming in my pants when he releases a moan.

"Stop!" he barks out, gripping my hips again. "I'm not going to find anything in there, am I?" His voice is low and gravelly, causing the hairs on my skin to prickle. "You just want to be a fucking slut."

His harsh words only cause my need to escalate that much higher. "Yes, but only *your* slut, Elijah. I only want *you* to touch me. I only want *you* to fuck me."

"That's enough!" he scolds, but the wavering in his voice does nothing to make me think he actually does want this to stop. I think he likes the idea of me being his slut to do with whatever he damn well pleases.

The heat from his body is lost as he steps back, causing me to turn around. I watch as his back retreats towards the door, his fists clenched beside him. Under different circumstances, I would take off all my clothes and let him see me completely naked for the first time ever. However, he's right about one thing: I am hiding drugs. And he's also right that they're nowhere near my pussy.

He reaches the door and is about to shut it when I say, "It will happen one day, Elijah. You can't fight fate, no matter what you do. I'll be your whore one day. Just you wait."

I'm thinking he's going to refute, deny that it will ever happen, but he doesn't. Instead, he simply shuts the door. I listen for the lock, but it never clicks. The fact that he didn't lock me in makes me nervous. Is he trying some reverse psychology shit on me?

Deciding not to dwell on it, I pull out the drugs from my bra then hide them beneath a loose floorboard under my bed. I then rush to the door and try opening it just to see if I'm right about him not locking me in. To my delight, it turns.

I walk out onto the empty landing. The only sound I hear is

running water from Elijah's bathroom. I tiptoe towards his room, my mind whirring and my excitement bubbling. I push his door open, revealing his empty king-sized bed which only he sleeps in since what my mom kindly did to me all those months ago.

I look towards his en suite bathroom, finding that ajar too. I walk over, then with my hand on the panel, I push it open more to reveal a bronzed, muscular god, his back to me, one hand against the wall of the shower while his other hand moves ferociously over his cock. I can't see his face, which fucking sucks, but his movements alone make what he's doing obvious.

Knowing he's probably releasing a dire need built up from our encounter makes me get to work too. Leaning against the bathroom wall, I delve my hands inside my panties and start to work my little nub, my moans bouncing off the walls along with his. His back arches, his muscles flexing with each movement as he milks his cock, desperate to find his release.

I'm right along with him.

He comes before I do, spinning around when he hears my moans. His eyes dart to mine, his cock still slightly hardened after climax. He doesn't say a word, but neither do I as I continue to work myself, the heat of his eyes causing an orgasm like no other to rip through me. Once my body finishes convulsing, I pull my hand out and lick my middle finger, eventually popping it in my mouth. His eyes never leave mine as I suck it until it pops out of my mouth. Then I turn and walk away, without a word uttered from either of us.

Elijah can deny the spark between us all he wants, but he can't hide from me much longer. He killed for me. He took a life ... all for me.

Now it's time for me to do the same in return.

CHAPTER THIRTY-TWO

ast

Elijah keeps my room unlocked, allowing me free reign of the house. I'm guessing it's because he's here, too, but whatever the reason is, I have this unwavering feeling that something's off. Maybe I'm just being paranoid, but the feeling is there.

By the time we sit down to have dinner, my mother still hasn't turned up. I hadn't thought she would. She's probably waiting it out in her little drugs den or getting fucked by God knows who while she's out cold, not even realizing her body's being used. I bet she doesn't even care.

I think back to my past before Elijah, which was a lot worse considering my dad was the one who go her hooked on that shit. When he started beating her and me, she decided to try to get her act together. She ran, taking me with her, stealing all the money she could from my dad in the process. We moved from Los Angeles to Kentucky, where my mom took a job waiting tables, trying to stay clean and start a new life with me. I've gotta admit, she did try. She even became a much better mother during that time. One day, Elijah walked into the café where she worked, and they started dating.

I was almost fourteen by then, going to the school I became to fucking hate but have always tolerated because I really did want a good education. Before Kentucky, I had missed a lot of school. They tried to put me in a lower grade, but when they realized I was brighter than a most of the kids my age, they decided against that, thank God. Still, it didn't stop the taunting and the bullying because I looked poor and uneducated. I also dressed way different which put yet another target on my back. At the time, I dressed in whatever my mother could gather together from thrift stores. I hated a lot of what I used to wear, but I put up with it because anything was better than the life I used to live back in L.A. Anything was better, period. But then, just as my mom got her life together and married Elijah, things started declining.

One evening around five months after they married, I came home from school after yet another shitty day only to walk in on my mom on the couch with another guy, both completely wasted with a needle stuck in her arm. When she bothered to pull her head up to see me—see the tears I had in my eyes—she just laughed. I turned and walked out of the house with the pain of knowing this was just the beginning. Boy, was I not wrong. Still, I can't say that her starting up that shit again was that bad. It inevitably crumbled whatever relationship she and Elijah had, ultimately bringing him and I closer together. That's definitely something I'll never grumble at.

Having just watched each other come only a few hours ago, things were kinda awkward between me and Elijah during dinner tonight. We both ate in relative silence, his brooding putting a damper on the evening. He's pissed because he knows full well that any control he has left at keeping a wedge between us won't last forever. He can't deny the pull between us. How can he when it was me he was waiting for all his life? The stars aligned, setting our paths to each other. It may have been through my mother, but ultimately it's me he belongs to. It's me he will forever belong to.

Which is why later, when we're in our beds and I hear my mother stumble through the door at three in the morning, I wait. I wait up for another hour, wondering if Elijah will go to her, question her about her whereabouts, but he never does.

Heart beating rapidly, I grab the shit I have been accumulating over the last couple of weeks then make my way down to her room. My heart is racing, but I continue my descent, clutching the drugs in my hand. Faint light illuminates my mom's room, so I cautiously push her door open. She's out cold, another needle stuck in her arm which houses purple marks from all of her abuse. Dark purple circles under her eyes match the color of her arm as she lays there, her mouth slightly parted.

Putting the contents on her bed, I place some latex gloves on then get to work, setting up the drugs I bought today. I unfortunately know exactly what to do, having watched my mother do it more times than I can count. After boiling a huge portion by cooking it under a spoon, I suck all of it into the needle I managed to steal from the drugstore I work at. It's more than she normally takes, so it should be enough to end her—especially since she's obviously already shot up enough shit as it is.

Breathing escalating at what I'm about to do, I approach her bedside to pull out the needle that's already in her arm. I place the one I made in her vein, and I'm just about to plunge the shit into her, ending her fucking miserable life when a hand reaches out, grabbing my arm.

Gasping, I look up to find Elijah, his eyes wide, his jaw clenched. "Go to bed, Bryce."

Determined, I don't release my hand. "I need to do this. I need to fucking end her pathetic fucking existence for you as well as for me. I fucking need this."

Witnessing the desperation in my eyes, he sucks in a breath, his nostrils flaring. "Once you take a life, there's no going back."

"I don't fucking care!" I bite back with a hiss.

"I fucking care," he growls, baring his teeth to me. "Go to fucking bed now, Bryce. I won't ask you a third time."

Releasing my hand from the needle, Elijah drops his hand from my arm, allowing me to take the gloves off. "Fuck you!" I seethe as I turn and walk out of the room. I don't wait for his response. I'm too fucking angry.

Taking to the steps, I angrily ascend two at a time until I reach my room, slamming the door shut behind me. I take my pajamas off and slip into my bed, my heart beating rapidly with adrenaline and rage. I'm so angry that I'm still awake an hour later, light starting to appear in my room. My door clicks open, and I don't have to look to know it's Elijah entering. His musky, cinnamon scent hits my nostrils, the electricity he exudes pulsing through the room.

Soon after he's entered, he rounds my bed, disappearing from sight before slipping in beside me. His arms wrap around my stomach, pulling me into his body, molding us together.

"I hate you," I whisper, tears threatening to sting my eyes.

A soft exhale hits the back of my neck. "I know you do."

Determination in my voice, I say, "I will kill her. You may have stopped me tonight, but you can't always be there. I promise you, Elijah. She's fucking dead."

"I know."

I'm surprised at the acceptance in his voice. So surprised in fact that it calms me. Aided by the fact he's here, snuggling up next to me, I eventually give in to sleep.

It's a few hours later when I awake to the sounds of sirens, doors opening and closing. Footsteps. Voices. Police and an ambulance at my house. I scramble out of bed, wondering what's happened.

During the night ... the night I was supposed to kill my mother, she died of a suspected drugs overdose.

CHAPTER THIRTY-THREE

resent

I must admit, I was pissed as hell at Elijah for taking my mother's life when it should have been me. We've never discussed what he did, but it's always been a niggling annoyance that never lets up. She wasn't my first victim, a fact that fucking killed me. I never hated Elijah for what he did. In fact, it only enriched the adoration I already felt for him. He killed for me. Twice. I just haven't been able to get rid of this incessant rage which constantly bubbles inside of me that I wasn't able to serve the justice she deserved. I may have set up the needle, and I even put it in her arm, but I wasn't the one who plunged the shit into her vein. I wasn't the one who watched as her life faded away until she drew her last, pathetic breath. I know Elijah did it to save me...

But you can't save the damned.

My eyes zip to the date on the calendar. The fateful day of Thursday, August 15 is practically humming off the page. All this preparation has led up to this date. "Operation Move" will hopefully take effect soon after if all goes well.

My heart skips a beat, feeling slightly nauseous at the possibilities of each outcome that today may bring. I've gone over every available possibility, all needing immediate action. If I'm quick enough, the game won't be given away, and all these months of planning won't be a waste of time.

Knowing time is of the essence, I make my way down to the basement, Elijah's gun in hand. I sit on the step, biting my nails as I check my watch what seems like every thirty seconds. I hear the door unlock, then footsteps sound along the hallway.

"Bryce!" Elijah calls out. After a few seconds of me not responding, he calls my name again. I don't answer. I can't answer. My phone vibrates in my hand, alerting me to his call, but I don't pick up. The call ends, but then it vibrates again. He's going to be so agitated that I'm not answering. He hates it when he doesn't know where I am. I don't know whether it's due to fear of what I'm doing or that he's just making sure I'm not out somewhere getting fucked by a man or having some random Duckface suck my tits.

Probably a bit of both.

Elijah curses under his breath, but my phone doesn't vibrate again. I had anticipated it would, that's why I set it to silent and vibrate. Another hour and three more calls from Elijah later, the anticipated ring of the doorbell surrounds the house, making me suck in a breath. This is when I need to act fast. This is when I really need to be fucking careful.

"Johnathan, what the fuck are you doing here? I thought I told you I would meet you later at the hotel."

Footsteps thump their way past the basement door, causing my heart to fly into my mouth. "I had to come see you now. It's important."

"Are you hurt?" Elijah asks. "Is everything okay?"

The voices trail into the living room, so I quickly get up and open the door as quietly as possible so I can fully hear what they're saying.

"Everything's not okay," Johnathan spits. "I only came so I could give you a message."

I silently emerge from the door, gun cocked and ready to take the shot.

"What message? Son, I don't know what you're talking about."

"Don't fucking call me son! I'm not your fucking son. You're just a sick, twisted, perverted cunt. You deserve nothing more than to rot in hell!"

Through the slit in the living room door, I watch Elijah holding his hands out in surrender as Johnathan—with his back to me—stands around ten feet away from him, pointing a gun in his direction.

"I don't understand what you're talking—"

And then he does it. Johnathan fires the fucking gun!

Elijah disappears from sight, and my vision blurs with anger. I almost scream, but I hold it together enough to emerge with Elijah's gun and without him seeing me enter. I aim it at the back of his head and pull the trigger.

Blood and parts of his brain splatter before Johnathan's body jerks, immediately falling down flat on his face.

"Elijah!" I scream, running towards where I saw him go down behind the couch.

This wasn't supposed to happen! This wasn't supposed to fucking happen!!

"Bryce?" Elijah rasps, his voice strained.

Thank fuck, he's alive.

I reach the back of the couch where Elijah lays clutching his left shoulder, blood oozing out and his face growing pale. I panic a moment, but then determination kicks in. "Hold on, I'll get you a towel."

He nods his head as I rush for the kitchen, along the way noticing a bag by the door that isn't ours. I grab a towel before running back to Elijah, taking a knee beside him while pressing it against his wound. He hisses in pain, his breaths uneven.

"Hold that, I'll go call 911."

Snatching the phone from my back jeans pocket, I dial 911, telling them there's been an attack in our home and now the man lies dead in our living room before hanging up. Knowing they're on their way, I kneel down beside Elijah again, taking his hand.

"Hang in there. The ambulance is on the way." He doesn't reply, just closes his eyes, nodding his head. "Who was that? Why did he shoot you?"

I'm hoping that Elijah will finally come clean to me, but he simply shakes his head. "I don't know," he lies, hissing in pain again. "I don't fucking know."

Disappointment clouds my thoughts a moment. Why he's continuing to hide shit from me, I have no idea. But I'm still reeling over Johnathan shooting Elijah so out of the blue that I can't think of anything but that right now.

"Okay," I concede, soothingly rubbing his good arm. "Just concentrate on you right now." I bite my lip, feeling a tug on my arm, so I look down.

"I'm sorry you ... had to ... do that. Fuck, this fucking hurts!"

I wince, watching him suffer. He's suffering because of me. I fucking did this to him.

Fuck!

"Don't be sorry. There was no way I was going to let him shoot you and get away with it."

"Where were ... you?"

I tsk at him. "Never mind that for now. We'll talk once you're taken care of."

Sirens sound in the distance, so I grip his hand. "I need to get up and open the door for them, okay?" Grimacing with pain, he nods his head.

I run to the door, wiping the blood from my hands onto my dress. I spot the bag again, so I quickly grab some latex gloves from under the kitchen sink before kneeling down to unzip the bag. Inside is a wallet, phone, and a hotel key. But most importantly, there are a bunch of letters wrapped up together with a piece of string.

My letters.

Glancing in the direction where Elijah is, I quickly take out the letters from Johnathan's bag and hide them under the kitchen sink for now—along with the gloves—before opening the door. An ambulance followed by three cop cars come racing down the street. Immediately, I put my hands up, waving like a crazy woman, trying to gain their attention. The ambulance screeches to a stop, and two paramedics, a man and woman, race out with all their gear.

"Please, he's inside and been shot. You have to help," I beg, anxiety gnawing away at me.

This wasn't supposed to happen!

"Where is he?" The female asks.

"In the living room," I reply, quickly turning around to race back inside.

They follow after me, bypassing the dead body on the ground. Considering half his brain is missing, they realize pretty quickly that they don't need to check his pulse, immediately racing over to deal with Elijah.

"You got yourself in quite the mess here, Chief," the male paramedic says, as he gets out a blood pressure machine and coaxes Elijah's hand away from the wound.

Elijah laughs back but winces. "Yep, I've definitely had better days."

They all laugh as the female goes to work, cutting open his shirt with scissors. "Don't you worry. We'll get you fixed up in no time."

Thudding boots pad into the room next, causing me to glance their way. Brent is here along with his blond partner and a few others I recognize.

"What happened?" Brent asks, taking in the scene in front of him, his eyes landing on a very dead Johnathan.

With a shaking hand, I point to him. "I came home to find him hollering at Elijah. When I noticed he had a gun, I quickly raced to get Elijah's so I could defend him when I heard a gunshot. As Elijah went down, I just ... fuck, I didn't think. I just pulled the trigger."

Brent's eyes widen before stepping forward and taking me into his arms. "Don't worry. You did the right thing. Your actions saved Elijah and possibly you, okay? Don't beat yourself up about it."

Normally Brent's nothing but banter, so I'm a little shocked by his sudden change in demeanor. I guess the seriousness of this fucked up situation changes things.

"You're being nice."

Brent's body vibrates with laughter, but he doesn't take his arms from me. "I can be nice when I want to be."

Glancing up, tears in my eyes, I tease him, "I don't think I like you like this."

This makes him laugh harder. "Always the alley cat, no matter what."

"That's better." I smirk back at him briefly before my attention snaps towards Elijah. "Will he be okay?"

By now they've got him bandaged up and ready to put on the stretcher. The female paramedic addresses me. "Luckily, it's just his shoulder. We've stemmed the bleeding, so he should be fine."

"Yeah, any excuse for a few days off. Huh, chief?" the blond guy jokes.

"Fuck off," Elijah snaps back, causing everyone to laugh.

"Yeah, he's definitely okay."

Brent talks into his radio, requesting forensics. He then turns to me. "Listen, you can't stay here for a couple of days because forensics is going to need to sweep and clean the scene. We can put you up in a hotel, so go on up and grab a few things. Can you change out of your dress?" He continues, pointing to it. "We're going to need to take it for evidence."

"We're taking him in," the male paramedic says. Elijah's now strapped to a stretcher, an IV already in and a clean bandage wrapped around his shoulder.

"I'll be there as soon as I can," I reply before turning my attention back to Brent. "Can you take me to the hospital once I'm ready?"

Brent smiles and nods. "Sure."

I approach Elijah, taking his hand. "I'll see you soon."

He grips my hand back. "Are you okay?"

"As long as you live then yes, I'll be fine." His lip curves up into a smile, but then he winces again. I turn my attention to the paramedics. "You'd better get him in."

I watch as they leave then quickly run upstairs to change my clothes. I grab a bag, packing a few items of clothing as well as my purse before running downstairs.

"I just need to grab something real quick," I tell Brent before rushing past him. As quickly as I can, I scurry to the kitchen, take out the letters I hid, then very carefully sneak them in my bag. I zip it all up then breathe out a much-needed exhale. Once back in the living area, I hand Brent my dress.

"Shall we go now?"

CHAPTER THIRTY-FOUR

ast

Four months ago, I buried my mother. A small affair which brought out some members of the community—most of whom were just being the fucking nosey shits that they are. Despite Elijah losing his wife, he continued going in to work as usual, quietly keeping his head down and burying himself in as much paperwork as he could. Everyone thought he was grieving over the loss of his wife and that was his way of coping.

I knew better.

He avoided me. Avoiding the inevitable coming together. He even managed to let my seventeenth birthday pass without so much as a touch of my hand.

Drastic action had to be taken.

Since my mother's passing, he has locked me in my room every single night. I know why. He's afraid I'll sneak into his room late at night and get under the covers of his bed. Of course, I would have done that, but still ... it pisses me off.

So one night I devise a plan where I wake up screaming during the middle of the night. Elijah—no doubt hearing my screams—will come to my aid, ready to tackle any possible threat.

I wait until it gets well past midnight before working myself up into a state of panic, desperate to get my eyes to water so that it all looks ... genuine.

Running my hands through my hair, I run around the room to get my heart rate up before dabbing my eyes with water for extra effect. Naked and back under the covers, I open my mouth and let out the most ear-piercing scream I can muster. Within ten seconds, the door is unlocking, and Elijah bursts through, his eyes wild as they wander around my room.

"What the fuck, Bryce!?" he shouts, running towards me.

"I had a nightmare. Dreamed that someone was in my room." The moment he sits on my bed, I throw my arms around him. "I'm so scared, Elijah. Hold me."

When his arms snake around my bare back, I nuzzle my head into the crook of his neck. His breathing is labored, no doubt from the fright I've just given him. Mine is, too, because he's holding me so close, his heart thudding against my chest.

"You scared the shit out of me," he whispers, trailing a hand through my hair.

"I'm sorry," I reply, trying to kick off my sheets so I can straddle him.

"No one's here. You're safe."

"I know. I'm safe because you're here." I breathe in his musky, cinnamon baked smell, my loins waking up and eager to ride the baloney pony. I pop my leg out and hoist myself up so I can throw that leg over his waist until I'm straddling him. I inhale his scent again, my groin reflexively rubbing over his cock. It's not hard ... yet, but the moment my naked body presses against his bare skin, his dick jumps to life.

"Bryce," Elijah warns, his hands gripping my waist.

Ignoring him, I spread kisses on the side of his neck and nibble his earlobe. "Elijah," I whisper back because I always have to say his name after he says mine.

"Stop this shit."

My lips twitch because despite him telling me to stop, he isn't physically doing anything about it. So again, I ignore him, circling my hips over the material of his boxer shorts, his cock now straining to get out.

"I want your cock inside me." My voice is a husky whisper, my words loud and clear.

Within an instant, he picks me up, spinning me around before throwing me back on my bed with a thump. He's angry, his eyes a blazing lavender as he hovers over me, his cock tenting his boxers.

"You didn't have a fucking nightmare, did you? It was just a ruse to get me into your bedroom."

I smirk up at him, spreading my legs for him to witness my bare flesh for the first time. "It worked, though, didn't it? Care to punish me for lying by making me come with your cock?"

His chest rising and falling with each breath, his eyes can't help but scan the contours of my body before landing on my very wet pussy. His nostrils flare, but then he closes his eyes.

"Looks like you lost this one, sweetheart."

He gets off the bed, turns, then heads towards the door, locking it again before his footsteps pad to his bedroom next door.

"Motherfucker!" I curse under my breath, my body still humming from our encounter. I grip my eyes shut a moment, pissed as hell, but then an idea pings in my head as I stare at my bedroom window. Bubbles of exhilaration burst in my belly as I slip out of bed and head for the window. Unlocking it, I push up the window then pop my head out. All is dark and quiet outside. Frank is probably still outside on his porch, but he's in the front yard so he can't see my window from there. And there are trees between us and the neighbors behind us, so I doubt I will be seen. Even if someone can see me, I don't fucking care. I have a rocking body, so why not put on a show?

Stepping out onto the awning, I notice all is dark in Elijah's room next door. Deciding to take a leaf out of Eddie Murphy's book, I start singing the song he sang in Coming to America "To be Loved". After the second line, a light flicks on in the house behind us, dogs barking in the distance. I'm just about to scream the, "to be loved" line, when an arm snakes around my waist and pulls me up and back through my window into my room so violently, that we both land on the floor.

Rugby tackling me, Elijah spins us around until my back is pressed to the floor, his hands pinning my wrists above my head, his breathing harsh and heavy.

"What the fuck do you think you're playing at?"

Deciding to keep up my childish antics, I poke my tongue out at him and wriggle my hips. His cock is still hard.

"You're ignoring me. I had to take drastic action to get your attention."

A muscle jumps in his cheek at my response, his nostrils flaring. However, I suspect his reaction is spurned on more by lust than anger.

"Well, congratulations, Bryce. You have my full fucking attention. Now what?"

He thinks I'm going to be taken aback by his question, but, apparently, Elijah underestimates me.

"Now you do what's been simmering on the surface between us for months." I arch my back, thrusting my heaving breasts up to him. "Go on, take one in your mouth. You know you want to."

His eyes can't help but dart to my breasts, my nipples hard and ready to receive whatever he can give. He takes in a deep inhale of breath before releasing my wrists with a grunt. Again, disappointment clouds me as he makes every effort not to look at me. Instead, he goes to my window, locks it, then starts to walk out the door.

"Go to fucking bed. I'm warning you."

His words only serve to increase my longing for him, desire spiking to extra high levels. I glance at his retreating frame, and before my brain can even engage, I'm up from the floor and running to him, jumping on his back the moment he's at the door.

"What the fuck?!" he bellows, trying to shove me off of him. It's too late, though. I have my legs wrapped around him so hard, I've almost become his second skin.

Realizing he can't physically get me off, his breaths come away in pants. "Bryce, get down from me now. I'm fucking warning you."

I smile as I press my head against his to whisper in his ear. "Do your fucking worst."

Throwing us back against the wall, he bashes me there twice until the wind is knocked out of me so much that I have no choice but to let go. I fall down into a heap, my breaths coming in gasps as my back vibrates from the impact. Instead of making me stop, it just adds fuel to my already lit fire. He wasn't violent with his moves, he didn't hurt me, but he knew just the right level of force needed to get me to drop.

Undeterred by his actions, I immediately get up, but the moment I do, a hand is placed around my neck, Elijah's eyes burning like a scorched flame as he flattens my back against the wall. All I do is smirk at him.

"I can go on like this all night," I taunt, my hand reaching out to grab his cock. My fingers wrap around his hardness, rubbing my hand up and down his shaft. The longer he just stands there letting me, the more my pussy aches for him.

His hand squeezes tighter and tighter around my neck, but it doesn't deter me. Elijah probably thinks I'm this little weakling who can't stand to be thrown around or abused. He's right, of course, but when it comes to him, I want *everything*. I want his fire, his rage, his tears, his joy, his gentleness, his violence. I want it fucking all.

"You're pushing for something that once it happens, it can't ever be undone," he growls.

I quirk an eyebrow at him. "Is that supposed to discourage me?" I'm challenging him, but I'm pretty certain he loves a good challenge.

"Bryce," he cautions, causing me to smile.

"Elijah," I bounce back.

His free hand cups my breast, kneading it in his hand before squeezing my nipple. I close my eyes, moaning at his rough touch.

"Is this what you want?!" he growls, his anger getting the better of him.

"Yes," I croak back.

The tighter he squeezes my nipple, the harder I work his cock. His breathing changes to the point that I know he's close to breaking.

"Fuck!" he hisses out, pulling me from the wall and towards my bed. There he spins me, his hand pushing me down so hard that I have to quickly fling my hands out to catch my body before I fall on the bed. He grabs the back of my neck, and that's when I feel it. The head of his cock at my entrance.

"This is what you're begging for, huh? To be fucked like the whore you are."

"Yes!"

My scream ricochets off the walls and then he slides in, his big, hard, cock filling me as I gasp out loud.

"Fuuuuuuuuuccccccccckkkkk!" he bellows, his cock hitting my womb. "You're so fucking tight."

"Fuck me!" I holler. "Fuck me hard like I know you want to!"

He doesn't disappoint. Keeping one hand possessively against the back of my neck, he thrusts forward, violent and unrelenting.

"Fucking bitch!" he grinds, grabbing and pinching my nipple, my desire spiking to new levels. He feels so fucking good and is fucking me so fast that an orgasm is bound to ripple through me at any moment. "Look what you fucking made me do."

"You made me a whore."

His breaths leave him in bursts, hips flexing inside me again and again. "Not just any whore. My. Fucking. Whore."

I moan out. "Oh, God, yes!" My body is tingling all over, my climax on the brink of letting loose.

"Say it, Bryce. Say the fucking words."

"I'm ... your ... whore," I pant.

"Say it fucking again. Louder this time."

"I'm your fucking whore ... ahhhhhhhhhh ... I'm going to come!" My body quivers and quakes with an orgasm to end all orgasms. I don't know how I'm able to hold my body up, but he continues to pound his cock into me as my body shudders under him.

"Fuck, Bryce! You're going to make me come. Fucking bitch!"

He jerks, roaring out his release inside me, his breaths uneven and deep.

Once he stills, his heaving body pressed to my back, we both take a moment, my eyes closed as I let the euphoria of my orgasm wash over me. I did it. I finally broke him.

And I've never felt so fucking good.

THWACK!

My eyes fling open at the sudden shock of his hand against my right ass cheek. The force of it so great that it catapults my body up off the bed.

"Now get to fucking bed."

Knowing he's on the move, I spin my body around just in time to catch his toned frame walking towards my bedroom door.

"Yes, Daddy," I tease back, right before he hits me with a glare and shuts the door with a violent bang.

Oh, he's mad.

Daddy's so mad that I made him fuck me.

I giggle at my sick, naughty thought as I throw myself down against my bed with a sigh, my body finally sated.

The only problem is, I know this one time will never be enough.

Now that I've had a taste of him, I won't ever be able to go without.

CHAPTER THIRTY-FIVE

resent

At the hospital waiting for news, I think back to that first night when I was finally able to get Elijah to give in to me. Too many incidences had happened between us, that same fire sizzling and humming between us. He felt it. I knew he could. That's why it was only a matter of time before he finally snapped.

That first morning after, I awoke to find him hovering beside my head, glass of water in hand, my contraceptive pill in the other. It was then that I realized he must have been rummaging through my things, no doubt spying on me to see if I was protected. After that, his control over me grew that much more—something I hadn't thought would be possible. Still, as I've said before, I don't mind. What he's never realized is that I control his life just as much. I've just always been a little more ... discreet about it.

Sitting in the waiting room, I bite my nails, anxious to hear that Elijah's okay. He's in here because of my actions, so I don't just feel anxiety but guilt too.

"Bryce Turner?" a doctor calls, my head snapping to her, my eyes wide with expectation. "It was a bit messy, but we've managed to get the bullet out. He's out of surgery and is asking for you. He's sleepy from the anesthesia, so be warned."

I nod my head, immediately getting up to follow her. "Thank you."

She smiles as she motions to the room he's in. I open the door to find Elijah laying on the bed, his chest bare, apart from the bandage round his shoulder and an IV giving him fluids. His eyes are closed, and he looks so young and peaceful. Happiness and relief flood me that he's okay. The color is back in his face again, and despite having been shot, he looks as healthy as usual.

I pull a chair closer to his bed then take his hand. "You fucking scared me a minute there."

At the sound of my voice, his eyes flutter open, his smile goofy when he sees me sitting beside him. "You're here."

I squeeze his hand. "I wouldn't be anywhere else."

"You saved my life."

My smile fades. I almost caused his death.

I'm about to tell him not to go there when he frowns. "I just ... don't get it. Why?"

His eyes dart between mine like he's seeking the answer to his question.

"I was hoping you'd be able to answer that question. Why did you let that guy into the house if you didn't know him?"

I should feel ashamed of myself for spouting all this bullshit to him. I just keep having to remind myself of the reason why. The reason for all of this.

Elijah closes his eyes and licks his dry lips. "He ... he was someone I ... arrested a few years ago. He said he just wanted to talk to me. I didn't think he would fucking shoot me."

My lips thin at his lie, but I don't call him out on it. There are so many questions I could ask, but I bite my tongue. At the end of the day, he's laying in this hospital bed because of me.

"I would suggest you don't let any known criminals in the house ever again."

He chuckles at that, but winces when his laughter causes him pain. "Yes, duly noted."

Swallowing hard, I have a burning question on my lips. A question I have been dying to ask for months but have held back until this very moment. A question that—depending on the answer—determines what course of action I take next.

"Elijah," I begin, my voice soft.

His drooping eyes flicker open, still doped up from the anesthesia. "Yes."

"Don't you think ... with all that's been happening right now that we should move? If we sell your house and Frank's house, you can get a transfer to a different state, and we can consolidate our money. Buy something special ... for us."

A crooked smile creases his face as he answers. "You wanna live with me, baby?"

I laugh at his stupid question. "Well, I kinda do now, don't I?"

When his eyes droop a little more, I silently berate myself for asking this fucking important question while he's under the influence.

"Bryce?" he asks, his eyes fully shut now.

"Yes?" I respond, hope building in my chest.

"Did you put dog poop on Mr. and Mrs. Grayson's living room floor?"

A rumble of laughter leaves me at his random question. Still, he's high, so why not be honest?

"She deserved it. Her and Duckface were trying to buy Frank's house because they didn't think it looked nice compared to the rest of the street. She put pressure on a dying man. I'm not sorry I did it."

A smile graces his lips before he sighs. "I always knew one day you'd be the death of me."

My body hunches in a grimace, because he has no clue how close to the truth his joke really is.

Exhausted from the whole day, I'm about to tell him to get some rest, but his shallow breathing tells me he's already fast asleep.

Deciding I need to leave since Brent's waiting to take me to the hotel, I get up, placing a soft kiss against his forehead. "I love you, Elijah."

It's the first time I have ever uttered those words, and despite knowing he's fast asleep, it feels good to get them out. It's supposed to be us.

Always us.

I gently stroke his face, feeling the little prickles of hair that are growing in before I kiss his hand and walk out the door. Brent is patiently waiting, a smile on his lips.

"How ya holding up, alley cat?"

I laugh at his joke but then sigh. "I've had better days, I must admit."

He closes the distance between us, his body giving us some privacy. "Listen, you already have a hotel lined up for the next two or three days, but you're welcome to stay at my place. You shouldn't be on your own after what happened today."

I smirk back at him, causing him to look surprised. "You'll do anything to get me alone, won't you?"

He snickers back at my joke, his hand placed upon his heart. "Ah, fuck. You've got me." His face then turns sincere. "Seriously, though, Bryce. You've just been through something that no eighteen-year-old woman should ever have to endure. Joking aside, the offer's there if you want it."

It gives me warm fuzzies to think that if Elijah could hear this conversation right now, he'd fucking blow his top. He would let me stay with him over his dead body—excuse the pun.

"I really appreciate that, Brent, but I'm going to decline. I think being alone right now is just what I need. Besides, I'll be surrounded by lots of people in a hotel. I won't feel alone there."

His forehead crinkles with uncertainty. "Are you sure?"

Placing my hand on his shoulder, I lean my head forward a little. "I'll be fine. I swear." Besides, I've still got something to do before I can lay my head down tonight.

He drives me to my hotel which thankfully is in the middle of town, so it's not far for me to walk to my destination. Before Brent leaves, he hands me his card, instructing me to call if I need him. He even makes me promise. It seems despite the bad boy image, there's a heart of gold in there somewhere. Either that or he really is desperate to get into my panties.

The room is adequate, the bed king size making me tempted to crawl in it now and just sleep. My body is seriously drained after today.

But like a lot of my days lately, I have shit I need to do first. So I grab my bag and quickly head out of the hotel. It's after midnight, so everything is quiet. I make the quick, ten-minute walk to the hardware store where I let myself in. I make my way to the back of the store then out to the backyard where the very handy burn barrel is.

Pulling out the letters I wrote to Johnathan, I open some of them up, reading the disgusting lies I fed him over the last few months, ultimately fueling his desire to kill Elijah.

Abuse.

Rape.

Torture.

Fear.

All those words and more that I poured into countless letters, the dirty, sick untruths that Elijah should kill me for.

As I'm throwing the letters in, one by one, I think back to the day I found out about Johnathan. You see, the thing is, Elijah can't hide anything from me. He tries, but I've made it my sole mission to know everything about him. All those times he would disappear for hours every two weeks or so had me curious, so one day I followed him to see what he was up to. I ordered an Uber while Elijah was getting ready, and we followed him to the airport. Since I couldn't tell where he was heading from in front of the airport, I told the driver to take me back home.

At home, I ransacked Elijah's bedroom, trying desperately to find any clues as to where he may have gone. I was just about to give up when I thought to run my hand underneath his nightstand, coming across a smooth envelope against my fingertips. It was a letter from the Wyoming State Penitentiary. The prison his twenty-three-year-old son was in for burglary.

When Johnathan's mom died a year ago, he decided to find then reach out to his dad, which ultimately had Elijah feeling obligated to go visit him every now and then. When I read this in the letter, I got so fucking angry that before I could even think straight, I was taking down his address and writing my own letter. I started slow and steady at first, reeling him in, his interest quickly piquing in regard to his stepsister. I sent him a fake photo of some random girl I found on the internet, a girl he eventually fell in love with as our letters became more frequent and even more intense.

One by one, I drop them in until every letter is inside the barrel. I douse them with lighter fluid then strike a match, dropping it inside, my eyes lighting up as the despicable untruths burn away, the evidence of all that's happened disappearing in beautiful, blue flames.

As they're burning, I take out one of Justin's cigarettes and light it up, inhaling that first puff that causes your eyes to close and a calm to wash over you. I sit and I smoke and I smile as I think about all that's been done and how everything is now coming together.

They say that you will do just about anything for love, and for me, that is certainly true. Now that every threat and distraction has been eliminated from Elijah's life, I can finally take him as mine. No one can fucking have him.

Least of all, his own son.

EPILOGUE

ix months later

"Go take the meat out for the barbecue. I'll grab the utensils and be right behind you."

A soft smile spreads my lips at my fiancé of only one month. I lean in, kissing him lightly, then with a husky voice, I answer, "Don't be long. I have plans or us later." I give him a mischievous wink before heading out to our new backyard, carrying said meat for the barbecue.

Outside, the sun shines, our beautiful pool glistening as its rays bounce off the water. We have only been here three days, and it's taken that long to sort out the furniture and whatnot. It's been totally exhausting but totally worth it. The house is the most incredible house I have ever encountered. With five bedrooms, four bathrooms, and a walk-in closet I could get lost in, it was a no brainer. I hadn't even seen the pool, and I already knew we had to buy it.

It was a bit tough, trying to convince Elijah to move, but in the end, he'd had so much pressure on him for not finding a suspect for Bitchface's murder. That coupled with all the bad memories the house we'd lived in possessed, I was able to convince him. "A brand-new start," I'd told him. "Somewhere we can be together and not be judged." Elijah had been wary, but then he made some tentative inquiries with other forces and hit the jackpot. He'd only put the word out that he was thinking of transferring when he had California, Florida, and even New York headhunting him to become their new chief of police. With the best pay and benefits, it was California that won out in the end. The perfect weather almost all year was a plus too. Moving had me putting Operation Baby on hold—a last ditch attempt at forcing him to move if he had dug his heels in. I'm sure he wouldn't want to stay in Kentucky knowing our baby was on the way.

Sprucing up Frank's old house a little, we placed both his and Elijah's house on the market, and within six weeks we had offers on both. I'd kept to my word and only allowed a family to purchase Frank's house—something which was easy enough considering everyone who looked at it were married couples. With the offers in, we flew to California so that Elijah could get the lay of the land at work and we could go house hunting. Our house had been the sixth one we'd looked at. I had gushed while Elijah laughed, telling the realtor that it looked like his fiancée had chosen this one. My shock was evident, considering that was the first time he'd ever mentioned anything about getting married. I asked him about it later that night, and his response was that he was still a single man despite being almost forty, so he needed to settle down—which I just laughed at. Despite moving across the country, apparently, he still felt he had to keep up with the pretenses. I can't complain, though, because it ultimately got me everything I've ever wanted. There are no obstacles in my way now. Elijah is finally mine, and in less than six months, I will become Mrs. Hawthorne. And better still, every fucker around here will know it.

I take in a deep breath, admiring our huge yard, the bright flowers, and perfectly manicured lawn. I place the meat down then turn around, wondering why Elijah hasn't come out yet.

Murmurs penetrate my ears, so I head back inside the house where the voices are coming from. I pass through our grand, modern kitchen, and down the long hallway as I creep towards the front door. Hidden by the staircase, I take a peek to find Elijah standing in the doorway, talking to a blonde woman who looks to be in her thirties, her tight green dress showing off her rounded hips and perky tits. She giggles at something Elijah says, her eyes lingering way too long on his chest, her own hand lightly dancing over hers in hopes that his eyes land there too. My eyes narrow, pure, jealous rage bubbling in my gut at this cunt's audacity. Everyone around here already knows about us. Knows that he's the new chief of police who recently moved here with his beautiful, young fiancée.

"Thank you for the blueberry muffins. I'm sure my fiancée and I will love them."

I cover my mouth to stifle a laugh. It seems we have another Duck-face on our hands. What is it with blonde women in their thirties baking blueberry muffins?

I continue watching as this bitch bites her lip seductively, the fiancée comment completely flying over that pretty, stupid head of hers. "If you ever need anything—and I mean *anything*—I'm only a five-minute drive up the road."

Elijah hangs onto the door, his body posture screaming at her to piss off. "We appreciate that. Thank you."

When her fingers dust over her breasts and she sways her hips a little, my eyes roll at her blatant flirtation. "Enjoy your barbecue now," she chirps before turning to walk away.

Just before Elijah shuts the door, I emerge, wrapping my arms around his shoulders. Elijah turns, taking me in his arms, and I snuggle my head to his chest as I watch my new, number one enemy swing her hips as she unevenly struts towards her car in her way too high pumps. She turns to gaze at our gorgeous house, no doubt also wanting to see if Elijah's still there watching her, only to find me in Elijah's embrace. Surprised, she stops dead in her tracks watching as I move my hand down to cup his ass possessively, an evil, murderous smirk coating my lips. Her eyes widen at my wicked expression, causing her to glance away before she gets into her car.

"Charming the new neighbors, I see."

Elijah chuckles as he inhales the scent on my neck, his hand caressing my ass. "Another one who likes baking blueberry muffins."

"So I see." My eyes glance over to the basket sitting on top of our mirror display by the door.

"You've got the sexiest ass, you know that?"

I moan as he pulls my groin to his hardened cock. All the while, I'm watching our new neighbor drive away.

I smile as I imagine all of things I could possibly do to her. All the things that will happen to her because she fucking *dared* to flirt with what's mine.

Hmm ... justice will be so sweet, I can almost taste it on my tongue.

This one, I believe I shall call Cuntface.

INTRODUCING ELIJAH HAWTHORNE

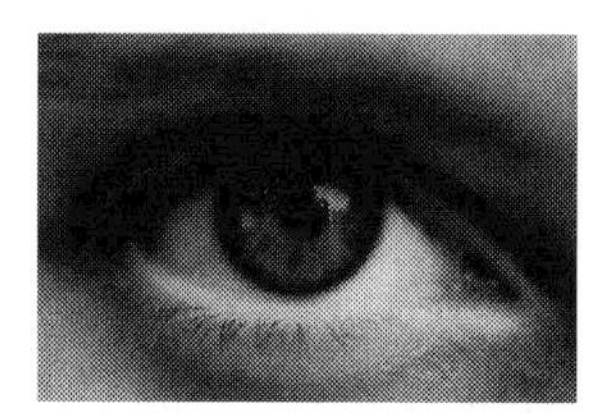

"Go take the meat out for the barbecue. I'll grab the utensils and be right behind you."

A subtle smile spreads across her stunning, heart-shaped face, her soft, flowing auburn hair perfectly framing her high cheekbones and helping to accentuate her sparkling, light blue eyes. She leans in, kissing me lightly on the lips, then with her sultry, fucking sexy voice only she knows how to command, she answers.

"Don't be long. I have plans for us later." She gives me a seductive wink before heading out to the yard.

I head into our living room—a room which is bigger than our old house back in Kentucky alone. A bit of an exaggeration, but still, at the moment it's unnecessarily big for just the two of us. But the moment we walked in and I saw Bryce's eyes light up like it was fucking Christmas, her gasps radiating around each room we walked in, I knew I would never be able to say no to her. Besides, what Bryce doesn't realize yet but will once we're married is that it won't be long before her perfect body will be blossoming further with my baby growing inside of it. That was the other reason for agreeing to buy this house. It's only us—for now—but I will be changing that very soon. The other reason to knock her up as soon as possible is to attempt to calm her unruly and damn right delinquent behavior. I've let her loose for far too long. Now that we've moved and starting a new life, all of that needs to stop. Does that make me controlling? Yes. Do I care? Fuck no. I make absolutely no apologies when it comes to Bryce. I survived months of turmoil while being attracted to my stepdaughter, but now, I refuse to view my behavior as sick or twisted. It is what it is, and I accepted that a long time ago. Long before Bryce even knew I had. It was just too much fun to watch her play.

Noticing that my phone is flashing with a notification, I grab it, seeing it's an email from the local mayor. He wants to meet me tomorrow at nine sharp to initiate introductions and the like. I click "accept", raking my hand through my hair with a sigh. I sure hope he's not like that fucker Schultz. He was yet another reason I decided I need to get Bryce knocked up as soon as we're married. She's a fucking danger to herself as well as others. Despite her reckless and obsessive antics fucking turning me on so much, I can't let them continue. All this time, she thought she was in charge, that only she had eyes on me. But little did she realize, I've had eyes on her all this time too.

The side of my lip coils into a smile, my cock jerking with thoughts of her flooding my head. It never takes much when it comes to her. She is—after all—the epitome of a woman. A lethal, fucking delicious cocktail of a pussy cat in a tigress's clothing. Regal, charming, and damn fucking alluring on the outside, but a potent poison of depravity and vengeance on the inside. She will lure you in with her beauty and charm, just like the widow spider she is. I have no misconceptions that if I ever crossed her, she'd kill me. I would never cross her anyway. Not because I'm scared of her—I can handle her better then she can handle herself—but because she's the only woman I have ever met who can push my buttons, make my head spin, and have me thinking about nothing but her. Everything stops with her. Would some call that love? I don't fucking know. All I know is my life hasn't been the same since she made me her target. Gone are the days when I viewed her as my timid, little stepdaughter who needed nurture and protection. Like the lotus flower, she bloomed from those muddy waters to become the most perfect specimen ever to grace the earth. And once she blossomed, her fate was sealed. Once she blossomed, she became mine. Only. Fucking. Mine.

I've killed three times for her, two of them she knows about. The other was her fucking deadbeat father who dared to turn up at my door after hearing that Bryce's mother had "passed". He wanted to take Bryce, spouting some shit about wanting to be her father again. I knew it was all bullshit, so there was no other choice but to eliminate the threat. No one can ever take her from me, so it was a no brainer. And I'll be more than willing to do it again if it means keeping her safe and well. and most importantly, by my side.

I think back to when she killed my son. I had missed the mark that day. One of the very few times I have ever been sidelined was that day. I had planned to go pick him up, take him to dinner, and then once he'd had his last supper, I would have taken him to the swamps and executed him. You see, I knew they were writing letters, knew he was head over heels in love with her, because I had intel in his prison who took pictures of all her lovey fucking dovey letters to him. I also knew that he could never, ever fucking have her. She was mine. Not even my own flesh and blood could come between us. It also fucking warmed my heart to know that Bryce was so obsessed with me that she was willing to remove anyone who could potentially get in the way of us solely being together. She reminds me of a lioness, taking out the potential mates of her cubs, erasing the chance of any other bloodline that threatens their future dominance. She's the sexiest, most deadly creature I have ever had the pleasure to encounter. She doesn't realize that I secretly worship at her feet, place her so fucking high on a pedestal that no-one could *ever* come even remotely close to taking her place. She is my Egyptian queen, my goddess of all goddesses. She has my soul, and I gladly fucking bow down to her.

I'm about to head back out to start the barbecue when the doorbell rings. I frown as we're not expecting company, but walk to the door to see who it could be. In the peephole, I see a blonde lady with big tits and a tight, coral-colored dress plumping up her hair. In her other hand is a basketful of what looks like blueberry muffins. I let out a groan, rolling my eyes before opening the door.

She steps back as she takes me in, her eyes making a show of taking in my torso, my fitted white t-shirt, and beige shorts, licking her lips as she goes. I seriously hate bitches like this. Bitches who don't care if I'm already taken or aren't fucking interested. Bitches like Duckface and Bitchface—as Bryce eloquently called them. I have to fight a smirk and shake my head at these errant thoughts.

"Can I help you?" I ask politely. I am the chief of police, after all. I have to make a show of being friendly around here, whether I like these assholes or not.

"Well, my, my," she coos, placing a hand on her chest to try to emphasize her assets. She may have big tits, but this woman has fucking nothing on Bryce. No women ever could. "I was told you were a handsome son of a bitch, but I didn't want to believe it till now." She giggles at her own joke, and I smile back despite itching to tell her to fuck off. "Where're my manners? Sorry, the name's Kylie Bassett. I live on the Bassett ranch about a mile down the road."

She offers me her hand, so I give it a firm shake. Her wide eyes tell me it surprised her, but she quickly recovers.

"I wanted to bring you these to welcome you to the community. I believe you and your fiancée will love it here."

I smile, taking the muffins and placing them on our mirror display by the door before moving back to speak to her. "Thank you for the blueberry muffins. I'm sure my fiancée and I will love them." They're going in the trash the moment she fucks off.

This Kylie woman bites her lip in an attempt to make her look more alluring. She's anything fucking but. She obviously doesn't give a flying fuck about the fact that I have a fiancée. She's probably one of those types who marries a man twice her age because he has lots of cash but will grab some dick whenever the opportunity arises because the last time she got good dick from her husband was ... well ... never.

"If you ever need anything—and I mean *anything*—I'm only a five-minute drive up the road."

The way she says 'anything' screams that she definitely doesn't mean coffee or a cup of sugar. I'm more than fucking tired of this woman already. I need to get back to my soon-to-be wife. The sooner the fucking better.

"We appreciate that. Thank you."

Her fingers lightly tap over her cleavage as she sways slightly. She's trying to be sexy, but instead, it makes her look pathetic. Bryce is the fucking sexy one. She could run rings around this stupid slut.

"Enjoy your barbecue now."

I let out a relieved breath when she finally realizes she's outstayed her welcome and starts to walk back to her car.

Just as I'm about to shut the door, a set of arms curl around my shoulders, making me smile, my body immediately relaxing. I close my eyes a millisecond, taking in her flowery scent, an aroma I could gladly live on for the rest of my life. My Bryce. My sustenance.

Eventually I turn, taking her in my arms as she snuggles her perfect head into my chest, making it inflate with pride.

Mine.

All mine.

"Charming the new neighbors, I see," Bryce quips, jealousy coating that sexy fucking voice of hers.

My laughter slips out before I take in the sweet scent of her neck, my hand caressing her perfectly rounded ass.

"Another one who likes baking blueberry muffins," I tell her, desperate to see her face so I can gauge her reaction.

"So I see," she responds, an element of danger in her voice that makes my cock come to life.

"You've got the sexiest ass, you know that?" I ask, needing to slide into that flawlessly tight pussy of hers.

She moans softly as I pull her against my hardened cock, wanting her to feel just how much of an effect she has on me. However, right now her attention is on something else—or I should say ... someone else.

Desperate to know what she's up to, I glance up to look in our mirror—a feature I'm glad I had hung by the door as it helps me spy on her when she thinks I can't see.

A surge of heat crawls up my spine when I witness the evil smirk that creeps up her face as she watches our new neighbor leave. It looks like my dazzling, exceptionally dangerous fiancée has a new target. Something I will need to nip in the bud considering we just recently moved here. We're starting afresh. There's no way I can let her go back to her usual ways, doing things like she did in Kentucky—despite the fact that it fucking makes my dick as solid as fucking rock for her.

I continue to watch as her eyes follow the car along the road, the speckles within her blue irises sparkling like the brightest of diamonds. I sigh because she's the most exquisite creature I have ever come across. How could I ever deny her anything?

Shit.

Maybe.

Just maybe ... I'll let her loose.

One last time.

WHAT HAPPENED WITH MISS PASHMORE?

Curiosity getting the better of me, I wait until the end of school, telling Adam that I have an appointment I need to head to before waiting outside for Miss Pashmore to exit. She comes out clutching her things then walks across the parking lot to her car. She awkwardly attempts to get her keys out of her pocket while carrying her purse and textbooks.

Rushing to her aid, I retrieve the books to free her hands. "Here, let me help you."

She breathes out a sigh, smiling. "Oh, thank you. You're a life-saver."

She uses her key to open her pink Mini before grabbing the books from me and placing them inside her trunk.

"Do you need a ride somewhere?" she offers, her hand resting on the driver's door.

I bite my lip, uncertainty momentarily halting my next words. "Actually," I begin, my heart skipping a beat. "I was wondering if you wouldn't mind going over today's lesson with me again. I hate to admit it, but I wasn't really listening because of not feeling well."

She steps forward, a frown reshaping her delicate mouth. "You should have said something. I would have let you leave. I'm not that much of an ogre."

Oh, there's nothing ogreish about this woman, that's for certain.

I almost laugh out loud at my own thoughts. I don't know what's gotten in to me lately, but I'm rolling with pretty much everything that comes to mind, and finding I'm actually damn fucking good at it.

"I didn't want to disturb you during class."

"You're a straight A student, Bryce. Missing one lesson probably wouldn't even cause a dent in your GPA."

I step forward so I'm closer to the car. "I know, but I would still like to go over it with you. That's if ... if you have the time?"

Uncertainty flashes over her eyes as she bites her lip. My eyes land on her mouth, the urge to ask her to dart her tongue out for me to see overwhelming me.

"I'm sorry, I've put you on the spot. I'll head home." I turn to walk away, but she calls after me, making me stifle a winning smile.

"I shouldn't do this, but... Get in the car. I don't have any plans for the rest of the day."

I want to ask her why she's not seeing the mystery women she kissed over the weekend, but I may end up scaring her off.

"Nice car," I comment as we're driving away.

"This is actually my car from college, would you believe it? She's like a faithful partner. It gets me from A to B, so as long as she still runs, I'm going to keep driving her."

"Where did you go to college?" I ask, my eyes watching her leg flex as she presses down on the clutch to change gears.

"Stanford."

I raise an eyebrow, impressed. I want to ask how much pussy she had while she was at Stanford, but again, I hold my tongue.

"Do you enjoy teaching?"

I'm not really interested in whether she does or not, but having some sort of conversation helps make time pass by.

"I do and I don't. I enjoy teaching students like you since you're eager to learn, but it's not enjoyable when I'm trying to teach someone who obviously doesn't want to be there."

"Yeah, that must be tough."

She smiles softly at my response, and soon after
the underground parking garage of her apartment
get out, I help her with all her books then we tak
sixth floor.

"It's not much," she begins, placing the key in the lock. "B
homey and comfortable, so it works well for me for now."

Swinging the door open, we step inside the living room kitchen combination. It is small but well-proportioned with its soft, warm colors and tons of cushions piled on the large couch she has opposite her big screen TV. Miss Pashmore catches me glancing that way and laughs.

"I'm a comfort girl. A big Netflix fan."

We both giggle. "I think I'd have my place just like this if I lived on my own too."

"Take a seat," she says, motioning towards the tiny dining table close to her kitchen. I do as she requests, sitting down on the wooden seat then setting my bag on the chair next to me. I watch as Miss Pashmore stacks her textbooks on a bookcase, keeping hold of one before eventually taking a seat next to me, her sweet citrus perfume hitting my nostrils and making me hum to life.

"Okay," she says, settling in. "Today I was talking about the Black Death of 1346 in England." She opens the textbook and sets it in front of me. "I don't know if you recall that I asked you all to read this little section here?" Her arm moves in front of my chest, placing her finger on a section of text. I do remember, but I must admit, my mind was on other things while everyone was reading.

"Yes, but I don't think it went in very well."

She smiles softly my way, motioning for me to read it again so that we can discuss it. Around twenty minutes go by while she points at parts of the book then we discuss them and I take notes, her perfume making me feel dizzy and hot with each minute that passes by.

"Excuse me," I whisper, pushing my chair back a bit. "I'm feeling a bit hot." Grabbing the hem of my hoodie, I pull it over my head, revealing my pink tank underneath. Having no bra on, my nipples will no doubt stick out through the thin material. As I set my hoodie on my bag, I glance across at Miss Pashmore whose face is flushed red, er eyes darting away from me. Did she just check me out? The thought that she may have turns me on.

She clears her throat and turns to the next page, pointing to another bit of text. "This was the next part I went over in the class." I lean forward, my nipple brushing against the back of her bare arm. She swallows, but keeps her hand on the book, her lips parting to say something when I stop her.

"Can I ask you a question?"

She slides her arm away, but I don't move out of her way, causing it to brush against my erect nipple. When it hits the back of her hand, she hitches in a breath, then shakes her head, composing herself.

"Yes, sure."

I twist my body so I'm facing her more, pushing my hair back so my breasts are on full display through my top. With hooded eyes, I lean slightly forward, hoping to create an intimate moment between us. Miss Pashmore stays still. A bit too still. I'm probably making her uncomfortable.

"It's actually a little embarrassing." I lick my lips, and she watches my movements, her breathing a bit halted. "I just figured, you being another woman, that you may be able to help me with something. You're older than me, so obviously you're more experienced."

She pulls her chair in a little more, making me think her nerves are getting the better of her. "I'm not sure about that, but what is it you want to know?"

Placing my hand on my bare chest, I stroke myself, hoping that her eyes will linger there. "I have trouble ... down there." I point towards my pussy.

She frowns. "In what way?"

"I've been trying all sorts to bring myself to orgasm, but nothing ever works. I don't think I'm doing it right."

Miss Pashmore glances away a moment, sucking in her lips. "I'm not sure it would be appropriate of me to go in to details on that with you, Bryce."

I place my hand on her arm, begging her with my eyes. "Please."

She releases a sharp breath. "Have you had any sort of encounters with boys at all? Tried anything with them?"

I bite my lip, shaking my head. "I'm not interested in boys. I just don't find myself attracted to them."

I'm not sure just how far I can push Miss Pashmore, but I'm certainly having fun trying.

Her eyes dart away for a moment, a nervous swallow dipping her throat. "I think what you need to do is lay down one day when you're all alone then explore your whole body. Find out what it is you like and what you don't like. Maybe..." She hesitates again. "Watch some videos?" She bites her lip. "Find something you ... enjoy. There're plenty of masturbation techniques you can find online if you do your research."

I nod my head before bringing my hands up to my breasts, squeezing my nipples between my fingers. "I like to play with my breasts. I always get worked up when I take my time with them." Miss Pashmore watches, her mouth parting slightly. "Do you think they're big enough?" I ask, her gasp telling me my question shocked her.

"What?"

I stick my breasts out. "My tits. Do you think they look big enough? I mean, do they look nice to you?" She doesn't answer, so I grab her hand and place it on my left breast. "Do you think they feel firm enough?"

Pushing her chair back, she gets up, her breathing harsh. "This is not appropriate behavior with a teacher, Bryce."

My excitement dwindling, I sag my shoulders. Miss Pashmore has always been one of the good teachers, so it shouldn't surprise me that she would turn down my advances.

"I'm sorry," I murmur, grabbing my stuff and getting up from my seat. The chair scrapes beneath me as I hold my stuff in my hands and walk towards her door. "I didn't mean to make you uncomfortable. I guess being close to you made me get a little carried away."

I get to the door, and I'm about to open it when a hand lands on my back. I turn around to see Miss Pashmore offering a soft smile. "You're gorgeous, Bryce. One of the most stunning young ladies I have ever come across. But you're not only very young, you're also my student."

I nod my head. "I understand. I'm really sorry."

She steps forward, laying a hand against my cheek. "No need to be sorry. I'm actually very flattered." She stares into my eyes, and we both just stand there a while. A part of me thinks that she's reconsidering turning me down, so holding that thought, I step forward and gently press my lips against hers. Miss Pashmore stays completely still, but when I dart my tongue out, she lets out a tiny moan, her tongue darting out to meet mine.

Fire raging in my belly, I step forward until we're chest to chest. I continue to kiss her softly, tenderly, her face in my hands. When she doesn't push me away, I move my hand down to her shirt and unbutton a couple of buttons before pushing my hand inside her bra and cupping her firm but soft breast. I swipe my thumb against her nipple, loving the way it instantly hardens against my touch.

"You feel so good," I whisper, my voice coated with need. I push her shirt open then bend down, taking her pert nipple into my mouth. She moans loudly, and my pussy throbs in response. Her breathing quickens as my tongue swirls around her nub. This experience is so weird but simultaneously extremely exhilarating.

After a beat, though, she pushes me back, putting her breast back into her bra, her chest heaving with need.

"I've let this go way too far. You need to leave."

She doesn't look my way as she says this, her face flushed with longing and embarrassment.

"Okay," I reply, turning and opening the door, my body still humming with a need for release. "I'm sorry," I say again, feeling like I need something to say.

I shut the door behind me then lean my head against it for a few seconds, trying to catch my breath. My pussy throbs, my body aches.

I need to come.

Taking my phone out, I search for Chesney's name. I know I said I would respect his need to stay away from me, but this is an ache I can't ignore. I'm pretty sure, if persuaded, I can get him to do another lesson in pussy eating—and I'll think of Miss Pashmore as he does it.

Thumb hovering over his number, I press the call button and head for the elevator.

"Chesney, I need to see you."

NOTES & ACKNOWLEDGEMENTS

Ever since I wrote *Siren*, I have been itching to write another twisted story. I never thought another idea would spring to mind, but then as I was busy completing the Take series, Bryce suddenly popped up and wouldn't let go. *i'm a CREEP* was born and so too was the journey I took with it. I seriously haven't had this much fun since *Siren*, so hopefully you've all enjoyed reading it as much as I enjoyed writing it.

As ever, I need to thank a few fantastic people. The first being my editor, Kim BookJunkie. As always, Kim, you were a superstar when it came to this book. I loved all the messages I received from you while you were editing. It seriously put a smile on my face. I love the final edits, and I love you, woman! Kiss.x

I also need to thank Dez Purington, from Pretty in Ink Creations. Dez, the cover you made for *i'm a CREEP* is one of my all-time favourites. It simply rocks! Thank you so much for this kick-ass cover.

Isa Jones and Joanne Mountford from Joandisalovebooks Promotions, thank you for the huge cover reveal that took place. I had SO much fun on that day, and it's thanks to you.

To Jena Gregoire from Book Mojo, thank you so much for the release blitz and book tour for *i'm a CREEP*. You've been extremely helpful, and for that, it's much appreciated.

To my family, thank you for supporting me to the fullest and allowing me to keep my dream alive. I love all you to bits!

And, to the readers, thank you *so much* for sticking with me through the good and the bad. I know some of my work hasn't been loved by all, so I'm eternally grateful for your loyalty. I will be bringing out more books as the year progresses, so I hope you will enjoy most of them. Whatever the outcome and whatever you think or feel, please know that I value your opinions. I will *always* value a reader's opinion. As I stated above, you are what enables me to grow and develop as an author. I know I can do better. I can always do better.

Love and light,

Jaimie xx

FOR LOVERS OF DARK AND TWISTED...

SIREN

Prologue

I stand over my father's grave, wiping the tears that threaten to fall onto the soil beneath my feet. I'm wearing a black dress, which is cut just above the knee, and on my feet is a pair of brand new, black and red Louboutin high heels. I scream *class*, but I am also the perfect image of a daughter in deep distress over her father's untimely death.

And what an untimely death it was.

I clutch my chest, heaving sobs of grief as I bend down to lay new flowers at his grave. I have been coming here every single day, bringing new flowers to replace the old ones. I pick up yesterday's flowers and toss them aside as I trace the line of my father's name on his headstone.

Here lies Richard Valentine, loving father to two daughters. Born 26th January 1970, Died 15th July 2016.

That was three weeks ago. His body was found buried in Virginia Water in Surrey—only nineteen miles or so from where I live. He was buried deep, but a storm sixteen days ago unearthed his decaying body. He had a stab wound in his back which was determined to be the cause of his death. It was murder, of course, and it is only now that the police are investigating.

At first, they thought he had run away—possibly met a girl, got swept off his feet, and was living by the beach, sipping cocktails with a buxom blonde. My sister kept on the case, though. She tried to tell them that it wasn't like him to just disappear without at least keeping in touch. I vouched for her to the police, but I also reminded her of that time when he disappeared for a year without a trace and came back just as suddenly as he had left. I knew the real reason why, but I didn't divulge it to my sister or to the police. That little secret was between Daddy and me alone. The two police officers gave each other that look ... The one that says, "Yeah, there's no foul play here." They just thought he had found the girl of his dreams and was busy acting the part of the doting boyfriend to his new plaything.

As I think on this, I stroke his grave tenderly and sweep away the leaves that have fallen from the nearby trees. I need to make sure that it is clean and tidy before kneeling down at his grave and throwing my arms over the gravestone. With my arms shielding me from anyone who may be watching, I take in a long, deep breath. A smirk rises on my face as I utter the words, "You always loved it when I threw my arms around you, didn't you?" I sigh, scooting up to get closer to his headstone before spitting on his grave.

"I hope you're enjoying your time in hell, Daddy."

FOR LOVERS OF DARK AND TABOO, TURN THE PAGE TO READ A SNIPPET FROM TAINTED LOVE...

PROLOGUE

"I don't want you to leave me," I whine, hating how pathetic my voice sounds.

My brother steps forward, a small but sad smile curving his lips. Within touching distance, he loops his fingers through my hair and places a strand behind my ear, lightly cupping my chin with his thumb and forefinger, holding my stare.

"Dad will look after you. And if not him, Uncle will."

I crane my neck behind me to make sure my parents aren't within listening distance. My brother, now twenty-one, has decided that I'm old enough in my fifteen years to look after myself—to leave me with a mother who likes to drink herself into a stupor, and a father who—although nice enough to me—enables my mother's habit because... well, I'm pretty sure he wants her dead. My brother always craved to join the army but stayed because of me. He stayed because he knew he would be the one and only one who could look after me properly. My mother can't, and my father tries his best, but he once gave me food poisoning when he cooked dinner. My brother, after that, cooked whatever we could gather at the time, until I was old enough to take over that chore myself.

"You know I've wanted this for a while, Bri. You'll be sixteen soon and doing your exams. The world is your oyster after that. Hell, you can even join me... if you want."

He winks, ruffling my hair like I'm a child. When I complain, he chuckles under his breath.

"Joining the army has been your dream. Not mine."

My brother glances over my shoulder towards our parents before his eyes land back on me. "It was a dream pushed on me."

I nod my head, a wave of sadness encasing me. I understand why he wants to leave. I will do the same once I turn sixteen, take my exams, and get myself a job. Seven more months and I will be able to leave home.

I can't wait.

"Just don't forget about me." My slightly raised eyebrows cause him to chuckle.

"Seriously, Bri, how could I ever forget you? You're my only sister. It's me who needs to worry about you. Without your protective brother around, all the boys will come flocking, asking you out on dates. You'll forget all about me soon enough."

I nudge his arm, scolding him. "Hey, that'll never happen, and you know it."

My brother extends his arm out to me and produces his little finger. "Pinky promise?"

I giggle and shake my head before latching my little finger round his. Ever since I was a little girl, about six years old, we have been pinky promising things to each other.

"Pinky promise," I reply, biting my lip. Fresh tears begin to sting my eyes, but I fight them because no matter how much I don't want him to leave, I also want him to be free of this shithole life we're in. When he first told me he was leaving to join the army, I had caused a scene, screaming and shouting, throwing things around the house. It was only when I calmed down that I realised what a selfish brat I was being. Just because I can't be free just now, doesn't mean my brother can't. Besides, if he hadn't joined now, he would have had to wait a few more months. I couldn't do that to him—no matter how selfish I want to be.

Wrapping his big, strong arms around me, my brother pulls me in for a hug. "I'll be back before you know it. And I'll send money when I can so you can set yourself up somewhere. I promise. All this is as good for you as it is for me. Once you have your own place, I'll come visit on my leave dates. We'll have so much fun, you and I." He pulls away before kissing me on the cheek. I grip his jacket, unable to let him go. I know I have to, but the selfish part of me is currently winning out.

"Right, everyone on the coach now!" a man in camouflage shouts. I look around, finding lots of people hugging, kissing, saying their goodbyes. I drown out the sniffles of the girlfriends. If I don't, it won't be long before I'm sobbing alongside them.

Just a few more minutes and he will be gone.

Just a few more minutes before I can cry.

"Take care of yourself, Son," my dad says from behind me.

My brother smiles as he shakes his hand. "I will, Dad. Thanks."

We both chance a look at my mother who, without my dad holding her, is swaying from the booze she's been drinking since eight this morning. It's currently ten, and apart from that, her only son is about to leave and join the army. You'd think she'd try and lay off the alcohol for him this one time. But no. Alcohol makes people selfish, and she's as selfish as they come.

With not so much as an acknowledgement from her, my brother sucks in a breath. "Well, I guess I better go." He then looks directly at me. "I'll message you once I'm there."

"You promise?" I ask, trying to smile.

"Pinky promise," he says, holding his little finger up. "I'll either call or message every day."

I attempt to smile at him, but the more time runs out before he has to leave, the more my heart hurts. He hugs me one last time, says a cursory goodbye to our parents, and then all I can do is watch. I watch as he walks towards the coach and queues up before taking his first step. I watch as he moves along the aisle until he finds a seat. I watch as he blows me a kiss through the window, offering that bright smile that always manages to lift my spirits. I watch as the coach leaves, and the last thing I see is his hand waving.

Then I cry. I cry all the way home with my mum complaining about the noise the whole journey. I cry when I'm on my bed with only my pillow to comfort me. I cry all the days and weeks that follow without him. I cry when years go by, and my brother does two tours of Afghanistan.

The second of which, I lose him forever.

CHAPTER 1

Years later

I close my eyes when I feel his tongue flick across my nipple, a slight moan leaving my lips. I feel his heavy breath above me, his slow, torturous hand caressing my other breast as it cascades down to my soaking pussy.

"Fuck, Bri, you're always so wet for me."

He inserts his finger into my wetness, causing my back to arch slightly. I'm so turned on. Always so turned on for this man.

Ever so slowly, his finger slides out of me, but only so he can start his leisurely strokes around my clit.

"Oh, God!" I cry out, loving the sensations flooding my body. His tongue darts out at my nipple again, flicking once, twice, three times before his lips wrap around my little nub and he starts sucking.

"Chris!" I shout, unable to hide my emotions from him. I've never, in this last year of living with him, been able to hide just how much pleasure he gives me.

"I'm going to fuck you, and you're going to come around my cock.

Got it?" he growls, plunging his finger back inside my pussy. I cry out, my breaths uneven and shallow. "Bri, I can't hear your answer."

Licking my lips, I nod my head, my hands fisting the dark blonde wavy locks I love to run my hands through.

"Say it, Bri. Say you want my cock inside you. Tell me you're going to love it so much that it'll make you come. Tell me!"

"Yes!" I scream, needing my release. Over the past twelve months, he's perfected the art of knowing exactly what my body wants and uses it to his advantage. He learnt what makes me tick and what doesn't. He's acquired the knowledge as to what will make me scream and my toes curl with heightened pleasure.

Opening my eyes, I find him staring down at me with a wicked grin, the dimple on his right cheek winking at me. His ice blue eyes caress my face as his finger pushes back inside my heated core. "I love you, Bri." His face lowers until his lips touch mine, his short stubble rough against my cheek. I touch the side of his face, stroking down his chiseled jawline, a vibratory moan rumbling through his mouth into mine. He pulls his finger out of my wetness, quickly finding my little nub, and once perfectly placed, he runs slow circles around my clit, causing me to thrust my hips. I want more. So much more.

As my head begins to dizzy, I groan into his mouth, needing so badly to scream out my arousal, but he halts me with his lips. His kiss hardens, and his finger starts to move quicker. His rough actions cause my body to quiver. He recognises that I'm close to orgasm. He knows exactly the right time I'm about to detonate.

When I'm almost there, he pulls his finger away, but only wasting enough time to thrust his big, hard cock inside of me. I scream out his name, and he groans out his pleasure. Every time, he can't help himself.

He's as obsessed as I am.

"You make me lose my mind, Bri. Fuck, you feel so fucking good."

He leans down, kissing my mouth again then begins his beautiful torture with his hips. The feel of his cock inside of me waves hello again to the orgasm I'd lost. It's back in full force, rearing its little head to the surface, taunting me—teasing me.

Chris flexes his hips, thrusting hard before both of us are moaning, clutching at each other as if one of us will be pulled away. With a free hand, Chris finds my hip and squeezes as he thrusts his cock again, our sweat meeting as our bodies unite.

He lifts his body slightly, but only so he can suck on my nipple as he thrusts harder and harder with each flex of his hips. Needing to touch him, I place one hand on his arse, and with every clench of his cheek as he thrusts his way inside of me, I feel my climax rising.

With my other hand, I thread my fingers through his hair as he carries on sucking my nipple. Everything... it's all... too much.

"Chris!" I scream again as my body starts to clench. He senses when I'm about to come because his own movements grow more rigorous. Skin slaps against skin as he grunts, his feral growl making my body heat and prickle with euphoria. Knowing we're both losing control, he pulls away from my nipple and solely concentrates on giving me his all. His cock slams into me, time and time again, and with each moan from his lips, my orgasm climbs, faster, harder.

"I'm going to make you come so hard, baby. So. Fucking. Hard," he pants between each thrust.

The familiar wave starts to ride my body, and just as it's at the precipice, I grip his arse with both hands and push him inside me. I come apart, screaming his name as an orgasm like no other rips me apart.

"Baby, you're going to be the death of me," he groans as his movements grow even faster. My orgasm rides on as he continues his onslaught, and right at the point when it's about to become too much, he flexes his hips one last time, releasing his climax inside of me.

With my eyes closed, all I feel is the giddy, calm sensation riding through me. That very same sensation that I try and hold on to as long as I possibly can before reality strikes.

"God, I fucking love you," he says again, kissing me on the cheek before rolling off me. For a while, we lie on the bed catching our breaths as we come down from our orgasms, the only sound is our steady exhales. I close my eyes, relishing the moment. Every single time, I let it come over me. I let the euphoria wash over me like a tidal wave. Because in a few minutes, I'll calm. In a few minutes, that reality will set in.

And then all I will feel is nothing but disgust.

ALSO BY JAIMIE ROBERTS

Until I Met You – Released 1st June 2014

DEVIANT – Released 31st October 2014

Redemption (Deviant #2) – Released 3rd April 2015

CHAINED – Released 17th July 2015

A Step Too Close – Released 17th September in 2015

Luca (You Will Be Mine) – Released 15th January 2016

Luca (Because You're Mine) – Released 26th February 2016

Scars – Released 23rd June 2016

Siren – Released 6th September 2016

Possession – Released 10th March 2017

A Surrogate Love Affair – Released 13th April 2017

Tailspin – Released 20th June 2017

My Valentine (Siren, #2) – Released 1st February 2018

Resurgence (A Siren Novella) – Released 13th March 2018

Headmaster – Released 17th May 2018

Amnesia – Released 28th December 2018

Scozzari (Deviant #3) Released 14th March 2019

Forbidden Desires - Released August 2019

Tainted Love - Released 15th October 2020

Take a Breath – Re-released 24th March 2021

Take it Deep – Release date 6th April 2021

Take the Gun - Release date 4th May 2021

i'm a CREEP - Release date 28th May 2021

ABOUT THE AUTHOR

Jaimie Roberts was born in London but moved to Gibraltar in 2001. She is married with two sons, and in her spare time, she writes.

In June 2013, Jaimie published her first book, Take a Breath, with the second released in November 2013. With the reviews, Jaimie took time out to read and learn how to become a better writer. She gets tremendous enjoyment out of writing, and even more so from the feedback she receives.

If you would like to send Jaimie a message, please do so by visiting her social media pages.

Made in the USA
Columbia, SC
22 July 2022